The Darling Buds of May

BY THE SAME AUTHOR

The Wedding Party

The Nature of Love

The Grapes of Paradise

The Wild Cherry Tree

The Four Beauties

Seven by Five

The Golden Oriole

The Jacaranda Tree

The Feast of July

The Sleepless Moon

Charlotte's Row

A Moment in Time

The Distant Horns of Summer

Fair Stood the Wind for France

Love for Lydia

The Purple Plain

The Scarlet Sword

The Triple Echo

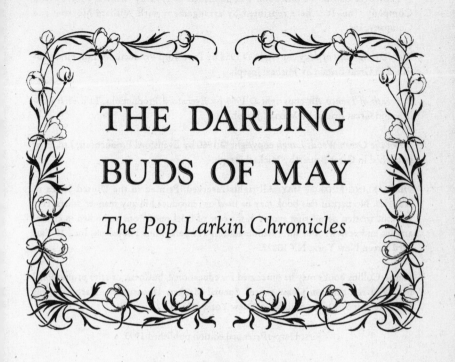

THE DARLING
BUDS OF MAY

The Pop Larkin Chronicles

H. E. BATES

HarperPerennial
A Division of HarperCollinsPublishers

HarperCollins books may be purchased for educational, business, or sales promotional use. For information please write: Special Markets Department, HarperCollins Publishers, Inc., 10 East 53rd Street, New York, NY 10022.

First HarperPerennial edition published 1993.

Designed by Dorothy S. Baker

Library of Congress Cataloging-in-Publication Data

Bates, H. E. (Herbert Ernest), 1905–1974.
    The darling buds of May : the Pop Larkin chronicles / H. E. Bates.
— 1st HarperPerennial ed.
        p.   cm.
    Contents: The darling buds of May — A breath of French air —
When the green woods laugh.
    ISBN 0-06-097596-2 (pbk.)
    1. Larkin family (Fictitious characters)—Fiction. 2. Larkin, Pop
(Fictitious character)—Fiction. 3. Country life—England—Fiction.
4. Family—England—Fiction. I. Title
PR6003.A965D28   1993b
823'.912—dc20   93-31525

93 94 95 96 97 RRD 10 9 8 7 6 5 4 3 2 1

Contents

The Darling Buds of May   7

A Breath of French Air   119

When the Green Woods Laugh   231

THE

DARLING BUDS

OF MAY

1

After distributing the eight ice creams—they were the largest vanilla, chocolate, and raspberry super-bumpers, each in yellow, brown, and almost purple stripes—Pop Larkin climbed up into the cab of the gentian blue, home-painted thirty-hundredweight truck, laughing happily.

"Perfick wevver! You kids all right at the back there? Ma, hitch up a bit!"

Ma, in her salmon sweater, was almost two yards wide.

"I said you kids all right there?"

"How do you think they can hear," Ma said, "with you revving up all the time?"

Pop laughed again and let the engine idle. The strong May sunlight, the first hot sun of the year, made the bonnet of the truck gleam like brilliant blue enamel. All down the road, winding through the valley, miles of pink apple orchards were in late bloom, showing petals like light confetti.

"Zinnia and Petunia, Primrose, Victoria, Montgomery, Mariette!"— Pop unrolled the handsome ribbon of six names but heard only five separate answers, each voice choked and clotted with ice cream.

"Where's Mariette? Ain't Mariette there?"

"I'm here, Pop."

"That's all right, then. Thought you'd fell overboard."

"No, I'm here, Pop, I'm here."

"Perfick!" Pop said. "You think I ought to get more ice creams? It's so hot Ma's is nearly melted."

Ma shook all over, laughing like shaking jelly. Little rivers of yellow, brown, and pinkish-purple ice cream were running down over her huge lardy hands. In her handsome big black eyes the cloudless blue May sky was reflected, making them dance as she threw out the splendid bank of her bosom, quivering under its salmon sweater. At thirty-five

9

she still had a head of hair like black silk cotton, curly and thick as it fell to her fat olive shoulders. Her stomach and thighs bulged like a hopsack under the tight brown skirt, and in her remarkably small delicate cream ears her round pearl drop earrings trembled like young white cherries.

"Hitch up a bit I said, Ma! Give father a bit o' room." Pop Larkin, who was thin, sharp, quick-eyed, jocular, and already going shining bald on top, with narrow brown side-linings to make up for it, nudged against the mass of flesh like a piglet against a sow. "Can't get the clutch in."

Ma hitched up a centimeter or two, still laughing.

"Perfick!" Pop said. "No, it ain't though. Where'd I put that money?"

Ice cream in his right hand, he began to feel in the pockets of his leather jacket with the other.

"I had it when I bought the ice creams. Don't say I dropped it. Here, Ma, hold my ice cream."

Ma held the ice cream, taking a neat lick at a melting edge of it with a red sparkling tongue.

"All right, all right. Panic over. Put it in with the crisps."

Packets of potato crisps crackled out of his pocket, together with a bundle of pound notes, rolled up, perhaps a hundred of them, and clasped with a thick elastic band.

"Anybody want some crisps? Don't all speak at once—anybody—"

"Please!"

Pop leaned out of the cab and with two deft backhand movements threw two packets of potato crisps into the back of the truck.

"Crisps, Ma?"

"Please," Ma said. "Lovely. Just what I wanted."

Pop took from his pocket a third packet of potato crisps and handed it over to Ma, taking his ice cream back and licking the dripping underside of it at the same time.

"All right. All set now." He let in the clutch at last, holding his ice cream against the wheel. "Perfick! Ma, take a look at that sky!"

Soon, in perfect sunlight, between orchards that lifted gentle pink branches in the lightest breath of wind, the truck was passing strawberry fields.

"Got the straw on," Pop said. "Won't be above anuvver few days now."

In June it would be strawberries for picking, followed by cherries before the month ended, and then more cherries through all the month of July. Sometimes, in good summers, apples began before August did, and with them early plums and pears. In August and again in September it was apples. In September also it was hops and in October potatoes. At strawberries alone, with a big family, you could earn fifteen pounds a day.

"See that, kids?" Pop slowed down the truck, idling past the long rows of fresh yellow straw. "Anybody don't want to go strawberry picking?"

In the answering burst of voices Pop thought, for the second time, that he couldn't hear the voice of Mariette.

"What's up with Mariette, Ma?"

"Mariette? Why?"

"Ain't heard her laughing much today."

"I expect she's thinking," Ma said.

Lost in silent astonishment at this possibility, Pop licked the last melting pink and chocolate-yellow cream from its paper and let the paper fly out of the window.

"Thinking? What's she got to think about?"

"She's going to have a baby."

"Oh?" Pop said. "Well, that don't matter. Perfick. Jolly good."

Ma did not seem unduly worried either.

"Who is it?" Pop said.

"She can't make up her mind."

Ma sat happily munching crisps, staring at cherry orchards as they sailed past the truck, every bough hung with swelling fruit, palest pink on the sunnier edges of the trees.

"Have to make up her mind some time, won't she?" Pop said.

"Why?"

"Oh! I just thought," Pop said.

Ma, who had almost finished the crisps, poured the last remaining golden crumbs into the palm of her left hand. Over the years, as she had grown fatter, the three big turquoise-and-pearl rings she wore had grown tighter and tighter on her fingers, so that every now and then she had to have them cut off, enlarged, and put back again.

"She thinks it's either that Charles boy who worked at the farm," Ma said, "or else that chap who works on the railway line. Harry somebody."

"I know him," Pop said. "He's married."

"The other one's overseas now," Ma said. "Tripoli or somewhere."

"Well, he'll get leave."

"Not for a year he won't," Ma said. "And perhaps not then if he hears."

"Ah well, we'll think of something," Pop said. "Like some more crisps? How about some chocolate? Let's stop and have a beer. Got a crate in the back."

"Not now," Ma said. "Wait till we get home now. We'll have a Guinness then and I'll warm the fish-and-chips up."

Pop drove happily, both hands free now, staring with pleasure at the cherries, the apples, and the strawberry fields, all so lovely under the May sunlight, and thinking with pleasure too of his six children and the splendid, handsome names he and Ma had given them. Jolly good names, perfick, every one of them, he thought. There was a reason for them all.

Montgomery, the only boy, had been named after the general. Primrose had come in the spring. Zinnia and Petunia were twins and they were the flowers Ma liked most. Victoria, the youngest girl, had been born in plumtime.

Suddenly he couldn't remember why they had called the eldest Mariette.

"Ma," he said, "trying to think why we called her Mariette. Why did we?"

"I wanted to call her after that queen," Ma said. "I always felt sorry for that queen."

"What queen?"

"The French one, Marie Antoinette. But you said it was too long. You'd never say it, you said."

"Oh! I remember," Pop said. "I remember now. We put the two together."

Ten minutes later they were home. With pride and satisfaction Pop gazed on home as it suddenly appeared beyond its scrubby fringe of woodland, half filled with bluebells, half with scratching red-brown hens.

"Home looks nice," he said. "Allus does though, don't it? Perfick."

"Lovely," Ma said.

"We're all right," Pop said. "Got nothing to worry about, Ma, have we?"

"Not that I can think of," Ma said.

Pop drew the truck to a standstill in a dusty yard of nettles, old oil drums, corrugated pigsties, and piles of rusty iron in which a line of white ducks, three gray goats, and a second batch of red-brown hens set up a concerted, trembling fuss of heads and wings, as if delighted.

"Just in time for dinner!" Pop said. It was almost four o'clock. "Anybody not hungry?"

He leapt down from the cab. Like him, everybody was laughing. He knew they were all hungry; they always were.

"Down you come, you kids. Down."

Letting down the backboard and holding up both arms, he took the youngest children one by one, jumping them down to the yard, laughing and kissing them as they came.

Presently only Mariette remained on the truck, wearing jodhpurs and a pale lemon shirt, standing erect, black-haired, soft-eyed, olive-skinned, and so well made in a slender and delicate way that he could not believe that Ma, at seventeen too, had once looked exactly like her.

"It's all right. I can get down myself, Pop."

Pop held up his arms, looking at her tenderly.

"Ah come on. Ma's told me."

"Let me get down myself, Pop."

He stood watching her. Her eyes roamed past him, flashing and dark as her mother's, searching the yard.

It suddenly crossed his mind that she was afraid of something, not happy, and he half opened his mouth to comment on this unlikely, disturbing, unheard-of fact when she suddenly shook her black head and startled him by saying, "Pop, there's a man in the yard. There's a man over there by the horse-box. Watching us."

Pop walked across the yard toward the horse-box. He owned two horses, one a young black mare for Mariette, the other a piebald pony for the other kids. Mariette, who was crazy about horses, rode to point-to-point races, sometimes went hunting, and even jumped at shows. She was wonderful about horses. She looked amazing on a horse. Perfick, he thought.

"Hullo, hullo, hullo," he said. "Good morning, afternoon rather. Looking for me?"

The man, young, spectacled, pale-faced, trilby-hatted, with a small brown toothbrush mustache, carried a black briefcase under his arm.

"Mr. Sidney Larkin?"

"Larkin, that's me," Pop said. He laughed in ringing fashion. "Larkin by name, Larkin by nature. What can I do for you? Nice wevver."

"I'm from the office of the Inspector of Taxes."

Pop stood blank and innocent, staggered by the very existence of such a person.

"Inspector of *what?*"

"Taxes. Inland Revenue."

"You must have come to the wrong house," Pop said.

"You are Mr. Sidney Larkin?" The young man snapped open the briefcase, took out a paper, and glanced at it quickly, nervously touching his spectacles with the back of his hand. "Sidney Charles Larkin."

"That's me. That's me all right," Pop said.

"According to our records," the young man said, "you have made no return of income for the past year."

"Return?" Pop said. "What return? Why? Nobody asked me."

"You should have had a form," the young man said. He took a yellow-buff sheet of paper from the briefcase and held it up. "One like this."

"Form?" Pop said. "Form?"

Ma was crossing the yard with a box of groceries under one arm and a bag of fruit in the other. Three big ripe pineapples stuck cactuslike heads from the top of the huge paper bag. The twins loved pineapple. Especially fresh. Much better than tinned, they thought.

"Ma, did we have a form like this?" Pop called. "Never had no form, did we?"

"Never seen one. Sure we never."

"Come over here, Ma, a minute. This gentleman's from the Inspector of Summat or other."

"I got dinner to get," Ma said and strode blandly on with groceries and pineapples, huge as a buffalo. "You want your dinner, don't you?"

Pop turned with an air of balmy indifference to the young man, who was staring incredulously at the receding figure of Ma as if she were part of the menagerie of hens, goats, ducks, and horses.

"No, never had no form. Ma says so."

"You should have. Two at least were sent. If not three."

"Well, Ma says so. Ma ought to know. Ma's the one who does the paperwork."

The young man opened his mouth to speak and for a moment it was as if a strangled, startled gurgle came out. His voice choked itself back, however, and in reality the sound came from a drove of fifteen young turkeys winding down from the strip of woodland.

"Won't hurt you," Pop said. "How about a nice hen bird for Christmas? Put your name on it now."

"This form has to be returned to the inspector," the young man said. "There is a statutory obligation—"

"Can't return it if I ain't got it," Pop said. "Now can I?"

"Here's another."

As he recoiled from the yellow-buff sheet of paper Pop saw Mariette walking across the yard, slender, long-striding, on her way to the wooden, brush-roofed stable where both pony and horse were kept.

"I got no time for forms," Pop said. "Gawd Almighty, I got pigs to feed. Turkeys to feed. Hens to feed. Kids to feed. I ain't had no dinner. Nobody ain't had no dinner."

Suddenly the young man was not listening. With amazement he was following the progress of Mariette's dark, yellow-shirted figure across the yard.

"My eldest daughter," Pop said. "Crazy on horses. Mad on riding. You do any riding, mister—mister—I never caught your name."

"Charlton."

"Like to meet her, Mr. Charlton?" Pop said. The young man was still staring, mouth partly open. Between his fingers the tax form fluttered in the breezy sunlit air.

"Mariette, come over here a jiff. Young man here's crazy on horses, like you. Wants to meet you. Comes from the Ministry of Revenue or summat."

In astonished silence the young man stared at the new celestial body, in its yellow shirt, as it floated across the background of rusty iron, pigsties, abandoned oil drums, goat-chewed hawthorn bushes, and dusty earth.

"Mr. Charlton, this is my eldest, Mariette. The one who's mad on horses. Rides everywhere. You've very like seen her picture in the papers."

"Hullo," Mariette said. "I spotted you first."

"That's right, she saw you," Pop said. " 'Who's that nice young feller in the yard,' she said."

"So you," Mariette said, "like riding too?"

The eyes of the young man groped at the sunlight as if still unable correctly to focus the celestial body smiling at him from three feet away.

"I say every kid should have a horse," Pop said. "Nothing like a horse. I'm going to get every one of my kids a horse."

Suddenly the young man woke from mesmerism, making a startling statement.

"I saw you riding over at Barfield," he said. "In the third race. At Easter. You came in second."

"I hope you won a bob or two on her," Pop said.

Again he laughed in ringing fashion, bringing from beyond the stable an echo of goose voices as three swaggering gray-white birds emerged from a barricade of nettles, to be followed presently by the half-sleepy, dainty figures of a dozen guinea fowl.

"Pity we didn't know you were coming," Pop said. "We're killing a goose tomorrow. Always kill a goose or a turkey or a few chickens on the weekend. Or else guinea fowl. Like guinea fowl?"

If the young man had any kind of answer ready it was snatched from him by the voice of Ma, calling suddenly from the house, "Dinner's nearly ready. Anybody coming in or am I slaving for nothing?"

"We're coming, Ma!" Pop turned with eager, tempting relish to the young man, still speechless, still struggling with his efforts to focus correctly the dark-haired girl. "Well, we got to go, Mr. Charlton. Sorry. Ma won't have no waiting."

"Now, Mr. Larkin, about this form—"

"Did you see me at Newchurch?" Mariette said. "I rode there too."

"As a matter of fact, I did—I did, yes—but, Mr. Larkin, about this form—"

"What form?" Mariette said.

"Oh, some form, some form," Pop said. "I tell you what, Mr. Charlton, you come in and have a bite o' dinner with us. No, no trouble. Tons o' grub—"

"I've eaten, thank you. I've eaten."

"Well, cuppa tea then. Cuppa coffee. Bottle o' beer. Bottle o' Guinness. Drop o' cider."

The entire body of the young man seemed to swirl helplessly, as if half intoxicated, out of balance, on its axis. "Oh yes, do," Mariette said, and by the time he had recovered he found himself being led by Pop Larkin toward the house, from which Ma was already calling a second time, "If nobody don't come in three minutes I'll give it to the cats."

"Know anybody who wants a pure white kitten?" Pop said. "Don't want a pure white kitten, do you?"

"So you were at Newchurch too," Mariette said. "I wish I'd known."

A moment later Pop threw up his hands in a gesture of near ecstasy at the overpowering beauty, which suddenly seemed to strike him all afresh, of the May afternoon.

"Beautiful, ain't it?" he said. "Perfick. I got a beautiful place here. Don't you think I got a beautiful place here, Mr. Charlton?"

* * *

In the kitchen a radio was loudly playing jazz. In the living room next door, where the curtains were half drawn, a television set was on, giving to the nine faces crowded about the table a gray-purple flickering glow.

"Have just what you fancy, Mr. Charlton," Pop said. "If you don't see it here, ask for it. Bottle o' beer? Glass o' sherry? Pass the vinegar, Ma."

Soon the young man, arms crooked at the crowded table, was nursing a cup of tea. In the center of the table stood the three pineapples, flanked on all sides by plates of fish-and-chips, more colored blocks of ice cream, pots of raspberry and strawberry jam, bottles of catsup and Guinness, bottles of Worcestershire sauce and cups of tea, chocolate biscuits and piles of icy buns.

"Perhaps Mr. Charlton would like a couple o' sardines with his tea?" Pop said. "Montgomery, fetch the sardines."

Mr. Charlton, bemused by the name Montgomery, protested faintly that he did not like sardines.

"Mr. Charlton saw Mariette riding at Barfield," Pop said.

"And at Newchurch," Mariette said.

"Funny we didn't see you there," Ma said. "We was all there."

"Mr. Charlton," Pop said, "loves horses."

"Turn up the contrast," Ma said, "it's getting dark."

In the television's flickering purplish light the young man watched the faces around the table as they munched on fish-and-chips, ice cream, catsup, and jam, becoming more and more like pallid, eyeless ghouls. Pop had placed him between Ma and Mariette and presently he detected under the great breathing bank of Ma's bosom, now mauve-salmon in the flickering light, the shape of two white kittens somehow nestling on the bulging precipice of her lap. Occasionally the kittens meowed prettily and Ma fed them with scraps of fish and batter.

Above the noise of jazz, television voices, kittens, geese honking at the kitchen door, and the chattering voices of the family he found it hard to make himself heard.

"Mr. Larkin, about this form. If you've got any difficulties I could help you fill it in."

"All right," Pop said, "you fill it in."

"It's still too dark," Ma said. "Turn it up a bit. It never stays where you put it nowadays."

"I'll give the damn thing one more week to behave itself," Pop said. "And if it don't then I'll turn it in for another."

Mr. Charlton spread the yellow-buff form on the table in front of him and then took out his fountain pen and unscrewed the cap.

"Ma, is there any more ice cream?" Primrose said.

"In the fridge," Ma said. "Big block o' strawberry mousse. Get that."

"Full name: Sidney Charles Larkin," Mr. Charlton said, and wrote it down. "Occupation? Dealer?"

"Don't you call him 'dealer,'" Ma said. "I'll give you dealer. He owns land."

"Well, landowner—"

"Farmer," Pop said.

"Well, farmer," Mr. Charlton said. "I'm very sorry. Farmer."

"Mariette, cut the pineapple," Ma said. "Montgomery, go into the kitchen and fetch that pint jug of cream."

While Mr. Charlton filled in the form Mariette stood up, reached for the bread knife, and started to cut the pineapples, putting thick juicy slices on plates over which Ma poured heavy yellow cream.

"Real Jersey," Ma said. "From our cow."

Every time Mariette reached over for another plate she brushed the sleeve of Mr. Charlton, who either made sketchy blobs on the tax form or could not write at all.

"How many children?" Mr. Charlton said. "Six? Is that right? No more?"

"Well, not yet, old man. Plenty o' time though. Give us a chance," Pop said, and again laughed in ringing fashion.

"Gone again," Ma said. "You can't see a blessed thing. Montgomery, Primrose—switch it off and change it for the set in our bedroom."

In the half darkness that now smothered the room Mr. Charlton felt something smooth, sinuous, and slender brush against his right calf. For one shimmering, unnerving moment he sat convinced that it was Mariette's leg entwining itself about his own. As it curled toward his thigh he felt his throat begin choking but suddenly he looked down to realize that already the geese were under the table, where Ma was feeding them with scraps of fish, half-cold chips, and crumbled icy buns.

Unnerved, he found it difficult to frame his next important question.

"Of course this is confidential in every way," he said, "but at what would you estimate your income?"

"Estimate, estimate?" Pop said. "Income? What income?"

Montgomery and Primrose, who had carried one television set away, now brought in another, larger than the first.

"Steady there, steady!" Ma said. "Watch where you're looking. Mind the cocktail cabinet."

"Hear that, Ma?" Pop said. "Income!"

Ma, as she had done in the truck, started laughing like a jelly.

"Outcome more likely," she said. "Outcome I should say."

"Six kids to feed and clothe," Pop said. "This place to run. Fodder to buy. Wheat as dear as gold dust. Pig food enough to frighten you to death. Living all the time going up and up. Vet's fees. Fowl pest. Foot-and-mouth. Swine fever. Birds all the time dying. Income, old man? *Income?* I should like some, old man."

Before Mr. Charlton could answer this, the second television set threw across the room its pallid, unreal glow, now in a curious nightmare green. At the same moment the twins, Zinnia and Petunia, demanded more pineapple. The geese made shoveling noises under the table and Mariette, rising to cut fresh slices, suddenly turned to Mr. Charlton with modest, almost whispered apology.

"I'm awfully sorry, Mr. Charlton. I didn't offer you any pineapple. Would you like some?"

"No thanks. I'm not allowed it. I find it too acid."

"What a shame. Won't you change your mind? They're nice ripe ones."

"Ought to be," Ma said. "Cost enough."

"I'm afraid I'm simply not allowed it," Mr. Charlton said. "I have to go very carefully. I have to manage mostly on eggs and that sort of thing."

"Eggs?" Pop said. "Eggs? Why didn't you say so? Got plenty of eggs, Ma, haven't we? Give Mr. Charlton a boiled egg or two wiv his tea."

"How would you like that?" Ma said. "A couple o' boiled eggs, Mr. Charlton? What do you say?"

To the delight of Ma, Mr. Charlton confessed that that was what he really wanted.

"I'll do them," Mariette said. "Three minutes? Four? How long?"

"Very light," Mr. Charlton said. "Three."

"Nice big 'uns—brown!" Pop called to Mariette as she went into the kitchen, where the geese presently followed her, brushing past Mr. Charlton's legs again as they passed, once more to give him that shimmering, shocking moment of unnerving ecstasy.

"About this income," Mr. Charlton said. "Can you give me an estimate? Just an estimate."

"Estimate it'll be an' all, old man," Pop said. "Lucky if we clear a fiver a week, ain't we, Ma?"

"Fiver? I'd like to see one," Ma said.

"We want boiled eggs, too!" the twins said, as in one voice. "Can we have boiled eggs?"

"Give over. Can't you see I'm cutting the pineapple?" Ma said.

Everybody except Mr. Charlton had large second helpings of pineapple, with more cream. When Ma had finished ladling out the cream she poured the remainder of it into a tablespoon and then licked the spoon with her big red tongue. After two or three spoonfuls she cleaned the spoon with her finger and fed one of the white kittens cream. On the television screen a posse of cowboys fired thirty revolvers into a mountainside and Mr. Charlton said, "I'm afraid we have to know what your income is, Mr. Larkin. Supposing—"

"All right," Pop said, "that's a fair question, old man. Fair for me, fair for another. How much do you get?"

"Oh well, me, not all that much. Civil servant, you know—"

"Nice safe job, though."

"Nice safe job, yes. I suppose so."

"Nothing like a nice safe job," Pop said. "As long as you're happy. Do you reckon you're happy?"

Mr. Charlton, who did not look at all happy, said quickly, "Supposing I put down a provisional five hundred?"

"Hundred weeks in a year now, Ma," Pop said, laughing again. "Well, put it down, old man, put it down. No harm in putting it down."

"Now the names of the children," Mr. Charlton said.

While Pop was reciting, with customary pride, the full names of the children, beginning with the youngest, Zinnia Florence and Petunia Mary, the twins, Mariette came back with two large brown boiled eggs in violet plastic eggcups to hear Pop say, "Nightingales in them woods up there behind the house, Mr. Charlton. Singing all day."

"Do nightingales sing all day?" Mr. Charlton said. "I wasn't aware—"

"All day, all night," Pop said. "Like everything else in the mating season they go hell for leather."

The plate holding the eggcups was embroidered with slices of the thinnest white bread and butter. Mariette had cut them herself. And now Mr. Charlton looked at them, as he looked at the eggs, with reluctance and trepidation, as if not wanting to tamper with their fresh, neat virginity.

"I've been looking at you," Ma said. "I don't think you get enough to eat by half."

"I live in lodgings," Mr. Charlton said. "It's not always—"

"We want to have some of your egg!" the twins said. "Give us some of your egg!"

"Now you've started summat," Pop said.

A moment later Mr. Charlton announced the startling discovery that the twins were just alike; he simply couldn't tell one from the other.

"You're quick," Pop said. "You're quick."

"It's gone dark again," Ma said. "Turn up the contrast. And, Montgomery, fetch me my Guinness. There's a good boy."

Soon, while Ma drank Guinness and Pop spoke passionately again of nightingales, bluebells that clothed the copses, "fick as carpets, ficker in fact," and how soon it would be the great time of the year, the time he loved most, the time of strawberry fields and cherries everywhere, Mr. Charlton found himself with a twin on each knee, dipping white fingers of bread and butter into delicious craters of warm golden egg yolk.

"I hope the eggs are done right?" Mariette said.

"Perfect."

"Perfick they will be an' all if she does 'em, you can bet you," Pop said. "Perfick!"

Mr. Charlton had given up, for the time being, all thought of the yellow-buff form. A goose brushed his legs again. Outside, somewhere in the yard, a dog barked and the drove of turkeys seemed to respond in bubbling chorus. Far beyond them, in broken, throaty tones, a cuckoo called, almost in its June voice, and when it was silent the entire afternoon simmered in a single marvelous moment of quietness, breathlessly.

"If you don't mind me saying so," Ma said, "a few days in the country do you a world of good."

"What are we having Sunday, Ma?" Pop said. "Turkey?"

"What you like. Just what you fancy."

"Roast pork," Montgomery said. "I like roast pork. With them brown onions."

"Or goose," Pop said. "How about goose? We ain't had goose since Easter."

In enthusiastic tones Pop went on to ask Mr. Charlton whether he preferred goose, turkey, or roast pork but Mr. Charlton, bewildered, trying to clean his misty spectacles and at the same time cut into thin fingers the last of his bread and butter, confessed he hardly knew.

"Well, I tell you what," Ma said, "we'll have goose *and* roast pork. Then I can do applesauce for the two."

"Perfick," Pop said. "Perfick. Primrose, pass me the catsup. I've got a bit of iced bun to finish up."

"Dinner on Sunday then," Ma said. "About two o'clock."

Mr. Charlton, who was unable to decide from this whether he had been invited to dinner or not, felt fate softly brush his legs again in the shape of a goose neck. At the same time he saw Mariette smile at him with intensely dark, glowing eyes, almost as if she had in fact brushed his leg with her own, and he felt his limbs again begin melting.

Across the fields a cuckoo called again and Pop echoed it with a belch that seemed to surprise him not only by its length and richness but by the fact that it was a belch at all.

"Manners," he said. "Pardon," and beat his chest in stern, suppressive apology. "Wind all of a sudden."

"What's on now?" Ma said. On the television screen all shooting had stopped and two men on horses, one a piebald, were riding up the valley, waving farewell hands.

"Nobody's birthday, Sunday, is it?" Pop said.

"Nobody's birthday before August," Ma said.

"Then it's mine," Mariette said. "I'll be eighteen."

"Pity it ain't nobody's birthday," Pop said. "We might have had a few fireworks."

Suddenly all the geese were gone from the kitchen and Ma, marveling at this fact, started laughing like shaking jelly again and said, "They did that once before. They heard us talking!"

"Tell you what," Pop said, "if you've had enough, Mr. Charlton, why don't you get Mariette to take you as far as the wood and hear them nightingales? I don't think you believe they sing all day, do you?"

"Oh yes, I—"

"Shall we ride or walk?" Mariette said. "I don't mind the pony if you want to ride."

"I think I'd rather walk."

"In that case I'll run and change into a dress," she said. "It's getting a bit warm for jodhpurs."

While Mariette had gone upstairs the twins abandoned Mr. Charlton's eggless plate and fetched jam jars from the kitchen.

"Going to the stall," they said. "Think we'll put honeysuckle on today instead of bluebells."

As they ran off, Pop said, "That's the flower stall they keep at the corner of the road down there. Wildflowers. Tuppence a bunch for motorists. Everybody works here, y'know."

"I think I passed it," Mr. Charlton said, "as I walked up from the bus."

"That's the one," Pop said. "Everybody's got to work here so's we can scratch a living. Montgomery, you'd better get off to your goats and start milking 'em."

Presently Ma, concerned at Mr. Charlton's air of retreat, uncertainty, and fatigue, spread hands like lardy legs of pork across her salmon sweater and said with earnest kindness, "Taking your holiday soon, Mr. Charlton? Where do you usually go?"

"I hadn't—"

"You should come strawberry picking with us," Ma said. "Do you the world of good. Else cherry picking. Best holiday in the world if the weather's nice. Make yourself a lot o' money too."

"Perfick," Pop said. "Don't cost nothing either. Here's Mariette. Perfick, I tell you."

Mr. Charlton rose from the table to find himself stunned by a new astral body, now in a lime-green dress with a broad black belt, a flouncing skirt, loose neck, and short scalloped sleeves. Her beautiful dark eyes were smiling at him splendidly.

"Is that your shantung?" Ma said. "You'll be warm enough in that, dear, will you?"

"Oh, it's hot," Mariette said. "It's nice to feel the breeze blowing around my legs again. You ready, Mr. Charlton?"

Mr. Charlton, the yellow-buff form forgotten, turned and followed Mariette, who actually stretched out a friendly hand. As they crossed a yard noisy with honking geese, mumbling turkeys, and braying goats being led to milking by Montgomery, Pop called, "Remember about Sunday, Mr. Charlton, won't you? Don't forget about Sunday."

"You really mean it?" Mr. Charlton halted and turned back, amazed. "Are you quite sure?"

"Sure?" Pop said. "Blimey, old man, I'm going to kill the geese any minute now."

"Thank you. Thank you very much."

"One goose or two, Ma?" Pop called. "Two geese be enough? Or shall we have three?"

Mr. Charlton, still stunned and amazed, turned to face the waiting figure of Mariette and saw it miraculously framed against piles of junk, rampant nettles, and in the near distance, deep strips of bluebells fenced away, in the strip of woodland, from flocks of red-brown marauding hens. Her legs, in pale beige silk stockings, were surprisingly shapely and slender. Her breasts protruded with grace from the soft lime shantung.

He could not believe in this figure. Nor, five minutes later, could he believe that the yard of nettles and junk, Pop's beautiful, incredible paradise, lay only a hundred yards away, screened by thickets of hornbeam and hazel, oaks in olive flower, and May trees carrying blossoms as rich and thick as Ma's lavish Jersey cream.

"You didn't really believe about the nightingales, did you?"

"No."

"Listen," she said. "You will."

Walking along the woodland path, Mr. Charlton could hear only a single untangled chorus of evening birdsong, unseparated into species, confusing as the tuning of orchestra strings.

"Let's stand here by the gate and listen," Mariette said. "Let's stand and listen here."

Mr. Charlton, transfixed, utterly bemused, stood by the gate and listened. Patches of evening sunlight, broken gold, sprinkled down through oakbranches like delicate quivering translations in light of the bird notes themselves.

"No, not that one," Mariette said. "That's a blackbird. Not the one over there, either. That's a wren. Now—that one. The one in the chestnut up there. The one with the long notes and then the long pause. Can you hear it now? That's a nightingale."

Mr. Charlton listened, hardly breathing, and heard for the first time in his life, in a conscious moment, the voice of a nightingale singing against a May evening sky.

Enthralled, still hardly believing it, he turned to see the deep black eyes holding him in utter captivation and heard her say again, "You really didn't believe it, did you?"

"I must say I didn't."

"I tell you something else you didn't believe either."

"What was that?"

"You didn't believe about me, did you?" she said. "You didn't believe I was the same girl you saw riding at Easter, did you?"

"No," he said. "How did you know?"

"I guessed," she said. "I could see it in your eyes. I was watching you."

She lifted her hands and held them suddenly against his cheeks without either boldness or hesitation but with a lightness of touch that woke in Mr. Charlton's legs exactly the same melting, unnerving sensation as that when the geese had brushed against him under the table. A moment later he saw her lips upraised.

"Who did you think I was?"

Mr. Charlton made a startling, embarrassed confession.

"I thought—well, I was actually told you were someone else in point of fact—that you were a niece of Lady Planson-Forbes—you know, at Carrington Hall—"

Mariette began laughing, in ringing tones, very much like her father.

"Now you've just found I wasn't."

"Well, yes—"

"You feel it makes any difference?"

"Well, in point of fact—"

"I'm just the same, aren't I?" She smiled and he found his eyes level with her bare, olive shoulder. "I'm just me. The same girl. Just me. Just the same."

Again she touched his face with her hands and Mr. Charlton took hurried refuge in a sudden recollection of the yellow-buff form.

"By the way, I mustn't forget to get your father to sign that form before I go—"

"You'll have to sign it for him," she said, "or Ma will. He can't write his name."

She laughed again and Mr. Charlton, his limbs melting once more as she lifted his hand to her bare warm shoulder, heard consciously but dizzily, for the second time in his life, a passionate burst of song from the nightingales.

At the same moment, back in the house, Pop returned to the kitchen after wringing the necks of three fat geese and poured himself a much needed glass of beer.

"A few days like this, Ma," he said, " 'll put a bit o' paint on the strawberries."

Ma was raking the kitchen fire, putting on to it empty ice-cream cartons, scraps of fish-and-chips, eggshells, pineapple tops, and Mr. Charlton's yellow-buff paper.

"I don't know as I shan't get a few bottles o' port wine in for Sunday," Pop said, "so we can celebrate."

"Celebrate what?"

"Well," Pop said, "what about Mariette?"

Ma laughed again, her sweater shaking like salmon jelly.

"The only thing is," Pop said, "I hope he won't want to take her away from here." He carried his beer to the kitchen door and from there contemplated, almost with reverence, the paradisiacal scene beyond. "Gawd A'mighty, Ma, you know we got a beautiful place here. Paradise. I don't know what we'd do if she were took away from here."

Standing in the evening sunlight, gazing across the pile of junk, the nettles, the rusting hovels, and the scratching, dusty hens, Pop sighed loudly and with such content that the sound seemed to travel with perfect definition across the surrounding fields of buttercups and may, gathering its echo at last from the mingled sounds of the remaining geese, the voices of cuckoos calling as they flew across the meadows, and the small, passionate, invisible nightingales.

"Perfick," Pop said. "You couldn't wish for nothing more perfick nowhere."

2

When Mariette and Mr. Charlton came down from the bluebell wood an hour later, Mariette carrying a bunch of bluebells and pink campion, Mr. Charlton bearing in his palm, with the tenderest care, two blue thrushes' eggs a bird had dropped in the grass at the woodside, Pop was washing pig buckets under the tap in the yard.

"Pigs look well," Pop said. "I think we'll kill one. Hear the nightingales?"

Mr. Charlton had not a second in which to answer this question before Pop said, "Wondering where you two had got to, Mr. Charlton. Tea's ready. Just in time."

A searching odor of frying kippers cut almost savagely through the warm May air.

"I thought we just had tea," Mr. Charlton said.

"That was dinner."

"I ought to catch my bus," Mr. Charlton said. "I must. The last one goes at eight o'clock."

"Ma won't hear of that," Pop said. "Will she, Mariette? Daresay Mariette won't either. Like to wash your hands? What you got there?"

Mr. Charlton revealed the thrushes' eggs, brilliant blue in his office-pale hands, and Mariette gave him a small dark smile of fascination that held him once more transfixed and speechless.

"Always run you home in the truck," Pop said. "Next time you come out you must bring your car. What kind of car you got, Mr. Charlton?"

Mr. Charlton confessed that he had no car. Pop was stunned.

"No car, no car?" he said. "That'll never do. Can't have that. Hear that, Mariette? Mr. Charlton ain't got no car."

"I don't think I'll have the time to come out again," Mr. Charlton said. "Do you think we could go into the question of the tax form before I go? It's very important."

"Tea first," Pop said. "Must have a cuppa tea first. Don't want to make Ma mad, do you?"

Pop finished drying his hands and gave Mr. Charlton the towel. Mr. Charlton put the two thrushes' eggs into his pocket and ran tap water over his hands, washing them with a gritty cake of purple soap. Mariette gave him another intimate, flashing smile and then went toward the house, calling that she was going to powder her nose, and Mr. Charlton, completely captivated by the delicate vision of green shantung retreating in the golden evening sunshine, forgot the thrushes' eggs and said, "I don't know if you appreciate how severe the penalties are for not making a tax return, Mr. Larkin."

"Ma's calling," Pop said.

Mr. Charlton listened but couldn't hear a sound.

"I shall have to make some sort of report to my office," Mr. Charlton said. "Then if you don't cooperate it'll be taken out of my hands and after that—"

"Beautiful evening, ain't it?" Pop said. Once again, caught in his own web of enchantment, he turned to stare at an evening distilled now into even deeper gold by the lower angle of light falling across still seas of buttercups and long-curled milky waves of may.

"I strongly recommend you—"

"Pair o' goldfinches," Pop said, but Mr. Charlton was too slow to see the birds, which darted past him like dipping sparks of scarlet, black, and gold.

In the kitchen Ma was frying a third batch of four fat tawny kippers in a brand-new aluminum pan while Mariette powdered her face over the sink, looking into a heart-shaped mirror stuck about with little silver, pink, and violet seashells.

"How'd you get on with Mr. Charlton, ducky?"

"Slow," Mariette said. "He's very shy."

"Well, he mustn't be shy," Ma said. "That won't get you nowhere."

"He would talk about horses."

"You'll have to find something a bit better than that to talk about, won't you?" Ma said. "Bit more stimulating."

Mariette, who was busy making up her lips with a tender shade of pink, not at all unlike the pink of the rose campion, that went well with her dress of cool lime shantung, did not answer.

"I think he looks half-starved," Ma said. "No blood in him. Wants feeding up. I'll find him a good fat kipper."

Mariette was wetting small wisps of short hair with her fingertips and winding them about her ears like black watch springs.

"Put some of my Goya on," Ma said. "The gardenia. Or else the Chanel. They both stand by my jewel box in our bedroom."

While Mariette went upstairs to dab perfume behind her ears and in the soft hollows of her legs, Mr. Charlton and Pop came in from the yard to join Montgomery, Primrose, Victoria, and the twins, who sat at the table licking thick bars of ice cream and watching a television program in which three men, a clergyman, and a woman were discussing prostitution and what should be done about it all.

"Strawberry picking on Monday over at Benacre, Pop," Montgomery said. "I heard from Fred Brown."

"That's early," Pop said. "Earliest we've ever been. I said this wevver'd soon put the paint on 'em."

Ma came in bearing a big dish of stinging hot kippers running with fat dabs of butter and on the television screen the woman shook a condemnatory finger at the gaping children and said, "The women are, on the whole, less to be blamed than pitied. It is largely the fault of man."

"Ma," Pop said. "Strawberry picking Monday. Better get that deep freeze, hadn't we?"

"Sooner the better," Ma said. "Better go in first thing tomorrow. It's Saturday." She began to serve kippers. "Start pouring tea, Primrose. Kipper, Mr. Charlton? Here we come. Nice fat one. Help yourself to more butter if you want to."

While Ma served kippers and Primrose poured tea, Pop rose from the table and fetched a bottle of whiskey from the cocktail cabinet.

"Milk?" he said to Ma.

"Please," Ma said. "Just what I need."

Pop poured whiskey into Ma's tea, then into his own, and then turned to Mr. Charlton, the bottle upraised.

"Drop o' milk, Mr. Charlton?"

"No, no, no. No really. Not for me. No, really not for me."

"Relieves the wind, frees the kidneys, and opens the bowels," Pop said blandly.

"No, no. No really. Not at this time of day."

"Do you all the good in the world, Mr. Charlton."

Pop, after filling up Mr. Charlton's teacup with whiskey, stood for a moment staring at the television screen and said, "What the ruddy 'ell are they talking about? Kids, how much money you make on the stall?"

"Eighteenpence. There was a policeman on a motorbike come along."

"Pity he hadn't got summat else to do," Pop said.

With elbows on the table, Victoria, who was trying to eat her kipper with a spoon, said in a shrill quick voice, "I don't like kippers. They're made of combs."

"Now, now," Pop said. "Now, now. Manners, manners. Elbows!"

"Pop has 'em at a word," Ma said.

Mr. Charlton sat held in a new constriction of bewilderment made more complex by the arrival of Mariette, fresh and lovely with new pink lipstick, face powder, and a heavy fragrance of gardenias that overwhelmed him in a cloud of intoxication as she came and sat at his side.

As if this were not enough she had brought with her the bluebells and the rose campion, arranged in an orange and crimson jar. She set the jar in the center of the table, where the flowers glowed in the nightmare marine glow of the television light like a strange sheaf of seaweed. The bluebells too smelled exquisitely.

"Sorry I'm late," she whispered to Mr. Charlton, and he could have sworn, in another moment of shimmering agony, that her silky legs had brushed his own. "Just had to make myself presentable."

"By the way, Mr. Charlton," Pop said, "what's your other name? Don't like this mistering."

"Cedric."

Ma started choking.

"Kipper bone!" Pop said. "Happened once before."

He rose from the table and struck Ma a severe blow in the middle of the back. She boomed like a drum.

"Better?" Pop said, and hit her a second time, rather more robustly than the first.

Except for bouncing slightly Ma did not seem to mind at all.

"Worst of kippers," Pop said. "Too much wirework. Fetched it up?"

On the television screen a man in close-up stared with steadfast earnestness at Mr. Charlton and the eight Larkins and said, "Well, there it is. We leave it with you. What do you think? What is to be done about these women? Is it their fault? Is it the fault of men? If not, whose fault is it?" and once again, for the third time, Ma started laughing, her sweater shaking like salmon jelly.

"Play crib at all, Mr. Charlton?" Pop said.

Mr. Charlton had to confess he had never heard of crib.

"Card game," Pop said. "We all play here. Learns you figures. Mariette plays. Mariette could show you how."

Mr. Charlton turned to look shyly at Mariette and found his vision, already blurred by the curious light from the television screen, clouded into more numbing and exquisite confusion by the thick sweet fragrance of gardenia. In return she gazed at him with dark silent eyes, so that he could not help trembling and was even glad when Pop said, "Like billiards? Or snooker? Got a nice table out the back there. Full size. We could have a game o' snooker after tea."

"You know," Mr. Charlton said, "I'm really awfully sorry, but I must catch this eight o'clock bus."

"No eight o'clock bus now," Montgomery said. "They knocked it off soon after petrol rationing started."

"That's right," Ma said. "They never put it back again."

Mr. Charlton half rose from the table, agitated.

"In that case I must start walking. It's eight miles."

"Walking my foot," Pop said. "I said I'll run you home in the truck. Or else Mariette can take you in the station wagon. Mariette can drive. Mariette'll take you, won't you, Mariette?"

"Of course."

Mr. Charlton sat down, mesmerized.

"Why don't you stay the night?" Pop said. "That's all right, ain't it, Ma?"

"More the merrier."

"Perfick," Pop said. "Ma'll make you a bed up on the billiard table."

"No, really—"

"It's so simple," Mariette said. "After all tomorrow's Saturday. You don't have to go to the office Saturday, do you?"

" 'Course he don't," Pop said. "Offices don't work Saturdays. They don't none of 'em know what work is no more."

"That's settled then," Ma said. "I'll put him on that new superfoam mattress Mariette has for sunbathing."

"Oh, that mattress is marvelous," Mariette said. "You sink in. Your body simply dreams into that mattress."

In another unnerving moment Mr. Charlton saw the girl, hands raised to her bare shoulders, luxuriously enact for him the attitudes of dreaming into the mattress. As her eyes closed and her lips parted gently he struggled to bring himself back to reality, firmness, and a state of resistance and he said, "No, I'm sorry. I really must be adamant—"

Pop stared with open mouth, powerfully stunned and impressed by this word. He could not ever remember having heard it even on television.

"Quite understand," he said.

In a single moment Mr. Charlton was raised greatly in his estimation. He looked at him with awe.

"Oh, won't you stay?" Mariette said. "We could ride tomorrow."

Groping again, struggling against the dark eyes and the fragrance of gardenia, powerful even above the penetrating sting of kippers, Mr. Charlton began to say, "No, really. For one thing I've nothing with me. I've no pajamas."

"Gawd Almighty," Pop said. "Pajamas?"

His admiration and awe for Mr. Charlton now increased still further. He was held transfixed by the fact that here was a man who spoke in words of inaccessible meaning and wore pajamas to sleep in.

"Sleep in your shirt, old man," he said. "Like I do."

Pop had always slept in his shirt; he found it more convenient that way. Ma, on the other hand, slept in nylon nightgowns, one of them an unusual pale petunia-pink that Pop liked more than all the rest because it was light, delicate, and above all completely transparent. It was wonderful for seeing through. Under it Ma's body appeared like a global map, an expanse of huge explorable mountains, shadowy valleys, and rosy pinnacles.

"I wear pajamas," Mariette said. "I'll lend you a pair of mine."

"No, really—"

Mr. Charlton became utterly speechless as Ma got up, went into the kitchen, and brought back four tins of whole peaches, which she began to open with an elaborate tin opener on the sideboard.

"Save some of the juice, Ma," Pop said. "I'll have it later with a drop o' gin."

"I think you're about my size," Mariette said, as if everything were now completely settled, so that Mr. Charlton found himself in the center of a shattering vortex, trapped there by the torturing and incredible thought that presently he would be sleeping in Mariette's own pajamas, on her own dreaming bed of foam.

Before he could make any further protest about this, Primrose poured him a second cup of tea, and Pop, leaning across the table, filled it up with whiskey.

"You ought to come strawberry picking," Pop said. Mr. Charlton suddenly remembered the tax form. It mustn't be forgotten, he thought, the tax form. On no account must it be forgotten. "This is very like the last summer we'll ever go strawberry picking, Mr. Charlton. We, you, anybody. You know why?"

Tax form, tax form, tax form, Mr. Charlton kept thinking. Tax form. "No. Why?"

On the television screen a voice announced, "We now take you to Fanshawe Castle, the home of the Duke of Peele," and Ma, ladling out the last of the peaches, crowned by thick ovals of cream, said, "Turn up the contrast. I want to see this. It's got dark again."

"Because," Pop said, "the strawberry lark's nearly over."

Tax form, tax form, tax form, Mr. Charlton thought again. How was it the strawberry lark was nearly over? Tax form.

"Disease," Pop said. "Sovereigns are finished. Climax is finished. Huxleys are finished. Soon there won't be no strawberries nowhere."

Tax form. "You mean that in this great strawberry-growing district—"

"This districk. Every districk. In two years the strawberry lark'll be over."

"Well, myself, I actually prefer raspberries—"

"The raspberry lark's nearly over as well," Pop said. "Mosaic. Weakening strain. And the plum lark. And the cherry lark. And the apple lark. They can't sell apples for love nor—"

"We're in the library," Ma said. "Pop, look at the library."

Tax form—Mr. Charlton, with piteous desperation, struggled with the power of all his declining concentration to see that the tax form was remembered. "I've got to go home," he thought. "I've got to start walking." Something brushed his leg. "I must remember the tax form." He was startled into a sudden shivering catch of his breath and a moment later the white kitten was on his knee.

"Gawd Almighty," Pop said. "What are all them on the walls?"

"Must be books," Ma said.

In mute staring concentration Pop sat involved by the picture on the television screen, noisily eating peaches and taking an occasional quickly sucked gulp of whiskey and tea.

"Never," he said. "Can't be."

"Beautiful home," Ma said. "I like the valances. That's what we want. Valances like that."

Tax form! Mr. Charlton's mind shouted. Tax form—!

"Books?" Pop said. "*All* books?"

"I'll go and find the pajamas and get them aired," Mariette said. Mr. Charlton emerged from a moment of acute hypnosis to feel her hand reach out, touch him softly, and then begin to draw him away. "Coming? We could try them against you for size."

"The man who owns that owes five million in taxes," Mr. Charlton said desperately and for no reason at all. "Mr. Larkin, that reminds me—we mustn't forget that form—"

"Perfick place," Pop said. "On the big side though. Suppose they need it for the books."

"Oh, the carpets. Look at the carpets," Ma said. "There must be miles of carpets. Acres."

"He'll have to give it all up," Mr. Charlton said. "The state will take it for taxes. You see what can happen—"

"Come on," Mariette said, and Mr. Charlton, struggling for the last time against the flickering, rising tides of sea-green light rolling across the table in mesmeric, engulfing flow, followed the girl blunderingly into the kitchen, the white kitten softly brushing his legs as he went, the thick night-sweet scent of gardenia penetrating to his blood, seeming to turn it as white as the flower from which it sprang.

3

At half past ten, just before television closed down for the night, Pop, Ma, and Mariette were still trying to teach Mr. Charlton the mysteries and arithmetic of crib. Utterly baffled—the only coherent thing he had been able to do all evening was to telephone his landlady to say that he wouldn't be coming home that night—Mr. Charlton found it quite impossible to understand the elements of the game, still less its language and figures.

"Fifteen-two, fifteen-four, fifteen-six, pair's eight, three's eleven, three's fourteen, and one for his nob's fifteen."

Pop dealt the cards very fluidly; he counted like a machine.

"I don't understand one for his nob."

"Jack," Pop said. "I told you—one for his nob. Two for his heels. Your deal, Ma."

Ma dealt very fluidly too.

"Got to use your loaf at this game, Mr. Charlton," Pop said. "I thought you was an office man? I thought you was good at figures?"

"Rather different sort of figures," Mr. Charlton said.

"Oh?" Pop said. "Really? They look all the same to me."

Pop picked up the cards Ma had dealt him, took a quick look at them, and said smartly, "Misdeal. Seven cards. Bung in."

"Pick 'em up!" Ma said, and threatened him with a hand as large as a leg of lamb. "Don't you dare."

"Wanted a Parson's Poke," Pop said.

"No more Parson's Pokes," Ma said. "Get on with it. Make the best with what you've got." Ma kicked Mr. Charlton playfully on the shins under the table, laughing. "Got to watch him, Mr. Charlton, playing crib. Parson's Poke, my foot. Sharp as a packet o' pins."

"Twenty-two, nine'll do. Twenty-five, six's is alive. Twenty-eight, Billy Wake. Twenty-seven, four's in heaven. Twenty-three, eight's a spree."

In the combined turmoil of counting and the glare of the television Mr. Charlton felt a certain madness coming back.

"What you got, Pop?"

"Terrible. What Paddy shot at."

"See what I mean?" Ma said. She kicked Mr. Charlton a second time on the shins, just as playfully as the first. "Misdeal my foot! No wonder he says you got to use your loaf at this game. Your deal next, Mr. Charlton. Your box."

Mr. Charlton, as he picked up the cards, was beginning to feel that he had no loaf to use. He felt awful; his loaf was like a sponge.

"Let's have a Parson's Poke!" Pop said.

"No more Parson's Poke," Ma said. "Too many Parson's Pokes are bad luck."

"Your box, Mr. Charlton. Give yourself a treat."

"Let him play his own game!" Ma said. "Play your own hand, Mr. Charlton. Use your own loaf. What's on telly now?"

"Something about free speech," Mariette said. "Freedom of the press or something."

Pop turned his head, looking casually at the flickering screen. On it four heated men were, it seemed, about to start fighting.

"Wherever conditions of uniform tolerance may be said to obtain—"

"Barmy," Ma said. "Want their heads testing."

"The trouble with telly," Pop said, "it don't go on long enough."

"You miss it when you're talking," Ma said. "You feel lost, somehow. Don't you think you feel lost, Mr. Charlton?"

Mr. Charlton had to confess he felt lost.

"I like this set better than the other," Ma said. "Better contrast."

"Thirsty, Ma?" Pop said. "I'm thirsty."

During the evening Pop had drunk the remainder of the peach juice laced with gin, two bottles of Guinness, and a light ale. Mr. Charlton had drunk two glasses of beer. Ma and Mariette had been drinking cider.

"I'll mix a cocktail," Pop said. "Mr. Charlton, what about a cocktail?"

"You don't want no more," Ma said. "You'll want to get out in the night."

"I'm thirsty," Pop said. "I'm parched up."

"You'll be pickled."

Pop was already on his feet, moving toward the expensive glass-and-chrome cocktail cabinet that stood in one corner. "Sit down and play your hand."

Pop stood by the cabinet, his pride hurt and offended.

"Never been pickled in me life," he said. "Anyway not more than once or twice a week. And then only standin'-up pickled."

Was there some difference between that and other forms? Mr. Charlton wondered.

"Layin'-down pickled," Pop said, "of course."

"I'm getting tired of crib," Mariette said. "It's hot in here. I'm going to cool off in the yard, Mr. Charlton." Like her father she found it difficult to call Mr. Charlton by his Christian name. "Like to come?"

"After he's had a cocktail," Pop said. "I'm going to mix everybody a special cocktail."

While Mariette packed up the cards, the pegs, and the pegboard Pop stood by the cocktail cabinet consulting a book, *A Guide to Better Drinking*, given him by Montgomery for Christmas. It was the only book he had ever read.

"Here's one we never tried," Pop said. "Rolls-Royce."

"That sounds nice," Ma said.

"Half vermouth, quarter whiskey, quarter gin, dash of orange bitters."

"Dash you will too," Ma said, "with that lot. It'll blow our heads off."

"Blow summat off," Pop said. "Not sure what though."

Once again Ma started laughing like shaking jelly.

"How do you like our cocktail cabinet, Mr. Charlton?" Pop said. "Only got it at Christmas. Cost us a hundred and fifty."

"Hundred and eighty," Ma said. "We got this model in the end. The one with the extra sets of goblets. The brandy lot. You remember. And the silver bits for hot punch and all that."

With confusion and awe Mr. Charlton stared at the cocktail cabinet, over which Pop hovered, mixing the drinks, in his shirt sleeves. The cabinet, he realized for the first time, seemed shaped like an elaborate glass and silver ship.

"Am I mistaken?" he said. "Or is it a ship?"

"Spanish galleon," Pop said. "Heigh-ho and a bottle o' rum and all that lark."

When the cocktail was mixed Pop poured it into four large cut-glass tumblers embellished with scarlet cockerels. He had mixed it double, he said. It saved a lot of time like that.

"Try it first," Ma said. "We don't want it if it's no good, Rolls-Royce or no Rolls-Royce. Besides, you might fall down dead."

Pop drained the shaker.

"Perfick," he said. "This'll grow hair."

"By the way," Ma said, "talking about Rolls-Royce, did you do anything about that one?"

"Sunday," Pop said. "The chap's a stockbroker. Colonel Forbes. He's only down weekends."

"Pop's mad on a Rolls," Ma explained to Mr. Charlton.

"By the way, Mr. Charlton," Pop said, "what was that about that feller on telly owing five million taxes? Was that right?"

"Perfectly correct."

"What for?"

"Death duties."

"Deaf duties!" Pop said. "Deaf duties! I feel like murder every time I hear deaf duties!"

Pop, snorting with disgust and irritation, struck the table with the palm of his hand and as if by a prearranged signal the light in the television went out. Ma uttered a sudden cry as if something terrible had happened. Mariette got up suddenly and switched the set off and there floated by Mr. Charlton's face, as she passed, a fresh wave of gardenia, warm as the evening itself, disturbed and disturbing as she moved.

"That made my head jump," Ma said. "I thought a valve had gone."

"Closing down, that's all," Pop said. "Eleven o'clock and they're closing down. Hardly got started."

Pop, giving another snort of disgust about death duties and the brief and contemptible daily compass of television, handed around the cocktails.

"Cheers, everybody," he said, raising his glass. "Here's to the strawberry lark. Roll on Monday."

Mr. Charlton drank. A wave of pure alcohol burned the roots of his tongue. He was utterly unable to speak for some moments and could only listen with undivided and searing agony to a question, first from Pop and then from Mariette, about whether he could be with them on Monday for the strawberry lark.

"I—I—I—"

A sensation as of a white-hot stiletto descending rapidly toward Mr. Charlton's navel prevented the sentence from developing beyond a single choking word.

"Make yourself fifteen or twenty quid in no time," Pop said. "All the strawberries you can eat. And a pound free every day. You can gather a hundred and fifty pounds a day."

"I—I—I—"

Burning tears came into Mr. Charlton's eyes. He succeeded in murmuring at last, with a tongue cauterized of all feeling and in a voice that did not belong to him, something about work, office, and having no leave.

"You could always come in the evening," Mariette said. "Plenty of people do."

As she said this she again turned and looked at him. The eyes seemed more tenderly, intensely, darkly penetrative than ever and he began flushing deeply.

"It's lovely in the evenings," Mariette said. "Absolutely lovely."

Another draft of alcohol, snatched by Mr. Charlton in another desperate moment of speechlessness, injected fire into remote interior corners of his body that he did not know existed.

"My God, this is a perfick pick-me-up," Pop said. "We must all have another one of those."

Mr. Charlton despaired and passed a groping hand over his face. His mouth burned, as from eating ginger. He heard Ma agree that the cocktail was a beauty. He actually heard her say that they owed everybody in the neighborhood a drink. "What say we have a cocktail party and give them this one? This'll get under their skin."

That, Mr. Charlton heard himself saying, was what was happening to him, but nobody seemed to hear a voice that was already inexplicably far away, except that Ma once again began laughing, piercingly, the salmon sweater shaking like a vast balloon.

"A few more of these and you won't see me for dust," she said.

"A few more?" Mr. Charlton heard himself saying. "A few more?"

"First refill coming up, Mr. Charlton. How do you like it? Ma, I bet this would go well with a herring paste sandwich."

Something about this remark made Mr. Charlton start laughing too. This enlivening development was a signal for Pop to strike Mr. Charlton a severe blow in the back, exactly as he had done Ma, and call him a rattlin' good feller. "Feel you're one of the family. Feel we've known you years. That right, Ma?"

That was right, Ma said. That was the truth. That was how they felt about him.

"Honest trufe," Pop said. "Honest trufe, Mr. Charlton."

A wave of unsteady pleasure, like a flutter of ruffling wind across water on a summer afternoon, ran through Mr. Charlton's veins and set them dancing. He drank again. He felt a sudden lively and uncontrollable desire to pick strawberries on warm midsummer evenings, no matter what happened. "My God, this is great stuff," he told everybody. "This is the true essence—"

Nobody knew what Mr. Charlton was talking about. It was impossible to grasp what he meant by the true essence, but it set Ma laughing again. Somewhere behind the laughter Mr. Charlton heard Pop mixing a third, perhaps a fourth refill, saying at the same time "Only thing it wants is more ice. More ice, Ma!"

Mr. Charlton, for no predetermined reason, suddenly rose and struck himself manfully on the chest.

"I'll get it," he said. "That's me. I'm the iceman."

When Mr. Charlton came back from the kitchen, carrying trays of ice, Pop mixed the new drink and tasted it with slow, appraising tongue and eye.

"More perfick than ever!"

Everything was more perfick, Mr. Charlton kept telling himself. The scent of gardenia was more perfick. It too was stronger than ever. He laughed immoderately, for no reason, and at length, looking for the first time straight into the dark searching eyes of Mariette with neither caution nor despair.

"Mariette," he said, "what is the scent you're wearing?"

"Come and sit over here and I'll tell you."

Mr. Charlton moved to sit on the other side of the table. Rising abruptly, he stood stunned. It seemed to him that something remarkable had happened to Pop. Pop, it seemed to him, had disappeared.

"I didn't see Pop go out," he said. "Where's Pop gone?"

Ma began shrieking.

"I'm under here!" Pop said.

"Under me! I'm sitting on his lap," Ma said. "Why don't you ask Mariette if she'll sit on yours?"

Mariette, who needed no asking, sat on Mr. Charlton's lap. The illusion of being caressed in a silken, sinuous, maddening way by the goose's neck returned to Mr. Charlton as he felt her silken legs cross his own. A sensation that for the second time his blood was turning white while being at the same time on fire, coursed completely through him. The soles of his feet started tingling. The scent of gardenia overwhelmed him like a drug.

"Tell me what the scent is," Mr. Charlton said.

"Gardenia."

"Gardenia? Gardenia? What's gardenia?"

"It's a flower. Do you like it?"

"Like it? Like it?" Mr. Charlton said madly. "Like it?"

With extraordinarily soft hands Mariette took his own and held them high around her waist, just under her breasts. With stupefying tenderness she started to rock backward and forward on his knee, with the result that Mr. Charlton could not see straight. His eyes were simply two quivering balls revolving unrestrainedly in the top of his head.

"Well, getting late," Pop said. "Hitch up a bit, Ma, and I'll mix another before we go to shut-eye."

Pop reappeared presently from underneath the salmon canopy of Ma and announced that he was going to mix a new one this time.

"How about a Chauffeur? Damnit, a Rolls has to have a chauffeur," he said. He stood earnestly consulting the *Guide to Better Drinking.* "One third vermouth, one third whiskey, one third gin, dash of angostura. Sounds perfick. Everybody game?"

Everybody was game. Mr. Charlton was very game. He said so over and over again. Mariette held his hands more closely against her body and a little higher than before and Mr. Charlton let his head rest against the velvety, downy nape of her dark neck.

"You're my goose. My gardenia," he said.

"Wouldn't you think," Mariette said, "that it was soon time to go to bed?"

Some moments later Mr. Charlton had drained the Chauffeur in two gulps and was addressing Ma and Pop in what he thought were solid, steadfast tones of gratitude.

"Can never thank you. Never thank you. Never be able to thank you."

He shook on his feet, grasped at air with aimless hands, and started jiggling like a fish.

"Should be a cocktail called gardenia! A sweet one—"

"I'll make one," Pop said. "I'll think one up."

"And one called Mariette," Mr. Charlton said. "Sweet one too!"

He staggered violently and some time later was vaguely aware of walking arm in arm to the billiard room with Mariette. There was no light in the billiard room. He felt filled with inconsolable happiness and laughed with wild immoderation, once again feeling her legs brush against him like the goose neck in the darkness. Once again too he called her a gardenia and stretched out groping hands to touch her.

Instead, unsurprised, he found himself kneeling by the billiard table, caressing in the corner pocket a solitary, cool abandoned ball.

"Where are you? Where are you?" he said. "Mariette—"

Mr. Charlton got up and fell down, breaking the thrushes' eggs in his pocket as he fell.

"Climb up," Mariette said. Mr. Charlton found it impossible to climb up and Mariette started pushing him. "Upsydaisy. Up you go. I'll get your collar off."

Meanwhile Pop, who was sitting up in bed in his shirt, thinking of the evening sunshine, the meadows shining so beautifully and so golden with buttercups and the prospect of summer growing to maturity all about his paradise, decided that the only thing to make the day more perfick was a cigar.

"I'm the same as Churchill," he said. "Like a good cigar."

He lit the cigar and sat watching Ma undress herself. The thing he really loved most about Ma, he had long since decided, was that she didn't have to wear corsets. She didn't need them; her figure was all her own; pure and natural as could be.

"Ma, I've been thinking," he said, "when does Mariette expect this baby?"

"She can't make up her mind."

"Well, she'd better," Pop said.

"Why?" Ma said.

From the depths of her transparent petunia canopy, as it floated down over the global map of her white, wide territory, Ma spoke with her customary air of unconcern.

Smoking his cigar, gazing thoughtfully through the open window to a night of warm May stars, as if pondering again on summer and the way it would soon embroider with its gold and green his already perfick paradise, Pop made a pronouncement.

"I'm a bit worried about Mr. Charlton. I don't think that young man's got it in 'im," he said. "At least not yet."

4

Mr. Charlton woke late and to a dark, disquieting impression. It was that he was lying alone in the center of a large flat green field. A cold storm was raging about him. Overhead drummed peals of thunder.

Agony taught him some minutes later that the thunder rolled from somewhere inside his own head and that the field was the billiard table, from which he was about to fall. He got up off the table and groped with uncertain agony about the semidarkened room, white hands limp at his sides, stringy and strengthless, like portions of tired celery.

He was wearing Mariette's pajamas, which were silk, of a pale blue color, with a pattern of either pink roses or carnations all over them— he was too distraught to tell which. He could not remember putting the pajamas on. He could only suppose Mariette had put them on. He could not remember that either.

Presently, after managing to pull on his trousers over his pajamas, he groped his way out of the billiard room. In the kitchen the apparition of Ma, now wearing a lavender-violet sweater instead of the salmon one, overrode all other objects, like a circus elephant. She was making toast and frying eggs and bacon. His hands trembled as they grasped a chair.

"Ah! there you are, Mr. Charlton. One egg or two?" Ma, in her customary fashion, started laughing like shaking jelly, her voice a carillon. "Two eggs or three? Sleep all right?"

Mr. Charlton sat down and thought that even if wild dogs had begun to chase him he would never again have the strength to move.

"Cuppa tea?" A heavy weight, like a descending pile driver, hit the table, shaking cups and cutlery. It was a cup. "Like a drop of milk in it?" With shaking bosom Ma roared happily again. "Cows or Johnnie Walker?"

Mr. Charlton prayed silently over the comforting fumes of tea.

"Mariette waited for you but you didn't seem to come, so she's gone for a ride now to get her appetite up," Ma said. "She'll be back any minute now. Pop's feeding the pigs. He's had one breakfast. But he'll want another."

Life, Mr. Charlton felt, was ebbing away from him. In his cup large tealeaves swam dizzily around and around, the black wreckage of disaster.

"You never said how many eggs," Ma said. "One or two? How do you like 'em? Turned over?"

"I—"

A moment later a rough sledgehammer hit Mr. Charlton in the middle of the back.

"How's the tax man?" Pop said. "How's my friend? All right, old man? Sleep well? Perfick morning, ain't it?"

Whereas overnight Mr. Charlton's veins had run white, in crazy, voluptuous courses, he now felt them to be some shade of pale, expiring green. There was something seriously wrong with his intestines. They were dissolving under waves of acid. He could no longer claim them for his own.

"I don't think Mr. Charlton feels very well," Ma said.

"No?" Pop said. "Pity. Didn't sleep very well? Potted the white, eh?" Pop barked with violent laughter at his joke. "Hair of the dog I should say."

Mr. Charlton had never heard of hair of the dog. Pop sat down at the table and drummed on it with the handles of his knife and fork, whistling "Come to the cook-house door, boys" through his teeth.

"What's your program this morning, old man? Like to come with me and take the pig over to the bacon factory?"

"I think I shall have to go home."

Faintly Mr. Charlton spoke for the first time, his voice full of pallid distress. Echoes of his words rang through his head in hollower tones, as through a sepulcher.

"Don't say that, old man," Pop said. "We was looking forward to having you the whole weekend. I want to show you the place. I got thirty-two acres here altogether. Lovely big medder at the back. Beautiful stretch o' river. Perfick. Do any fishing?"

While Pop was speaking Ma set before him a plate of three eggs, four six-inch rashers of home-cured bacon, three very thick brown sausages, and a slice of fried bread. Pop attacked this with the precipitate virility and desperation of a man who has not seen food for some long time. In an excruciating moment the last of Mr. Charlton's intestines got ready to dissolve.

Suddenly Pop slapped down his knife and fork, troubled.

"Something wrong?" Ma said.

"Don't taste right."

"You forgot the catsup, you loony, that's why."

"Gorblimey, so I did. Knowed there was summat wrong some-where."

Pop reached out, grabbed the catsup bottle, and shook an ocean of scarlet all over his breakfast.

Mr. Charlton shut his eyes. This grave mistake made him think that he was on the deck of a sinking ship, in a hurricane. He opened his eyes with great haste and the deck came up at him.

"Hullo there, bright eyes. Good morning. How are we this morning?"

The astral figure of Mariette, fresh in yellow shirt and jodhpurs, was all that Mr. Charlton felt he needed to set him weeping. The pristine, cheerful voice was beyond his range of thought. He tried to say something and failed, faintly.

"Mr. Charlton doesn't feel all that well," Ma said. "He says he might have to go home."

Pop belched with enormous pleasure, as usual surprising himself.

"Manners. Early-morning breeze. Pardon me." He struck his chest with the handle of the fork, as if in stern reproval. "Home, my foot. Stop worrying, old man. That's the trouble with you office fellers. You all worry too much by half. After all, here today and gone tomorrow."

It was not tomorrow, Mr. Charlton thought, that he was worried about. Unless he could find some speedy, drastic remedy he would, he was convinced, be gone today.

"Heavens, I'm hungry," Mariette said.

She sat down at the table, stirred a cup of tea, and started laughing. Her voice put stitches into Mr. Charlton's head: stabbing lines of them, on hot needles.

"See something funny out riding?" Pop said. "Like the brigadier's sister?"

"I was just smiling at Mr. Charlton. He's still got the pajamas on." She started laughing again and Mr. Charlton could not help feeling there was some sinister, hidden meaning in the word "smiling." "Oh, that was a laugh, getting them on last night. First we couldn't get one lot of trousers off and then we couldn't get the other lot on. Oh, Mr. Charlton, you were a scream. Absolute scream."

Mr. Charlton, who began to feel among other things that he was not grown up, did not doubt it. Everything was a scream. His whole body, his entire mind, and his intestines were a scream.

"Most of the time you were making love to a billiard ball in the side pocket."

Pop started choking.

"I said you potted the white, didn't I?" he shouted. "Ain't that what I said, Ma?" With immense glee Pop beat a tattoo on the tablecloth with the handles of his knife and fork. "Potted the white. Damn funny. Just what I said."

"Tonight I'll make you a proper bed up," Ma said. "In the bottom bathroom. Nobody uses it very much now we've got the new one upstairs."

"I really think," Mr. Charlton said, his voice limp, "I'd better go home."

In a sudden gesture of fond solicitude Pop put an arm around Mr. Charlton's shoulder.

"You know, Charley boy," he said, "I wish your name was Charley instead of Cedric. It's more human. I can't get used to Cedric. It's like a parson's name. Can't we call you Charley?—after all it's short for your other name."

"Please call me Charley if you wish," Mr. Charlton said and felt once again like weeping.

"What I was going to say, Charley boy," Pop went on, "is this, old man, I think you need a Larkin Special."

Mr. Charlton had no time to ask what a Larkin Special was before Pop was out of the room, across the passage, and into the living room on the other side. Presently there were noises from the Spanish galleon, the monster cocktail cabinet that could have only been molded, Mr. Charlton thought, by a man of evil, demoniac designs.

"That'll put you as right as a lamplighter in no time," Ma said. "Acts like a charm."

"A nice walk after breakfast," Mariette said, "and you'll be on top of the world." Mr. Charlton felt sure that that in fact was where he was, but in the act of falling. Mariette was now eating bacon, eggs, large burnished brown sausages, and fried bread. "We could walk across the meadow and have a look at the motorboat if you like."

"Motorboat?" At the same moment some curious reflex of thought made Mr. Charlton remember the yellow-buff tax form. He hadn't seen it since sharing his boiled eggs with the twins the previous day. "You've got a motorboat?"

"Nice one. Little beauty. We keep it in the boathouse on the other side of the meadow."

"Pop took it in exchange for a debt," Ma explained.

"Mrs. Larkin," Mr. Charlton began to say. He felt suddenly, in a guilty fashion, that he ought to make some sort of atonement with himself for all that had happened. He was actually bothered by a sense of duty. "I don't suppose you've seen that yellow-buff form—"

"Coming up, coming up, coming up," Pop said. "There you are, Charley, old man. Larkin Special. Don't ask what's in it. Don't stare at it. Don't think. Just drink it down. In ten minutes you'll feel perfick again."

Pop set before a demoralized Mr. Charlton, on the breakfast table, what Mr. Charlton could only think was a draft of bull's blood.

"I think I should go and lie down—"

"Don't think a thing!" Pop said. "Drink it. Say to 'ell wiv everything and drink it."

Mr. Charlton hesitated. His intestines rolled.

"I can vouch for it," Ma said.

The soft dark eyes of Mariette smiled across the table. The familiar astral vision of cool olive skin against the light lemon shirt, of dark hair and the firm treasured breasts that Mr. Charlton had almost clasped the previous evening, revived an inspiring, momentary recollection of his lost white fire.

He ducked his head and drank.

"Now I must get cracking," Pop said. "I got a bit of a deal to do about some straw. I got the new deep freeze to pick up. And the pigs. And the port."

With fond assurance he laid a hand on Mr. Charlton's shoulder.

"Charley, old man," he said, "by the time I get back you'll feel perfick."

For some time Mr. Charlton sat in tentative silence, reawaking. A feeling of slow intestinal restoration made him give, once or twice, a tender sigh. He grasped slowly that the thunder in his head had now become mere singing, like distant vespers in a minor key.

"Feeling more yourself now?"

Mariette was eating toast and golden marmalade. As she opened her mouth to eat he saw, for the first time, how beautifully white her teeth were and how pink, in a pure rose-petal shade, her tongue now appeared as it darted out and caught at golden shreds of marmalade.

He even found himself thinking of gardenia, its compelling, torturing night scent and the pure whiteness of its flower.

"It's absolutely wonderful in the woods this morning," Mariette said. "All the bluebells out. Millions of them. And the moon daisies.

It's hot too and the nightingales had already started when I was coming back. You're not really going home today?"

A lyrical wave passed over Mr. Charlton. With distaste he remembered his office: the in tray, the out tray, the files, the other chaps, the ink-stained desks, the chatter of typewriters.

"If you're sure it's no trouble—"

"Trouble!" Ma said. "We *want* you. We love to have you."

"I've finished," Mariette said. "Like to get a breath of air?"

Mr. Charlton went to the door and stood in the sun. With reviving heart he stared across Pop's paradise of junk, scratching hens, patrols of geese, and graveyards of rusty iron, in the middle of which Montgomery was milking goats under a haystack. Over all this a sky as blue as the thrushes' eggs that had come to disaster in his pocket spread with unblemished purity. The near fringes of meadows had become, overnight, white with moon daisies, drifts of summer snow. A cuckoo called and was answered by another, the notes like those of tender horns, the birds hidden in oak trees, among curtains of thickest olive flower.

"How do you feel now?" Mariette said.

The pale face of Mr. Charlton broadened into its first unsteady daylight smile.

"A little more perfick than I was."

By Saturday night the deep freeze was installed. By Sunday morning, three nine-pound geese, well stuffed with sage and onion, were sizzling in a pure white electric oven that could have spoken, Mr. Charlton thought, if spoke to. A light breeze drove with frailest spinnings of air through the bluebell wood and bore across the hot yard the delicious aroma of roasting birds.

Ma, who loved color, cooked in a canary yellow pinafore with big scarlet pockets and at intervals shouted across the yard, either to Pop or Mariette, Mr. Charlton or the children, or whoever happened to be there, a demand for instructions about the meal.

"What sort of vegetables do you fancy? Asparagus? I got green peas and new potatoes but shout if you want anything different." It turned out that Montgomery wanted brown braised onions, the twins Yorkshire pudding, and Primrose baked potatoes. "Fair enough," Ma said, "as long as we know."

At eleven o'clock, by which time Pop was no longer in the yard, Ma shouted that it was already so hot in the kitchen that she'd be sick by the time the meal was served.

"What say we have it outside?" she called. "Under the walnut tree?"

By noon Mariette, dressed in neat sky-blue linen shorts and an open-necked vermilion blouse, her legs bare, was laying a white cloth on a long table underneath a walnut tree that overshadowed, like a faintly fragrant umbrella, the only civilized stretch of grass near the house, on the south side, beside which Ma would later grow patches of petunia and zinnia, her favorite flowers. It was cool and dark there under the thickening walnut leaves, out of the sun, and Mr. Charlton helped her by bringing cutlery from the house on papier-mâché trays brightly decorated with hunting scenes, race meetings, or pointers carrying birds.

At half past twelve Pop startled everybody by driving into the yard in a Rolls-Royce, a prewar landaulet in black, with straw-colored doors that actually looked as if they had been made of plaited basketwork. The horn, sounding with discreet harmonious distinction, brought everybody running to the center of the rusty, dusty graveyards of junk and iron.

Pop stopped the car and dismounted with triumphant, imperial pride.

"Here it is!" he shouted. "Ourn!"

Before anyone could speak he leapt down to the doors, proudly pointing.

"Monogram," he said. "Look, Ma—monograms on the doors."

"Royal?" Ma said.

"Duke, I think," Pop said. "The feller didn't know. Anyway, duke or viscount or some toff of some sort."

Ma was dazzled. She took several paces forward and touched the gleaming bodywork.

"All in!" Pop said. "Everybody in! Everybody who wants a ride get in!"

Everybody, including Mr. Charlton, got into the Rolls-Royce. On the wide spacious seats of dove-gray upholstery, upon which heavy cords of tasseled yellow silk hung at the windows, there was plenty of room for everybody, but the twins sat on Mr. Charlton's lap. Ma herself sat in the center of the backseat, her pinafore spread out crinoline-wise, almost in royal fashion, her turquoise-ringed hands spread on her yellow pinafore.

Soon an entranced look crept like a web across her face, only her eyes moving as they rolled gently from side to side, taking in the smallest details.

"I wish I had my hat on," she said at last. "I don't feel right without my hat on."

"Got a big picnic basket in the boot," Pop said. "Corkscrews an' all."

"It's got vases for flowers," Ma said. She leaned forward and fingered with delicacy a pair of silver hornlike vases fixed below the glass screen that divided the backseat from the front.

"Notice anything else?" Pop called. "Have a good dekko. All around. Want you to notice one more thing, Ma. Have a good dekko."

After several seconds of silence, in which Ma's eyes revolved on a slow axis of exploration, in pure wonderment, Ma confessed that she saw nothing more.

"That thing like the bit off the end of a carpet sweeper!" Pop yelled. In his own delight he laughed in his customary ringing fashion. "Mind it don't bite you."

"No," Ma said. "No." Her mouth expired air in a long incredulous wheeze. "No—"

"Speakin' tube!" Pop said. "Pick it up. Say something down it. Give me an order. Say, 'Home James!'—summat like that."

Ma, in possession of the end of the speaking tube, sat utterly speechless.

"Give me an order!" Pop said. "I can hear whatever you say perfickly well in front here. Go on, Ma. Give me an order!"

Ma breathed into the speaking tube in a voice pitched in a minor key of desolation.

"I don't know whether I like it," she said. "They'll be putting the price of fish-and-chips up when they see us roll up in this."

"Never!" Pop said. "They'll be paying us."

The receiving end of the speaking apparatus was just above the head of Mr. Charlton, who was sitting next to Pop in the driving seat. The voices of Victoria and Primrose began to shriek into his ears like a gabble of excited young ducks.

"Take us for a ride! Take us for a ride! Take us for a ride!"

Pop let in the clutch and started to steer a course of slow elegance between a pile of discarded oil drums and a big galvanized iron swill tub. No breath of sound came, for a full minute, from either the Rolls or its passengers.

Then Ma said, "Like riding on air. Not a squeak anywhere. Must be paid for."

"Cash down!" Pop said.

He pressed the horn. An orchestration of low notes, harmonious, smooth as honey, disturbed into slight flutterings a batch of young turkeys sunning themselves in the lee of the pigsties.

"That's the town one," Pop explained. He flicked a switch with a fingernail. "Now hark at this. Country. Open road."

A peremptory, urgent snarl, like the surprise entry of symphonic brass, tore the peaceful fabric of the yard's livestock to pieces. A whole flotilla of white ducks sprang into the air and raced like hurdlers over rusty junk, empty boxes, and feeding troughs. Brown hens flew like windy paper bags in all directions, shedding feathers.

"Special fittin'," Pop explained. "Chap who owned it once lived in Paris or somewheres."

He completed with slow imperial pride the course of the yard, now blowing the town horn, now the snarl.

"Comfortable in the back, ain't it, Ma? Make a nice bed, don't you think?"

Ma, who had recovered equilibrium, now spoke down the speaking tube, like shaking lemon jelly.

"Home, James. Else them geese'll burn."

Pop responded with the honeyed notes of the town horn and the Rolls, like a ship gliding to anchorage in smooth waters, skirted with a final swing of silent elegance past a strong black alp of pig manure.

"Perfick, ain't it?" Pop said. "Ain't it perfick?"

Ma, who had stopped laughing, breathed hard before she spoke again.

"I got to have flowers in the vases," she said, her voice full of a pleasure so deep that it was at once loving and lovable in humility. "Every time we go out we got to have flowers."

Back at the house everybody alighted and Ma once again stroked, with touching affection, the shining chariot wings, her huge body reflected in their black curves with a vast transfiguration of yellow and scarlet, distorted as in a comic mirror at a fair.

"Gorblimey, I must run," she said suddenly. "I haven't even started the applesauce."

As Ma ran toward the house Mariette remembered the table under the walnut tree and took Mr. Charlton's hand. Pop remembered the port and called after a dutifully retreating Mr. Charlton, "Charley boy, like to do summat for me while you're helping Mariette? Put the port on ice, old man, will you? Three bottles. Two red and one white. You'll find two ice buckets in the cocktail cabinet. Give 'em plenty of ice, old man."

At the same time Montgomery stood staring across the yard in the direction of the road.

"Pop," he said, "I think we got a visitor. I think it looks like the brigadier."

Across the yard a straight, six-foot human straw was drifting. It was dressed in a suit of tropical alpaca, once yellowish, now bleached to whitish fawn, that looked as if it had recently been under a steamroller.

It was the brigadier all right, Pop said, and leaned one hand on the front wing of the Rolls with casual pride, raising the other in greeting. He wondered too what the brigadier wanted and where his sister was and said he betted the old whippet had left him for the day.

"General!" he called. "What can I do you for?"

"Hail," the brigadier said. The voice was low and cryptic. "Well met, Larkin."

At closer range it was to be seen that the brigadier's elbows had been patched with squares of paler colored material that appeared to have been torn from pillow slips. The cuffs of his jacket sleeves had been trimmed more or less level with scissors and then sewn back. His socks were yellow. The hat worn on the back of his head resembled more than anything a frayed beehive and seemed to be worn so far back in order to avoid his extraordinary extensive white eyebrows, altogether too large for the rest of his cadaverous face, which stuck above his pale blue eyes like two salty prawns.

These prawns were repeated on his upper lip in a stiff mustache, which contrasted sharply with cheeks consisting entirely of purple veins. The chin was resolute and looked like worn pumice stone. The neck was long and loose and held entirely together by a rigid bolt of fiery crimson, the Adam's apple, which seemed over the course of time to have worn the soiled shirt collar to shreds.

The brigadier shook hands with Pop, at the same time recognizing in Pop's demeanor the divinity of new possession. He held the Rolls-Royce in flinty stare.

"Not yours?"

"Just got it."

"Good God."

Pop made breezy gestures of pride. He wanted instantly to reveal possession of the monograms and then decided against it. It was too much all at one time, he thought.

"Hellish costly to run?"

"Well, might be, can't tell, might be," Pop said. "But worth it. Always flog it."

Sooner or later, in his energetic way, Pop flogged most things.

"Good God." The brigadier looked at the car with closer, microscopic inspection. "What's all this?"

"Monogram."

"Good God." In moments of humor the brigadier drew on dry resources of solemnity. "No crown?"

The remark was lost on Pop, who was dying to demonstrate the horn's orchestral variations.

"Well," the brigadier said, "I mustn't linger. Down to staff work."

Pop laughed in his usual ringing fashion and said he betted a quid the general wanted a subscription.

"Wrong," the brigadier said. "Not this time."

"Well, that's worth a drink," Pop said. "What about a snifter?"

"Trifle early, don't you think?" the brigadier said. "Not quite over the yardarm yet, are we?"

"When I want a drink," Pop said, "I have a drink. Wevver it's early or wevver it ain't."

The brigadier, after a minor pretense at refusal, chose to have a whiskey and soda. Pop said first that he'd have a Guinness and then changed his mind and said he'd have a beer called Dragon's Blood with a dash of lime instead. The brigadier looked astonished at this extraordinary combination but followed Pop into the house without a word.

In the sitting room he found it hard to concentrate even on the whiskey and soda because of powerful, torturing odors of roasting geese that penetrated every corner of the house, delicious with sage and onion stuffing. He sat most of the time with his glass on his right knee, where it successfully concealed a hole that mice might have gnawed.

"Might as well come straight to the point," the brigadier said. "Fact is, Larkin, I'm in a god-awful mess."

"Wimmin?"

The brigadier looked extremely startled. The prawns of his eyebrows seemed to leap out. He seemed about to speak and then drank with eagerness at the whiskey and soda instead.

"No, no, no," he said eventually. "Bad enough, but not that bad."

Pop knew that the brigadier's sister, who resembled more than anything a long hairpin on the top of which she generally wore a cloche hat that looked like a pink thimble, was presumed to lead him a hell of a dance on most occasions and in all directions. Among other things he felt that she never gave the brigadier enough to eat: a terrible thing.

"No, it's this damn gymkhana," the brigadier said. "The Bolshie Fortescue had a god-awful row with the committee Friday and has withdrawn from the field."

"Always was a basket."

"Not only withdrawn *from* the field," the brigadier said, "but withdrawn *the* field."

"Means you've got nowhere to hold the damn thing."

"Bingo," the brigadier said.

In a soft voice Pop called Mr. Fortescue a bloody sausage and re-membered Mariette. The gymkhana was in a fortnight's time. It might be the last chance she'd ever get to ride in the jumps before she had the baby. She was mad on jumping; her heart was set on horses and all that sort of thing.

"Nothing to worry about," Pop said. "You can hold it in my med-der."

"Don't let me rush you into a decision, Larkin," the brigadier said. "You don't have to decide—"

"Good grief," Pop said. "Nothing to decide. The medder's there, ain't it? All I got to do is get the grass cut. I'll get the grass cut this week and things'll be perfick."

The brigadier was so much touched by this that he nervously held his glass in his left hand and started poking a finger into the hole in his right trouser knee, a habit about which his sister had already scolded him acidly twice at breakfast.

"Can't thank you enough, Larkin," he said. He several times used the words "eternal gratitude" in a low muttered voice, as in prayer. He coughed, drank again, poked at the hole in his knee, and called Pop a stout feller. He knew the committee would be eternally grateful. "Never be able to thank you."

Out of politeness he rose to go. Before he was on his feet Pop was insisting on another snifter, and Ma, hearing the tinkle of ice in glasses, called from the kitchen, "What about one for the old cook in here? What's she done today?"

The brigadier, under indeterminate protest, had a second whiskey and soda. Pop had a change of mind and had a whiskey and soda too. Ma ordered beer because she was parched from cooking and came to the sitting room door to drink it from a big glass that spilled foam down her hands.

"Bung-ho," she said to the brigadier. "How's your sister today?"

"Gone to see an aunt," the brigadier said. Now that Ma had opened the kitchen door the smell of browning goose flesh was attacking him in even more frontal, more excruciating waves. "Over in Hampshire. Day's march away."

"Sunday dinner all on your lonesome?" Ma said.

"Not quite that bad." Torturing waves of sage-sharp fragrance from the roasting geese made him suddenly feel more heady than even the whiskey and soda had done on his empty stomach. "I shall waffle down to the pub and grab a bite of cold."

"Cold on Sundays?" Ma was deeply shocked. "You wouldn't catch Pop having cold on Sundays. Why don't you stay here and eat with us?"

"No, no, really no. No, thanks all the same, really—"

"Encore," Pop said. "More the merrier. Perfick."

"Bless my soul, with all your brood—"

"Of course," Ma said. "Cold, my foot."

"Ma," Pop said, "pity you didn't put that leg o'pork in after all." Ma had calculated that, within reason, three nine-pound geese ought to be enough. "Too late now I suppose?"

He seemed quite disappointed as Ma said, "Not unless you want to eat about five o'clock," and went away kitchenward. He hated having to skimp on joints and things; it made it hard work for the carver.

From the kitchen Ma called a minute later, "Come here a minute, Pop, I want you. Lift the geese out of the oven for me, will you? I want to baste them."

Pop went into the kitchen, realizing as soon as he went through the door that the call was after all merely a ruse to get him away from the brigadier. Ma was standing by the window, arms folded like huge white vegetable marrows across her bolstered bosom, looking toward the walnut tree.

"Take a look at that," she said.

Under the tree, at the dinner table, cloth and cutlery having been laid, Mariette and Mr. Charlton were coolly sitting some distance apart from each other, absorbed in the Sunday papers.

Ma made noises of puzzled disgust, which Pop echoed.

"What's wrong with 'em?"

"Wrong? Don't he know his technique?" Ma said.

"Very like do better on the boat this afternoon," Pop said. "There's some very good quiet places up the river."

Ma, as if she could not bear the sight any longer, turned away to stir the applesauce with a wooden spoon as it simmered away in a new bright aluminum pan. After looking at it critically she decided it needed a touch of something and dropped into the steaming olive-yellow purée a lump of butter as big as a tennis ball.

"Brigadier looks seedy, I think, don't you?" she said. Pop agreed. He felt immensely sorry for the brigadier. "Trouble with these people they never get enough to eat. Like Mr. Charlton. Half-starved."

Pop agreed with that too. "Cold at the pub Sundays," he said, as if this was the depths of deplorable gastronomic misery. "Can you beat it?"

Ma said she could. "Because if I know anything about it he wasn't going near the pub. He was going home to a marmite sandwich and a glass o' milk. Perhaps even water."

A moment later she turned to reach from a cupboard a new tin of salt and Pop, watching her upstretched figure as it revealed portions of enormous calves, suddenly felt a startling twinge of excitement in his veins. He immediately grasped Ma by the bosom and started squeezing her. Ma pretended to protest, giggling at the same time, but Pop continued to fondle her with immense, experienced enthusiasm until finally she turned, yielded the great continent of her body to him and let him kiss her full on her soft big mouth.

Pop prolonged this delicious experience as long as he had breath. He always felt more passionate in the kitchen. He supposed it was the smell of food. Ma sometimes told him it was a wonder he ever got any meals at all and that he ought to know, at his age, which he wanted most, meals or her. "Both," he always said. "Often."

This morning, against the shining white stove, the glistening aluminum pans, and the background of sunlight on the young coppery green leaves of the walnut tree, he thought she looked absolutely lovely. She was his dream.

He started to kiss her passionately again. But this time she held him away. The brigadier, she said, would be wondering what was happening. He was to go back to the brigadier. "The twins'll be back with the ice cream any moment too," she said. The twins had gone to the village, a quarter of a mile down the road, with orders to bring back the largest blocks of strawberry and chocolate they could buy.

"Take the brigadier a few crisps," Ma said. "They'll keep him going for half an hour."

With reluctance Pop went back to the brigadier, who sat staring into an empty glass, elbows on his knees, his trouser legs hitched up so that his socks and thin hairy shins were revealed. Pop saw now that the socks were odd, one yellow and one white, and that both had potatoes in the heels.

"Crisp, General?" he said, and held out a big plastic orange dish of potato crisps, glistening fresh and salty.

The brigadier, who belonged to two London clubs that he used only twice a year and spent most of the rest of his time wearing himself to a skeleton chopping wood, washing dishes, clipping hedges, mowing the lawn, and cleaning out blocked drainpipes because he couldn't afford a man, accepted the crisps with formal reluctance that actually concealed a boyish gratitude.

Pop also suggested another snifter.

"No, no. Thanks all the same. No, no," the brigadier said. "No really," and then allowed his glass to be taken away from him with no more than dying stutters of protestation.

Half an hour later two of the three geese were lying side by side, browned to perfection, deliciously varnished with running gravy, in a big oval blue meat dish on the table under the walnut tree. Other blue dishes stood about the table containing green peas and new potatoes veined with dark sprigs of mint, baked onions, asparagus, roast potatoes, Yorkshire pudding, and broad beans in parsley sauce. There were also big blue boats of applesauce and gravy.

There had been times in his life when the brigadier would have been prompted, out of sheer good form, social constraint, and various other preventive forces of upbringing, to describe the sight of all this as rather lacking in decency. Today he merely sat with restrained bewilderment, tortured by odors of goose flesh and sage and onions, watching the faces of Pop, Ma, Mr. Charlton, and the entire Larkin brood while Pop carved with dextrous ease at the birds, themselves not at all unlike brown laden galleons floating in a glistening gravy sea.

Even the stiff prawns of his eyebrows made no quiver of surprise as Pop, flashing carving knife and steel in air, suggested that if Charley boy wanted to help he could pour the port out now.

Mr. Charlton put the port on the table in its champagne bucket, all beady with ice dew.

"Mix it," Pop said. "It makes a jolly good drink, red and white mixed together."

Mr. Charlton went around the table, pouring and mixing port. He had been introduced to the brigadier by a more than usually facetious Pop as "a late entry—chap on the tax lark."

"Actually a real pukka tax gatherer you mean?" the brigadier said, as if astonished that there could be such a person.

"Inspector's office," Mr. Charlton said.

"Tried to rope *me* in on that swindle yesterday," Pop said. He laughed derisively in his customary ringing fashion. "I should like, eh, General? What do you say?"

The brigadier confessed, with a certain sadness, that he paid no tax. At least, hardly any.

"And rightly so!" Pop thundered.

Succulent pieces of bird were now being carved and dispatched about the table with breezy speed.

"That all right for you, General?" The brigadier found himself facing an entire leg of goose and a large mound of sage and onions.

"Start!" Pop ordered. "Don't let it get cold, General!" To the goose Mariette came to add peas, beans, Yorkshire pudding, and two sorts of potatoes, so that finally, when gravy and applesauce had been ladled on, no single centimeter of naked plate could be seen.

A moment later the brigadier, faced with superior forces and not knowing where to attack, saw Ma, like some huge yellow and scarlet butterfly glowing in the walnut shade, come up on his flank, bearing a deep dish of fat and buttery asparagus. With dry humor he started to confess to being outnumbered, a problem that Ma at once solved by placing the dish between the brigadier and the head of table, where she herself now sat down.

"We'll share, shall we, General?" she said. "Help yourself from the dish. Everybody else has had some."

It was some moments before the brigadier, deeply touched and painfully strung up by the first delicious tortures of eating, could relax enough to remember formality and lift his glass to Ma.

"Mr. Charlton, I think we should raise a glass to our hostess."

"'Ear, 'ear," Pop said. "Cheers to Ma."

The brigadier bent upward from the table, raising his glass to Ma. Mr. Charlton also half rose and raised his glass and at the same moment Victoria said, pointing to the brigadier, "You got potatoes in your socks, I saw them."

"Now, now," Pop said. "Manners. Elbows!"

Victoria was silent.

"Pop's got 'em at a word," Ma said proudly. "And now *eat* your potatoes," she said to Victoria. "Never mind about the general's."

"This is most superb cooking," the brigadier said. "Where did you learn to cook, Mrs. Larkin?"

"She learned at The Three Cocks hotel at Fordington," Pop said. "That's where she learned. I can tell you. And it's never been the same since she left there."

"I can only say the cock's loss is your gain," the brigadier said, a remark that Ma found so amusing that she started choking again, her mouth jammed by a piece of asparagus.

"Hit her, General!" Pop said. "Middle o' the back!"

The brigadier was utterly startled by this sudden and unnatural order. He moved vaguely to action by putting down his knife and fork, but a second later Ma had recovered.

"All right, Ma?" Pop said. "Drink a drop o' wine."

Ma, sipping wine, said thanks, she was all right again.

"Ma's got a very small gullet," Pop explained to the brigadier, "compared with the rest of her."

"Have you told the children about the gymkhana, Larkin?" the brigadier said.

"Good God, went clean out of my head," Pop said. Waving a dripping wing bone, which he had been busily sucking for some moments past, he informed the entire table in proud, imperial tones, "Going to hold the gymkhana in the medder, kids. *Here.*"

Before anyone could speak an excited Mariette was on her feet, running around the table to Pop, whom she began kissing with great fervor on the lips, hardly a degree less passionately than Pop, in the kitchen, had kissed Ma.

"Lovely, lovely man. Lovely, lovely Pop."

Mr. Charlton sat tremulous, completely shaken. A curious wave of emotion, at first hot, then cold, lapped entirely through him from the small of his back to his brain. Unaccountably he found himself both jealous, then afraid, of the unquenchable demonstration that had left Pop, laughing loudly, hugging Mariette in return. He was not used to unquenchable demonstrations.

"That's the loveliest, loveliest news. Don't you think so. Mr. Charlton?"

"You should really thank the general," Pop said. "His idea."

"Committee—"

The word had hardly broken from the lips of the brigadier before Mariette was at his side, kissing him too. The brigadier, looking formally delighted, began to wipe his mouth with his serviette, but whether to wipe away kiss or asparagus butter it was not possible to say. He was still dabbing his mouth when Mariette kissed Ma, who explained to the brigadier, "Mad on horses, General. Absolutely stark raving mad on horses," and then came around the table to where Mr. Charlton sat concentrating with every nerve on scraping the last tissues of goose flesh from a leg bone.

Mr. Charlton was all mixed up. He was fighting to concentrate. He was fighting to disentangle one thought, one fear, from another. There had crossed his mind, for no sensible reason at all, the uneasy notion that the goose he was now eating might well be part of the same living bird that had so sinuously, shimmeringly wrapped its neck about his legs the previous day, with the shattering sensation of their being caressed by silk stockings. It was the most disturbing thought of his life and he knew that he was blushing. He knew he was afraid.

"Oh, Mr. Charlton, I'm so happy I think I'll kiss you too."

Mariette, to the unconcealed delight and satisfaction of Ma and Pop, bent and kissed Mr. Charlton briefly, but with purpose, full on the lips. Mr. Charlton recoiled in a crimson cloud, hearing about him trumpets of disaster. Everyone was laughing.

When he came to himself he knew he could never forget that moment. He was trembling all over. It was impossible to describe what the full soft lips of Mariette had felt like against his own except that it was, perhaps like having them brushed by the skin of a warm firm plum, in full ripeness, for the first time.

While Mr. Charlton was still blushing Pop retired to the kitchen and fetched another goose. He began to carve for the brigadier several thin extrasucculent slices of the breast. This one, he started saying, as he slid the knife across the crackling dark golden skin, was the tenderest of them all and a moment later confirmed Mr. Charlton's worst fears by laughing uproariously, "This must be the joker that was under the table yesterday and heard us talking. Eh, Ma? Think o' that."

"Knowing birds," Ma said, and turned to the brigadier to ask, "What was it you was going to say, General, about the committee?"

"Oh, merely that I was elected to be spokesman. To ask your husband—"

"Who's on the committee?" Ma said.

"Well, Edith is secretary. Edith Pilchester. I expect she'll be coming to see you."

"Oh, I love old Edith," Pop said. "Edith's a sport."

"You be careful she don't love you," Ma said. "I wouldn't put anything past her."

"Ah, perfickly harmless," Pop said.

"Splendid organizer," the brigadier said.

"That's what she thinks. She fancies she could organize a stallion into having pups," Ma said, "but that's where she's wrong," and once again, as she did so often at her own jokes, laughed with jellified splendor.

"Then there's Mrs. Peele and George Carter," the brigadier said.

"Still living together I suppose?" Ma said.

"I understand the arrangement still holds."

"Disgusting."

Ma made tutting noises as she sucked a final piece of asparagus. Pop belched with sudden richness and said, "Manners." It was terrible the way people carried on, Ma said and Pop agreed.

"Then there's Freda O'Connor."

"She's another tart if you like," Ma said. "Showing off her bosom."

"And Jack Woodley."

"That feller's another so-and-so," Pop said. "Just like Fortescue. A complete b—"

"Not in front of the twins," Ma said. "I don't mind Victoria. She's not old enough to understand."

"And then Mrs. Borden. That makes the lot."

Ma, eating the last of her peas with a tablespoon, made more noises of disgust and asked if Mrs. Borden was still keeping as sober as ever? Supposed she was?

"With the same fishlike capacity, I understand," the brigadier said.

"Terrible," Ma said. "Shocking. Terrible state of affairs when you let drink get you down like that."

"Disgusting," Pop said. "Disgusting."

It was time for ice cream. Mariette rose to fetch it from the kitchen, together with a jug of real Jersey, hoping that Mr. Charlton would seize so good an opportunity and come with her, but Mr. Charlton was still all mixed up. The day had grown exceptionally humid and warm, the air thick with the stirring breath of growing leaves and grasses. Mariette felt the sweetness of it tingling madly in her nostrils and remembered the kiss she had given Mr. Charlton. She was sorry for Mr. Charlton and wondered if it would ever be possible to make love with him. Making love might ease his mind. In the meadow beyond the house she had noticed how high the buttercups were growing, thick and sappy and golden among the grasses' feathery flower, and she wondered what it would be like to make love to Mr. Charlton in a buttercup field. She thought she could but try. She was growing fonder and fonder of Mr. Charlton. His eyes were soft, endearing, and sometimes even sad and she found herself fascinated by their brown, delicate paintbrush lashes.

"Cuppa tea, General?"

After the ice cream Ma was sitting back with a great air of content, as if really getting ready to enjoy herself.

"No, no, no. No really, thank you."

"No trouble. Always have one after dinner."

The thought of tea after two plates of goose, asparagus, sage and onions, ice cream, and everything else provoked in the brigadier's stomach a restless thunderstorm. He suppressed a belch of his own.

Pop was not so successful and a positive bark leapt out, causing Primrose to say, "I love sage and onions. You keeping having a taste of it all afternoon. And sometimes all night too."

Mariette went away to the house to make tea, hoping again that Mr. Charlton would go with her, but Mr. Charlton was still battling for courage and concentration. Ma hoped so too and made pointed remarks about the heaviness of cups and trays. Mr. Charlton, soporific as well as fearful, made no hint of a move and Ma gave it all up, at last, in disgust. He just didn't know his technique, that was all.

When at last Mariette came across the garden with the tea the brigadier was moved to admiration of the dark, delicious little figure advancing with shapely provocation under the pure hot light of early afternoon.

"Remarkably pretty she looks," he told Ma, who agreed with surprisingly energetic warmth, saying, "I'm glad somebody thinks so. She's been hiding her light under a bushel long enough."

"Well, I don't know," Pop said, "as you can say that." He was thinking of the news Ma had told him two days before. Well, he supposed it was hiding her light in a way. Keeping it dark anyway.

Everybody except the brigadier had tea, which Mariette poured out thick and strong, with Jersey cream. To Mr. Charlton's surprise, nobody suggested Johnnie Walker milk, though Pop stirred into his own cup two teaspoonfuls of port. It was still icy.

"Helps to cool it down," he explained. "Ma can't do with it in a saucer."

An afternoon of delicious golden content folded its transparent envelope more and more softly about the paradisiacal Larkin world, over the outlying meadow scintillating with its million buttercups and the shady fragrant walnut tree. Pop sighed and remarked how perfick it was. If only the gymkhana was as perfick it would be marvelous, he said. Should they have fireworks? "Tell the committee I'll provide the fireworks," he said to the brigadier. "That'll make it go with a bang."

The brigadier, who did not answer, was almost asleep. The twins and the younger children had already slipped away. Ma was falling slowly asleep too, her head falling sideways, so that she was now less like a bright expansive butterfly than a vast yellow parrot tucking its head under its sleepy wing.

"Look at that sky, Charley," Pop said, and indicated with the tip of an unlighted cigar the exquisite expanse of all heaven, blue as flax flower. "There's summat worthwhile for you. Perfick. Blimey, I wonder how you fellers can work in offices."

Mr. Charlton was beginning to wonder too.

"Cigar?"

Mr. Charlton declined the cigar with low thanks.

"Ought to have given the general one," Pop said. The brigadier was now fast asleep. Bad manners to have forgot the general, he thought. He liked the general. The old sport might not live very grand but he was unmistakably a gent. Not like George Carter and Jack Woodley and a few other baskets he could name. Nor Freda O'Connor and Mrs. Battersby and Molly Borden and that crowd. They didn't think much of people like him and Ma. That's why they'd sent the general along as spokesman. He knew.

He liked Edith Pilchester though. Edith was a sport. He laughed softly as he thought that if they had fireworks at the gymkhana he would put one under Edith's skirts, just to see what happened. "Probably never turn a hair," he thought. "Probably get a thrill."

"Put the cigar on the general's plate, Charley," he said to Mr. Charlton, "when you get around to going."

"I think we're going now," Mariette said to Mr. Charlton, "aren't we?"

Mr. Charlton, who had been in a mix-up all afternoon, abruptly fumbled to his feet, expressing agreement by taking the cigar and laying it beside the brigadier's head, reclining now in flushed oblivion on the table.

"Going on the boat?" Pop said.

"Might do," Mariette said. "Might not get that far."

"Perfick anyway," Pop said, "wherever you go."

As they crossed from the garden to the big meadow beyond, Mariette took Mr. Charlton's hand. In the startled fashion of a young colt he almost jumped as she touched him. A wave of fragrance blew on the lightest breath of wind from the direction of the river, driving into her quickening nostrils odors of hawthorn bloom, clover, an entire valley of rising grasses, and distant invisible fields of early May.

It was so exquisitely strong that suddenly she bent down, took off her shoes, and started running.

A moment later, Mr. Charlton, running too, realized how pretty, how exciting, her naked feet were.

5

That evening Pop, after a half hour of twilight spent with Ma in the bluebell wood, listening to a whole orchestra of nightingales, came back to the house to urge on Mr. Charlton the virtues of a little sick leave.

"Ma and me don't think you look all that grand," he said.

Ma followed this up by saying that she didn't like the look around Mr. Charlton's cheekbones. There were white spots on them. White spots were a bad sign, but of what she didn't say.

Pop went on to urge on Mr. Charlton to use his loaf and take proper advantage of what he called "the National Elf lark," a service that, after all, Mr. Charlton paid for. Pop was certain Mr. Charlton had already paid out millions to this swindle in weekly contributions. It must have cost him a fortune in stamps. With warmth he urged Mr. Charlton not to be a mug about it. It was, after all, the state that had started this lark—why not go sick, he urged, and have a bit of fun?

Mr. Charlton might have resisted these arguments if it hadn't been that, just before midnight, Mariette pinned him up against the newel-post of the dark stairs, kissed him again, and said his hands were hot. Like white spots on the cheekbones, hot hands were a bad sign. Mr. Charlton tried to protest that his hands were invariably hot, especially at that time of year, but Mariette kissed him again, pressing her warm plumlike mouth for a long time against his lips, leaving him in another terrible turmoil of divided emotions about the buttercup field, the nightingales, and the affair of the goose neck entwining his leg.

"You could stay a week, lovey," she said. She had begun to call him lovey in the buttercup field. "And then all next weekend."

Mr. Charlton tried to explain that he had a vast and frightful number of papers on his desk at the office that had to be attended to and how there would be an awful stink if he didn't get back.

"Think if you broke your leg," she said.

Mr. Charlton said he didn't want to think of breaking his leg. He was talking about loyalty, duty, pangs of conscience, and that sort of thing.

"Sounds silly," Mariette said, and Mr. Charlton, trembling on the dark stairs, under the influence of the pressing, plumlike lips, was bound to admit that it did.

The result was that he got up next morning to a massive breakfast of two fried eggs, several slices of liver and bacon, much fried bread, and enormous cups of black sugary tea.

Pop was already breakfasting when he arrived at table. Poised heartily above a sea of catsup, under which whatever he was having for breakfast was completely submerged, he praised for some moments the utter beauty of the first young strawberry morning. It was going to be a perfick day, he said. The cuckoo had been calling since four o'clock.

The only thing that troubled Mr. Charlton as he ate his breakfast was that he felt there was absolutely nothing wrong with him. He could honestly complain of neither sickness nor exhaustion. He had never felt better. "I don't know what to tell the office," he said. "Honestly there's nothing wrong with me."

"Then you must make summat up," Pop said, "mustn't you? Like lumbago."

Mr. Charlton protested that he had never had lumbago in his life, and was not likely to have.

"Oh yes you are," Pop said, and laughed in hearty, ringing fashion. "You'll have it chronic tonight. After the first day in the strawberry field."

At eight o'clock Mr. Charlton found himself sitting in the back of the gentian blue, home-painted truck, together with Mariette, the twins, Montgomery, Victoria, and Primrose. Ma and Pop sat in the cab in front, and Ma, who was in great spirits and was dressed in enormous khaki denim slacks with an overall top, laughed and said it was a pity they couldn't all go in the Rolls, just to shake everybody. Mariette was in slacks too, bright salvia blue ones, with a soft blue shirt and a spotted red-and-white kerchief over her hair. Over the khaki overalls Ma was wearing the salmon sweater, just because the ride might be cool in the morning air, and a great pudding bag of an orange scarf on her head.

"Everybody all right in the back there?" Pop yelled, and got his customary handsome ribbon of voices in answer. "Hang on by your toenails, you kids!"

The truck had hardly rolled out of the yard before everyone began singing. It was Pop who started the song, which was "We Ain't Got a Barrel o' Money," and everyone took it up in shrill voices. Mr. Charlton was embarrassed. He had never ridden in the back of a truck before. Still less had he ever sung in a truck on a public highway.

He wondered what on earth would happen if he was seen by someone who knew him, someone perhaps from the office. It would be terrible to be seen by any of the chaps.

Half a mile down the road the truck drew up with a sharp whistle of brakes and everyone stopped singing and started shrieking loudly instead. Mr. Charlton looked over the sideboard of the truck to see what the trouble was and saw Pop in the road, lifting up in his arms the tiniest woman Mr. Charlton had, outside a circus, ever seen.

"Room for a little 'un?" Pop said, and threw the little lady up into the truck. She shrieked like a laughing doll as she landed between the twins and Mr. Charlton. "That little two penn'orth," Pop explained, "is Aunt Fan."

Aunt Fan to whom? Mr. Charlton wondered but never discovered. His immediate impression was that the little two penn'orth had a face like a small brown shellfish of the winkle sort. It was all round and crinkled and twisted up. She too was wearing slacks, tiny dark maroon red ones, and a man's gray tweed cap on her head, fixed there by two large pearl hatpins. Her ginger-brown eyes shone like shoe buttons and her chest was flat.

"Everybody all right in the truck there? Hang on, Aunt Fan!"

Once again everybody, including the little two penn'orth, started singing. By this time the sun was well above the miles of surrounding orchards, chestnut copses, and fields of rising oats and barley, and as it shone down on the truck and on the laughing, singing faces, Mr. Charlton saw a tiny creature popping in and out of Aunt Fan's mouth, exactly like a pink mollusk emerging from its shell. This was the little two penn'orth's tongue and it helped to work the shrillest voice he had ever heard. It was a voice like a wild train whistle shrieking to be heard on a far mountaintop.

"Don't you sing, mister?" she said.

Mr. Charlton, grinning feebly, did not know what to say. His hair was flying about in all directions. The truck was wildly bumping over a hard clay track, jolting Aunt Fan and the children to new laughter. Mr. Charlton did sing. He flattered himself, excusably, that he sang rather well. His voice, belying his bony, very average physique, was a deep, soft baritone. But now his mouth and throat felt like pumice stone and he was not sure, with the wild bouncing of the truck, quite where his breakfast was.

"You're new, ainyer?" The little two penn'orth said.

Mr. Charlton confessed that he was new.

"Thought you was. On 'oliday?"

"Sort of," Mr. Charlton said.

Another mile of this, he thought, and he wouldn't need an excuse for the National Health lark. His breakfast would be up.

To his great relief the truck came to a halt, two minutes later, between a copse of tall chestnut saplings and a big open strawberry field. A sudden sensation of dizziness found Mr. Charlton unready as he jumped from the truck. He groped at the air and was suddenly surprised to see the little two penn'orth flying down from the back of the truck, straight into his arms.

He clasped at the toylike body instinctively, as at a ball. The little two penn'orth landed straight on his chest, winding him temporarily. Everyone began laughing and the little two penn'orth shrieked with delight. Ma started shaking like jelly and Pop warned Mr. Charlton that he'd better watch out or else Aunt Fan would have him on the floor in no time.

"Just what I'd like on a nice warm day," the little two penn'orth said. "Just what I bin waiting for."

Mr. Charlton did his best to focus the shimmering strawberry field. He was now convinced that a terrible day lay in front of him. The sun was clear and hot under the shelter of the barrier of woodland; by noon it would be blistering down. Yesterday had been the hottest thirtieth of May, so the papers all said, for forty years. Today would be hotter even than that.

"You can eat all the strawberries you like," Mariette said. "But you'll soon get tired of that."

Mr. Charlton did not feel at all like eating strawberries. He longed to be able to sit down, if possible to lie down, in some cool quiet place under the chestnut saplings.

"Keep near me," Mariette said, and gave him a dark low stare which he was too sick to appreciate or return.

He followed her, the rest of the family, and the little two penn'orth into the strawberry field. Already, along the yellow alleys of straw, twenty or thirty girls and women, with an odd man or two, were picking. Flagwise a strange assortment of shirts and blouses, yellow and red and green and brown and even violet, was strung about the field. A green canvas tent toward which Mr. Charlton looked with pitiful desperation, as at an oasis, stood in the center of the field, piled inside with fresh white chip baskets.

Bending down, Mr. Charlton started to pick strawberries, deciding at the same time that he would never again eat pig's liver and bacon for breakfast. The hot summery distances were full of calling cuckoos. The field trembled like a zither with chattering women's voices. A man decided to strip his shirt off and the sudden sight of his pure naked torso set every female voice laughing, catcalling, or simply whistling in admiring wonder.

"Why don't you do that, lovey?" Mariette said. "You'd be all that much cooler. In time you'd get marvelously brown."

"I think I'll try and get acclimatized first," Mr. Charlton said.

The process of getting acclimatized took him through a sickening forty minutes of sweat. His spectacles misted over. The little two penn'orth's voice, piercing as a drill, cut the hot air about him, as it seemed, every several seconds. Broad belts of Ma's quivering laughter slapped across the field.

Lying on their fresh beds of straw, the squarish fat crimson strawberries shone in the sun with a too-perfect beauty, exactly, as Pop said, as if painted, and now and then Mr. Charlton looked up to see the lips of Mariette parted half in laughter, half in the act of biting into some glistening arc of lovely dark ripe flesh.

"Heavens, I'm getting hungry," she told him several times. "I hope Ma brought the rest of the cold roast goose for dinner."

He was very slow, he presently discovered, at the picking. Mariette could fill, with swift deft ease, three small baskets to his one.

"You're not very fast, are you?" she said. "Don't you feel very well?"

Mr. Charlton confessed with a small wry smile that he was not quite a top note.

"I thought as much," she said. "It's just what we were telling you yesterday. You need some sick leave. Come on—let's go along to the tent and get the baskets weighed. You have to get them weighed and checked there."

It turned out that this, the tent, was Mr. Charlton's salvation. Pop, who was also at the tent getting his first baskets checked, introduced him to the foreman, a youngish energetic man in khaki shirt and slacks, as "Charley boy. Friend of ours, Mr. Jennings. Office feller from the tax lark."

Mr. Jennings appraised Mr. Charlton, of the tax lark, with interested swiftness. You didn't often get office fellers in the strawberry field.

"Chap I'm looking for," he told Mr. Charlton. "What about sitting here and doing my job? All you do is weigh and book the baskets. How about it? I got a million things to do besides sit here and check these ruddy women."

"There y'are, Charley boy," Pop said, clapping him on the shoulder and laughing in ringing fashion. "Got you promoted already."

Mr. Charlton felt intensely relieved. To his astonishment, Pop shook his hand.

"Well, got to run along now, Charley boy. Got to see a man about some scrap iron. Don't do anything I wouldn't do. See you all about five."

Pop departed across the field to the truck and Mr. Charlton, sitting down at the table in the green shade of the tent, at once felt much more himself, much more at home. With a chair under his bottom it was almost like being back in the office again.

"It's pretty simple," Mr. Jennings said, and went on to explain what he said was the easy, straightforward procedure of checking, weighing, and recording the baskets. Mr. Charlton thought it was simple too. "Nothing to it," Mr. Jennings said. "You just got to keep a record in the book here, with the names, that's all, so we can pay out at the end of the day."

Mr. Jennings departed too after saying that he'd come back in an hour or so to see how Mr. Charlton was getting on, though he didn't think, on the whole, he'd have any trouble at all.

"One or two of the old faggots might try a bit of cheek on you," he said, "but if they do, be firm. Don't let 'em spit in your eye."

Mr. Charlton said he thought he had it taped all right and sat back and cleaned his glasses and combed his hair. Across the field he could see all kinds of women, fat ones, scrawny ones, pretty ones, old ones, very young ones, together with children, bending and laughing in the long strawberry rows, their blouses and slacks stringing out flagwise, in brilliant colors, under a hot cloudless sky. It was a very pleasant, peaceful, pastoral scene, he thought, and there was a delicious fragrance of ripe strawberries in the air.

"Forgotten me?"

He was startled. He had utterly forgotten Mariette, who had been standing behind him all the time.

"Afraid I had. So absorbed in the new job and all that—"

"Well, don't," she said, "or I'll be miserable." She kissed him lightly on the cheek. "Feeling better now?"

"Absolutely all right."

"You see, I told you," she said. "All you want is rest and fresh air and good food and you'll be as right as rain."

She stood at the door of the tent, so prettily framed against the clear sky beyond that Mr. Charlton wished he were back with her in the buttercup field.

"See you soon," she said. "And mind what you're up to. Don't get mixed up with other women."

Mr. Charlton, who had no intention whatsoever of getting mixed up with other women, started to apply himself earnestly to the task of checking and weighing the baskets of fruit as they came in. It seemed that he got on very well for a time. All the women seemed very polite and some actually called him "ducky." They spelled their names out carefully when he wasn't quite sure of them. They said how hot it was and one of them, a big sloppy woman named Poll Sanders, with gold-filled teeth and small gold earrings, laughed in a voice like a street trader selling mackerel and said, "Sweat—I can feel it running down my back. Goes on like this we'll have to strip out again—like we did that 'ot year afore. Remember that, Lil?"

Lil remembered. "And that wasn't as 'ot as this though." Lil was tall, yellow, and hollow-faced. She too had small gold earrings. She was much thinner than Poll but this made no difference. She sweated as much as Poll did. "Runs orf yer like water."

Mr. Charlton wrote in the book that Poll Sanders had brought in two dozen baskets and then, looking up, saw that Lil had gone. He realized that he had forgotten exactly how many baskets Lil had brought in. He dropped his rubber-tipped pencil on the table and ran after her, catching her up twenty yards across the field.

He said he was frightfully sorry but he had forgotten the number of baskets.

She gave him a look as hard as flint and her mouth opened and shut like a spring trap.

"Two dozen," she said.

"That's what I thought," he said and she gave him another look, harder than the first, and he left it at that.

"You want to get your arithmetic working," she said.

His arithmetic wasn't working very well with Poll Sanders either. When he got back to the tent and sat down to write Lil's figures he discovered he had penciled down three for Poll Sanders instead of two. Poll had disappeared.

He was so sure the figure was two that he ran after her too.

"Three," she said. She too gave him that same flat, unflinching look he had seen on the face of Lil. "I was standing there when you writ it down, wasn't I? Use your loaf, man."

He decided he'd better use his loaf as much as possible, but he was soon overbusy and it was very stifling in the little tent. He had to keep a sharper, keener eye on the figures as the women came in, bringing scores of baskets. Once the little two penn'orth came in, bent double by two dozen baskets in boxes almost as large as herself, so that they hung from her little hands like overladen panniers from the sides of a tiny gray donkey. The entire Larkin family also came in, all of them eating potato crisps and big orange lollipops on sticks, except the twins, who were eating peanuts, strawberries, and bread and jam.

Ma offered Mr. Charlton an orange lollipop on a stick and seemed surprised, even pained, when he said no thanks, he didn't think so.

"You'll be glad of it," she said. "You ain't had nothing since breakfast." Mr. Charlton still had moments when he found it impossible to remember breakfast with anything but pain. "Anyway I'll leave it here on the table. You might be glad of it later."

"Toodle-oo," the twins said, "if you don't want it we'll eat it next time we come," and ran after Ma, begging for ice creams.

Mr. Charlton looked up, sometime later, to see a pretty, fair-haired, well-made girl standing in the tent. She was wearing tight black jeans and an even tighter thin black woolen sweater. The outlines of her breasts under the sweater were as pronounced as if carved. Her hair was tied up in a long shining ponytail, the fluffy sun-whitened ends of it brushing her bare shoulders.

"Pauline Jackson," she said, "two dozen."

Her eyes were big and blue. Her very smooth skin was deep brown from working in the fields. Her forearms were covered with tender, downy golden hairs. Her tongue played on her straight white teeth when she had finished speaking.

While Mr. Charlton was writing in the book she said, "New here, aren't you? Never seen you here before."

"Sort of on holiday," Mr. Charlton explained.

"Nice to be some people."

She had a slow, drowsy way of talking. It somehow matched the way her tongue remained playing on her lips and the way her hair fell on her shoulders.

"Mind if I ask you something?" she said.

"No," Mr. Charlton said. "What would that be?"

"Is your name Cedric? They all say your name's Cedric out there."

The blush that ramped through Mr. Charlton's face and neck made every pore of his body break with sweat.

"Oh no," he said. "Goodness no. Who told you that one?"

"That's what they all say. I said there was no such name."

She was laughing at him, he thought, in her drowsy, large-eyed way. He was sure of that. He fumbled about nervously with book, baskets, and papers and said, "Good Lord no. Charley. That's me."

She reached out a brown long-fingered hand and took a strawberry from a basket. She bit into it and then stood staring at the white-crimson juicy inner flesh.

"Don't you like strawberries?" she said.

"Ask the Larkins," he said. "Ask Mariette. They all call me Charley."

"Oh, her. She knows you, does she?"

She put the rest of the strawberry in her mouth and pulled out the clean, white plug.

"Last feller who was here did nothing but eat strawberries. Every time you came in here that feller was bolting strawberries."

Mr. Charlton, confused again, murmured something about having no time. Having something else to do.

"Such as what?"

Mr. Charlton didn't know.

She moved nearer the table to pick up another strawberry and then changed her mind and picked up Ma's orange lollipop instead.

"Don't you like these either?"

"Not frightfully—"

"Don't like anything, do you?" She laughed, her voice drowsier than ever in her throat, the tongue drifting idly across her mouth. "Not much!"

A moment later she started twisting the lollipop around and around in her brown fingers.

"Suppose you'd think I was greedy if I asked you whether I could have it?"

"Oh no, please," Mr. Charlton said. "Take it if you want. By all means."

"Thanks." She laughed again, once more with that drowsy softness that made Mr. Charlton feel dreadfully congested, sweating, and messy, sure that she was mocking him. "That's the way to be nice to anybody. First time."

Unaware of it, Mr. Charlton said an extremely foolish thing, "Aren't people always nice to you first time?"

"Depends."

Mr. Charlton, unaware of it again, said another foolish thing, "Depends on what?"

She turned sideways, so that for the second time in his life Mr. Charlton found himself confronted by an astral body of alarming shape, this time as firm and dark as ebony.

"On whether I let them."

She had already started to peel the paper from the orange lollipop when Mariette came in, carrying two baskets.

"Oh, company," the girl said.

Peeling the last of the paper from the lollipop, she stared with flat cool eyes at Mariette. Mr. Charlton thought Mariette's eyes looked, in reply, like two infuriated black bees.

"Well, I'll push off," the girl said. "See you later, Charley." She tossed her hair from one side of her shoulders to another, at the same time giving Mr. Charlton a glad, cool, backward look. "If not before."

She was hardly out of the tent before Mariette banged the two baskets on the table and shouted, "Tart!"

Mr. Charlton was very much shaken.

"Steady," he said. "She'll hear—"

"She's meant to, the so-and-so, isn't she?"

"I really didn't want the thing," Mr. Charlton said. "I told her to take it—"

"She'd take anything. She'd take the skin off your back—and a bit more if you let her!"

He had never seen Mariette angry before. Her voice sounded raw.

"She's nothing but a—" Mariette choked at some impossible word and then decided Mr. Charlton wouldn't understand it. "No, I won't say it. It's too good. I'll bottle it in. She's no virgin though," she shouted, "everybody knows that!"

Mr. Charlton, who was not accustomed to hear the word "virgin" bandied about very much, especially in public, was relieved to see two more women approaching the tent, but was disappointed a moment later to see that they were Poll and Lil. He had made up his mind to remonstrate as tactfully as possible with Poll about rubbing out and altering the figures in the book from two to three and thus twisting him. He was convinced that that was what had happened.

But when he saw the two earringed women, one tall and scrawny as a scarecrow, the other brawny as a bare-armed fishwife, both as brown as gypsies, he suddenly lost heart and said to Mariette, "Don't go for a minute. Stay until these two have gone. I want to talk to you—"

"I've got to cool off!" Mariette said. "I'm going into the wood to cool off!"

"Wait just a minute—"

"I've got to cool off! That's where I'll be if you want me."

A moment later he was alone with Poll and Lil, who had been having a conference as to whether they could twist him a second time so soon or whether they should leave it for a while and do a double twist next time. Between them they knew a few good ones and they generally worked better, for some funny reason, in the afternoon.

"Hullo, ducky," they said. "Here we are again."

By the middle of the afternoon it was so hot that Mr. Charlton got Montgomery and the twins to bring him a bucket of water drawn from a standpipe by the gate of the field. He drank a big draft or two of water and then plunged his head several times into the bucket and then dried his face on his handkerchief and combed his wet, cooled hair. After this, he cleaned up his spectacles, polishing them on the driest piece of his shirt he could find, and went to stand at the door of the tent, slightly refreshed, to get a breath of air.

The sun hit the crown of his head like a brass cymbal. He had never known it so hot in May. It seemed to affect his eyesight for a moment and when he looked across the strawberry field he was astonished to see a startling change there.

Almost all the women had done what Poll and Lil had said they would do. They had stripped off their blouses and shirts in the heat and were working in nothing but bodices and brassieres. The effect was that the lines of colored flags had now become like lines of white washing hung out in the blazing sun to dry.

Mr. Charlton went back into the tent and tried to satisfy his curiosity about what Pop called the strawberry lark by adding up how many pounds of strawberries had been in and out of the tent that day. He calculated, astonishingly, that he had checked in more than a ton. That meant, he reasoned, a pretty fair lump for the pickers.

His trained mind wondered what the tax position about *that* was. He would have to ask Pop. He was sure Pop would know.

He was still thinking of this when he looked up and saw Pauline Jackson standing in the door. She was not wearing a black sweater now. Like the rest of the women she had stripped down to her brassiere. She had very fine sun-tanned arms and shoulders but the lower part of her deep chest was as white as the inside of a young apple by comparison.

It was this startling whiteness that made his heart start bouncing. She smiled. She came to the table and said in her lazy way, "Not much cooler, is it?"

She put twenty-four pounds of strawberries on the table. He started to fumble with pencil and paper, his eyes downcast. She leaned forward as if to see what he was writing down and said, "How many does that make for me today? Eight dozen?"

He started to say, "I've got an idea it's more than that, Miss Jackson," determined to keep it as formal as possible, and then looked up to see, not ten or twelve inches from his face, most of her bared, white, perfectly sculptured bust, blazingly revealed, heaving deeply.

Like Ma, Miss Jackson did not seem unduly perturbed.

"Two more dozen," she said, "and I think I'll pack it up for the day."

"I see. Are you paid every day, Miss Jackson, or do you leave it till the weekend?"

"What makes you keep calling me Miss Jackson?"

He started to write in the book again when she said, "What time are you knocking off? Going back to Fordington? If you are, I could give you a lift on my Vespa."

Where on earth did these people get the money from? Mr. Charlton started thinking. He supposed—

"What about it?" she said.

Too nervous to think clearly, Mr. Charlton said, "I don't know what time I'll finish. I did want to go to Fordington to fetch some clothes from my room, but—"

"Might go on and have a swim at the pool," she said, "afterward. How about that?"

He said, "Well—"

"I could wait." The sculptured breasts rose and fell heavily and came an inch or two nearer, their division so deep and the pure whiteness so sharp in the shade of the tent, against the dark brown upper flesh of her shoulders, that Mr. Charlton was utterly mesmerized. "No hurry for half an hour one way or the other. Just tell me when."

She swung her body away. He saw the splendid curves turn full circle in such a way that he was dizzy in the heat. She laughed and reached the door as he stuttered, "You know, I actually couldn't say if—I mean, there's nothing definite—"

"Just say when," she said. "All you got to do is tell me when."

She had hardly disappeared before Poll and Lil came in. They too had stripped down to the bust and Poll had an unlighted cigarette dangling from her lips. They had decided to work a new one on Mr. Charlton.

"Hullo, ducky," they said, and Poll took the cigarette from her lips, broke it in half, and gave one half to Lil. "Last one, dear. Not unless Charley can help us out. Haven't got a gasper, ducky, I suppose?"

Mr. Charlton, who smoked moderately at the best of times, had recently given it up altogether because he was scared of cancer.

"Afraid not. Don't smoke now—"

"Came out without a bean this morning," Poll explained. "Too early for the damn Post Office. Else we'd have got the kids' allowances."

"How many baskets?" Mr. Charlton said.

"Three dozen." Poll lit her cigarette and then gave Lil a light, both of them exhaling smoke in desperate relief. "Gawd, it's hot out in that field. You want a drag every two minutes to keep you going at all. Don't suppose you could lend us five bob so's Lil can nip down to the shop on her bike, can you? Pay you back first thing tomorrow."

Mr. Charlton wrote desperately in the book while the two bare-chested women watched him, though he did not know it, like two brown, hungry, calculating old dogs watching a bone. There probably wasn't much meat on Mr. Charlton; they'd better get it off while they could.

"Five bob, ducky. Gawd, it's hot out in that field. Two women fainted. Did you hear about that, ducky? Two women fainted."

"Work it orf as dead horse," Lil started to say.

Touched, nervous, and swayed against his better judgment, Mr. Charlton was just thinking of lending Poll and Lil the five bob to be worked off as dead horse when he heard, from the field, a sudden pandemonium of yelling and shrieking.

He followed Poll and Lil to the door of the tent. Thirty yards from the tent a ring of seminaked vultures were shrieking and flapping in the sun. "Somebody's at it. Somebody's catching a packet." Poll said, and Mr. Charlton caught a glimpse, somewhere in the vultured circle, of two bare-shouldered girls fighting each other, like wild white cats.

Poll and Lil started running. Mr. Charlton started running too. Then, after ten yards or so, he suddenly stopped as if his head had been caught by an invisible trip wire.

One of the white cats was Pauline Jackson; the other was Mariette. Like cats too they were howling in the unrestricted animal voices that belong to dark rooftops. With alarm Mr. Charlton saw streams of blood on the flesh of hands, faces, bare shoulders, and half-bare breasts, and then suddenly realized that this was really the scarlet juice of mashed strawberries that the girls were viciously rubbing into each other's eyes and throat and hair. The fair ponytail was like frayed red rope and the neat dark curls of Mariette that he cared for more and more every time he saw them were being torn from her face. Somewhere in the center of it all the colossal bulk of Ma was shouting; but whether in encouragement, discouragement, or sheer delight he never knew.

Half a minute later he heard the highest shrieking of all. It came from behind him. He turned sharply and saw the little two penn'orth running from the shelter of the wood, waving her tiny arms in excitement. That high-pitched voice of hers was more like a train whistle than ever.

When she reached him she started bobbing wildly up and down like a child too small to see over a fence, and Mr. Charlton realized that she could not see any part of the cat-and-strawberry horror that by now had him completely spellbound.

"Hold me up, mister!" she shrieked. "I s'll miss it!"

He took her by the arms and the tiny body rose into the air like a spring.

"Blimey, it's good!" she shrieked. "It's good!" By now she was actually sitting on Mr. Charlton's shoulder, her tiny short legs drumming continually on his chest and her fists in his hair. "That'll take some getting out in the wash. Git stuck into her, Mariette! It's good! It's good! It's good!"

Mr. Charlton didn't think it was good. He was afraid Mariette would get seriously hurt and he felt a little sick at the thought of it. Suddenly he felt constrained to rush in and separate the two combatants, all scarlet now and weeping and half-naked, before they disfigured each other forever, and he said, "I've got to stop them. I've got to make them stop it. Anyway, what on earth are they fighting *for?*"

"Gawd blimey, don't you *know*, mister?" The little two penn'orth shrieked. "Don't tell me you don't *know!*"

Even when he was riding home that evening in the back of the truck Mr. Charlton still could not really believe that he knew. The notion that two girls would fight for him still had him completely stunned.

Everybody had been sternly briefed by Ma, before the truck arrived, not to say a word to Pop. "Might give her a good leatherin' if he knew," Ma explained, "and it's hot enough as it is."

Everybody agreed; they were all for Mariette. Mr. Charlton was all for Mariette too; he felt himself grow continually more proud of her as the truck, driven at Pop's customary jolting speed, rocked homewards through fragrant hedgerows of honeysuckle, the first wild pink roses, and may. He kept smiling at her and watching her dark, pretty, red-stained hair. Somebody had lent her a green sweater to wear over her ripped bodice and you could hardly tell, now, that she had been in a fight at all.

In a curious way it was Mr. Charlton who felt he had been in a fight. A total lack of all feeling of uncertainty, together with an odd sensation of actual aggression, began to make him feel rather proud of himself too.

"Well, how was the first day, Charley?" Pop said. In the sitting room Pop had poured out a Dragon's Blood for himself and one for Mr. Charlton, who felt he really needed it. He was as hungry as a hunter too. "How was the first day? Everything go orf all right? Smooth an' all that? No lumbago?"

"No lumbago," Mr. Charlton said. "Everything smooth as it could be."

"Perfick," Pop said.

He drank Dragon's Blood to the day's perfection and called through to the kitchen to Ma, "How long'll supper be, Ma? I'm turning over."

"About an hour yet. Roast beef's only just gone in."

"How'd you get on today, Ma? Good picking?"

"Earned fourteen pounds ten," Ma said.

"Hour yet," Pop said to Mr. Charlton, "plenty o' time for you to take Mariette for a stroll as far as the river. They'll be cutting the grass in that medder tomorrow."

Mr. Charlton agreed; he had his thoughts very much on the butter-cup field.

Just before going outside, however, he remembered that he had a question to ask of Pop. It was the one about tax on the strawberry lark.

"An awful lot of money gets paid out to these people," he said. "Strawberries. Cherries. Hops and so on. Take, for example, all these Cockneys coming down for the hops. Strictly, in law, they ought to pay tax on that."

"Pay tax?" Pop said. He spoke faintly.

"I mean if the law is to be interpreted to the strict letter—"

"Strick letter my aunt Fanny," Pop said. "Damnit if they was taxed they wouldn't come. Then you wouldn't have no strawberries, no cherries, no nothink. No beer!"

The logic of this argument dashed the last of Mr. Charlton's reasoning as he went away to find Mariette, who was just coming downstairs, dressed now in the cool green shantung of which he had grown so very fond.

As Mr. Charlton and Mariette disappeared across the yard in the evening sun Ma's only complaint, as she watched them from the kitchen window, was that she hadn't got a pair of field glasses so that she could watch "how that young man's getting on with his technique. If he's getting on at all."

Pop, after pouring two gills of gin into his second Dragon's Blood in order to pep it up a bit, retired to watch television. It had been on for some considerable time, out of natural habit, though no one was watching it, and now there was a program on the screen about life in Central Africa, about wild animals, pygmies, and their strange, baffling customs.

Pop sat back happily in the greenish unreal semidarkness. He had had a very good day going a big lark in scrap that showed 600 percent with not a very great deal of trouble. He would tell Ma all about it later. Meanwhile he was perfectly content to sit and sip his beer and watch the pygmies, all of whom hopped around the jungle and the village compounds with unconcern, without a stitch on, all the women barebreasted. There was hardly a program he liked better than those about strange hot countries, wild animals, and queer tribes, especially those who had never seen civilization.

Out in the buttercup field Mariette and Mr. Charlton were lying in the tall brilliant flowers and the even taller feathery grasses. Mariette, so dark and so pretty in her green shantung, was drawing Mr. Charlton very gently to her and Mr. Charlton was responding with a proud, searching look on his face so that Ma, if she could have been watching him at that moment through binoculars, would have seen that he had gone some way, in certain directions, toward improving his technique.

6

When Pop got home the following evening he found Miss Pilchester waiting in the yard.

"Isn't it absolutely ghastly?" Miss Pilchester said.

The evening seemed warmer than ever, but Miss Pilchester was wearing a thick thorn-proof skirt of cabbage green and a cable stitch woolen cardigan to match. Pop did not ask her what was absolutely ghastly and she did not offer to tell him either.

There was no need. Everything to Edith Pilchester was always absolutely ghastly. She lived alone and kept numbers of laying hens. The hens were absolutely ghastly, and so, even worse, was living alone. It was absolutely impossible to get any help in the house, in the garden, or with the hens. She couldn't afford to run a car because of taxes and the price of petrol and oil and servicing and repairs. She could just afford a solitary hack of her own, but she couldn't afford a groom. It was all absolutely ghastly. Before the war she had kept a little maid in the house, a man in the garden, and a groom-cum-chauffeur-cum-cook who was an absolute treasure in all sorts of ways, including bringing her early-morning tea and hot whiskey last thing at night in bed. Now all of them had gone and she could hardly afford the whiskey. It was absolutely ghastly. Everybody went out to work in the fields at strawberry picking, cherry picking, plum picking, apple picking, bean picking, hop picking, or at the canning factories in the town, earning mountains more money than they knew what to do with and in any case more than she could pay. It was all absolutely ghastly.

One of the results of everything being so absolutely ghastly was that Miss Pilchester, who was a fortyish, slightly mustached brunette shaped like a bolster, threw herself into an amazing number of projects with an energy quite ferocious, desperately trying to put the whole ghastly business to rights again. Prowling from committee to committee, charity to charity, bazaar to bazaar, she was like some restless, thirsty lioness seeking prey.

"Hot again, ain't it?" Pop said.

"Absolutely ghastly."

When Pop suggested that Miss Pilchester should come into the house and have a drink and cool off a bit, Miss Pilchester said no thanks, not for the moment, it was absolutely ghastly. She thought they ought to do the field; there wasn't much time left, thanks to that bounder Fortescue letting them down at the last moment and the committee, with the exception of the brigadier, having been very nearly as bad. The whole thing was simply too ghastly.

Over in the meadow the grass had been cut and baled during the day. Big fragrant cotton reels of hay lay scattered everywhere between the house and the river. Only a white-and-yellow fringe of moon daisy and buttercup remained standing at the edges, pretty as a ruffle under the hedgerows of hawthorn, rising honeysuckle, and wild rose.

"Damn good field, Larkin," Miss Pilchester said. "No doubt about that. Just the job."

She surveyed it with a critical, organizing eye, seeing on it a vision of jumps, judges' tents, show rings, beer tents, and horses. It was awfully decent of Larkin to do it, she said, otherwise everything would have been an absolute shambles.

"Always like to oblige," Pop said, and laughed in cheerful fashion.

Miss Pilchester laughed too. One of the things she always liked about Larkin was the man's inexhaustible cheerfulness. Friendly chap.

"What about the car park though?" she said. "That's always another nightmare."

"Use the other field," Pop said. "Next door. The little 'un. Simple."

Swallows were flying high above the meadows and the river, swooping in the blue hot sky, and Miss Pilchester might almost have been one of them in the quick, darting glances of gratitude she gave to Pop.

"All yours," Pop said. "Come and go just as you like. Any time."

Another thing Miss Pilchester liked about Pop was the terrific easy generosity of the chap. Good sport. She had once been casually kissed by Pop at a Christmas village social, in some game or other, and the experience, for her at least, had been something more than that of two pairs of lips briefly meeting. It gave you the same feeling, she thought, as smelling bruised spring grass, or new-mown hay, for the first time.

"All we want then is a fine day," Miss Pilchester said. "If it's wet it'll be absolutely ghastly."

"Can't control the tap water I'm afraid," Pop said, and laughed again, at the same time remarking how thirsty he was. "Might put something in it, though, if you feel like it now. Drop o' gin? Drop o' whiskey? Glass o' port?"

Miss Pilchester darted toward Pop another rapid, swallowlike glance of approval, half-affectionate, half-grateful, her eyes so momentarily absorbed in the baldish, perky profile with its dark side-linings that she quite forgot to say that anything was absolutely ghastly.

Back in the yard a van from the bacon factory had just delivered all of Pop's two pigs—he had decided after all that one would be gone almost before you could wink—except the four sides and two hams, which had been left for curing. In the kitchen, Ma, now a white-aproned expansive butcheress, was busy trimming several score pounds of pork and pork offal; cheerful as ever, she stowed it away in the new deep freeze. As Pop put his head through the kitchen door he was confronted by a blood-stained mountain of legs, loins, heads, chitterlings, and trotters and the sight gave him enormous pleasure.

Ma said, "Dr. Leagrave's in the sitting room. I said you wouldn't be long."

"Come to see Mariette?"

"No, pipe down, you loony. Nobody knows anything about that. No, just on his way back from the golf course. Just passing."

"Thirsty, I expect," Pop said. "Still, just the job—we can get him to run the rule over Mr. Charlton."

In the sitting room Pop introduced Miss Pilchester to Dr. Leagrave, who was a heavyish man in his fifties, rather red-necked in a Teutonic sort of way, and completely bald. The doctor, who played a good deal of golf as a pretense of getting exercise and keeping his weight down, though in reality preferring the comforts of the clubhouse, remarked that it was warmish. Miss Pilchester said it was absolutely ghastly and flopped into an easy chair with the grace of a cow.

Television was on, out of natural habit, and the program was one of opera, the composer being a man named Wagner, of whom Pop had never heard. Pop gave the screen a cursory, whipping glance—the programs were never much catch Tuesdays—and wondered if everybody on it had gone stark, staring mad.

It was a relief to turn to drinks and Miss Pilchester.

"Now, Miss Pilchester. Edith." Miss Pilchester bloomed softly, smiling as Pop called her Edith. "What shall it be? Drop o' whiskey? Drop o' gin? Drop o' Guinness? I can make you a cocktail."

Miss Pilchester said she thought cocktails were absolutely ghastly. "No, whiskey for me. And soda please."

Dr. Leagrave chose the same. Pop, in brief thought over the cocktail galleon, wondered if he should mix himself a real snorter, such as a Rolls-Royce or a Chauffeur, but finally decided to have his favorite Dragon's Blood with lime.

"Your day off, Doc?" he said.

Dr. Leagrave thanked God it was and took his whiskey with uncertain but eager hands.

"It must be absolutely ghastly in this heat," Miss Pilchester said, "sick visiting and all that."

"Not that so much," the doctor said. "Trouble is it's a nice fine evening. By now my waiting room'll be jam-packed as a cinema with Lolla showing."

Sipping whiskey, an astonished Miss Pilchester asked why that should be and got the answer not from Dr. Leagrave, but from Pop, himself as quick as a swallow. "Ain't got nothing better to do. That's why."

"Hit it plumb on the head," the doctor said.

"You mean it makes a difference," Miss Pilchester said, "what the weather is?"

"More perfick the wevver," Pop said, "the more they roll up. You told me that once afore, didn't you, Doc?"

The doctor said indeed he had.

"Absolutely ghastly," Miss Pilchester said.

"Fast becoming a nation of hypochondriacs," the doctor said, and Pop looked so suddenly startled at yet another word he had never even heard on television that he couldn't speak. That was the second within a few days.

"Pill takers. Drug takers."

"Ghastly."

"Then there are young doctors," Dr. Leagrave said, now launching on a tried-and-favorite theme, "men of not very great experience, who are prescribing a hundred, two hundred, capsules of new and highly expensive drugs to patients who take two and put the rest into the kitchen cupboard."

"Ghastly."

With something like venom Dr. Leagrave finished his whiskey, his seventh since six o'clock, and said it was no wonder the country was on its beam-ends. Miss Pilchester warmly agreed and Pop took away the doctor's empty glass to fill it up again, at the same time glancing at the television screen, unable to make any sense whatever of a single note or gesture coming out of it.

As soon as he had poured the doctor's whiskey he decided to switch the sound off. He couldn't bear to switch the picture off in case something should come on, like pygmies or football or chorus girls, which he liked. In consequence, the screen became a pallid mime of open-mouthed puppets singing silently.

"By the way, Doc," he said, "we got a young friend of ours staying here who's bad abed and wuss up. Think you could have a look at him?"

"What's wrong?" the doctor said. "Not another pill addict, I hope."

"Lumbago," Pop said.

"Ghastly," Miss Pilchester said. "I get it. I sympathize."

Pop said he would try to find Mr. Charlton and started to go out of the room, remembering as he did so the kitchen piled with pork.

"Nice piece o' pork for you when you go, Doc," he said. "How about that? You too, Edith. Like chitterlings?" Pop laughed in his infectious, rousing fashion. "How about a nice piece o' pig's liver and a basin o' chitterlings?"

Miss Pilchester, who had not yet been reduced to eating chitterlings, nevertheless laughed too. Always made you feel happy, that man, she thought. When Pop came back with a rather hesitant but sun-scorched Mr. Charlton, red-faced from a second day in the strawberry fields and more ravenously hungry than he had ever been in his life, the doctor was just saying to Edith Pilchester, again with a sort of evangelical, venomous uncertainty, "This county alone is spending over a million a year on drugs! This one county—"

"Here's our young friend," Pop said. "Friend of Mariette's. Mr. Charlton. Been very poorly."

"Well," the doctor said, "perhaps we can have a look at you." He glanced uncertainly around at Miss Pilchester. "Is there somewhere—"

"Upstairs," Pop said. "I'll lead the way."

Mr. Charlton followed Pop and Dr. Leagrave upstairs. On the landing Pop paused to whisper confidentially to the doctor that there would be a whole leg of pork if he wanted it; he hadn't very well been able to say it in front of Edith—the doc would understand?

The doctor, swaying a little, said he understood, and Pop opened the first door on the landing without knocking. "This'll do," he said. "Mariette's room."

Fortunately the room was empty and presently Mr. Charlton,

stripped to the waist, found himself lying face downward on Mariette's bed, his sensations very like those he had experienced when the geese had entwined their necks about his legs, when he had worn Mariette's pajamas and when, in utter ecstasy, he had breathed the fragrance of gardenia for the first time. The hot room was thick and intoxicating with that same deep, torturing fragrance now.

The doctor, who had not bothered to fetch his bag from the car, pressed his fingers gently into Mr. Charlton's lumbar region.

"Much pain?"

Mr. Charlton confessed that he had no pain whatever. A day in the strawberry fields had in fact improved him so much, both physically and mentally, that he had actually spotted the double twist Poll and Lil were going to work on him almost before they had started.

"Comes and goes? That it?"

"Sort of like that."

"Suppose you'd like to go on sick benefit for a couple of weeks?"

To the doctor's astonishment, Mr. Charlton said no, he didn't think so. He was, though he didn't say so, having a wonderful time in the strawberry field. He was earning money. If he went on sick benefit he wouldn't earn any money and he wouldn't have half the fun. He was learning to use his loaf.

"Well," the doctor said, "try to keep out of drafts when you're hot." He laughed briefly, swayed tipsily, and thought of how perhaps it would be possible to snatch another quick one downstairs before he took the leg of pork and went home. "And avoid lying in wet grasses."

Some time after the doctor had gone Pop wrapped up two pounds of loin of pork, about a pound of liver, and a pair of pig's trotters and said that, if Edith was ready, he would run her home. Edith Pilchester, charmed with three whiskeys, more than she usually had in a week, and enough food to last her until Sunday, was more than ready and completely forgot, for the second time, to say how absolutely ghastly anything was.

"Got a Rolls now," Pop said.

Miss Pilchester confessed she had seen it in the yard.

"I said to myself it couldn't be yours."

In the yard, Pop spent some time, with touches of imperial pride, showing Miss Pilchester the Rolls's burnished monograms, the silver vases for flowers, and the speaking tube.

"If you'd like to sit in the back," he said, "you can say things down the tube to me. Orders and all that."

"I don't want to sit in the back," Miss Pilchester said. "Not on your life. I want to sit in the front with you."

As they drove along Pop demonstrated first the town horn, the sweet one, then the country, the snarl. Miss Pilchester enjoyed this but said, "Not so fast. I don't like driving so fast," remembering that she lived less than a mile away. Accordingly Pop slowed down, driving with one hand and with the other half caressing, half pinching Miss Pilchester's knee. Since she wore only loose lisle stockings, this, he found, was not half so delicious an experience as pinching Ma, who wore nylons and very tight ones at that, but to Miss Pilchester it seemed to be a source of palpitating pleasure.

She again became like a swallow, darting nervous, rapid glances.

A few minutes later the Rolls drew up at Bonny Banks, Miss Pilchester's cottage, tiny, thatched, and low-pitched, which she had converted out of a fallen-down cow byre in prewar days, when things were cheap. Creosoted beams and a gimcrack front door studded with what appeared to be rusty horseshoe nails were designed to give the little loaf-shaped house an appearance of Tudor antiquity or of having come out of a fairy tale. But in the evening light, after the hot day, its garden ill-kept, the lawn unmown, the paths a flourish of dandelions, the rosebeds pitted with dustbaths made by escaping hens, it looked shabby even by comparison with Pop's paradise.

Miss Pilchester begged Pop over and over again not to look at it. It was simply ghastly, absolutely ghastly.

"You'll come in for a moment though, won't you?"

Pop had always wanted to see the inside of Miss Pilchester's cottage but when he groped his way through the kitchen, which smelled stale from unwashed dishes, and into a living room as dark and cramped as a bolthole, even he was surprised. A flock of sheep might well have passed through the place an hour before. Bits of wool—raw, unwashed sheep's wool—lay everywhere. It was one of Miss Pilchester's hobbies to gather wool from field and hedgerow and on long winter's nights clean, spin, and wind it for making into socks and sweaters, which she dyed in subdued rough shades with lichen.

"Do take a pew if you can find room, won't you?"

It was difficult, if not impossible, to find a pew. Miss Pilchester hastily removed a basin of eggs, a half-finished sweater, two skeins of wool, the *Times*, a sewing basket, some gray underwear, and an unplucked brown fowl from various chairs.

"Sit you down. I'll have a drink for you in a jiff. Don't mind anything. I'll just find a plate for the pork and then get some glasses."

Remains of a boiled egg, a cup of cocoa, and a burned raspberry tart, the leftovers either of breakfast or lunch, or both, lay scattered about the table. Miss Pilchester gathered up eggs and cocoa, dropped the shell into the cocoa and then upset the resulting mess into the raspberry tart.

Some seconds later she was calling from the kitchen, "Absolutely ghastly having no help. But nobody does, do they? Only Professor Fane."

Fane, a professor of physics, with some distinguished degrees, including foreign ones, used the house next door as a weekend cottage only, coming down on Friday evenings to be bullied for three whole days by an ex-naval artificer and his wife, acting as chauffeur and cook, who borrowed the car all day on Sundays to visit other naval men by the sea or watch dirt-track racing on the hills. The professor spent most of the time in a ten-by-six attic under the roof, listening to Bach and Beethoven, while the ex-artificer and his wife used the drawing room downstairs, watching the television set that the professor had had to install in order to get them to stay in the house at all.

"He's lucky," Miss Pilchester called. "I can't get a soul."

She was looking in various cupboards for a bottle of whiskey, which she knew was there. It wasn't there and it was some moments before she found it tucked away behind another pile of underclothes, a basket of clothes pegs, and a vegetable marrow left over from last year.

An inch of whiskey lay in the bottom and Miss Pilchester remembered she had not bought another bottle since she had had a cold at Easter, over six weeks before.

She put another inch of tap water into the bottle and then poured the whiskey and water into two glasses, and called, "Just coming. Sorry I kept you so long," went out of the kitchen to find Pop glancing at the *Times*, a newspaper he had never heard of before.

"No television?" Pop said.

"Couldn't possibly afford it."

"Terrible," Pop said.

With sudden irritation Miss Pilchester remembered some stock exchange figures she had been reading at breakfast and found herself in half a mind to ask Pop what he thought she ought to do with her 3½ percent War Stock. He seemed so clever about money. He must be. The stock was another government swindle. She had bought it at ninety-six, and now it stood at sixty-seven—that was the way they treated you for being prudent, thrifty, and careful.

It was perfectly true, as someone or other had remarked to her only the other day, that all governments were dishonest.

"Don't you think all governments are dishonest?" she said. She handed Pop the whiskey and explained about the shares. "All they think about is getting out of you the little you've got. What do you think?"

"What do I think?" Pop said. "I think you want to get it out o' *them* afore they have a chance to get it out o' *you*."

Miss Pilchester laughed. She said, "Cheers," and, drinking an economical sip of whiskey, thanked Pop once again for being so nice about the field.

"Going to pay your hunt subscription next season? Hope so."

Pop said of course he was going to pay a subscription, and one for Mariette too.

"Thank the Good God there are a few chaps like you."

The hunt, Miss Pilchester said, was going down. Hardly anybody had any time. The Christmas meet last year had been an absolute rag-tag-and-bobtail. It was simply ghastly.

"Captain Prettyman's retiring as master next year," she said, and thanked the Good God a second time. "Never has been any good. Never got hold of the right end of the stick from the beginning."

She darted Pop another of her rapid, swallowlike glances.

"You're the sort of chap they ought to have. New blood to pep them up."

Pop could hardly bear it. In an uncertain spasm of ambition he actually had a swift vision of himself as Master of Fox Hounds. It was dazzling. At the present time he paid a subscription but never rode to hounds, though Mariette always did. The incredible idea of his being master had never once occurred to him.

"Here, steady on, old girl," he said. "You'll get me started thinking things."

Miss Pilchester, remembering the brief interlude when Pop had pressed her knee in the car, laughed as softly as she could.

"Well, that's always nice, isn't it?" she said.

Suddenly Pop did the thing Miss Pilchester feared most: He drained his whiskey in a single gulp, smacking his lips with pleasure, as if ready to go. There was no more whiskey left, not even a drop to water down, and she experienced a second of panic before he got up from the chair.

"Well, I must push back. Got a few things to do before bedtime."

"Oh, must you go?"

With uncertainty Miss Pilchester got up too. She had been careful to sit with her back to the little cottage window, but now twilight was falling rapidly enough to make it almost impossible to distinguish the

smaller details of her face. Only her eyes were bright as they gave Pop
yet another quick, swallowlike dart.

"You've been an absolute lamb," she said. "Don't know how—"

She turned suddenly to find herself wrapped in Pop Larkin's arms,
being kissed in splendid silence, with something of the effect of a velvet
battering ram. This was the way Pop always kissed Ma but Miss Pilchester, for her part, had never experienced anything quite like it. It
had on her something of the effect of Pop's cocktail on Mr. Charlton:
It explored with disquieting fire a few corners of her body that she
hardly knew existed before.

When it was over Pop retired a few inches, took breath, and said, in
almost exactly the tones he always used when mixing drinks at the
glittering Spanish galleon, "How about one more?"

"Please."

"Perfick," Pop said.

Five minutes later a palpitating but very happy Miss Pilchester,
trebly kissed—one more for luck, Pop had said—came to the gate of
the little garden wilderness to wave him good-bye. If it had been possible she would have kissed him good-bye but she knew that even in the
gathering May twilight the ex-artificer's wife would be watching from
a window. Not that she cared a damn now. She felt dedicated for ever,
with abandon, to the generous, passionate Mr. Larkin.

"See you soon!" she waved.

"Any time," Pop said. She laughed merrily. "Don't do anything I
wouldn't do. Keep your hand on your ha'penny."

The last of Miss Pilchester's darting glances, this one almost of fire,
seemed actually to set the Rolls in motion and with a neat, sidelong
wink he drove away.

At first he drove rather fast and then, suddenly subdued by the
immensely incredible notion that he might one day become Master of
Fox Hounds, slowed down to a silent crawl. He didn't want anybody
to think he was drunk in charge. Two minutes later he passed a policeman on duty. Seeing the Rolls, the policeman saluted. Pop saluted in
reply.

He'd have to tell Ma, he thought, about the Master of Fox Hounds
lark. No, he wouldn't though. He'd keep that after all; she'd say he was
flying too high. What he would tell her, though, was about the inside
of Miss Pilchester's house; that terrible, cramped, untidy, woolly,
televisionless little bolt-hole. Perfickly awful how some people lived,
he would tell Ma, perfickly awful.

When he arrived home Ma was sitting outside the kitchen door, enjoying a Guinness and a few potato crisps after her battle with the pork. It was still hot in the semidarkness, but Pop feared he could hear, in the distance, a few muted notes of thunder.

"Where's Mr. Charlton?" he said.

"Been writing letters," Ma said. "Just gone off with Mariette to post them."

"*Writing letters?*"

Another high, incredible mark of credit for Mr. Charlton.

"Whatever's he got to write letters for?"

Impossible to understand how anybody could write letters.

"I think he'd been writing to the tax office."

"Not about us," Pop said. "He ain't got nothing to write there about us."

"Oh, no," Ma said. Enjoying her Guinness, she was quite unperturbed. "I think he's gone and extended his sick leave. That's all. Since he saw the doctor. Going to stay another week or two."

"Perfick," Pop said. "Jolly good."

Pop, to whom Mr. Charlton was rapidly becoming a more and more agreeable figure, quite exceptional in his literacy, went into the house to pour himself a Dragon's Blood. When he came back, Ma said, "Well, did you kiss her?"

"Course I did."

"I thought you would." Ma sat with the Guinness balanced on the precipice of her rolling stomach like a little black doll, again completely unperturbed. "Do her good. Make her sleep all the sweeter. What was it like?"

Pop considered. He remembered how, in the twilight, some portion of Miss Pilchester's mustache had brushed against him.

"A bit like trying to catch a mole," he said, "in a dark entry."

Ma dug him sharply in the ribs and started laughing like shaking jelly. Pop laughed too at his own joke and then stared up at the sky, his attention rapt for some moments by the young, unquenchable summer stars. A few drops of rain fell, as if by a miracle, from a cloudless heaven, and then ceased in a whisper. Laughing made Pop give a sudden belch and far away, across miles of windless fields, somewhere on the dim hills, nature echoed him in a scarcely audible double note of thunder. Ma looked at the stars too and Pop started to tell her, true amazement in his voice, about Miss Pilchester's Tudor bolt-hole and how perfickly awful it was.

"Never credit it, Ma," he told her. "Never credit it. Still, what I always say: You don't know, do you, until you get a look inside?"

For a few moments longer they sat in silence, until at last Ma said, "Well: I'm waiting."

"What for?"

"Don't you think it's about time you kissed *me?*"

Pop said he supposed it was. He drained his Dragon's Blood and set the empty glass behind his chair. Then he leaned over and clasped in his right hand as much of Ma's vast bosom as he could hold.

"It's coming to something," Ma said, "when I have to ask you for one. Are you tired?"

Pop demonstrated that he was far from tired by kissing Ma with prolonged velvety artistry. Ma responded by settling back into her chair into a cocoon of silence unbroken except for an occasional exquisite breath of pleasure, exactly like the murmur of a kitten in a doze.

In the far distance new waves of thunder rolled. From the cloudless heaven a few fresh warm drops of rain fell. For some moments they splashed the two faces as lightly as a sigh but Pop and Ma, like the youngest of lovers, did not heed them at all.

7

On the day of the pony gymkhana Mr. Charlton was up at half past four. The morning was humid, dreamy, and overcast, with low mist on the river. Pop, who had already been up an hour, giving swill to pigs and fodder to the Jersey cow, and was now staunching back the first pangs of hunger with a few slices of bread and Cheddar cheese doused half an inch thick with catsup, said he thought "the wevver looked a little bit thick in the clear" but otherwise, with luck, it ought to be all right by noon.

Mr. Charlton breakfasted on two lean pork cutlets, some scrambled eggs cooked by Mariette, fried potatoes, and four halves of tomato.

"In the old days," said Pop, whose estimation of Mr. Charlton rose almost every time he talked to him, especially on occasions like coming down to breakfast at a good time and getting outside a reasonable amount of food, "my dad used to tell me that they always had beer for breakfast. Like a glass o' beer?"

Mr. Charlton thanked him and said he didn't think he would. Mariette had just made tea.

"Well, I think I will," Pop said. "I don't think a lot o' tea is all that good for you."

Pop, after pouring himself a Dragon's Blood, had much the same breakfast as Mr. Charlton, except that there was a lot more of it and his plate was gay with mustard, catsup, and two kinds of Worcestershire sauce. Mariette, who looked pretty and fresh in dark green slacks and a pale yellow shirt blouse, said she was so excited she could hardly eat but nevertheless managed two eggs and bacon, a pint of milk, and four slices of bread.

Ma was not yet down but had sent word that as the day was going to be a long one she was having a lay-in, which meant she would be down by half past six.

Toward the end of breakfast Pop turned to Mr. Charlton, who had not been able to keep his eyes off Mariette for more than two seconds since she had come into the kitchen tying up her hair with a thin emerald ribbon, and said, "Are you two going to feed and water the donkeys? I've got forty thousand jobs to do and Miss Pilchester'll be here by six."

Mr. Charlton said of course they would feed the donkeys and helped himself to a fifth slice of bread and covered it half an inch thick with fresh Jersey butter made by Ma. Pop watched this process with immense admiration, telling himself he had never seen such a change in a man's health as he had witnessed in three weeks in Mr. Charlton.

Mr. Charlton was still on sick leave.

"Oh! Those sweet donkeys," Mariette said.

The donkeys that she and Mr. Charlton were going to feed were not the rest of the Larkin household but four animals Pop had secured for racing. Pop thought that gymkhanas were sometimes inclined to be on the dull side, what he called "a bit horseface like—so many folks with long faces you can't very often tell the mares from some of the old women"—and that therefore something was needed to enliven the customary round of trotting, riding, leading rein, jumping, bending, and walk, trot, canter, and run.

This was why he had thought of the donkeys and why, later on in the day, he thought of introducing a few private harmless jokes of his own. What these were he was keeping to himself; but he had not forgotten the one about putting a firework under Miss Pilchester.

To his grievous disappointment the committee had turned down his offer of fireworks. It might well be, they had pointed out, that a few ponies would be late leaving the ground and that some fireworks would in any case go off early and the ponies be distressed. Pop saw the reason in this but if there was going to be one firework and only one it was, he was determined, going to be Miss Pilchester's.

"What time is the cocktail party, Pop?" Mr. Charlton said.

Pop was delighted that Mr. Charlton now called him Pop.

"Ma thinks eight o'clock would be the perfick time."

"What a day," Mariette said. "All this and cocktails too."

She went on to confess that she had never been to a cocktail party and Pop said, "Come to that neither have I. Neither has Ma."

"What do people normally drink at cocktail parties?" Mariette said.

"Cocktails," Mr. Charlton said slyly, and before he could move she gave him a swift playful cuff, exactly like that of a dark soft kitten, across the head.

"Not at this one you don't," Pop said.

Both Mariette and Mr. Charlton were too excited to remember that the whole question of what was drunk at cocktail parties had been discussed a week before.

Since Pop had been unable to indulge himself with fireworks he and Ma had decided that there must, if possible, be something in their place. A cocktail party, Pop said, would be the perfick answer. Ma agreed, but said they ought to keep it very select if possible. Not more than thirty people, she thought, at the outside; mostly the committee and their families and of course nice people like the Misses Barnwell and the Luffingtons and the brigadier. And what about eats?

Neither Pop nor Ma had any idea what you ate at cocktail parties; therefore Mr. Charlton was consulted.

"Canapés, vol-au-vents, pistachios, and that sort of thing," Mr. Charlton said.

A lot more marks for Mr. Charlton, Pop thought, as once again he heard words he had never even heard on television.

"You mean nuts and things?" Ma said. "They won't keep anybody alive very long. I'd better cook a ham."

Pop warmly agreed; the ham was firmly decided upon. Ma could cut plenty of the thinnest white and brown sandwiches, with nice Jersey butter. And what else?

Mariette said she thought small pieces of cold sardine on toast would be nice. "They're absolutely marvelous hot too," Mr. Charlton said, and got himself still more marks by also suggesting small squares of toast with hot Welsh rarebit, chicken sandwiches, and little sausages on sticks.

Most of this, to Pop, seemed rather light, unsatisfying fare.

"We want to give 'em enough," he said. "We don't want 'em to think we're starving 'em. What about a leg o' pork?"

To his disappointment Mr. Charlton said he rather ruled out the leg of pork.

"All right," Pop said. "What about drinks?"

Pop was all for making plenty of Rolls-Royces and that sort of thing, good, strong ones, together with two new ones he had recently tried out from the *Guide to Better Drinking*: Red Bull and Ma Chérie. Red Bull was a blinder. That would curl their hair.

Mr. Charlton said he thought it made it so much simpler if you stuck to two, or at the outside, three good drinks: say, sherry, port, and gin and tonic. He suggested the port in case the evening was cool.

He got no marks this time. Pop thought it was all about as dull as flippin' ditchwater. With sudden enthusiasm he said, "What about champagne?"

Both Ma and Mariette said they adored champagne. That was a brilliant idea. Something extra nice always happened, Mariette said, when you had champagne, and it seemed to Pop that he saw her exchange with Mr. Charlton an intimate glance of secret tenderness that left him baffled and unsatisfied. Couldn't be nothing in the wind?

"Well, champagne it is then!" Pop said. "Might as well do the thing properly."

Here Mr. Charlton remarked with tact that since not everybody liked champagne it might be just as well to have some other drink in reserve.

"I'll make a few hair curlers," Pop said. "Red Bull—remember that one?—and Ma Chérie."

Mr. Charlton remembered Red Bull. It had rammed him one evening after a hardish day in the strawberry field. It was not inaptly named.

It was half past five before Mr. Charlton and Mariette got up at last from breakfast and went across the yard to feed the donkeys. The four little donkeys had been tied up in the stable that Pop had built with his eye on the day when all the family, with the possible exception of Ma, would have a pony or a horse to ride. That would be the day. Two donkeys had been hired by Pop; two had been brought over by their owners the previous night. Three more, it was hoped, were still to come.

As soon as Mariette and he were in the half-dark stable, among the donkeys, Mr. Charlton took her quickly in his arms and kissed her. His arms and hands, as they tenderly touched her face, breasts, and shoulders, were as brown as her own.

Mariette laughed, trembling, and said she'd hardly been able to wait for that one, the first, the loveliest of the day. Mr. Charlton, with something like ecstasy, said he hadn't been able to wait either. He could hardly wait for anything. Above all he could hardly wait for the afternoon. "Nor me," Mariette said, and held her body out to him again.

Quietly, as the second kiss went on, the donkeys stirred about the stable, swishing tails, restless. Hearing them, Mariette partly broke away from Mr. Charlton and said with half-laughing mouth, "I suppose there's a first time for everything. I've never been kissed among donkeys before."

Quick as a swallow himself, Mr. Charlton answered. It was the answer of a man sharpened by three weeks in the strawberry field, living with the Larkins, and using his loaf.

"Wait till the cocktail party," he said.

It was almost half past ten before Miss Pilchester fell bodily out of the taxi she had hired in desperation, four hours late, to bring her to the meadow. Pop, who was helping the brigadier to string up gay lines of square and triangular flags about and among the tents, stared in stupefaction at a figure that might have been that of a tired and collapsing mountaineer descending from a peak. Miss Pilchester was armed with shooting stick, rolled mackintosh, a leather holdall containing a spare cardigan, her lunch, and a red vacuum flask, an attaché case containing the judging lists, the *Times*, several books, and a basket of pot eggs. The pot eggs, evidently brought for use in some pony event or other, rolled about the squatting Miss Pilchester exactly as if, in a sudden overspasm of broodiness, she had laid them all herself.

It was all absolutely ghastly, but both Pop and the brigadier were too stupefied to go over and pick up either Miss Pilchester or the eggs; and Pop, for once, was utterly without words. It was the brigadier who spoke for him.

"Good God, Larkin," he said. "Edith must be either tight or eggbound."

Five minutes later Miss Pilchester, the great organizer, was at her work. With indecisive excitement Miss Pilchester rushed from tent to tent, inquiring if someone had seen this, somebody that, had the caterers arrived, and above all wasn't it ghastly?

The caterers had been on the field since seven o'clock; all of them had knocked off for tea. Where then, was the loudspeaker for announcements? Hadn't that arrived? It had arrived and Miss Pilchester tripped over two lines of its wires. Canceled entries—were there any canceled entries?—all entries, she wailed, should have been canceled by nine o'clock.

It was now, the brigadier was heard to point out dryly, half past ten.

Where then, Miss Pilchester wanted to know, were the donkeys? Were the donkeys here?

"Some donkeys," the brigadier was heard to remark, "have been here all night," but the remark was lost on Miss Pilchester, who rushed away to inquire if the ladies' conveniences had been installed. "They are most important," she said, and disappeared into a far tent as if feeling it suddenly necessary to prove it for herself.

At half past eleven the sun broke through, beginning to dry at last the heavy dew on the grass, the trees of the bluebell wood, and the hedgerows. From the completely windless river the last transparent breaths of mist began to rise. A few water lilies were in bud, their heads rising above wet leaves, and they looked like pipes, gently smoking.

It was then discovered that Miss Pilchester had completely forgotten to meet a London train, as she had faithfully promised, at ten forty-five. The train was bringing a judge who had, in counties west of London, a great reputation for judging such things as the Horse of the Year Show. The committee had specially asked for him.

Now Ma came hurrying from the house to say she'd had a bulldog on the phone. "And *did* he bark. And, *oh,* the language."

"Why the 'ell couldn't he come by car?" Pop said.

"Said he flipping well couldn't afford one under this flipping government."

"*We must do something!*" Miss Pilchester said. "It's absolutely ghastly!"

"Mariette and Mr. Charlton can fetch him in the station wagon," Pop said. "They've got to collect more champagne anyway. Ma don't think we've got enough."

"Champagne? What champagne? Who ordered champagne?"

"I did."

"*Not for this show?*"

"Cocktail party," Pop said. "Me and Ma. Instead of the fireworks tonight. You got your invite, didn't you? Mariette and Mr. Charlton sent all the invites out."

The word "fireworks" dragged Miss Pilchester back to Pop's side like a struggling dog on a lead.

"Now you will promise, won't you, no fireworks?"

"No fireworks," Pop said.

Miss Pilchester, remembering Pop's delicate investigation of her knee in the Rolls, the velvety battering ram of the kiss that, as Ma had predicted, had made her sleep so much more sweetly, now permitted herself the luxury of a half smile, the first of her hurried day.

"I know you. Sometimes you're more than naughty."

Sun twinkled on Pop's eyes, lighting up the pupils in a face that otherwise remained as dead as a dummy.

"Not today though," Pop said. "Got to behave today."

"And promise no fireworks?"

"No fireworks."

"Not one?"

"Not one," Pop said, and fixed his eyes on the hem of her skirt as she rushed away to attend once again to the matter of the ladies' conveniences, which were not quite what she had hoped they would be. It was a matter of some delicacy.

As she disappeared Pop reminded the brigadier of how he had said Miss Pilchester was a splendid organizer and all that.

The brigadier was more than kind, "Well, in her own sweet way I suppose she is. Fact is, I suppose, she's the only one who can spare the time. Nobody else has the time."

That was it. Nobody had the time. In the crushing, rushing pressure of modern life, nobody, even in the country, had the time.

A few moments later the brigadier glanced hurriedly at his watch, saw it was after twelve o'clock and said he must rush back for a bite of cold. Pop begged him to come to the beer tent for a quick snifter before he went, but the brigadier was firm. Nellie would be waiting. He was going to be adamant this time.

Pop, watching him depart with bemused admiration, remembered that word. The brigadier had one shoelace missing and had replaced it with packing string. His hair badly needed cutting at the back, and his shirt collar was, if anything, more frayed than before. But the word "adamant" shone from him to remind Pop once again of all those wonderful fellers who could use these startling words. He envied them very much.

Going to the beer tent he found that the bulldog of a judge had arrived and was drinking with two members of the committee, Jack Woodley and Freda O'Connor. The judge was a squat ebullient man in a bowler hat. With Woodley, a ruddy, crude, thick-lipped man who was wearing a yellow waistcoat under his hacking jacket, he kept up a constant braying duet, swaying backward and forward waving a pint mug of beer. Woodley was evidently telling smoke room stories, at the same time gazing with rough interest at the notorious O'Connor bosom, which protruded by several white marble inches above a low yellow sweater. The coarser the stories the more the O'Connor bosom seemed to like them. Like a pair of bellows, its splendid mass pumped air into the hearty organ of her voice, setting the air about her ringing.

All three ignored Pop and he knew why. He and Ma hadn't invited them to the cocktail party. Not caring, he said in a loud voice, "How's everybody? Fit as fleas?" as he went past them. Nobody answered, but Pop didn't care. He believed in treating everybody alike, fleas or no fleas.

Glass of beer in hand, he found a companion some moments later in Sir George Bluff-Gore, who owned a large red-brick Georgian mansion that was too expensive to keep up. He and his wife somehow pigged it out in a keeper's cottage instead. Bluff-Gore, yellowish, funereal, stiff, and despondent, had the face of a pallbearer cramped by indigestion. He was not the sort of man you could slap on the back to wish him well.

Nevertheless Pop did so.

Bluff-Gore, recoiling with dejection, managed to say that it was nice of Larkin to invite him and Lady Rose to this cocktail party. They didn't get out much.

"More the merrier," Pop said, and then remembered that the Bluff-Gores had a daughter—Rosemary, he thought her name was—a big puddeny girl with sour eyes and a blond fringe, whom he had sometimes seen riding at meetings or pony gymkhanas with Mariette. He wondered where she was; he hadn't seen her lately.

"Hope the daughter's coming too?" he said. "Welcome."

"Rosemary? Afraid not. Lives in London now."

"Oh?" Pop said. "Doing what? Working?"

With increasing gloom Bluff-Gore gazed at the grass of the beer tent and thought of his only daughter, who had suddenly decided for some utterly unaccountable reason to give up a perfectly sound, happy, normal home to go and paint in Chelsea. It had practically broken her mother's heart; it was utterly unaccountable.

"Gone over to art," he said.

It was as if he spoke of some old despicable enemy and Pop could only say he hoped it would turn out well.

Drinking again, deciding that art could only be some man or other that Rosemary had run off with, he suddenly switched the subject, charging the unready Bluff-Gore with a startling question.

"When are you going to sell Bluff Court, Sir George?"

Bluff-Gore looked white. For some moments he could find no suitable words with which to tell Pop that he had no intention of selling his house, Bluff Court, even though it was far too large to live in. Bluff Court had sixty rooms, an entire hamlet of barns, dairies, and stables, half a mile of greenhouses and potting sheds and an orangery where, for fifty years, no oranges had grown. You needed a hundred tons of coal to heat it every winter and eighteen gardeners to keep the place tidy and productive in summer. You needed to keep twenty servants to wait on you and another twenty to wait on them. It was dog eat dog. You couldn't get the servants anyway and you couldn't have afforded to pay them if you could.

But to give it up, to sell it, even though you hadn't a bean, was unthinkable. It was a monstrous idea; it simply couldn't be entertained. Among its miles of neglected beeches, elms, and oaks, Bluff Court must and would stand where it did. It might be that one day it would be possible to let it to one of those stockbroker chaps who played at farming, made colossal losses but in the end came out on the right side because he got it out of taxes. Everybody was doing it and it was all perfectly legitimate, they said. It just showed, of course, what the country was coming to. It was grim. No wonder everybody you met was worried stiff. The country was committing suicide. "What makes you think I have any intention of selling Bluff Court?"

"Well, you don't live in the damn thing," Pop said, straight as a bird, "do you? And never will do if you ask me."

Bluff-Gore indicated with funereal acidity that he was, in fact, not asking him.

"Damn silly," Pop said. He started to say that it was like having a car you never rode in and then decided on a more illuminating, more contemporary metaphor and said, "Like having a television set you never look at."

The illustration was, however, lost on Sir George, who had no television set. "There are certain aspects other than material," he said, "that have to be borne in mind."

Pop said he couldn't think for the life of him what they were, and Bluff-Gore looked at the perky, side-lined face with tolerant irony and an oysterish half smile. "You were not thinking of buying the place, by any chance, were you?"

"Course I was." The gentry were, Pop thought, really half dopes sometimes. "What d'ye think I asked you for?"

The oysterish smile widened a little, still ironically tolerant, for the next question. "And what would you do with it, may I ask?"

"Pull the flippin' thing down." Pop gave one of his piercing jolly shouts of laughter. "What else d'ye think?"

"Good God."

By now Bluff-Gore was whiter than ever. The eyes themselves had become oysters, opaque, sightless jellies, wet with shock, even with a glint of tears.

"Lot o' good scrap there," Pop said. "Make you a good offer."

Bluff-Gore found himself quite incapable of speaking; he could only stare emptily and with increasing dejection at the grass of the beer tent, as if mourning for some dear, unspoken departed.

"Cash," Pop said. "Ready as Freddy—why don't you think it over?"

Laughing again, he made a final expansive swing of his beer mug, drawing froth, and left the speechless, sightless Bluff-Gore standing dismally alone.

Outside, in the meadow now gay with strung flags of yellow, scarlet, blue, and emerald, the tents and the marquees standing about the new green grass like white haystacks, Pop found the sun now shining brilliantly. Over by the river, well away from the ring, Mariette was having a practice canter. She was in her yellow shirt and jodhpurs and her bare head was like a curly black kitten against the far blue sky. Mr. Charlton was in attendance and suddenly Pop remembered the little matter of the baby. He supposed she wouldn't have to ride much longer and he wondered mildly if Mr. Charlton knew. He'd forgotten about that.

Suddenly, from far across the meadow, he heard a rousing, familiar sound. It was Ma beating with a wooden spoon on a big jam saucepan.

It was time to eat. It was hot in the midday sun and there was a scent of bruised grass in the air.

"Perfick," Pop thought. "Going to be a stinger. Going to be a wonderful afternoon."

All afternoon Mr. Charlton watched Mariette taking part in the riding and jumping events she had chosen. Once again, as she took her pony faultlessly through the walk, trot, canter, and run, he could hardly believe in that astral delicious figure, yellow, fawn, and black on its bay pony. Impossible almost to believe that it was the girl who had undressed him on the billiard table, scratched the eyes out of Pauline Jackson, and worked with him in the strawberry field. Once again she looked so perfectly aristocratic that she might have been the niece of Lady Planson-Forbes and he had never been so happy in his life as he watched her.

Ma was happy too. Who wouldn't be? All the children were properly dressed for the occasion, wearing riding habits, jodhpurs, and proper riding caps, even though only Mariette and Montgomery were going to ride. Each of them went about sucking enormous pink and yellow ice creams; and the twins, who took so much after Ma, had large crackling bags of popcorn and potato crisps.

Nor were there any flies on Ma. She was wearing a silk costume in very pale turquoise, with slightly darker perpendicular stripes. She had chosen a rather large dark blue straw hat that shaded her face nicely and, as the milliner had predicted, "helped to balance her up a bit." Her shoes were also blue, almost the color of her hat, and her hair had been permed into stiffish little waves. The only thing that really bothered her was her turquoise rings. They had started to cut into her fingers again. She would have to have them off.

Beside her the brigadier's sister looked, as she always did, in her beige shantung and pink cloche hat, like a clothes peg with a thimble perched on top of it.

"Not going in for this 'ere ladies' donkey derby, are you?" Ma said. Her body quivered with resonant, jellying laughter.

An invitation to strip down to the bare bosom could hardly have brought less response from the sister of the brigadier.

"I think Miss Pilchester's going in," Ma said. "Anyway Pop's trying to persuade her to."

The ladies' donkey derby was a late, inspired idea of Pop's. He had managed to persuade the committee that they owed it to him in return for the field. He had also found a silver cup. He had once bought it at a sale, thinking it would be nice to stand on the sideboard. It was engraved with the details of an angling competition, but Pop didn't think it mattered all that much.

While Ma wandered about with the children and Mr. Charlton watched the various events, listening with pride every time the loud-speakers spoke the name of Miss Mariette Larkin, Pop was spending some time behind the beer tent, trying to induce Miss Pilchester to ride in the donkey derby.

"I honestly couldn't. It would be absolutely ghastly."

"I thought you liked a bit o' fun?"

"I think you are trying to be very naughty."

Irresistible though Miss Pilchester always found him, she could not help thinking that this afternoon, in the brilliant sun, Pop looked even more so. He was wearing a suit of small, smart brown-and-white checks, an orange-brown tie, and a new brown Edwardian cap. Like Ma, he compared very favorably with other people: with, for instance, the brigadier, who was wearing a snuff-colored sports jacket patched at the elbows with brown leather, his washed-out university tie, and a pair of crumpled corduroys the color of a molting stoat.

For the second or third time Pop urged Miss Pilchester to be a sport. "Just one more rider to make up the seven."

"Who else is riding? I have never even ridden a donkey in my life before."

"All girls of your age."

Miss Pilchester darted one of her rapid glances at Pop. The cast of suspicion died in her eyes as she saw the new brown cap. How well it suited him.

"What about that time I took you home in the Rolls?"

"What about it?"

"Best kiss I've had for a long time."

"You make me feel shy!" Miss Pilchester said.

"Beauty," Pop said. "Haven't been able to forget it."

Miss Pilchester hadn't been able to forget it either; she had even wondered if it might ever be repeated.

"I admit it was far from unpleasant, but what has it to do with the donkey derby?"

Pop started to caress the outer rim of Miss Pilchester's thigh. With upsurgent alarm Miss Pilchester felt an investigating finger press a suspender button.

"People will be looking!"

"Coming to the cocktail party?"

"I think so. Yes, I am."

"Repeat performance tonight at the cocktail party. Promise."

"I know those promises. They're like piecrust!"

At four o'clock Miss Pilchester was ready to ride in the ladies' donkey derby.

A quarter of an hour before that Montgomery and Mr. Charlton had ridden in the men's donkey derby. Most of the donkeys, including Mr. Charlton's, had had to be started with carrots and the race had been won by a pale sagacious animal named Whiskey Johnny, who didn't need any carrots. Mr. Charlton had ridden three yards and then fallen off. His mount had instantly bolted, ending up in a stirring style far beyond the tea tent, by the river, where already a few lovers, bored by the events and stimulated by a warm afternoon of entrancing golden air, were embracing in the long grasses by the bank, profitably dreaming out the day in the world of rising fish, wild irises, and expanding water lily blooms.

When Pop went to collect the animal, which was called Jasmine, he found it staring with detached interest at a soldier and a passionate, well-formed young blonde, both of whom were oblivious, in the grasses, of the presence of watchers. Jasmine, Pop thought, seemed so interested in what was going on that after being led away some paces she turned, pricked up her ears, and looked around, rather as if she wanted to come back and see it all again.

After all this Pop selected Jasmine for Miss Pilchester to ride. The animal stood dangerously still at the starting point, in stubborn suspense, while Pop gave earnest ante-post advice to Miss Pilchester, who sat astride.

"Hang on with your knees. Don't let go. Hang on tight. Like grim death."

Miss Pilchester, already looking like grim death, gave a hasty glance around at the other competitors, dismayed to find them all young, effervescent girls of sixteen or seventeen. She herself felt neither young nor effervescent and the donkey was horribly hairy underneath her calves.

"Don't mind them, Edith. Don't look at them. Look straight ahead—straight as you can go. Hang on like grim death."

Miss Pilchester became vaguely aware of carrots, in orange arcs, being waved in all directions. A few animals trotted indifferently up the track, between shrieking, cheering rows of spectators. One trotted at an incautious speed for thirty yards or so and then, as if inexplicably bored about something, turned and came back. Another sidled to the side of the track and leaned against a post, allowing itself to be stroked by various children, including Victoria and the twins. Two girls fell off, screaming, and there were gay momentary glimpses of black and apricot lingerie.

Jasmine stood fast. "Git up, old gal!" Pop said, and started to push her. "Git up there, Jasmine!" Pop put his weight against her rump and heaved. Nothing happened, and it seemed as if Jasmine had sunk her feet into the ground.

It was all absolutely ghastly, Miss Pilchester was just thinking when over the loudspeaker a voice started up an announcement about Anne Fitzgerald, aged three, who had lost her mother. Would Mrs. Fitzgerald please—

The loudspeaker gave a few snappy barks. Jasmine cocked her ears and broke through with frenzy the final waving arcs of carrots, leaving Pop on the ground and everybody scattered.

Miss Pilchester, as Pop had so earnestly and correctly advised, hung on firmly and desperately with her knees, just like grim death, and in thirty seconds Jasmine was back at the river, once more staring into the world of grasses, water lilies, irises, and a soldier's summer love.

Half dismounting, half falling, a disheveled and demoralized Miss Pilchester stood staring too. It was all absolutely and utterly ghastly and it only made things worse when the soldier, disturbed in the middle of his technique, looked up calmly and said, "Why don't you go away, Ma? Both of you. You *and* your sister."

8

Pop, uncertain as to quite who had been invited to the party and who had not, spent most of the rest of the afternoon hailing odd acquaintances, generously clapping them on the back, and saying, "See you at eight o'clock. See you at the party." The result was that by half past eight the billiard room was a clamorous, fighting mass of fifty or sixty people, one half of whom had never received a formal invitation.

"I never thought we asked this lot," Ma said. "Hardly enough stuff to go around——"

"Let 'em all come!" Pop said.

The billiard room was the perfick place, he thought, for having the party. The billiard table, covered over by trestle table boards and then with a big white cloth, was just the thing for the eats, the champagne, and the glasses. One of the doors led back into the house, in case people wanted to pop upstairs, and the other into the garden, so that those who felt inclined could dodge out and take the air.

Through the thickest fog of smoke Pop had ever seen outside a smoking concert, he and Ma, helped by Mariette, Mr. Charlton, and Montgomery, served food, poured out champagne, and handed glasses around. Every now and then people collided with each other in the crowded fog and a glass went smashing to the floor. Nobody seemed to care about this and Ma was glad the glasses had been hired from caterers. That was another brilliant idea of Mr. Charlton's.

Now and then someone, almost always someone he hardly knew, came up to Pop, squeezed his elbow, and said, "Damn good party, Larkin, old boy. Going well," so that Pop felt very pleased. Ma too moved everywhere with genial expansiveness. In the crowd she seemed larger than ever, so that whenever she moved her huge body from one spot to another a large open vacuum was formed.

In one of these spaces, alongside a wall, Pop found the two Misses Barnwell, Effie and Edna, who, to his infinite pain and surprise, had no crumb or glass between them. The Misses Barnwell, who were thinking of applying for National Assistance because times were so bad, were two genteel freckled little ladies, daughters of an Indian civil servant, who had been born in Delhi. Among other things they kept bees and their little yellow faces, crowded with freckles, looked as if they were regularly and thoroughly stung all over.

"Nothing to eat? Nothing to drink?" Pop could hardly believe it; he was shocked.

"We were just contemplating."

"Contemplate my foot," Pop said. "I'll get you a glass o' champagne."

"No, no," they said. "Nothing at all like that."

"Terrible," Pop said. "Nobody looking after you. I'll get you a sandwich."

Coming back a moment or two later with a plate of Ma's delicious buttery ham sandwiches, he returned to the painful subject of the Misses Barnwell and their having nothing to drink at all.

"Glass o' beer? Drop o' cider? Glass o' port?"

"No, no. No thank you. We are quite happy."

"Have a Ma Chérie."

The air seemed to light up with infinite twinkling freckles.

"What is a Ma Chérie?"

Ma Chérie was hardly, Pop thought, a drink at all. It was simply sherry, soda, and a dash of something or other, he could never remember quite what. It was nothing like a Red Bull or Rolls-Royce or Chauffeur, the good ones.

"Soda with flavoring," he said.

"That sounds quite nice. Perhaps we might have two of—"

Pop was away, pushing through the foggy crowd to the living room, where he presently mixed two Ma Chéries, double strength, adding an extra dash of brandy to hold the feeble things together.

"There you are. Knock that back."

The Misses Barnwell, who hardly ever had much lunch on Saturdays, took their glasses, chewing rapidly, and thanked him. The air danced with freckles. He was, they said, infinitely kind.

"I'll keep 'em topped up," Pop said.

A moment later a firm gentle hand fixed itself to his elbow and drew him away.

"Mr. Larkin, isn't it?"

A tallish lady in a small gray tweed hat with a peacock feather in it smiled at him over a piece of cheese toast and a glass of champagne.

"Lady Bluff-Gore. You remember?"

Pop remembered; they had met occasionally at village Christmas socials.

"Ah, yes," Pop said. "Lady Rose."

"Afraid we don't run across each other very often."

She smiled again; her ivory teeth were remarkably long and large.

"I hear you made an interesting suggestion to my husband this afternoon."

"Oh! About the house? That's right. Time it was pulled down."

"So I heard."

All afternoon she had been thinking what an interesting suggestion it was to pull the house down. She had so long wanted to pull it down herself.

"Who wants these old places?" Pop said.

Who indeed? she thought. She had so often longed to pull hers down, and all the miles of silly greenhouses, unused stables, and drafty barns. Perhaps if it were pulled down, she thought, they might have a little money in the bank instead of living on overdrafts. Perhaps Rosemary would come back. Perhaps they could really live in comfort for a change.

"Would it be too much to ask what you feel it's worth?"

"Could take a squint at it tomorrow," Pop said, "and let you know."

Nothing like striking the iron while it was hot, Pop thought. That's how he liked to do things. In a couple of hours he could get a rough idea what bricks, tiles, doors, flooring, and hard core he would get out of it. In two shakes he could be on the blower to Freddy Fox and do a deal with Freddy.

"Yes, I'll take a squint at it—"

"Do you suppose—could we talk elsewhere?" she said. Her voice was quiet. "It's a little public here."

Elsewhere, at Pop's suggestion, was under the walnut tree. The evening was overcast and humid, with a feeling of coming rain. Cuckoos were still calling across the fields in their late bubbling voices and a few people were wandering among Ma's flower beds, taking the air.

"You see it wouldn't be at all an easy business to persuade my husband."

"No?"

"Not at all an easy man."

Pop didn't doubt it at all.

"All the same I think I might persuade him."

If he could persuade Miss Pilchester to ride the donkey, Pop thought, it ought to be possible to persuade Bluff-Gore to do a little thing like pulling a mansion down. Nothing to it. Perhaps by much the same process too?

"It's just a thought," she said, "but supposing I did?"

"Don't get it," Pop said.

"Mightn't it be an idea to come to some little arrangement? You and I?"

Women were clever, Pop thought. That showed you how clever women were. All the same under their skins. He snagged on now. Lady Five Percent he would call her now.

"I get you," Pop said.

"Good. Shall I let you know when we might have another little talk?"

Back in the smoky, clamorous fog he discovered the Misses Barnwell gazing at empty glasses. How had they liked the Ma Chéries? Quite delicious, they thought; and he went away to get them more.

In the comparative quiet of the sitting room, where it was getting dusk, he got the impression that the entire billiard room would, at any moment, blow up behind him. The place was a whirring dynamo, rapidly running hot.

"And what about me?"

It was Miss Pilchester, furtive against the Spanish galleon. Another one come to collect her interest, Pop supposed.

"Having a nice time?"

"It'll be nicer when you've kept your promise."

Might as well get it over, Pop thought.

"Lovely party. Such luck with the weather. Best gymkhana we've ever had."

Pop put down the two Ma Chéries and braced himself. Miss Pilchester simply didn't know how to hold herself for the act of kissing and Pop seized her like a sheaf of corn. There was a momentary bony stir of corsets and Miss Pilchester gave a short palpitating sigh. She had determined, this time, to give everything she'd got.

For all the velvet artistry he put into it Pop could make little impression on lips so well fortified with teeth that he felt they might at any moment crack like walnuts underneath the strain.

"Thanks. That was just what the doctor ordered. Time for one more?"

"Last one," Pop said. "Must get back to the party."

With thrilling silence Miss Pilchester gave everything she'd got for the second time. It was almost too much for Pop, who throughout the kiss was wondering if, after all, he might indulge in a firework or two. Finally Miss Pilchester broke away, gazing wildly up at him.

"And in case I don't get another chance of seeing you alone again, thanks for everything. Marvelous day. All your doing. Simply wouldn't have been anything without you. Best gymkhana we've ever had. And this party. Made me very happy."

The length of the speech suddenly seemed to take away the rest of her capacity for calm. She gave something like a sob, patted Pop's cheek, and rushed hurriedly away and upstairs, brushing past two women already on their way up. Once more she had forgotten to say how absolutely ghastly everything was.

"You simply must see the polly," one woman was saying. "Purple and yellow tiles with big blue hollyhocks coming out the top. And pink nymphs on the bath mirror."

"Oh God!" Miss Pilchester said.

Taking the two Ma Chéries back to the Misses Barnwell, Pop found them laughing merrily, chewing at their seventh ham sandwich.

"Going positively to drag you away if you'll let me."

The longest, slimmest, coolest hand Pop had ever touched suddenly came and took him sinuously away from the munching Misses Barnwell, now eagerly sipping their second Ma Chéries.

"They tell me you practically organized this whole bun fight single-handed."

A tall aristocratically fair girl, so fair that her hair was almost barley-white, with a figure like a reed and enormous pellucid olive eyes, had Pop so transfixed that, for a moment, he was almost unnerved. He had never seen her, or anyone like her, before.

"The thing positively went like a bomb."

The cool, long hand still held his own. The large pale eyes, languidly swimming, washed over him an endless stream of softer and softer glances.

"And this party. What a slam."

Her dress was pure clear primrose, with a long V neck. She wore long transparent earrings that swung about her long neck like dewy pendulums.

"Going to have a party of my own next week. Say you'll come."

Pop, who so far had not spoken a word, murmured something about he'd love to, trying at the same time to decide where and when he'd seen this unheralded vision before, deciding finally that he never had.

"Gorgeous party. Do you dance at all?"

"Used to fling 'em up a bit at one time."

"Scream."

She laughed on clear bell-like notes.

"My dear. Absolute scream."

Bewitched, Pop again had nothing to say. A vacuum left by Ma, three or four feet away from him, made him feel quite naked before it filled up again.

"That donkey ride, they tell me, was your idea. Blistering success."

Pop, with a certain touch of pride, admitted it.

"The seven foolish virgins. Scream. Couldn't stop laughing. Practically needed changing—"

Again she laughed on pure bell-like notes, the dewy earrings dancing.

"Just what it needed. They can be absolute stinkers, gymkhanas, don't you think? Everybody jog trotting around. Fond mothers biting lips because little Waffles doesn't win the trotting on Pretty Boy. Oh, absolute stinkers."

She held him captured with moist splendid eyes.

"But you thought of the virgins. That was the stroke. Absolute genius. Absolute scream, the virgins."

She suddenly gave Pop what he thought was a fleeting sporting wink.

"So few, after all, aren't there?"

To Pop it now began to seem that he might have met, under the sheer primrose sheath, the dancing earrings, the aristocratic voice, and the shining languid eyes, a character something after his own heart and kind.

"But seriously, dear man, what I came to say was this. My name's Angela Snow. Elmhurst Valley. We've got one of these pony trots coming off in August—what say you come over and bring the donkey outfit and make that one go with a bang?"

The word "bang" made Pop remember something. It was, he thought, the one thing needed to make the day a perfick one.

"Like fireworks?"

"Love 'em. Adore 'em."

"Stay here," Pop said, "while I fetch you a drop more champagne." He started to struggle through the smoky screen hemming him in on all sides and then remembered something and came back to her. "Or a cocktail? Rather have a cocktail?"

"Adore one. Just what I need."

"This way."

He started to lead the way out to the sitting room, but halfway he was stopped by Mr. Charlton and Mariette, who said, "Pop, Charley has something he'd like to say to you."

"Not now," Pop said. "Busy now."

"It's terribly important. It's something he's *got* to ask you."

Mr. Charlton looked unexpectedly strained and tense. Must have found out about the baby, Pop supposed. Pity.

"Be back in five minutes," he said, and followed the tall, reedy, primrose figure into the sitting room.

There, over his Spanish galleon, he asked the dewy, languid girl which she would rather have—a Rolls-Royce, Red Bull, or Chauffeur. Red Bull was the blinder, he said.

"Red Bull then, dear," she said. "What names they give them nowadays."

Pop mixed two double Red Bulls and in the falling twilight the elegant Angela Snow knocked hers back with the coolest speed, like a man.

"One more of these, dear boy, and I'm ready."

Pop was ready too. Ten minutes later the first firework went off like a bomb under Ma, who showed hardly any sign of disturbance at all. The two ladies who had been to investigate Ma's impossible bathroom met a Roman candle on the stairs. The tall reedy girl put two jumping crackers under the brigadier's sister and another under Sir George Bluff-Gore. Ma started laughing like shaking jelly and Pop put a Mighty Atom under the billiard table where it set the glasses ringing like a xylophone. The two Misses Barnwell started giggling uncontrollably and said it reminded them of a pujah in Delhi and Miss Pilchester was heard saying she knew this would happen and that it was absolutely ghastly and she'd hide under the stairs. People started running from the smoky house into the garden, where the tall, languid girl had a big fizzing Catherine wheel already going on the walnut tree and was now getting ready to put a Roman candle as near as she could without killing him under a man named Jack Farley, who was a complete slob and had tried to pinch her three times in the tea tent early in the afternoon. A few rockets started shooting up from empty champagne bottles into a sky now summery dark, cuckooless, and completely canopied with cloud. Pop did what he had so long wanted to do and put a beauty under Miss Pilchester, who started shrieking she was burned. Upstairs Primrose, Victoria, and the twins hung out of the bedroom windows, shouting, laughing, and eating the day's last ice cream, potato crisps, and apple tart. In the middle of it all Mariette and Mr. Charlton tried once again, with little success, to speak with Pop, who was running about the flower beds waving a Golden Rain, calling like a Red Indian, happy as a boy.

When finally Pop had thrown the Golden Rain over a damson tree Mr. Charlton said, "Pop, I want to speak to you. Ma says I can marry Mariette if you'll let her—"

"Perfick," Pop said. "Let her? Course I'll let her."

The tall, willowy girl was everywhere, selecting victims. The sky was comet bright with sprays of silver stars, rockets, and Golden Rain. A Roman candle went off with shattering concussion behind the walnut tree and Mr. Charlton begged of Pop, "Pop, Ma says if you agree will you announce it? She says now's the perfect time."

"Perfick it is an' all," Pop said. "Never thought of that."

A quarter of an hour later Pop was standing on a chair outside the billiard room, announcing to the gathered guests, in the smoky garden, with a touch of imperial pride in his voice, together with a certain sadness, that Mr. Charlton was going to marry his daughter Mariette and had everybody got their glasses filled?

"Give you the toast!" he called into the smoky summer air. "Charley and Mariette."

As he lifted his glass a stunning explosion split the air, knocking him backward.

"One for his nob!" Mr. Charlton shouted.

"What Paddy shot at!" Ma screamed, and started choking in helpless laughter.

It was the last devastating Roman candle of the cool, tall, primrose girl.

"Quite perfect," she said.

9

When it was all over, and even television had closed down, Ma and
Pop sat alone in the kitchen. Ma now and then shaking all over as she
remembered the donkeys, Miss Pilchester, and the way Pop had been
blown flat on his back by the Roman candle.

"Nothing at all to eat?" Pop inquired.

"Think there's another apple tart," Ma said, and got up to get it from
the fridge. The apple tart was large and puffy, with white sugar sprinkled on its lid of crust. With it Ma brought two plates, a knife, and,
out of sheer habit, the bottle of catsup. "By the way, who was that girl
in the yellow dress? She was a spark."

"Never seen her in me life. Somebody said her father was a judge."

"Oh?" Ma said. "Well, I suppose there's a throwback in every
family."

Pop cut two six-inch slices of pie. He gave one to Ma, and then
started to eat the other in his fingers, at the same time ignoring, much
to Ma's surprise, the bottle of catsup.

"Don't you want no catsup?"

"Gone off catsup a bit," Pop said.

"Oh?" Ma said. "How's that?"

"Makes everything taste the same."

Ma, who thought this was odd, went on to say what about port?

"Don't say you've gone off port as well."

"No," Pop said. "Just got some more in. Started to order it in
two-gallon jars now."

He got up, found the jar of port under the stairs, and poured out two
nice big glasses, inquiring at the same time where Mr. Charlton and
Mariette were.

"Having a quiet few minutes in the sitting room."

Pop said it was very nice about Mr. Charlton and Mariette and had
Mr. Charlton found out about the baby.

"She's not going to have a baby now," Ma said. "False alarm."

"Jolly good," Pop said. "Perfick."

Ma sat meditatively fingering her turquoise rings, which seemed to be getting tighter every day, while Pop listened to the sound of the first gentle summery feathers of rain on earth and leaves as it came through the open kitchen door.

"I am though," Ma said.

Pop looked mildly, though not disagreeably, surprised.

"How did that happen then?"

"*How?* What do you mean, *how?*"

Pop said he meant when did it all date back to.

"That night in the bluebell wood," Ma said. "Just before Mr. Charlton came. You said you thought there was a wild duck's nest up there and we went to have a look."

"That night?" Pop said. "I never even thought—"

"You don't know your own strength," Ma said. "Have some more apple tart. Pass the catsup."

Pop cut himself another biggish slice of apple tart. Ma, he noticed, hadn't quite finished hers. She was always a slow eater. She was still fingering her turquoise rings, as if for some reason she was engaged in thinking, though Pop couldn't imagine what about, unless it was the baby.

The turquoise rings, however, put a thought into his own mind, and he gave a short soft laugh or two, no louder than the summery feathers of rain.

"If this lark goes on much longer," he said, "you and me'll have to get married as well."

Ma said she thought it wouldn't be a bad idea perhaps.

"I've got to have my rings cut off again anyway," she said. "We might as well do it then."

For some moments Pop sat in complete silence, still listening to the rain and wondering about the baby and if Ma wanted a boy and what names they would pick for it when it came.

Ma sat wondering too, mostly about what it would be like to be married. She couldn't imagine at all.

Eventually Pop spoke. "Thought up any names for it?" he said.

"It?" Ma said. "I've got a funny feeling it might be twins."

"Marvelous. Perfick," Pop said.

Ma, who had in fact thought a very great deal about names, went on to say that if it did turn out to be just a boy, which she hoped it wouldn't, or just a girl, what about Orlando and Rosalind—out of that play they saw on television the other night? A very nice play.

Pop said he thought they were jolly good names, just the sort of names he liked. And what if it was twins?

"Well," Ma said, "I've been thinking. If it's girls I thought of Lucinda and Clorinda. I think they're very nice. Or if it's boys I wouldn't say no to Nelson and Rodney. They were admirals."

"Not so bad," Pop said. "I like Lucinda."

The rain was falling a little faster now, though still softly, the dampness bringing out of the air the last lingering smell of firework smoke. At one time the house had seemed full of the stench of gunpowder.

"Couldn't very well make it a double wedding, I suppose, could we?" Ma said.

"Might ask Mr. Charlton."

"Why Mr. Charlton?"

"He knows about things. Look what he knew about the party."

Pop had just finished his second slice of apple pie and was vaguely wondering about a third—there wasn't so much of it left and it was a pity to let it go begging—when Mr. Charlton and Mariette came in from the sitting room. He said how glad he was to see them and how he could congratulate them now it was quieter. He said he and Ma weren't half glad about things and that it didn't seem five minutes since Mr. Charlton had arrived.

"How about a glass of port, you two?"

While he was pouring out two more nice big glasses of port he couldn't help thinking how pretty Mariette looked in her black semi-fitting cocktail dress with its white cuffs, collar, and belt. He hoped all the girls would take after Ma. He thought too how nice it was about Mariette and the baby—just as well to start with a clean sheet about these things.

"Well, cheers," he said. "God bless," and with a sudden affectionate impulse got up and kissed Mariette. "Couldn't be more perfick."

Ma, who said she wasn't going to be left out, then got up and kissed both Mariette and Mr. Charlton; and then Mr. Charlton and Pop shook hands.

"Got a bit of news of our own now," Pop said. "Shall we tell them, Ma?"

"You tell them."

"Well," Pop said, "we thought we'd get married too. Ma's going to have another baby."

Mr. Charlton, who only a month before would have been more than startled by this announcement, didn't turn a hair. Nor did Mariette seem unduly perturbed. The only thing that suddenly occurred to Mr. Charlton was that this was a time when it was essential, if ever, to use his loaf.

"Now wait a minute," he said, "this wants thinking about."

"There you are, Ma," Pop said. "I told you."

"Why does it want thinking about?" Ma said.

Mr. Charlton took a thoughtful sip of port.

"I was thinking of the tax situation," he said. "You see, it actually doesn't pay to get married. It actually pays to live in—"

He was about to say "sin" but abruptly checked himself, too late to prevent Ma, however, from being a little upset.

"Don't use that word," she said severely. "I know what you were going to say."

Mr. Charlton apologized and said what he really meant was that if he were them he'd keep the status quo. This was the first time Pop had ever heard such astonishing un-English words used under his roof, but it meant more marks for Mr. Charlton. Ma, forgetting that she had been very nearly outraged a moment before, could only look on in silent, fervent admiration.

"Quite happy as we are, I suppose, eh, Ma?" Pop said. "Nothing to worry about?"

Not that she could think of, Ma said.

"All right. Let's go on in the old sweet way."

Mr. Charlton agreed.

"By keeping to the old way," Mr. Charlton said, "you'll be better off when the time comes."

"When what time comes?" Pop said. "For what?"

"To pay your tax," Mr. Charlton said. "It's bound to catch up some day."

"That's what you think!" Pop said.

"I'm afraid they'll take notice of the Rolls. They're bound to say—"

"That old thing?" Pop said. "Never. Took it for a debt!"

Suddenly Pop started laughing as heartily as Ma had when the girl in the yellow dress had blown him off the chair with the Roman candle.

Ma laughed piercingly too and said, "Oh, that reminds me. Are you going back to that office?"

"That's right, Charley," Pop said. "Are you ever going back to that lark?"

Mr. Charlton, thoughtful again, said he supposed if he didn't go back he'd lose his pension.

The word "pension" made Pop laugh even more than the idea of the tax lark. "You mean sit on your backside for forty years and then collect four pounds a week that's worth only two and 'll only buy half as much anyway?" He urged Mr. Charlton to use his loaf. Mr. Charlton could not help thinking that it was high time he did. "I tell you what," Pop said. "I'll be doing a nice little demolition job very soon. Some very good stuff. Big mansion. What say we pick the best out and build you and Mariette a bungalow in the medder, near the bluebell wood?"

"Oh, wonderful, wonderful, Pop!" Mariette said, and, with eyes impulsively dancing, came to kiss his face and lips and hair, so that Mr. Charlton knew that there was, really, nothing more to say.

"Well, that's it then," Pop said. "Perfick. Now who says one more glass o' port? And then we go to bed."

He was intensely looking forward to going to bed. It would top it all up to have a cigar and watch Ma get into the transparent nylon nightgown.

"Yes, time to get a little beauty sleep," Ma said.

Pop poured four more nice big glasses of port, saying at the same time how glad he was about the rain. They could do with the rain. It was just what the cherries, the plums, and the apples wanted now.

"Shall you come cherry picking too?" Mariette said to Mr. Charlton, but in answer he could only look at her olive skin, the dark shining eyes, the kittenish hair, and the firm young breasts with silent fascination.

Some moments later Pop took his glass of port to the kitchen door, staring out at the summer darkness and the rain. Mr. Charlton felt an impulse to join him and stood there staring too, thinking of how spring had passed, how quickly the buds of May had gone, and how everything now had blossomed into full, high summer.

"Listen," Pop said. "Perfick."

Everybody listened, and in the dark air there was the sound of nightingales.

A BREATH OF
FRENCH AIR

1

Little Oscar, Ma Larkin's seventh, to whom she hoped in due course to give a real proper ribbon of names, probably calling him after some famous explorer, admiral, or Roman emperor, or even the whole lot, lay in his lavish silvery pram in the kitchen, looking remarkably like a very soft, very large apple dumpling that has been slightly overboiled.

Continual small bubbles of spittle oozed softly like pink juice from his lips and Pop, coming in to breakfast after giving morning swill to the pigs, paused affectionately to wipe them off with a feeder worked all over in royal blue daisies and a bright scarlet picture of Miss Muffet, the big spider, and the curds and whey. Ma, who looked if anything six inches wider since having the baby than she had even while carrying it, had worked the feeder herself. She hadn't all that much time to spare with seven on her hands but she was surprisingly clever with her plump olive fingers that were almost hidden in pearl and turquoise rings.

"Soon be as fat as a Christmas gander," Pop said, at the same time pausing to give his son-in-law, Mr. Charlton, his customary open-handed clout of greeting in the middle of the back. Mr. Charlton, who sat patiently looking through his spectacles at the *Times* while waiting for his breakfast, took the salutation without flinching. Nearly a year in the Larkin household had hardened him a lot.

Ma, in a bright purple blouse and pink apron and with her dark rich hair still in curling pins, had three pounds of sausages in one frying pan, several rounds of fried bread and seven or eight rashers of bacon in another, and a basket of fresh pink field mushrooms waiting for a saucepan. Just before Pop bent to kiss her full on her handsome mouth and wish her good morning, she dropped half the mushrooms into the saucepan, where they at once started hissing at an intruding lump of butter as big as a tennis ball, cooking fragrantly.

"Mariette not down?" Pop said. "Kids off to their riding lessons? Going to be a beautiful day. Perfick. Mushrooms smell good."

Outside it was raining in drilling summer torrents. Nothing could be seen of the far side of the junkyard, the woods, and the surrounding meadows in the cloudy, steamy air. Nearer to the house the only visible moving things were a few hens shaking damp brown feathers under a straw hovel, a line of six or seven Chinese geese wandering dopily in and out of a wet jungle of rusty iron and nettles, and a small flock of sparrows bathing with sprinkling wings in muddy pools of water.

This was July, Ma thought, and it was enough to give you the willies. It was a real thick'un, or what she sometimes called bad courting weather. Not that she had any intention of going courting, but it reminded her of times when she had. Wet summer days and evenings frustrated you that bad you felt all bottled up. You couldn't let yourself go at all. The fact that she had let herself go with splendidly fruitful effect over the years didn't occur to her at all. It was just that she hated rain in July.

Pop, irrepressibly optimistic that the day was going to be a beautiful one, inquired again about his eldest daughter Mariette. She was nearly always up with the lark, out riding or something, and he missed her when she didn't come down. It wasn't like her.

"Not feeling all that good," Ma said. "Bit peaky."

Pop pricked up his ears sharply. Not good? He wondered what it could be? Morning sickness perhaps. He hoped so.

"Oh?" he said. "Thought she looked a little bit below par yesterday. Anythink I ought to know about?"

Pop gave a sharp, inquiring look at Ma and then a still sharper, even more searching look at Mr. Charlton. But neither Ma nor Charley seemed to think it was anything he ought to know about and Ma went on moodily prodding at sizzling mushrooms and Mr. Charlton with the *Times*.

"She needs a change," Ma said. "Ought to have a holiday. Weather's getting her down."

"Soon clear up," Pop said. "You'll see. Be perfick by midday. Beautiful."

"Don't you believe it," Ma said. "It's one of them Julys. I've seen 'em before. They never get right. By the time you get into August it's like they have in India. What are they called, Charley, them things?"

"Monsoons," Mr. Charlton said.

"That's it." Ma, with a gesture of unaccustomed impatience, threw four more links of sausage into the frying pan. "I don't know as I shan't be screeching for a holiday myself if this lot goes on."

The sausages hit the frying pan with the sound of red-hot irons plunging into freezing water and immediately little Oscar began to cry.

Pop rushed at once to pick him up but Ma said breakfast was ready and began to serve the first of the bacon, the sausages, the fried bread, and the mushrooms to Mr. Charlton, who was still deep in the *Times*.

"I know what he wants," Pop said. "He wants his morning Guinness."

"Well, he'll have to wait for his Guinness, that's all," Ma said. "Like other folks do."

Oscar cried out plaintively again and Pop asked with some concern if he shouldn't give him a piece of fried bread? Ma said, "Not on your nelly," in a voice very near to severity. It wouldn't hurt him to cry for a bit and in any case he'd have to learn to be patient. You had to learn to be patient in this world. Anyway, sometimes.

"He wants his drop o' Guinness," Pop said. "I know."

Mr. Charlton, who had heard nothing of this conversation, folded the *Times* into quarter-page size, then suddenly pointed to a picture in it and said that that was a most extraordinary thing.

"What is?" Pop said. "Wanting a drop o' Ma's Guinness?"

Pop laughed uproariously, as if in fact it was.

"How many sausages, Pop?" Ma said. "Four? Shall I do you a couple of eggs before I sit down?"

Pop said five sausages and he would manage with two eggs.

"What's extraordinary?" Ma said.

"This picture," Mr. Charlton said. "It's a picture of a little place called St. Pierre le Port. I used to go and spend every summer holiday there when I was a boy. My aunt and uncle used to take me."

"Let's have a look," Ma said.

"This is the actual view I used to see from my bedroom window. The actual view—here—along the quay."

"Seaside?"

"On the Atlantic. The sea goes out for miles at low tide and you can paddle on lovely warm sand and there's a funny little train comes from somewhere inland and goes trundling from place to place along the coast." Mr. Charlton had forgotten sausages, bacon, fried bread, and mushrooms, and even the cries of Oscar in a delicious ecstasy of recollection. "Oh, I hope they haven't done away with that train. I loved that little train. That train *is* France for me."

Pop, openmouthed, stopped biting sausage and looked completely startled at the word "France," as if it were something he had never heard of before.

"France? You went abroad?" he said. "For your holidays? Didn't your Pop and Ma want you?"

"I lost them both when I was six," Mr. Charlton said. "I think I told you."

At this moment Oscar started to cry again and Ma said she would switch on the radio to soothe him down. She turned the switch and "The Blue Danube" bellowed out at full blast.

"Uncle Arthur and Aunt Edna adored France," Mr. Charlton said. "I think they loved it even more than England. They went so often in the end you'd have taken them *for* French. Especially Uncle Arthur."

In a low voice Pop asked Mr. Charlton to pass him the mustard. He could think of nothing else to say.

"It brings it all back," Mr. Charlton said, "that picture in the *Times*."

Pop, still submerged in disbelief at the astonishing course of the conversation, now became aware of another remarkable thing. Ma was not eating breakfast.

"Ma, you're not having anythink," he said. "What's up?"

Ma got up from the breakfast table. Oscar was crying more loudly than ever, undrowned by "The Blue Danube."

"Not very peckish," Ma said. "I think I'll give Oscar his first. Perhaps I'll feel better after that."

"Hope so. Terrible. What's up with everybody? Everybody looks pale round the gills."

Without speaking Ma, who did indeed feel pale round the gills, went over to the pram and picked up little Oscar, who belched sharply and stopped crying immediately. Then she kissed him softly in the nape of his neck and sat down again at the table, at the same time undoing her blouse.

All this time Pop had been silently dipping sausage into mustard, staring at his plate, unable to think of a word to say, but now he looked up in time to see Ma extract from her blouse a large expanse of olive bosom twice as large as a full-ripe melon. Into this mass of tender flesh Oscar buried his face and settled down.

"Was it healthy?" Pop said.

"France you mean?" Mr. Charlton said. "Oh, very. The air's wonderful there in Brittany. All hot and sultry. It was awfully cheap too. And marvelous food. Wonderful food."

"Did you say hot?" Ma said.

"Some summers we'd never see a drop of rain. And the sea—I

always remember how blue the sea was. Vivid. Just the color you see on travel posters."

"I should like to feel it hot again," Ma said. "Like last year. I haven't felt the sun hot on my chest since that day you and Mariette were married in September."

"Always hot in Britanny," Mr. Charlton said. "That's my recollection. You can bet on that."

Oscar pulled at his mother's breast with steadfast sucks of contentment and an occasional rich, startling plop! like that of cork coming out of a bottle. In silence Pop dipped pieces of sausage into mustard and found himself brooding over a remembrance of the day Mariette and Charley had been married.

A very lovely day that had been, as Ma had said: all light and hot sunshine, with a big marquee in the garden and plenty of iced port, cold salmon, and champagne. He would remember forever Mariette's striking and unconventional dress of yellow silk, so suited to her dark hair, and her bouquet of stephanotis and cherry-red nerines that appeared to have gold dust sprinkled all over their petals. Everybody was there that day and Mariette's sisters, Zinnia, Petunia, Victoria, and Primrose, were bridesmaids, each in deep cream, with headdresses of small golden roses and posies of lily of the valley. Ma, like Miss Pilchester and several of their friends, wept openly at the sight of these touching things and even Pop had a tear in his eye.

It was less than a week after Mariette and Charley were back from honeymoon when Pop began to inquire of Ma if anything was happening yet?

Ma said she should think not—everybody wasn't like him.

"You've only got to start eyeing me across a forty-acre field," she said, "and I start wondering whether I'm going to have twins or triplets."

You'd got to give them a chance, she went on, and Pop could only reply that he thought a fortnight was plenty of chance. He murmured something about the question of Charley's technique, of which in view of his great shyness before marriage Ma had entertained considerable doubts, but Ma replied blandly that she thought that if there was anything Charley didn't know by this time Mariette would soon teach him. Pop said he should hope so.

Ever since that time there hadn't been a day when Pop had been increasingly fired with the hope that Ma would soon have some interesting news to tell him. But nothing ever happened and now at last Pop had begun to have considerable doubts about Charley's desire, or even ability, to make him a grandfather. He thought the whole situation was getting everybody down. Ma seemed mopey and was always complaining of the summer rain. Mariette looked decidedly pale too and even seemed, he thought, a shade thinner and lacked that plumlike bloom that even at seventeen had given her such a dark and luscious maturity.

"Got your watch on you, Charley?" Ma said. "How long's he had on this side?"

Mr. Charlton looked briefly up from reading the *Times* to glance at his wristwatch. With unconcern he gave another glance at Oscar, nestling into Ma's bosom like a piglet into the side of a vast pink sow, and said he thought it was about ten minutes.

Deftly Ma released Oscar from her bosom. There was another rich, milky plop! as Oscar let go the cork of her nipple and then a sudden complaining wail of hunger as she slipped her breast back into her blouse.

"Let me get the door open for goodness sake, child," Ma said.

"Never known anybody like him for his Guinness," Pop said.

"Oh," Ma said, "haven't you?"

A moment later Oscar was buried again in rosy flesh, all contentment, while Ma held him close to her with one hand, trying at the same time to pour herself a cup of tea with the other.

Mr. Charlton was quick to see her difficulties and got up at once to pour it for her himself. That was one of the things Ma liked about Charley: these little touches of nice manners. They did you so much good.

After Charley had poured the tea she took two or three sips slowly, as if in contentment or deep thought or both, and then made a sudden pronouncement that set Pop choking.

"I should like to go to France," she said.

"God Almighty," Pop said. "What for?"

Hot mustard stabbed at the back of his throat and set him coughing.

"For a holiday of course," Ma said. "I think it would do us all good to get some sun."

Pop could think of nothing to say. He sat in meditative, flabbergasted silence while Mr. Charlton let out a positive crow of delight and approval at what Ma had said.

"Heavens, that would be marvelous," he said. "That would be great. That little train again, that beach, that warm sea. Those little sweet grapes and the peaches. That food—"

He was suddenly overcome with an emotional desire to strike Pop in the back and actually did so. It was a thing he had never felt urged to do before, but its effect on Pop was only to stun him into a deeper more confused silence than ever.

" 'Come unto these yellow sands and then take hands,' " Charley started quoting, at the same time getting up from the breakfast table. "I've simply got to tell Mariette."

Charley was off, Pop thought. That feller Keats again.

"We haven't gone yet," Ma said.

"I'll call her anyway."

While Mr. Charlton went upstairs to call Mariette, whistling all the way up, and Ma sipped at her tea and little Oscar at his mother, Pop sat thinking. The first stunning surprise of Ma's pronouncement had passed. It now began to occur to him that the situation was not at all unlike that in which Charley, soon after his marriage, had suggested that Pop should give up the *Daily Mirror* as his daily newspaper and start instead to take the *Times*.

At the time that too had seemed a surprising, unthinkable, revolutionary thing to do. Then Pop remembered that quite a number of other people in the village, including Miss Pilchester, the brigadier, and Sir George Bluff-Gore, all took the *Times* too and if they could do so why not he? Miss Pilchester was as poor as a church mouse; the brigadier hadn't had a new suit for twenty years and generally wore socks that didn't match; and Sir George Bluff-Gore was so hamstrung with taxes that he couldn't afford to keep the ancestral Gore Court going and had had to sell it to Pop himself for demolition and then go and live in a stable. They were the aristocracy, of course, these people, they were the toffs; but if they could afford the *Times* so could he.

Now he didn't regret taking the *Times* at all. It gave you something, the *Times* did, though he wasn't quite sure what. Ma liked it too, though she still took the *Mirror* herself, otherwise she would never know what was in her stars. Nevertheless she got a big thrill out of the Saturday *Times* advertisements for rich and exotic foods and was always sending away for lists and catalogues. Such things didn't inspire Pop and he still thought there was nothing so good as roast beef and Yorkshire, rice pudding, lamb and mint sauce, and plenty of roast goose and applesauce on Sundays. He supposed he might have to change some day, though he didn't see why.

Oscar had taken another five minutes of his mother when Ma pulled the cork of her nipple away from him with another gentle plop and turned him over to lie against her shoulder. The result of this was a series of sudden belches, each richer, louder, and milkier than the first.

Ma said that that was better and it must be the gin she'd had last night.

Instinctively Oscar renewed his nuzzling for the breast. Ma said she might just as well turn herself into a four-ale bar and be done with it and gave a sudden deep sigh that had in it a certain note of weariness and even despair.

Pop felt suddenly concerned at this sigh and said, "Ma, don't you really feel well? Tell me, my old duck."

In reply Ma could only ask him how he would feel if someone had played football inside him for nine months, but it was a question for which Pop could think of no sensible answer and he was both glad and relieved to hear Mariette and Charley coming downstairs.

"As well as turning yourself into a bar three or four times a day. Somehow I think I'm getting too old for this lark."

Ma, he thought, had never talked like this before. It struck him as being chronic. Too old? Damnit, she was only thirty-six.

"The trouble is this one's like you," Ma said. "Never satisfied."

A moment later Mariette came in, her dark hair still loose from sleep, wearing a green silk dressing gown and crimson slippers. In a new state of excitement she ran straight to Pop, who had a mouth full of sausage, mushroom, and mustard, and started kissing him with a warm fervor that reminded him of Ma when he had first met her at the age of fifteen.

"Oh, wonderful, wonderful, Pop. Oh, you're always so wonderful."

What had he done now? Pop started to say.

"France!" she said. "I've always wanted to go to France. When do we start? Do we all go?"

"Who said we were going to France?"

"You did, Charley did." She turned excitedly to Ma, at the same time kissing Oscar on the back of his neck. "You want to go to France, don't you, Ma?"

"That's what I just told Pop."

"There you are—everybody wants to go. Oh, for that sun"—Mariette rolled her handsome body to and fro under its dressing gown, her breasts rising in voluptuous expectation—"I can't wait for that sun. It's amazing what that sun can do for you. Oh, to feel the heat of that sun."

Pop listened with keen alertness. Perhaps it was, after all, the sun that she and Charley had been missing.

"Ah, the heat of the sun," Charley said, " 'Fear no more the heat of the sun—' "

Off again, Pop thought. Keats again. Mr. Charlton started laughing happily and Mariette again rolled her shoulders ecstatically in her dressing gown, laughing with him. Oscar made succulent noises at his mother's breast and Ma sipped with relish at her tea, so that suddenly, for some reason, Pop felt rather out in the cold about things. He couldn't get worked up at all.

"Is it right they eat frogs?" he said.

"Of course," Charley said. "And absolutely delicious they are too."

"Good God." Pop felt mildly sick.

"Just the legs," Charley said. "They're exactly like chicken."

Involuntarily Pop burst out laughing in his customary ringing fashion.

"Hear that, Ma? Frogs! Just like chicken."

"They eat snails too," Ma said, "don't they?"

"Certainly. *Escargots de Bourgogne.* Wonderful too they are."

Pop sat stunned over the breakfast table, openmouthed at the sound of a new, strange language coming from Charley's lips.

"That was French," Mariette said with both excitement and pride. "Did you know Charley speaks French?"

"French? Where'd he pick that up?"

"Playing with French children," Charley said. "Every holiday."

Ma said she was greatly relieved.

"That was the only thing that was worrying me," she said. "How we'd make ourselves understood."

"He's going to teach me," Mariette said. "Anyway, why don't we all learn?"

"Why not?" Charley said. "I could teach you all a few simple phrases."

Pop was speechless. Charley boy speaking French, Charley boy quoting Keats and Shakespeare and spending holidays abroad—there was no end to the surprises of his son-in-law.

Pensively Pop helped himself to marmalade and made a tentative suggestion that Charley boy should give him an example of one or two of the simple phrases.

"Certainly," Charley said. *"Bonjour, comment ça va, Monsieur Larkin?"*

"Eh?" Pop said.

Ma sat in silent admiration at these few but impressively fluent words, bemusedly rocking little Oscar backward and forward at her bosom. Marveling too, Pop said, his mouth full of marmalade, "And what the pipe does all that mean?"

"Good morning. How goes it? How are you?"

"I'm damned if I know," Pop said. "I'm getting a bit tangled up with this Froggy lark."

Ma started laughing, her body shaking like a vast quivering jelly, so that for a moment little Oscar lost his grip on her. With a deft movement she heaved him back into his place at the bosom and said she could never get her tongue around that lot.

"Nor me neither," Pop said.

"Oh, it's simple, it's easy," Charley said. "Just say it."

"Me?" Pop said.

"Yes. Go on. Just repeat it. *Bonjour. Comment ça va?* or *comment allez-vous?* if you like. Same thing."

"One thing at a time," Pop said, "as the girl said to the soldier. *Bonjour*—that it?"

"Splendid. *Bonjour. Comment ça va?*"

"*Bonjour. Comment ça va?*" Pop said, grinning now, his perkiness and confidence coming back. "Any good?"

"Marvelous. You'd have a jolly fine accent in no time."

Pop, feeling suddenly proud, started preening himself before Ma, languidly stroking his side linings with the back of one hand.

"Having French lessons now, Ma. Eh? What price that?"

Ma was proud too and looked at Pop in gleaming admiration.

"Oh, Pop, you'd pick it up in no time," Mariette said.

"Always quick to learn," Ma said. "Sharp as a packet o' needles. No flies on Pop."

Pop, increasingly thirsty for knowledge, preened himself again and said what about some more examples, Charley boy.

"*Au revoir,*" Charley said. "*À bientôt.*"

"What's that mean?"

"Good-bye. See you soon."

"*Au revoir. À bientôt,*" Pop said swiftly. "Easy. Like water running off a duck's back."

Charley said again how marvelous it was and how, very soon, in no time at all, Pop could acquire an accent. Mariette actually applauded, so that suddenly there was no holding Pop, who got up smartly from the breakfast table, bowed to Ma and said,

"*Bonjour, madame. Comment ça va? Au revoir! À bientôt!*"

"Jolly fine!" Charley said, and Ma started laughing so much that little Oscar lost his grip on the bosom again. Milk flowed down his pink dumpling face as Ma rocked up and down.

"Can you see us, over there, Ma?" Pop said. "Eating frogs' legs and snails and me talking Froggy?"

"Oh, I can't wait!" Mariette said, and again her body went through its voluptuous rolling under the dressing gown. "I just can't wait. I'll just lie all day in the sun in a bikini."

"That's what I'd like to take too," Ma said. "A bikini. A bit of sun would firm me up."

The prospect of Ma being firmed up in a bikini fired Pop so madly that he almost shouted at Charley, "All right, Charley boy, when do we start?"

"Well, the children will finish up in August—that's if we're all going."

"Of course we're all going," Ma said. "It'll be education for the lot of us. Like telly is."

"All right then. I suggest the third week in August."

"Perfick!" Pop said. "*À bientôt!*"

Pop, sitting down at table again, poured himself another cup of tea while Mr. Charlton marveled once more how swiftly, fluently, and excellently Pop had acquired himself an accent.

"How do we get there?" Pop said. "Swim?"

"I suggest we take the Rolls if it's all right with you."

"Good God," Pop said. "Never thought of that."

"They won't overcharge us, will they," Ma said, "if they see the Rolls?"

"I'll get the Beau Rivage to quote everything first," Charley said. "Taxes, *taxe de séjour*, service, everything. I think Mr. Dupont will be fair—that's if he's still there. But in France it's always as well to fix everything beforehand."

A great fixer, Charley. A marvelous fellow for figures, discounts, bills, and all that. In the last six months Pop had left him to deal with all paperwork, forms, returns, and what Pop called the dodgy stuff. A great help, Charley.

Pop in fact was more than pleased that Charley, after marrying Mariette, had had sense enough to throw up his job at the tax inspector's office to take up more respectable, more sensible employment. It was worse than awful to think of having anybody in the family connected with the tax lark. Wouldn't do at all. Worse than having somebody who'd been doing time.

In recognition of Charley's sensible behavior Pop had given him and Mariette five hundred laying pullets. That had set them up in the egg lark. It paid pretty well on the whole, the egg lark, if you worked it right. It was another way of getting doh-ray-me out of the government before they had a chance to get it out of you. In less than a year Charley and Mariette had made enough profit to buy themselves another five hundred pullets and were doing very well for themselves, except that Charley would insist on making proper income tax returns about it all, which was a very bad habit to get into, Pop considered, whichever way you looked at it.

As to the house he had promised to build them out of material from Sir George Bluff-Gore's mansion at Gore Court, when he pulled it down, he'd been much too busy on a variety of other larks even to get around to the house's demolition. It would have to wait a bit. Most of his time had been taken up with a big deal about army surplus, the surplus consisting of all sorts of unlikely things like tins of beetroot in vinegar, rattraps, body belts, brass collar studs, gherkins in mustard, rubber shoe heels, and bottles of caper sauce: the sorts of things that nobody else seemed to think that anybody wanted. Pop knew better. There was always somebody who wanted something somewhere. He had to admit the beetroot in vinegar and the gherkins in mustard were turning out a bit sticky though.

But there was no doubt about the change from taxes to eggs suiting Charley all right. Charley had put on a bit of weight and looked brown. He always ate hearty breakfasts and had stopped worrying over his health and whether he was going to wake up every morning with appendicitis or not. He looked in every way a fit, virile young man. All the more puzzling, Pop thought, that he didn't seem to be able to translate it all into the proper channels. He had to admit that Charley had always been a slow starter—but married nearly a year and no children, that was really a bit dodgy. He wouldn't have thought a young healthy couple like them would have found it all that hard.

"Of course," Charley said now, "there's the trouble of passports."

"Trouble?" Mariette said. "What trouble?"

With as much tact as he could muster, Mr. Charlton reminded them all of the delicate and rather difficult situation concerning Pop and Ma.

"Perhaps it would have been better if you'd got married after all," he said.

"Well, I suppose we still could," Pop said, but not with apparent enthusiasm. "But it's a bit of a palaver."

"I'm willing," Ma said blandly. "Always was."

Mr. Charlton pondered briefly on this and finally said he supposed the solution was that all the children could go on Pop's passport, leaving Ma to take hers out in her maiden name, though he was still not quite sure what that was.

Placidly Ma fondled the head of her seventh child against her large cheek, not unduly concerned.

"Well, I suppose if everybody had their rights," she said, "I'm still Flo Parker."

Pop looked painfully startled, almost embarrassed, more at the word rights than anything else, but also as if he were actually being introduced to Ma by name for the first time. It was a bit unnerving, hearing Ma called Flo Parker.

"Oh, well," Ma said, "I expect it'll sort itself out in the wash."

"The Froggies are broad-minded," Pop said, and laughed uproariously. "If all I hear is true. Paris and all that lark, eh?"

"Leave it to Charley," Mariette said. "He'll arrange everything. Not the clothes though, Ma, I'll need masses. I'll need a million new frocks."

Ma had now finished giving little Oscar his breakfast. The huge melons of her bosom were back in the folds of her purple blouse.

"Talking about clothes, Pop," she said, "I think it would be nice if you took your yachting cap. The one you bought once for that fancy-dress ball."

That was a jolly good idea, Pop said. Perfick. Just the thing for the Froggy seaside.

A moment later Ma was putting little Oscar back into the luscious folds of his pram and Pop was at the door, suddenly remembering there was work to do.

"Must go. Got to see Joe Rawlings about the straw deal at half past nine." He stood erect and perky, holding the doorknob, and then permitted himself the luxury of a bow.

"*Au revoir!* see you *bientôt!*"

"*Au revoir,*" Mr. Charlton and Mariette said together, laughing. "*A bientôt! Adieu!*"

At the same time little Oscar made a series of noises compounded of wind, slobber, and his mother's milk, so that Ma said if they weren't all careful they'd have him at it too.

Outside the rain had slackened, almost ceased. Pop drove the Rolls from a junkyard deep in puddles to a road overhung by oak shadow from which dripped great drops of humid July rain.

Half a mile down the road a figure was walking under an umbrella, wearing a military raincoat of the kind once known as a gorblimey and carrying a gray string bag in his hands. It was Pop's old friend the retired brigadier.

Like Ma, Pop always felt uncommonly sorry for the brigadier: always so erect and yet so down at heel, with odd socks, patched elbows, darned shirt collars, and that half-lost, undernourished leathery look about him. But today, under the umbrella, in the tattered raincoat, and carrying the empty string shopping bag, he looked, if anything, more like a walking skeleton than ever.

Reaching him, Pop drew up the Rolls, leaned out of the window, and said, "*Bonjour*, General. *Comment ça va?*"

The brigadier stopped sharply and looked immensely startled. "*Très bien, merci*, Larkin," he said. "*Et vous aussi j'espère?*"

At this Pop looked even more startled than the brigadier and could think of nothing to say at all except, "*Au revoir! À bientôt!*"

"Bless my soul, Larkin, you're in a hurry, aren't you?" the brigadier said. "What's all this?"

"Started to learn Froggy," Pop said. "All going to France. For a holiday. Place in Brittany."

"Entire brood?" the brigadier said.

"The whole shoot," Pop said. "Baby an' all."

"Cost you a pretty penny, won't it?"

"Who cares?" Pop thundered. "Ma wants to go. Mariette wants to go. Charley wants to go. Everybody wants to go. What about you? Why don't you come too? More the merrier, general!"

The brigadier, who found it hard on his meager pension to afford a day in London every six weeks or so and who couldn't remember the last time he had had a holiday at all, much less one in France, merely stood bemusedly in the rain, involuntarily shaking his head and having no word of any kind to say, until Pop, with a burst of expansive exuberance, invited him to hop in.

"No. No thanks. I like the walk. Part of my constitutional."

"Still raining. Glad to drop you."

The brigadier bemusedly thanked him again and said he really rather preferred shanks if Larkin didn't mind.

"Just what you like best, General," Pop said breezily. "How about France though? Do you a power o' good, General. Get some sun on that back of yours." The general he thought, didn't look half well as he stood there in the rain. No doubt about it, the mackintosh and the rain made him look, if anything, more drawn than ever. "Find room for a little 'un like you in the Rolls. Return trip won't cost you a penny."

In a low circumspect voice the brigadier inquired if Pop really meant he was contemplating taking the Rolls.

"Course," Pop said. "Going to fly the damn thing over. New idea. Over there in two ticks of a donkey's tail."

"Good God," the brigadier said. His white mustaches seemed to bristle and the stiff prawns of his eyebrows leapt upward sharply. "Bless my soul."

"Got to get out and see life, General!" Pop said suddenly, in a burst of enthusiastic admonishment. "See how the other half lives. See the world. What about it?"

The brigadier, who had spent the better part of forty years in places like Delhi, Singapore, Hyderabad, and Hong Kong, had seen all of the world he wanted to see and could only thank Pop a third time in polite, irresolute tones, adding at the same time that he thought the thing was hardly in his line.

"Well, plenty o' time to change your mind, General old boy," Pop said. "Get me on the blower if you do. Not going to hop in after all?"

"Thanks all the same, I won't. Only going as far as the shop to get a little mousetrap."

Pop said he was sorry to hear that the brigadier was troubled with mice. Ma hated them.

"Meant the cheese," the brigadier explained. He would dearly have loved a cheese of a better, more imaginative kind than mousetrap, but the budget wouldn't run to it. "You'll have beautiful cheeses in Brittany. Delectable."

Pop had never heard of the word "delectable." He marveled silently and then started to push in the car gears.

"Ah, well, can't stop. Must push on. *Au revoir*, General! See you *bientôt!*"

Pop raised his hand in breezy, friendly farewell and the Rolls drove opulently away. The brigadier, cadaverous, upright, and still both bemused and startled, stood for some time under the umbrella in the lessening rain, forgetting even to say *"Adieu!"* and merely thinking of the delicious, delectable cheeses one could eat in Brittany and listening to the sound of the Rolls hooter, melodious and triumphant as a hunting horn, cutting through the dripping quietness of the meadows, the oak woods, and the steaming country lanes.

How should he have the mousetrap? On toast or *au naturel?* Still shaken by the opulence of Pop's entrance, news, and exit, he decided to have it on toast. In that way he could fool himself, perhaps, that it was really *Camembert.*

2

When Pop drew up the Rolls outside the Hôtel Beau Rivage at half past six in the evening of the last day of August a gale was raging in from the Atlantic that made even the sturdy blue fishing boats in the most sheltered corners of the little port look like a battered wreckage of half-drowned matchsticks.

Dancing arches of white spray ran up and down the gray quay walls like raging dinosaurs forty feet high. Rain and spray beat at the windows of the little hotel, crashing pebbles on the shutter boards. A wind as cold as winter ran ceaselessly around the harbor with unbroken shriekings and occasional whistles like those of Mr. Charlton's much-loved, long-distant little train.

"For crying out gently, Charley," Pop said. "Where's this? Where the pipe have we come to? Lapland?"

With a sudden feeling of low, cold dismay Mr. Charlton stared silently at the Beau Rivage. The hotel seemed altogether so much smaller, so much shabbier, so much more dilapidated and inexclusive than he remembered it being in the last summer before the war. It seemed to have shrunk somehow. He had fondly pictured it as large and gay. Now it looked dismal, dark, and pokey. Its style of creosoted Tudor looked incredibly flimsy and insecure and now and then the blistered brown shutters sprang violently on their hooks and seemed, like the rest of the hotel, ready to collapse, disintegrate, and wash away. On the little outside terrace rows of colored fairy lights, strung necklace fashion between half a dozen plane trees pollarded to the appearance of yellowish skinning skeletons, were swinging wildly about in the wind, one or two of them occasionally crashing on to the concrete below. There was very little Beau about it, Mr. Charlton thought, and not much Rivage.

"Well, I suppose we ought to go in," he said at last, and suddenly led the way with an appearance of remarkably enthusiastic alacrity into the hotel, hastily followed by Ma carrying little Oscar, then Primrose and Montgomery submerged under one raincoat, the twins, Victoria and Mariette, under one umbrella, and finally Pop carrying two suitcases and a zip canvas bag.

Pop was wearing thin blue linen trousers, a yellow sleeveless shirt, yellow canvas shoes, and his yachting cap in anticipation of a long spell of French hot weather. In the short passage from the car to the hotel he half rowed, half paddled through rising lakes of Atlantic rain and spray. Several times he was convinced he was going under. Once he slipped down and one of the suitcases was blown out of his hands and began to wash away along the quayside. He grabbed it, battled on, and a few moments later found himself shipwrecked inside the vestibule of the hotel, where he was at once assailed by a powerful smell of linseed oil, drainpipes, French cigarettes, and leaking gas. One single electric bulb burned above the reception desk in the gloom of early evening and this was flickering madly up and down.

When Pop was able to get to his feet again he was more than glad to observe that Charley was already in charge of things at the reception desk. Charley, even if he didn't feel it, looked calm, self-possessed, even authoritative. He was speaking in French. Pop liked it when Charley spoke in French. It seemed to ease and resolve the most anxious of situations.

"*Et les passeports, M'sieu?*"

Behind the reception desk a small, bald, paste-colored man in pince-nez, with gray, hungry cheeks and brown molelike eyes, spoke to Mr. Charlton in a voice of schoolmasterly irritation, as if hoping to catch him out. But in a split second Mr. Charlton had everything weighed up. Swiftly the passports were on the desk: Mr. and Mrs. Charlton's, Pop's with the six children included on it, and Ma's in her maiden name of Flo Parker.

"*Et qu'est-ce que vous avez comme bagage?*"

With a commanding, irritated palm the man in pince-nez struck a large desk bell such a resonant blow that little Oscar, startled, began loudly weeping.

Ma, sitting reposefully in one of several decrepit basket chairs, at once decided that the best way of meeting the situation was to give him a little refreshment.

A few moments later an astonished elderly concierge in gum boots, sou'wester, and plastic mackintosh arrived from dark regions somewhere behind the reception desk in time to see little Oscar bury his face in the contented continent of Ma. The hungry-faced man in pince-nez looked astonished too.

Pop then remembered that there was a good deal of baggage in the car, Ma and Mariette having brought three suitcases each, mostly full of beachwear, swimwear, and summer dresses, and he followed the concierge into the driving, howling August rain.

Coming back, both shoes full of water, he saw Charley in process of being lectured, as it seemed, by the man in pince-nez. He looked extremely annoyed and seemed to be accusing Charley of some act of irresponsibility.

"What's up?" Pop called.

"He says he wasn't aware that one of the children was so small."

"Tell him we've only just had him," Ma said, and moved herself as if to expose her bosom to larger, fuller, and more public gaze. "I'm trying to fatten him up as fast as I can."

Earnestly, in French, Mr. Charlton spent some moments explaining to the cold eyes behind the pince-nez the reasons for little Oscar's immaturity. The man in pince-nez seemed not only unimpressed by this but more irritated than ever and began to snatch various huge brass-lobed keys from their hooks.

"And tell him we want a cup o' tea," Ma said, and moved with squeaks of wicker irritation in her chair. "I'm dying for one."

With mounting impatience the man in pince-nez crashed the keys back on their hooks.

"He says—"

"Don't he speak English?" Ma said. "I'll bet he does or else he wouldn't have understood what I said just now. You speak English, don't you?"

"*Oui, madame.* Yes."

"All right then, why don't you speak it? Instead of standing there talking a foreign language?"

"*Oui, madame.*"

"We all want a nice cup of tea. Quick. And if you can't make it, I soon will."

"But in twenty minutes you may have dinner, madame."

"I daresay I may, but that's not tea, is it?"

The man in pince-nez snatched at a telephone, as if about to pour rasping orders into it, and then stopped.

"*Combien de*—how many teas, madame?"

"Everybody," Ma said. "All ten of us."

With piercing but sightless frigidity the man in pince-nez stared at the sight of little Oscar busily engaged in taking refreshment.

"Even the baby, *madame?*"

"Oh, he'll have gin," Ma said. "He likes it better."

With cold and extravagant restraint the man in pince-nez put the telephone back in its place and walked out, at the same time calling to the concierge. *"Dix-sept, dix-neuf, vingt-quatre, vingt-huit,"* as if these were orders for prisoners going to an execution.

Pop stood looking at his new canvas shoes. They were full of water. It was running out of them in a stream. Water was coursing down his backbone, through his trousers, and out of his shirt and socks.

There was a sudden smell of fried fish in the air and Ma, catching it, said, "Smells like fish-and-chips for dinner, Pop. Why don't we cancel the tea and have it later? Go down well with the fish."

An old, premarital nervousness seized Mr. Charlton.

"I doubt very much if we ought to countermand the order now—"

"Oh no, don't let's," Mariette said. "I'm dying for a cup."

"Me too," Ma said. "All right."

"Like a nice glass of hot port," Pop said. "I know that. With cloves and cinnamon. Like I rigged up last Christmas."

"Or else a Guinness," Ma said.

A fusillade of pebbles, sharp as shrapnel, hit the half-closed shutters. A cold blast chiseled at the door cracks and the smell of fried fish grew stronger. The smell reminded Ma that she was hungry. She said so in a loud voice and Mr. Charlton thought it a good moment to draw her attention to various framed certificates, diplomas, and illustrated addresses hanging about the walls, so much evidence of the excellent, even high-class cuisine of the Beau Rivage.

"Diplôme d'Honneur Strasbourg 1907. Lyon 1912 and 1924. Marseilles 1910, '27, and '29. Paris, six times. Dijon, 1932. Chevalier de Taste Vin—*Foire Gastronomique* 1929—"

"See, Ma?" Pop said. "Cooking prizes."

"Anything for this year?" Ma said.

Mr. Charlton was saved the necessity of finding an answer to this pertinent question by the arrival of the tea.

The tea was in a huge white metal coffee pot, with thick white coffee cups to drink it from, and the bill was on the tray.

While Mariette sugared and milked the cups, Pop, moving like a deep-sea diver who has only just surfaced, dripping water from every thread, picked up the bill and gazed at it.

"How much is two thousand three hundred and fifty francs, Charley boy?"

At this moment Victoria started crying.

"You take her, Mariette," Ma said. "You know how she is."

Whispering consolatory noises, Mariette took Victoria out, and Mr. Charlton, trying in the circumstances to be both discreet and casual, said, "Oh, about two pounds. Just over."

"For *tea?*" Ma yelled.

For one moment her bosom seemed to rise into air like an outraged, affronted puffball.

"I thought you said it was cheap." Pop said.

"Well, of course, you've got to remember—in France—"

"Here," Ma said. "Hold Oscar."

Mr. Charlton found himself suddenly holding Oscar. Oscar, like Pop, was wet. Ma hastily covered up her bosom and bore down on tea and teacups, stunned to impotent silence while Mr. Charlton said, "After all, tea in France is probably a pound a pound. Perhaps twenty-five shillings. I was reading in the *Times* only the other day—"

"And hot milk!" Ma said. "Feel this! They brought hot milk."

No one had any time to comment on this outrage before Mariette and Victoria came back, Mariette tightly holding her sister's hand.

"Hot milk, Mariette!" Ma said. "Two pounds and over for a cuppa tea and they bring hot milk. Hullo, what's the matter with you?"

"Nothing."

Mariette looked white and shaken.

"Look as if you'd seen a ghost or something. Look as if you'd had the bill and not Pop."

Mariette's lip was trembling. She was taking long, hard breaths.

"Whatever's the matter?" Ma said.

"I'd rather not talk about it. Just something out there."

"You can't sit down!" Victoria said. "You have to stand up!"

"Good God," Ma said. "Think of me."

There was nothing for it but to give Mariette the strongest cup of tea she could pour out. This was several shades paler than straw and looked and tasted like discolored water flavored ever so faintly with boiled onions.

After that Ma swished the teapot powerfully around and around in an effort to bring strength where it was most needed, saying at the same time, "It'll be mice next. I know. I smelled 'em when we came in."

As if in answer to an outrageous signal the man in pince-nez appeared out of a door marked BUREAU with the habit of a hungry burrowing mole. He busied himself for some moments behind the desk, sniffing and rattling keys, and then asked Mr. Charlton if he had yet filled out the forms.

Mr. Charlton had not filled out the forms. There were ten of them. He now gave Oscar to Montgomery, took out his fountain pen, and sat down in one of the many decrepit, disintegrating wicker chairs. His hands were damp from Oscar.

As he started on the forms Ma called, "I bet they haven't got television. Ask him, Charley. Ask him if they got telly."

Mr. Charlton looked up and asked the man in pince-nez, in French, if they'd got television.

"*Pas de télévision.*"

"No telly, Ma, I'm afraid."

Pop was stunned. For crying out gently.

"Terrible. You'd never believe it," he said. "Never believe it, Ma, would you?"

"Well, good thing Montgomery brought the radio," Ma said. "Turn it on, somebody. Let's have a tune. Should have brought the new hi-fi."

Primrose switched on the portable radio at full blast and dance music roared forth, momentarily louder than the wind, now punctuated by occasional thunder, that ripped like a half hurricane across the port.

Involuntarily startled, the man in pince-nez rang the desk bell, setting Oscar crying again.

"Ask him if there's a bar," Pop said.

Mr. Charlton, who in the confusion was having difficulty in remembering the date of his own birthday, looked up to ask the man in pince-nez if there was a bar.

"*Oui, m'sieu. Par ici.*"

With one thin finger he indicated that the bar lay somewhere in regions beyond the bureau, in the direction where Mariette and Victoria had found life so inconvenient for their sex.

"Yes, it seems there's a bar."

"Good egg," Pop said. "That's something." With relief he abandoned the tepid, onioned tea. "I think I'll buzz around and have a snifter."

"Not on your nelly!" Ma said. "Take hold of Oscar. I expect he wants changing. That's why he's roaring again."

The concierge came back. Pop took over Oscar. It was now so dark that Mr. Charlton could hardly see to write the forms. A tremendous crash of thunder broke immediately above the hotel, setting the shutters rattling, the radio crackling, and the single dim light beside the telephone quaking even more like a candle in a wind.

The man in pince-nez spoke suddenly in French, with a slight sense of outrage, as if still offended by Ma's charge about speaking in a foreign language. Mr. Charlton translated, "He says you can go up to your rooms now if you want to."

"Well, what the merry Ellen does he think we're sitting here waiting for?" Ma said. "Christmas?"

Oscar had stopped crying. The concierge picked up the remainder of the baggage and the children their things. Mr. Charlton said he'd come up soon, since the forms would take him at least another twenty minutes to finish, not that he'd even finish them then, in view of remembering all the birthdays.

"My belly's rattling," Petunia said. Zinnia said hers was too and they couldn't stand it much longer.

"We won't bother to unpack," Ma said. She knew Pop was starved. She was getting pretty well starved herself. "I'll just change Oscar and wash and then we'll all come down."

Everybody was ready to go upstairs except Ma and Mr. Charlton when a fresh and more stupendous crash of thunder occurred. The light above the telephone went completely out, came on, went out, came on, and repeated the process six more times before going out altogether.

In the comparative silence after the thunder a strange new sound crept into the air. It was that of one of the wicker chairs squeaking, like a horde of mice, in protest.

It was the chair containing Ma.

"Here, hold Oscar, somebody," Pop said. "Ma's stuck."

Mariette took Oscar. Pop went over to Ma, solicitous but unsurprised; it had happened before. Ma had always had difficulty in getting her two-yard bulk into the confines of strange furniture and still more difficulty in getting it out again.

"Give us a hand, Charley," Pop said, "before she goes under for the third time."

Pop and Charley started to pull at Ma, who began to laugh with huge jellified ripples. The man in pince-nez looked on with frigid, withdrawn, offended eyes. Pop and Charley pulled at Ma harder than ever, but with no result except to set her laughing with louder shrieks, more fatly.

Presently Ma went strengthless. It became impossible to budge her. Above the telephone the light came on again, illuminating Ma as a collapsing balloon that would never rise.

"Ma, you're not helping," Pop said. He pleaded for some small cooperation. "If you don't help you'll have to go around with the damn thing stuck on your behind for the rest of your natural."

Ma laughed more than ever. The vast milky hillock of her bosom, deeply cleft, rose and fell in mighty breaths. Her whole body started to sink lower and lower and suddenly Pop realized that even if she survived the chair never would.

He started to urge Charley to pull again. In a sudden wrench the two of them pulled Ma to her feet and she stood there for some seconds with the chair attached to her great buttocks like a sort of tender.

Suddenly, with shrieks, she sank back again. Another peal of thunder, more violent than any other, rent the air above the hotel. The man in pince-nez pleaded *"La chaise, madame—je vous prie—la chaise!"* and for the ninth or tenth time the light went out.

When it came on again Ma was on her feet. Behind her the chair was flatter than a doormat and by the telephone the man in pince-nez had his head in his hands.

"Madame, madame, je vous—" he was saying. In distress the necessary language for the occasion did not come to him for some moments. When it did so his English was sadly broken up. "Madame, please could—Oh, madame, I ask—I please—"

With incredible swiftness Pop came forward to defend Ma. Irately he strode over to the man in pince-nez and struck the desk a severe blow with his fist, speaking peremptorily and with voluble rapidity.

"Qu'est-ce qu'il y a?" he shouted, "and *comment ça va* and *comment allez-vous* and *avez-vous bien dormi* and *qu'est-ce que vous avez à manger* and *à bientôt* san fairy ann and all that lark!"

The little man in pince-nez looked as if he'd been hit with a poleax. His mouth fell open sharply, but except for a muted gurgle he had nothing to say. A moment later Pop and Ma started to go upstairs, followed by the children, Ma still laughing, Pop glad in his heart of the excellent tuition given by Charley in various French phrases likely to be of use in emergency.

At the foot of the stairs he paused to turn with pride and perkiness to look back.

"Accent all right, Charley boy?"

"Perfick," Mr. Charlton said. "Absolutely perfick."

Pop waved a mildly deprecating hand.

"Très bon, you mean, *très bon*," he said. "Don't forget we're in France now. Charley boy. We don't take lessons for nothing, do we? *À bientôt!"*

3

Nearly an hour later, when Ma brought the children downstairs for dinner, closely followed by Charley and Mariette, Pop was already sitting moodily in a corner of the *salle à manger*, a room of varnished, ginger-colored matchboard and glass built like a greenhouse shrouded with yellowing lace curtains against the westward side of the hotel. Some squares of glass were colored blue or ruby. A few, broken altogether, had been patched up with squares of treacle-brown paper and it seemed generally that the whole ramshackle structure, battered by the Atlantic storm, might at any moment fall down, disintegrate, and blow away.

Driven by ravenous hunger and thirst to the bar, Pop had found it furnished with a solitary stool, a yard of dusty counter, a dozing gray cat, and a vase of last year's heather. The stool had two legs instead of three and all about the place was that curious pungent odor that Ma had been so quick to notice earlier in the day—as if a drain has been left open or a gas tap on.

In the *salle à manger*, in contrast to the silent half-darkness of the bar, a noisy, eager battle was being waged by seven or eight French families against the howl of wind and rain, the tossing lace curtains, and more particularly against what appeared to be dishes of large unpleasant pink spiders, in reality *langoustines*. A mad cracking of claws filled the air and one plump Frenchman sat eating, wearing his cap, a large white one, as if for protection against something, perhaps flying claws or bread or rain.

Three feet from Pop's table a harassed French waitress with a marked limp and loose peroxide hair came to operate, every desperate two minutes or so, a large patent wooden-handled bread slicer about the size of an old fashioned sewing machine—a cross somewhere between a guillotine and a chaff cutter.

This instrument made crude groaning noises, like an old tram trying to start. Slices of bread, savagely chopped from yard-long loaves, flew about in all directions, dropping all over the place until harassed waiters and waitresses bore them hurriedly off to eager, waiting guests. These, Pop noticed, at once crammed them ravenously into their mouths and even gluttonously mopped their plates with them.

Presently the rest of the family arrived: Mariette immaculate and perfumed in a beautiful sleeveless low-cut dress of emerald green that made her shoulders and upper breast glow a warm olive color, Ma in a mauve woolen dress and a royal blue sweater on top to keep out the cold. Ma had plenty of Chanel No. 5 on, still convinced that the hotel smelled not only of mice but a lot of other things besides.

As the family walked in all the French families suddenly stopped eating. The French, Charley had once told Pop, were the elite of Europe. Now they stopped ramming bread into their mouths like famished prisoners and gaped at the bare, astral shoulders of Mariette, Ma's great mauve and blue balloon of a body, and the retinue of children behind it.

Most of the older French women, Pop thought, seemed to be wearing discolored woolen sacks. The younger ones, who were nearly all tallow-colored, bruise-eyed, and flat-chested, wore jeans. It was hard to tell any of them from boys and in consequence Pop felt more than usually proud of Mariette, who looked so fleshily, elegantly, and provocatively a girl.

Presently the waitress with the limp brought the menu and then with not a moment to spare hopped off to work the bread machine.

"Well, what's to eat, Charley boy?" Pop said, rubbing his hands. "Somethink good I hope, old man, I'm starving."

Mr. Charlton consulted the menu with a certain musing, studious air of English calm.

"By the way, Charley," Pop said, "what's 'eat' in French? Haven't learned any words today."

It was Pop's honest resolve to learn, if possible, a few new French words every day.

"*Manger*," Charley said. "Same word as the thing in the stable—manger."

Pop sat mute and astounded. Manger—a simple thing like that. Perfickly wonderful. Unbelievable. Manger. He sat back and prepared to listen to Charley reading out the menu with the awe he deserved.

"Well, to begin with there are *langoustines*. They're a kind of small lobster. Speciality of the Atlantic coast. Then there's *saucisson à la mode d'ici*—that's a sort of sausage they do here. *Spécialité de la maison*, I shouldn't wonder. Hot, I expect. Probably awfully good. Then *pigeons à la Gautier*—I expect that's pigeons in some sort of wine sauce. And afterward fruit and cheese."

"Sounds jolly *bon*," Pop said.

Charley said he thought it ought to satisfy and Ma at once started remonstrating with Montgomery, Primrose, Victoria, and the twins about eating so much bread. She said they'd never want their dinners if they went on stuffing bread down.

"What shall we drink?" Charley said.

"Port," Pop said. He too was stuffing down large quantities of bread, trying to stave off increasing stabs and rumbles of hunger. Ma agreed about the port. It would warm them all up, she said.

"I doubt if they'll have port."

"Good God," Pop said. *"What?* I thought you said the Froggies lived on wine?"

"Well, they do. But it's their own. Port isn't. I suggest we drink *vin rosé*. That'll go well with the fish and the pigeon."

The harassed waitress with the limp, freed momentarily of bread cutting, arrived a moment later to tell Charley, in French, that there were, after all, no *langoustines*.

"Sorry, no more *langoustines*," Mr. Charlton said. "They've got *friture* instead."

"What's *friture?*"

"Fried sardines."

Ma choked; she felt she wanted to be suddenly and violently sick.

"Oh, fresh ones, of course," Charley said. "Probably caught this afternoon."

"In that lot?" Pop said, and waved a hand in the general direction of the howling, blackening gale that threatened increasingly to blow away the *salle à manger*.

A second later a vast flash of lightning seemed to sizzle down the entire length of roof glass like a celestial diamond cutter. A Frenchwoman rose hysterically and rushed from the room. The chaff cutter guillotine attacked yet another loaf with louder and louder groans and a long black burst of thunder struck the hotel to the depth of its foundations.

Alarmed too, the children ate more bread. Pop ate more bread and was in fact still eating bread when the *friture* arrived.

"They're only tiddlers!" the twins said. "They're only tiddlers!"

"Sardines never grow any bigger," Charley said, "otherwise they wouldn't be sardines."

"About time they did then," Ma said, peering dubiously at piled scraps of fish, "that's all."

"*Bon appétit!*" Mr. Charlton said, and proceeded enthusiastically to attack the *friture*.

Pop, turning to the attack too, found himself facing a large plateful of shriveled dark brown objects which immediately fell to pieces at the touch of a fork. Scorched fragments of fish flew flakily about in all directions. The few crumbs that he was able to capture, impale on his fork, and at last transfer to his mouth tasted, he thought, exactly like the unwanted scraps left over at the bottom of a bag of fish-and-chips.

"Shan't get very fat on these," Ma said.

In a low depressed voice Pop agreed. Ma's great bulk, which filled half the side of one length of the table, now and then quivered in irritation and presently she was eating the *friture* with her fingers, urging the children to do likewise.

The children, in silent despair, ate more bread. Savagely the chaff cutter-guillotine worked overtime, drowning conversation. And presently the limping waitress brought the *vin rosé*, which Charley tasted.

"Delicious," he said with mounting enthusiasm. "Quite delicious."

Ma drank too and suddenly felt a quick sharp stream of ice descend to her bowels, cold as charity.

At last the multitudinous remains of the *friture* were taken away, plates piled high with brown wreckage, and Ma said it looked like the feeding of the five thousand. Pop drank deep of *vin rosé*, raised his glass to everybody, and unable to think of very much to say remarked mournfully, "Well, cheers, everybody. Well, here we are."

"We certainly are," Ma said. "You never spoke a truer word."

After a short interval the *saucisson à la mode d'ici* arrived. This consisted of a strange object looking like a large pregnant sausage roll, rather scorched on top. Slight puffs of steam seemed to be issuing from the exhausts at either end.

Ma remarked that at least it was hot and Pop, appetite now whetted to the full by another sharp draft or two of *vin rosé*, prepared to attack the object on his plate by cutting it directly through the middle.

To his complete dismay the force of the cut, meeting hard resistance from the surface of scorched crust, sent the two pieces hurtling in the air. Both fell with a low thud to the floor.

"Don't touch it! Don't touch it!" Ma said. "Mice everywhere."

"I'll order another," Charley said. "*Ma'moiselle!*"

In silent patience Pop waited, but by the time a waitress could be spared from the bondage of bread cutting the rest of the family had finished the battle with the *saucisson à la mode d'ici.*

With gloom, drinking more *vin rosé* to fortify himself, Pop waited while Charley explained to the waitress the situation about the unfortunate disappearance of his second course.

The waitress seemed dubious, even unimpressed. She simply stared coldly at Pop's empty plate as if knowing perfectly well he had eaten what had been on there and crushingly uttered the single word *"supplément."*

"She says if you have another you'll have to pay extra," Charley said.

"Better order another bottle of vin rosy instead, Charley," Pop said.

Weakly he started to eat more bread. He had, he thought, never eaten so much bread in his life. He no longer wondered why the guillotine worked overtime.

Suddenly thunder roared again, faintly echoed by the rumblings of his own belly, and presently the little man in pince-nez appeared, making his furtive molelike way from table to table. When he saw the Larkins, however, he stood some distance off, in partly obsequious retreat, an uneasy grimace on his face, his hands held together.

Once he bowed, Mr. Charlton bowed too and Ma grinned faintly in reply.

"Nice to see that," Mr. Charlton said. "Typical French. He's come to see if everything's all right."

"Why don't we tell him?" Ma said.

"What do we have next?" the twins said. "What do we have next?"

"Pigeons," Pop said. The thought of stewed pigeons made his mouth water. In wine sauce too. "Pigeons."

"We want baked beans on toast!" the twins said. "And cocoa."

"Quiet!" Pop thundered. "I'll have order."

A moment later a waitress, arriving with a fourth plate of bread, proceeded to announce to Mr. Charlton a fresh and disturbing piece of news. There were, after all, no pigeons.

Pop felt too weak to utter any kind of exclamation about this second, deeper disappointment.

"There's rabbit," Charley told him, "instead."

Instantly Pop recoiled in pale, fastidious horror.

"Not after myxo!" he said. "No! Charley, I couldn't. I can't touch 'em after myxo!"

Myxomatosis, the scourge of the rabbit tribe, had affected Pop very deeply. No one else in the family had been so moved by the plague and its results. But to Pop the thought of eating rabbits was now as great a nausea as the thought of eating nightingales.

"It started here in France too," he said. "The Froggies were the ones who first started it."

"Have an omelet," Charley said cheerfully.

"They don't suit him," Ma said. "They always give him heartburn."

Pop could only murmur in a low, dispassionate voice that he had to have something, somehow, soon. Heartburn or no heartburn. Even an omelet.

"A steak then," Charley said. "With chips."

At this Pop cheered up a little, saying that a steak would suit him.

"*Alors, un filet bifteck pour Monsieur,*" Charley said, "*avec pommes frites.*"

"Biff-teck! Biff-teck!" the twins started shouting, punching each other, laughing loudly. "Biff-teck! Biff-you! Biff-you! Biff-teck!"

Pop was too weak to cry "Quiet!" this time and from a distance the man in pince-nez stared in disapproval at the scene, so Ma said, "Sssh! Mr. Dupont's looking."

"That isn't Mr. Dupont," Charley said. "He's only the manager. Mr. Dupont's dead."

"Die of overeating?" Ma said.

Pop laughed faintly.

"The hotel is run by a Miss Dupont—Mlle. Dupont," Charley explained. "But it seems she's away in Brest for the day."

"When the cat's away," Ma said.

"Well," Charley said, "I wouldn't be at all surprised if that didn't explain a slight lack of liaison."

Pop, too low in spirits even to admire Charley's turn of phrase, drank deeply of *vin rosé.*

"Better order some more of the juice, Charley old man," he said. "Got to keep going somehow."

"Biff-teck! Biff-teck! Biff-you! Biff-teck!"

"Quiet!" Pop said sharply, and from across the *salle à manger* several French mamas looked quickly around at him with full sudden glances, clearly electrified.

Half an hour later he had masticated his way through a bloody piece of beef roughly the shape of a boot's sole, the same thickness, and about as interesting. He ate the chips that accompanied it down to the last frizzled crumb and even dipped his bread in the half-cold blood.

Ma said she hoped he felt better for it but Pop could hardly do more than nod, drinking again of *vin rosé*.

"Don't even have catsup," he said, as if this serious gastronomic omission were the final straw.

Soon the twins, Primrose, Victoria, and Montgomery, tired out from the journey, went up to bed and presently Pop began to throw out broad hints that Mariette and Charley ought to be doing likewise.

"It's only nine o'clock," Mariette said.

"I used to be in bed at nine o'clock at your age," Pop said.

"Don't tell me," Ma said.

"We thought there might be dancing," Charley said, "somewhere."

"There's sure to be a night spot in the town," Mariette said. "Something gay."

With a queer low laugh and a wave of the hand Pop invited the two young people to look and listen at the signs and echoes of the little port's mad, nighttime gaiety: the howl of Atlantic wind and rain on the glass roof of the *salle à manger*, the whirling curtains, the crash of spewed foam on the quayside, and the intermittent lightning and cracks of thunder that threatened every few moments to put the lights out.

"Gorblimey, hark at it," Pop said, and once again urged on Charley and Mariette the fact that they would be much better off, in all respects, in bed.

Mr. Charlton evidently didn't think so.

"I'd rather like some coffee," he said.

"Me too," Mariette said.

Pop agreed that perhaps it wasn't a bad idea at that. At least it would save him from going to bed on a completely empty stomach.

"I expect we can get it in the lounge," Mr. Charlton said.

In the lounge, in flickering semidarkness, various French couples were furtively drinking coffee, talking and playing whist, vingt-et-un, and things of that sort. A few discouraged moths fluttered about, and above the howl of wind and rain no other sound could be heard except a sudden metallic clash as someone lost patience and struck a patent coffee filter a severe blow on top in order to encourage the flow.

While waiting for the coffee, which Mr. Charlton ordered, Ma sat staring at the moths and wondering what on earth she and the rest of the family were going to do with themselves for a month. It was Pop who had suggested coming for a month. It would give Mariette and Charley more of a chance, he thought.

Presently, after the lights had taken another alarming dip toward absolute darkness, the coffee arrived in four patent filters, once silvered but now worn very brassy at the edges. The top half of the filter was full of water and the lid was too hot to hold.

"What the hell do we do with these?" Pop said.

"The coffee should come through," Mr. Charlton said. "If not, you strike it. The filter I mean."

Five minutes later everyone looked inside the filters and found that the water level hadn't dropped a centimeter. This was often the way, Mr. Charlton assured them, and went on to explain that the trouble could often be cured by pressure.

"Like this," he said, and pressed the top of the filter firmly with the palm of his hand. "That ought to do the trick."

Pop wondered. Whenever he pressed the filter the top of it scalded the palm of his hand. There was never any sign of coffee coming through either.

"They vary," Mr. Charlton explained. "Mine's coming through quite happily."

After another five minutes both Ma and Mariette said theirs was coming through quite nicely too. Pop peered several times at the unchanged water level in his own with a gloom unbroken except by the arrival of a cognac, thoughtfully ordered by Charley when the filters came. The cognac was, by Pop's standards a mere thimbleful, but it was better than nothing at all.

"No luck?" Mr. Charlton said, and Pop peered for the ninth or tenth time into the top of the filter, to discover once more that the water level hadn't varied a bit.

"Better give it a tap," Mr. Charlton suggested.

Unaccountably maddened, Pop proceeded to strike the lid of the filter a sudden almighty blow such as he had seen several of the French couples do. The lid at once went leaping vertically into the air and Pop, in an involuntary effort to save it, knocked the bottom of the filter flying, spilling hot water, closely followed by coffee grounds and the cognac, into the upper parts of his trousers.

"Ma," he said after this, "I think we'd better go up. I don't know wevver I can last out much longer."

It wasn't his lucky day, he said as he and Ma went into the bedroom, but Ma instantly and peremptorily shushed him, urging him to be careful and not to wake little Oscar.

"I'm just going along," she said. "Don't put the light on. You can see to get undressed without it."

"Can't see a damn thing," Pop said.

"Then you must feel," Ma said. "That's all."

Pop was still feeling when, three or four minutes later, Ma came back. He had got as far as taking off his jacket, collar, and tie but had decided to go no further until he got some further guidance from Ma.

"Where is it?" he said.

"Along the corridor and turn left and then down three steps. Mind the steps. The light isn't very good."

The light certainly wasn't very good and in fact suddenly went out altogether under a fresh clap of thunder, leaving Pop groping helplessly along the unfamiliar walls of the corridor.

When he finally decided to feel his way back he found himself unsure about the bedroom door but fortunately little Oscar turned and murmured in his sleep and Pop, pushing open the door, said, "Where are you, Ma? Undressed yet?"

Ma said she wasn't undressing that night. It was too risky. She was sleeping in her dressing gown.

Pop, demoralized, taking off his wet trousers in complete darkness, didn't comment. Life was suddenly a bit too much: no light, no sight of Ma undressing, no telly, no chance of having a cigar and reading the *Times* for half an hour before turning in. This was the end.

"Did you find it?" Ma said.

No, Pop said, he hadn't found it. That was the trouble.

"There must be a doings in the bedroom somewhere," Ma said. "You'd better try and find that."

Pop started to grope about the completely darkened room, knocking against bed, chairs, and chests of drawers, feeling for what Ma had called the doings.

"Sssh!" Ma said. "You'll wake Oscar. Can't you find it?"

"Don't seem to be nothink nowhere." Pop was in despair. "Have to find somewhere soon."

"You'd better try the window," Ma said.

Pop, after a few more minutes of groping, managed to find a window. With some difficulty he opened it and then stood there for some time in concentrated silence except for an occasional earnest sigh or two, facing the Atlantic, its wind, and its rain.

During this time he was too busy to speak, so that at last Ma called, "You all right? You're a long time. What's happening?"

Pop, sad and remote at the window, murmured something about he was having a bit of a battle with the elements. Ma thought this was very funny and started laughing like shaking jelly, rocking the bed springs, but there was no answering echo from Pop except another earnest sigh or two.

"Are you winning or losing?" Ma called.

"Think it's a draw," Pop said.

"Fair result I suppose," Ma said, laughing again.

A moment later Pop brought the long day to a silent close by creeping into bed with Ma, tired and damp but hopeful that little Oscar wouldn't wake too soon for his early-morning drop of refreshment.

4

Pop rose from an uncheerful breakfast of one croissant, one roll of bread, two cups of coffee, and a small pot of red currant jelly. in very low spirits. This, it seemed to him, was no breakfast for a man and moreover he had slept very badly.

Outside, the day was slightly less violent. The wind had dropped a little, though not completely, and now rain was merely coming down in a mad, unremitting waterfall, a gray curtain obscuring all but the closer reaches of harbor, sea, and sky.

In the small hotel lounge, behind rattling doors, among a cramped forest of decrepit wicker chairs, Mariette and Charley were looking at French fashion magazines; the twins were playing patience with Victoria, and Montgomery and Primrose noughts and crosses. Several French children were running noisily backward and forward or were reading and playing too, constantly pursued by the voices of remonstrating mamas calling them by name: "Hippolyte! Ernestine! Jean-Pierre! Marc-Antoine! Celestine! Fifi!"

Pop thought these names were plain damn silly and moodily congratulated himself that he and Ma, who was still upstairs giving Oscar his breakfast, had given their children sensible solid names like Zinnia and Petunia, Primrose and Montgomery, Victoria, Mariette, and Oscar.

At last he could bear it no longer. He put on his yachting cap and mackintosh and went out into a gray rain that had in it the chill of December, hopeful of somewhere finding himself an honest, solid breakfast.

The entire length of dark gray *pavé* running along the little harbor was as deserted as the deck of an abandoned ship. Down in the harbor itself the black figures of a few fishermen in oilskins were busy tightening the moorings of their blue sardine boats, on the masts of which the furled sails were rolled like copper umbrellas.

In the morning air was a raw saltiness which sharpened the appetite with a sting. Seagulls made continuous mournful cries as they quarreled above the boats, hungry too. From a café at the end of the promenade came the smell of coffee, bitter, strong, deliciously mocking.

Inside the café Pop found himself to be the only customer. Presently a waiter who looked as if he had been awake all night and was now preparing to sleep all day came and stood beside his table.

"*M'sieu?*"

"Three boiled eggs," Pop said. "Soft."

"*Comment?*"

Thanks to Mr. Charlton, Pop knew what this meant.

"Soft?" he said. "*S'il vous plaît.*"

"*M'sieu?*"

"Three boiled eggs. Soft," Pop said.

"*Ex?*"

"*S'il vous plaît,*" Pop said. "Soft." He held up three fingers. "Three. *Trois.* Soft boiled."

"*Ex?*"

"Yes, old boy," Pop said. "*Oui.*"

With his forefinger he described what he thought were a few helpful circles in the air and at this, he felt, the waiter seemed to understand. In a sort of ruminating daze he went away, muttering, "*Ex,*" several times.

Two minutes later he came back to bring Pop a large treble brandy.

"*Ça va?*" he said, and Pop could only nod his head in mute, melancholy acquiescence, deeply regretting that among the French words Mr. Charlton had taught him there had so far been none relating to drink and food. It was an omission that would have to be remedied pretty soon.

With increasing depression, as yet unrelieved by the brandy, Pop walked back to the hotel. It would be a pretty good idea, he thought, to buy himself a pocket dictionary and he was about to go over and consult Charley on the subject when the man in pince-nez came hurrying forward from behind the reception desk, molelike, blinking nervously.

"*Bonjour,* Monsieur Larkin. It is possible to speak with you?"

"*Oui,*" Pop said. "What's up?"

"Please to step one moment into the bureau."

Pop followed the man in pince-nez through the door marked BU-REAU. The door was carefully shut behind him and the little office at once struck him as being markedly untidy, full of dust, and without a breath of air. Piles of dusty brown paper parcels were everywhere stacked on shelves, tables, and even chairs and in one corner stood a high heavy oak desk with a fretted brass grille running around three sides.

Behind this the man in pince-nez perched himself, less like a mole than a little inquisitorial monkey.

"Monsieur Larkin, it is merely a little matter of the passports."

"I see," Pop said, and then remembered something. "By the way, what's your name?"

"Mollet."

"Molly," Pop said. "Always nice to know."

"Monsieur Larkin," M. Mollet said, "I am finding some little difficulty in saying which of your passports is which." He held up a passport for Pop to see. *"Par exemple*, this one. Mr. and Mrs. Charlton. This is not relating to you and Madame?"

No, Pop explained, it wasn't relating to him and Madame, but to his daughter and her husband, Charley.

"I see. And this one—Sydney Charles Larkin. This is relating to you?"

That was it, Pop said. That was him all right.

"With the six children?"

"With the six children," Pop said.

"Then what," M. Mollet said, "is this one relating to? Florence Daisy Parker?"

"That's Ma."

"Pardon? Comment?"

"That's my missus. My wife," Pop said. "Ma."

M. Mollet peered with startled, troubled, inquisitorial eyes above the top of the grille.

"Your wife? A single lady? With another name?"

"That's it," Pop said. By this time the brandy had made him feel more cheerful, more his perky self. "Any objections?"

"You are taking a double room in this hotel to share with a single lady while you yourself have six children?"

Pop actually laughed. "Right first time," he said.

M. Mollet, again looking as if he'd been poleaxed, took off his pince-nez, hastily wiped them with his handkerchief, and put them on again. When he spoke again it was with an uncertain quiver of the lips, his eyes looking down through the spectacles.

"In this case I regret that I must ask you to leave the hotel."

"Not on your nelly," Pop said. His cheerfulness had begun to evaporate. He had a sudden sneaking notion that the Froggies thought he and Ma weren't respectable. He began to wish he'd had another treble brandy. "Not on your flipping nelly."

"Nelly? What is that?"

"Rhubarb," Pop said. "Don't bother."

By now his cheerfulness had evaporated completely; suddenly he was feeling hot and bristly.

"If you will leave without complications we will dismiss the matter of the bill. There will be no charge. Not even for the chair that Madame—the lady—was destroying yesterday."

"Destroying!" Pop said. "Good God, it might have destroyed Ma! It might have injured Ma for life!"

"Please not to shout, Monsieur Larkin. If you will agree to—"

"Agree my aunt Sally," Pop said. Suddenly, in an inspired flash of anger, he remembered Mlle. Dupont. "Is this Miss Dupont's doing or yours? Where the pie is she anyway? Is she back?"

"Mlle. Dupont is back. I have tried to spare her the unpleasantness—"

"Unpleasantness? Damnit, I thought Froggies were broad-minded," Pop said. "Paris an' all that lark."

"This," M. Mollet said severely, "is not Paris."

"Bet your nelly it's not," Pop said. "It's brighter in The Bricklayers Arms at home on a foggy Monday."

"That I do not know about, Monsieur Larkin. I only know—"

"Get Mlle. Dupont," Pop said. "Go on, get her on the blower, you whelk." M. Mollet, unaware what a whelk was, stood in a state of restless suspension behind the grille. "Go on, get her, I want to talk to her."

"Very well, Monsieur Larkin."

With no other words M. Mollet extricated himself with dignified stiffness from behind the grille and went out on legs as bent as wires.

It was nearly five minutes before Mlle. Dupont came into the bureau. She seemed, Pop thought, about thirty-eight, rather plump and of medium height, and was wearing a black dress with pure white collar and cuffs—an arrangement that might well have been a considered attempt to make herself look a trifle younger.

"Monsieur Larkin? *Bonjour, m'sieu.*"

She spoke formally, but with nervousness; she played now and then with a large bunch of keys suspended from a chain attached to the belt of her dress.

"*Bonjour.* Good morning. Hope you speak English." Pop said.

"I speak some English. Yes."

"Good egg." Pop felt more cheerful again. He always felt more cheerful in the presence of women anyway. "Well, I hear you're throwing us out?"

Mlle. Dupont, completely embarrassed and transfixed at the sheer directness of this remark, could not speak. She looked unreal. Her skin had that clay-colored, slightly unhealthy appearance so common in French women, giving them faces like half-cooked dough. Her hair, parted sharply down the middle, was very black and inclined to be greasy. Her eyes seemed, at first, to be black too, but when seen more closely, as Pop discovered later, they were like two thick pieces of glass, carved from an intensely green-black bottle.

"There are times, *m'sieu,* when one has to exercise a certain discretion."

Pop, smiling, looked Mlle. Dupont straight in the eyes. This was when he first discovered their unusual intensity and the fact that they were really more green than black.

There was a certain intensity about Pop's gaze too, so that Mlle. Dupont at once started to play again with her keys.

A moment later Pop put to her a sudden, simple, alarming question, "If Ma and me don't mind why should you?"

Mlle. Dupont had no answer; she did not even begin to move her lips in reply.

"Ma and me ran away when she was sixteen. Eloped. Spent the night at Brighton. She was thinner then. More like you. More your size." Once again he transfixed Mlle. Dupont, looking straight into her eyes with a gaze of exceptionally friendly, perky intensity. "Same dark hair as you too. Same sort of skin. Lovely."

Involuntarily Mlle. Dupont drew a deep breath. Without being in the least aware of it she selected a single key from her bunch and started pressing it hard into the palm of one hand.

"Telling you my life story already," Pop said. "What a lark. Why should I do that?"

For a moment Mlle. Dupont appeared to be thinking in French, for she suddenly said, "*Je ne sais—*"

"I thought you were going to be a bit sticky about me and Ma. I don't know—bit awkward. Were you?"

Mlle. Dupont simply didn't know if she was or not. Pop was talking now in his intimate quick-knitted fashion, smiling all the time, and

Mlle. Dupont stood listening as if partially mesmerized.

"It was so rough last night we thought of going back home anyway," Pop said. "Blimey it was rough. Never thought it could be so rough and cold here in France."

"Oh, but it will improve!" she said. "It will get better! It isn't always so!"

"Will it? Ah, but when?" Pop said. "Blimey, look at it now."

Once again Mlle. Dupont, utterly confused, appeared to be thinking partly in French.

"*Dans deux ou trois jours*—two or three days. The storms come and go and then suddenly all is over and then—*le soleil, toujours le soleil—toujours, toujours, toujours—*"

"*Soleil?*"

"Sun—the sun. In French *soleil*—"

Softly Pop said he wished he could speak French like Mlle. Dupont and she in turn stood once again as if mesmerized.

"In July it was so hot you could not bear it," she said. "You could not bear the heat on the flesh—"

"No? Bet I could," Pop said, and gave Mlle. Dupont a look of rapidity so near a wink, that she retreated sharply into herself and began to think in French again.

"*Et l'orage,*" she started saying, "*vous n'avez pas peur pour les enfants?*"

"*Comment?*" Pop said, and remarked that Mlle. Dupont had got him there, he was afraid.

Mlle. Dupont apologized, began to speak in English again, and said she hoped the children had not been frightened by the storm.

"Slept like tops," Pop said. "Wish Ma and me had."

"You did not sleep well?"

"Terrible."

"I am sorry. It was the storm?"

"The beds," Pop said. "And that room. We'll have to change that room, Ma and me, if we're going to stay here."

For the third or fourth time Pop transfixed her with a smile that was at once perky, soft, and full of disquieting penetration, so that Mlle. Dupont found herself torn between the question of the unsatisfactory room and its bed and that brief, tormenting scrap of reminiscence about Pop and Ma eloping and how Ma and she had the same creamy skin and the same dark soft hair.

This flash of romantic reminiscence confused her all over again, so that she pressed the key harder than ever into the palm of her hand and said, "It is *très, très difficile.* I have no more rooms, Monsieur Larkin. Not one more."

"Couldn't spend another night in that 'orrible room," Pop said. He thought of his battle with the elements. He hadn't been dry all night. "And Ma won't, what's more."

Mlle. Dupont, without knowing why, felt suddenly ashamed. She felt inexplicably sorry that there had ever been any thought of ejecting M. Larkin and his family.

"Nothing for it but the beach, I suppose," Pop said. "Bit difficult with Oscar, though."

Mlle. Dupont inquired if Pop meant sleeping on the beach and who Oscar was.

"The baby," Pop said, and added that he thought Oscar was a bit young to start night work.

Mlle. Dupont said, in French, how much she agreed. For some inexplicable reason she felt like weeping. She pressed the key harder and harder into the palm of her hand and listened confusedly while Pop inquired if there were other hotels.

"*Mais oui, certainement,*" she said, starting to think in French again, "*mais ils sont tous pleins*—all full. I know. All are full."

"Like the sky," Pop said, and with a slow wearying hand directed Mlle. Dupont's glance through the window, beyond which the relentless Atlantic was stretching with still grayer thickness its imprisoning curtain over port, quayside, and *plage.* "Fancy sleeping out in that lot. Eh?"

Mlle. Dupont found herself confronted by an emotional and physical dilemma: She was overcome by a violent desire to sneeze and at the same time wanted to weep again. She compromised by blowing her nose extremely hard on a very small lace handkerchief, almost masculine fashion, with a note like that from a trombone.

This stentorian call startled Pop into saying, "Sound as if you've caught your death. Well, this rain'll give the car a wash anyway."

Outside, in the hotel yard, the Rolls stood with expansive professorial dignity among a shabby crowd of down-at-heel pupils, the muddy family Citroëns, the Peugeots, the Simcas, the Renaults of the hotel's French guests.

"That is your car? The large one?"

Pop confessed that the Rolls-Royce was his and with a wave of modest pride drew Mlle. Dupont's attention to the gilt monograms on the doors. These, he assured her, gave the car both class and tone.

"Some duke or other," he said. "Some lord. Feller I bought it from wasn't sure."

At the word "lord" Mlle. Dupont found herself flushing, not from embarrassment or shyness, but from sheer excitement. It was on the tip of her tongue to inquire if Pop was actually an English milord or not but she checked herself in time, content merely to stare down at the monogrammed aristocracy of the Rolls, so distinctive and splendid among the muddy plebeian crowd of family four-seaters parked about it.

Nevertheless she found it impossible to stop herself from supposing that Pop was, perhaps, a milord. She had once before had an English milord, a real aristocrat, stay in the hotel. All day and even for dinner he had worn mud-colored corduroy trousers, much patched, a French railway porter's blue blouse, a vivid buttercup yellow neckerchief, and open green sandals. He had a large golden ambrosial mustache and thick, chestnut hair that was obviously not cut very often and curled in his neck like fine wood shavings. Mostly he smoked French workmen's cigarettes and sometimes a short English clay. He also took snuff and invariably blew his nose on a large red handkerchief.

From this Mlle. Dupont had come to the conclusion that the English were to some extent eccentric. All the lower classes tried to behave like aristocracy; all the aristocracy tried to behave like workmen. The higher you got in the social scale the worse people dressed. The men, like the milord, dressed in corduroys and baggy jackets and workmen's blouses and had patched elbows and knees and took snuff. The women dressed in thick imperishable sacks called tweeds, flat boatlike shoes, and putty-colored felt hats, or, if the weather became hot, in drooping canopies of cream shantung that looked like tattered sails on the gaunt masts of ships becalmed.

The English were also very unemotional. They were immensely restrained. They never gave way. The women said, "My deah!" and the men "Good God" and "Bad show" and sometimes even "Damme." They were bluff, unbelievably reticent, and very stiff. They were not only stiff with strangers, but much worse, they were stiff with each other and this, perhaps, Mlle. Dupont thought, explained a lot of things.

It might explain, perhaps, why some of them never got married. It might be that the milords, the true aristocrats, were a law unto themselves. As with the corduroys and clay pipes and snuff, they could set aside the mere conventions of wedlock lightly.

Suddenly she was quite sure in her own mind that M. Larkin was one of these: a milord whose only outward symbol of aristocracy was the Rolls and its flourishing gilded monograms. In no other way could she explain the charm, the ease of manner, the captivating, even impetuous inconsistencies.

"I have been thinking," she said. "There is perhaps just one room that possibly you and Madame could have."

"I hope it's got something for emergency," Pop said, thinking again of his elemental battle the night before.

"Please to come with me."

With a final sidelong glance at the Rolls—every time she looked at it now it shone like a princess, she thought, among a shabby crowd of kitchen workers—she led Pop out of the bureau and upstairs.

Once or twice on the way to the second floor—Ma and Pop and the children were all high up on the fourth—she apologized for the lack of an *ascenseur*. She supposed they really ought to have an *ascenseur* one day. On the other hand it was surprising how people got used to being without it and even, in time, learned to run upstairs.

"I haven't caught Ma at it yet," Pop said.

Following Mlle. Dupont upstairs, Pop was pleased to make two interesting discoveries: one that her legs, though her black dress was rather long, were very shapely. They were, he thought, not at all a bad-looking pair. From his lower angle on the stairs he discovered also that he could see the hem of her underslip. It was a black lace one.

This, he decided, was a bit of all right. It was perfick. It interested him greatly, his private theory being that all girls who wore black underwear were, in secret, highly passionate.

He set aside these interesting theoretical musings in order to hold open a bedroom door which Mlle. Dupont had now unlocked with one of her large bunch of keys.

"Please enter, Monsieur Larkin. Please to come in."

The room, though not so large as the one he and Ma were occupying two floors above, was prettily furnished and a good deal lighter. It had one large mahogany bed, a huge Breton linen chest, several chairs covered in rose-patterned cretonne, and curtains to match. It also had a basin with running water. It lacked, Pop noticed, that odor of linseed oil, drainpipes, French cigarettes, and leaking gas that penetrated every other part of the hotel. It seemed instead to be bathed in a strong but delicate air of lily of the valley.

"The room is not large," Mlle. Dupont said. She patted the bed with one hand. "But the bed is full size."

That, Pop said, was the spirit, and almost winked again.

"And you see the view is also good."

She stood at the window, still pressing a single key into the palm of her hand. Pop stood close beside her and looked out on a view of *plage*, sea, sand dunes, and distant pines. As he did so he couldn't help noticing that Mlle. Dupont herself also smelled deeply of lily of the valley.

"Very nice," Pop said. "I'm sure Ma would like this room."

"I hope so," she said. "It is my room."

Pop at once protested that this was far too good of her and under several of his rapid disquieting smiles of thanks Mlle. Dupont felt herself flushing again. There was no need to protest, she said, only to accept. The pleasure was entirely hers—and a great pleasure indeed it was. She merely wanted him to be happy, to be comfortable there.

"And you see there is even a little annex for the baby—in here," she said, and showed Pop into a sort of box room, just large enough for little Oscar to sleep in.

Laughing richly, Pop said he was absolutely sure they would be very comfortable in that pleasant room, with that nice bed, with that nice smell of lily of the valley.

"*C'est curieux, c'est extraordinaire,*" she said, starting to think in French again. "How did you know this?"

Pop drew a deep breath and told her, in a swift flick of description, almost ecstatic, how he had a kind of sixth sense about flowers and their perfumes.

"Acts like a key," he said. "Marigolds—I smell marigolds and in a jiff I'm back in Ma's front garden where I first met her. Bluebells—straightaway up in our wood at home. Cinnamon—and it's Christmas. Violets—only got to smell 'em and I'm back in the woods as a kid. The same," he concluded, "with your lily of the valley. Never be able to smell it again without thinking of this room."

Averting her face, watching the distant pines that she had already assured Pop several times were so exquisite in the strong Atlantic sunsets, Mlle. Dupont diffidently confessed that they were her favorite flowers, *le muguet*, they were all of springtime to her, as roses were of summer.

"They suit you," Pop said, and without waiting for comment or answer thanked her again for all her kindness about the room.

It was perfick, he said, he was tremendously grateful, and suddenly, feeling that mere words were not enough, he gave Mlle. Dupont an affectionate playful touch, half pinch, half pat, somewhere between the waist and the upper thigh.

Mlle. Dupont's reaction to this was to experience a small but exquisite palpitation in the region of her navel. She could find no coherent word either of English or French to say and she confusedly apologized once again about the stairs, "I am sorry it was so hard for Madame— the stairs. But it is old, the hotel. So much needs doing and one does not know what to do."

Pop, resisting an impulse to pinch Mademoiselle a second time and with more purpose, merely gazed at the rain-sodden landscape and said, "I know what I'd do."

"Yes?" Mlle. Dupont said. "What?"

"Pull it down," Pop said. "Pull the whole flipping lot down."

Mlle. Dupont, too shocked to speak, turned on him a face in which the mouth had fallen wide open. A moment later she was biting her tongue.

"But it belonged to my father and my grandfather. My family have always owned it."

"They're dead. It's dead," Pop said airily. "No use being sentimental. Comes a time—"

"I know we need an *ascenseur*. We need so much. But the money— here in France everything is so expensive. *C'est formidable.*"

"Always raise the money," Pop said. "Only want the ideas."

Mlle. Dupont laughed—Pop thought rather ironically.

"That may be for English milords and people who have Rolls-Royces."

"When you want anythink bad enough," Pop said blandly, "you'll always get it."

This casual statement of philosophy plunged Mlle. Dupont into a fresh silence of embarrassment, in which she played again with the key.

"Well, I'll go and tell Ma," Pop said, "she'll be tickled to death, I know."

His final disquieting perky smile caught Mlle. Dupont in a state of unreadiness again, so much so that she actually made several quick brushes at her greasy hair with the tips of her fingers, as if to show how calm and indifferent she was. Her ears, Pop saw, were pale and pretty and faintly flushed at the edges.

"I will see that your things are moved. Please tell Madame not to bother. And if there is something—"

"Only the wevver," Pop said. "The sun. That's all we want. Sol—"

"*Soleil.*"

"*Soleil,*" Pop said. "Masculine or feminine?"

"Feminine—no, no, masculine of course. Masculine. How stupid of me."

"Should have been feminine," Pop said, and gave her a last, brief, quick-knitted smile.

Long after he had gone downstairs Mlle. Dupont still stood at the window watching the unrelenting rain, trying with difficulty to reshape her thoughts on English milords, the strange, unaccountable, eccentric habits of the English, the Rolls-Royce and its monograms, and the way M. Larkin, who seemed so unlike the English of tradition, possessed the secret of a key through the scents of flowers to events and places long-distant, forgotten, and even lost, as for example with lilies of the valley, *les muguets*, her favorite flowers.

5

After three days the sun began to shine, though not very much, mostly in fitful bursts, still whitish and watered down. A steady temperate wind blew in from the Atlantic, generally raising clouds of sand and at times bristling saltily. The evenings were like December.

From time to time it was just warm enough for Mariette and Ma to shed wraps and sweaters and lie in bikinis on the little smooth-sanded *plage*. Mariette's figure, in spite of what Pop thought about its slight narrowing down since marriage, was well suited to the bikini. Her breasts were round but firm, girlishly fresh but quite mature. Her waist was delicate and narrow, with hips of pear-shaped line. From behind she appeared to have a beautiful little saddle, to which the lower of the bikini's three scarlet triangles was tied with the slenderest of strings.

Ma was not so lucky. She hadn't been able to get a bikini quite large enough to fit her. They didn't go quite as high as Ma in size. But there was, as she remarked, nothing much to them and she had consequently run up two for herself: one in bright petunia purple, her favorite color, and the other in brilliant salmon rose.

Primrose, Petunia, Zinnia, and Victoria all wore bikinis too, in shades of royal blue, green, pink, yellow, and pure white which they changed from day to day. Ma wasn't having her children outdone by any Froggy kids, some of whom she noticed had their hair dyed, generally red, blond, or black, sometimes to match their mother's.

On the whole Ma wasn't much impressed by Froggy women, young or old. The young girls who lay or pranced about the *plage* all looked what Pop called pale about the gills; they were very pasty, like Mlle. Dupont, and looked decidedly unwell about the eyes; they either wore no lipstick at all or far too much of it in the palest of puce and parma violet shades.

Their necks always looked surprisingly yellow too. Ma thought, a funny suet sort of color, and she was certain sure they all slept in their

makeup. Their hair looked uncombed and tatty and they seemed generally to wear it long, either untied or in ponytails, but occasionally they
wore it crimped up, in curious frontal rolls that achieved the effect of
making their foreheads recede or disappear.

And their figures were nothing, Ma thought, absolutely nothing.
"Compared with our Mariette's," Ma reckoned, "you'd think they
were boys with a few pimples here and there. I thought French girls
were supposed to be so chick and all that. Blow me, some of 'em don't
even shave where they ought to."

She felt quite sorry for Pop in this respect. There was hardly anything for him to look at on the *plage*. Even Edith Pilchester had more
to call her own, Ma thought, than some of these. Even Mlle. Dupont
had a certain firmness of chest and lower line. She did at least look neat
and tidy, whereas most of the mamas who sat about in beach chairs or
even in the shelter of red-and-white-striped tents, intensely gossiping
and knitting, either looked hopelessly overdressed, with two extra
cardigans to keep out the temperate westerly wind, or like molting
hawks restlessly awaiting a false move by younger prey.

The young men, on the other hand, were magnificent. Ma had never
seen anything like it. All of them seemed to be tall, athletic, bronzed,
and lissome. Innumerable protruding knots of muscle stuck brownly
out from all over them, accentuating arms, shoulders, chest, and buttocks. Their hair was always perfectly crimped and waved and around
their middles they wore nothing but skintight pudding bags tied with
string.

The young men occupied the beach all day, tirelessly exercising
themselves. They leapt in perpendicular fashion in the air, scissoring
brown legs. They stood on their heads, did statuesque handstands, or
pranced about like restless straining racehorses. They played leapfrog
or ran about square-chested, like Grecian runners, hair slightly flowing,
breasting the wind. They climbed invisible ropes with arms plaited
with brown muscle or did long, silent, earnest, dedicatory breathing
exercises for the abdomen and chest.

But mostly they played with balls: large, highly colored balls, two or
three feet in diameter, in segments of scarlet and green, or yellow and
violet, so inflated and so light that the Atlantic wind, when it caught
them, rolled them swiftly away across acres of bare beach into distances of sea and dune and pine. When this happened they showed new
high prowess as athletes, running after the balls in fleeting file or in
handsome echelon, Greek-like again, hair flowing, racing the wind.

Mr. Charlton, who could see no point in these exercises, was glad merely to relax with Mariette in the sun, reading detective stories or occasionally turning an eye on Mariette, moving her perfect young body over to brown on the other side, like a young plump chicken on a spit. He felt mostly relaxed and contented, even when sometimes aroused by the voice of Ma, "Fetch everybody ice cream, Charley, will you? There's a dear. Big ones. Bring two for everybody. And some nuts."

One of the few things Ma was agreeably surprised about in France was the fact that they had ice cream and nuts. She had been afraid they wouldn't. At least that made it a bit more civilized.

Pop too was content. He liked merely to lie in the sun and look at the sky. With his hypersensitive, keenly developed sense of smell he could lie for hours breathing the scent of sea and seaweed, sun-dried rocks and pines, tarry boats and fish being unloaded at the quay. He could translate these things into separate living scenes without opening his eyes at all, just as he could smell lily of the valley in imagination and recapture Mlle. Dupont clear and close to him.

Over the past day or two it had struck him that Mlle. Dupont had become more and more refreshingly attentive. She laughed whenever he met her on the stairs. Was the food right for M. Larkin? Did Madame and the family like it? Were the children happy? Was there some special dish they would like? Pop hadn't the heart to tell her he thought the food was mostly a terrible mistake and that what he really wanted was rice pudding, stewed plums, and roast beef and Yorkshire. He merely joked, "Ma says it suits her a treat. She's slimming. Taken off pounds."

"If there is something special you prefer at any time please to tell me. Sans supplément, of course. Please just to say."

On the fifth morning she called him into the bureau in order to give him back the passports, apologizing at the same time for keeping them so long. She also said, "I have been thinking that you might care to take an excursion on the eighth—that is, to Le Folgoët. There is a great pardon there that day. It is the greatest and most beautiful pardon we have in Finistère."

"Pardon?" Pop had no idea what a pardon was but he listened respectfully as Mlle. Dupont went on to explain its religious significance and beauty.

"Not much on religion," he confessed. "Don't care for dog collars."

"Perhaps Madame and the children would care to go," she said. "You must please tell me if they do. I can give them all directions."

Up to that moment, rather absentmindedly, Mlle. Dupont had kept the passports in her hands. Suddenly she remembered them and handed them back to Pop, giving a little nervous laugh at the same time.

Pop grinned quickly as he took the passports and asked to know what had amused her.

It was quite a little thing, Mlle. Dupont said, just something that had occurred to her.

"What?" Pop said.

"*Ce sont les passeports,*" she said, starting once again nervously thinking in French. "It is rather *curieux.* A little bit funny."

"Oh?" Pop said. "How's that?"

"It was when I was looking at the passports this morning," Mlle. Dupont said. "It was *très curieux*—very *curieux*—but it occurred to me that if you are not married you are still a single man?"

She laughed quickly and rather self-consciously and Pop, in his customary rousing fashion, laughed too. That, he confessed, had never occurred to him either.

"Single chap, eh?" he said. "Well, well."

That afternoon, when he went back to the *plage* after having a short after-lunch nap with Ma on the bed, he found Mr. Charlton in a state of unusual restlessness.

Charley, who had hitherto been fairly content, had made a disturbing discovery. He had rumbled what the business of the big sailing colored balls was all about. They were all part of a design for the ensnarement, if not seduction, of Mariette.

The young Frenchmen, he had at last discovered, had every wind direction beautifully worked out. In that way they could be sure that the balls would always float toward her, so that every five minutes or so they would find it necessary to invade the precious territory of scarlet bikini and naked flesh and, with voluble apologies, laughter, and much athletic show, recapture them.

Mr. Charlton made it clear he didn't care for it at all.

On the morning of the eighth Pop lay alone on the *plage*, basking for the first time in the true heat of the sun. The sky was actually the color Mr. Charlton had so confidently predicted it would be. It hung overhead like a cornflower, brightest blue to the very distant edges of a sea that seemed to have receded across miles of new-bleached sand to the hazy rim of the world.

The extrasensory impressions that were so lively in him that morning told him that this was perfick. It couldn't possibly be more perfick anywhere, even to go off to a *pardon,* however beautiful, as Ma and all the rest had done. Only Mariette, it seemed, had shown any reluctance to go to the great *pardon* of Le Folgoët, largely on the ground that it would interfere with her scheme for browning her body all over, but Charley had rumbled that. He had shown swift and admirable marital firmness and had, to Pop's great satisfaction, insisted she should go.

So by ten o'clock the Rolls was away, Mariette driving, the boot packed with a large picnic lunch of Mlle. Dupont's preparing, together with several bottles of *vin rosé* and bags of peaches, sweet white grapes, and pears. The children now liked *vin rosé* as much as ice cream and much more than orange juice and Ma was very glad. She thought it was very good for them.

As the Rolls drove away she was already busy giving little Oscar a drop of refreshment and with a free hand waving "Have a good time" to Pop, who called back that he had the *Times* of the day before yesterday and that it wouldn't be long before he went down to read it over a snifter and watch the Breton women dozing in their stiff white hats and the sardine boats bringing in their catches to the quay.

"Perfick," he kept saying to himself in the sun. "Perfick. Absolutely perfick." He could actually feel the early September heat, bristling with its heavy Atlantic salt, burning his chest and thighs and shoulders. "Perfick. Good as champagne."

Twenty minutes later he was asleep on his face and woke only just before midday—a time when the *plage* always emptied itself so suddenly and completely of people that it was as if a plague had struck it—to hear an elegant voice saying, "Hullo, there. *Comment ça va, mon chéri?* How's the beauty sleep, darling? It's me."

Pop turned and looked up. Above him a hatless vision, in shirt and slacks of a warm pale shade of apricot, was sitting on the seawall above the *plage*. Down over the sand dangled the long, languid legs of Angela Snow, his kindred spirit of the summer party of a year before.

Pop was instantly glad of Charley's brief tuition in French and promptly leapt to his feet and said,

"*Très bien, merci! Et vous aussi,* my old firework?"

"Scream," she said. "You speak the language!"

"Just enough," Pop said. "Count up to ten and ask for vin rosy."

"Been dying to see someone who's fun and here you are."

Angela Snow gave a serpentine twist of her body and leapt down to the sand. Her hair had a glorious gold-white sheen on it and she gave the impression of having chosen the slacks and shirt not to match it but to heighten it and make it shine more brilliantly. Her pretty feet were bare except for flat yellow sandals that simply slipped on, Chinese fashion, without a tie.

When she sat down her long legs curled themselves loosely underneath her. Her clear olive eyes seemed even larger than Pop remembered them and she seemed to embrace him with them as she asked him all about himself, how he came to be there, in this hole, and all that.

"Holiday," Pop said.

"Not alone?" Her usually languid voice was quick, even eager.

Pop at once explained about the family and how everyone else had gone to the great *pardon* at Le Folgoët.

"Iris too," she said. "My sister. Terribly religious, Iris. Got the most god-awful relidge, Iris has."

Smiling to the uttermost edges of her large pellucid olive eyes, she asked Pop, in turn, if he was very relidge.

Pop said he wasn't very.

"No particular brand, you mean?"

Pop confessed he had no particular brand. He supposed if it came to a definition he would say that being alive was his relidge—that and earth and woods and flowers and nightingales and all that sort of lark and enjoying it and not preventing other people doing so.

"Wouldn't do for Iris," Angela Snow said. "Couldn't have that, darling. Couldn't sell her that. She's an Ill-fare Stater. The iller you fare the gooder you are."

Pop shook his head. Family throwback? he suggested.

"Got to lacerate yourself, according to Iris. Beds of nails. Fakir stuff."

"Sackcloth and ashes?" Pop suggested.

"Dishcloth and wet breeches," Angela Snow said, "that's Iris. A positive wetter. Even says damp prayers. Sobs away half the time."

Not much of a chum on holiday, Pop suggested. Why did she come?

"My idea," Angela Snow said. "Thought I might find some arresting Breton fisherman to bed her down with. Sort of cure. Don't know of an arresting somebody, *chéri*, do you?"

Pop said he didn't and laughed. He much enjoyed being called darling and *chéri* by Angela Snow.

"And how," she said, "are the virgins?"

Throwing back her head, Angela Snow laughed with all the rippling limpidity of a carillon about the virgins. She'd never forgotten the virgins. Seven of them and so foolish, riding on the donkeys at Pop's derby in the summer gymkhana a year before. Almost needed changing still, she confessed, every time she thought of them. Dear virgins.

"Iris is one," she said. "The dears do make such hard work of it."

"This place is full of 'em," Pop said.

"You don't say?"

Pop referred her to the boyish female skinnies, largely unwashed, who disported themselves listlessly about the *plage*. Ma and he had discussed them thoroughly. Terrible little show-offs, they thought, with nothing to show. And French girls supposed to be so chick an' all. And fast. Even young Montgomery was bored.

"Terribly strict country still," Angela Snow said. "Big mother is watching you and all that."

"Nothing for the Froggy boys to do but make eyes at Mariette."

"Can't blame 'em," she said. "She's inherited all her father's virtues."

Virtues? Pop laughed and said he didn't think he'd got very many of them.

"No?" Angela Snow said, and gave him a smile of luscious simplicity.

Free to look about him again, Pop saw that the *plage* had miraculously emptied itself, as always, at the stroke of noon. In five minutes every *salle à manger* in the place would be full of ravenous masticators. The *potage cultivateur* would be on, stemming the first pangs of the *pensionnaires*. Everywhere the bread slicers would be working overtime.

Suddenly overcome by a sharp recollection that if you weren't there on time you fell behind in the noon race for nourishment and never really caught up again, Pop half got to his feet and said, "Suppose I ought to get back to the Beau Rivage. Before the troughs are empty."

"Any good?" she asked, "the Beau Rivage?"

Pop was obliged to confess he thought it terrible.

"Bad grub?"

That was the worst part of it, Pop said. He yearned for a good drop of—

"Complain, sweetie, complain."

Pop confessed that he hadn't the heart to complain to Mlle. Dupont. She probably did her best.

"You must, darling. It's the only way. I'm the great complainer of all time. The great table banger. And who's this Dupont?"

Pop explained about Mlle. Dupont while Angela Snow listened with detachment, unsympathetically.

"All too obviously another one," she said. "Like Iris. Plain as a pikestaff, sweetie."

Pop's insides were light with hunger. Sleep and the bristling air of morning had made him feel empty and fragile as a husk.

"Invite me to lunch one day," she said, "and I'll give a demonstration of the arch-complainer."

What about lunch today? Pop said. He couldn't go on much longer.

"Only place in this hole is Pierre's," Angela Snow said. "Out there, toward the forest. About ten minutes, if you don't mind walking."

Pop said he hoped his legs would carry him. Angela Snow laughed in reply, again in her high, infectious rippling fashion, and actually took Pop's arm in her soft, slender fingers.

"I'll see you don't fall by the wayside, chum. Lean on me, *chéri*."

Thus fortified, Pop bore up remarkably well until they reached Pierre's, which stood in a clearing where forest and sand joined at the deep central cup of the bay. All his hypersensitive impressions, heightened still further by the growing heat of sun, baking sand, seaweed, and pines, were now fused together in wild galloping pangs of hunger.

Pierre's appeared to be a shack built of bits of bamboo, pine boughs, and old orange boxes. It looked, Pop thought, remarkably like an abandoned coal shed.

Outside it a few tables without cloths, apparently knocked up out of driftwood, were sheltered by the same number of blue and white umbrellas. Charcoal was smoking away slowly under an iron grid built above bricks. A sign stuck on a pole said TOILETTE and pointed to a flimsy arrangement of almost transparent sacks slung up behind a tree.

Angela Snow and Pop sat down at a table and Angela Snow said this was the greatest place for food you ever came across. The only problem was whether Pierre would like you. If he didn't he wouldn't serve you. He liked to pick his customers.

"Mad on me," she said.

"Hullo, lousy," Pierre said. "Why bloody hell you turn up?" and then stood over the table to slop into thick glasses two large *camparis* which nobody had ordered.

Angela Snow shook back her sumptuous golden hair and with her slow drawling voice and luscious smile gave back as good as she got.

"How now, brown sow?" she said. "This is my friend Mr. Larkin. Mr. Larkin—Pierre. Mr. Larkin keeps pigs—he'll understand you."

Pop actually half rose to shake hands but relapsed at once when

Pierre said, "Hope you enjoy yourself. What you want to eat? I know. Don't say. Rossbiff, eh?"

This was exactly what Pop did want and his juices at once started flowing madly in anticipation.

"Well, you won't get, see? Today you get *moules, châteaubriant*, and the best *brie* your English bloody nose ever stank of and like it."

"Scream," Angela Snow said. "Killing."

She laughed again in her high-ringing fashion and Pierre gave a grin part sugary, part lascivious, his thick lips opening to reveal a row of blackened teeth punctuated in the center by a positive doorknob of gold. The rest of his sunburned body, which Pop thought was almost as wide as Ma's, suffered from these same unclean extravagances. His blue-striped sweatshirt seemed to have been dipped in candle grease. His uncut black hair could have been knotted in his neck. Glimpses of a belly both hairy and sweaty appeared from time to time between the bottom edge of his shirt and the tops of his trousers, which were held up by some sort of bellrope, bright scarlet and hung with gilded tassels.

"And what wine you want?"

"Vin rosy," Pop said.

"Rosy, rosy, rosy," Pierre said. "Well, we don't have rosy, rosy, rosy. Here you bloddy well have what you get and like it."

"Mad," Angela Snow said. "Killing me."

Pop thought it would kill him too and was openly relieved when Pierre went away, dragging one foot, like a potbellied crab crawling across the sand.

"Going to bring Iris here one day," Angela Snow said. "Pierre's the type for her. Half an hour with him and she'd never be the same again."

Pop was positive she wouldn't be.

"Fun, isn't it?" Angela Snow said. "Don't you think so? Awful fun. And the food celestial."

Pop was busy drinking *campari* for the first time and decided he didn't like it.

"These are the only places," Angela Snow said. "Real France. All the atmosphere. Piquant somehow—delish."

Scooping up his mussels and thinking, like Ma, that he wasn't going to get very fat on this lark, Pop watched Pierre grilling the *châteaubriant* over a glowing bed of charcoal. Now and then Pierre scratched his long black hair or the hairs on his chest and sometimes he spat over the grill into the sand.

Watching him, Pop was reminded of Charley's opinion that the

French were the elite of Europe. France was the place. Everything so cultured.

"Two bloddy steaks for two bloddy English. *Bon appétit.*"

A certain belching contempt filled the glowing autumn air. This, however, was merely yet another signal for Angela Snow to break into fresh peals of laughter and say what awful fun it was.

"A change from the deadly Dupont and all that anyway, darling," she said.

It certainly was, Pop said, and then turned with intense relish to tackle the *châteaubriant* and its accompanying *pommes frites*. After a struggle of five minutes or so it struck him that the meat was, perhaps, a piece of dog. The charred rectangle, when cut, was icy blue inside and exuded large quantities of blood. This, like the *pommes frites*, was stone-cold. The inner sinews of the meat itself, so tenaciously bound to each other that nothing could separate them, were stone-cold too.

"Terribly naughty of me," Angela Snow said. "You'd have liked mustard, wouldn't you?"

Pop still struggling, said it didn't matter. Nevertheless Angela Snow said she'd ask for it, and it turned out to be English when it came.

"Suppose it's *très snob*, wouldn't you think perhaps?" she said. "English mustard?"

Pop, masticating hard at bits of dog, supposed it was. *Très snob*—rather good expression, he thought. He must tell Ma.

"How about some cheese? Or fruit perhaps?"

Pop, who was feeling a little less light, but not much, said he fancied both.

For the next half hour it was delicious to sit in the open air, on the edge of the pines, and eat cheese, peel big yellow peaches, and suck grapes; and also, Pop thought, to watch newly arrived customers struggling with their rectangles of charred dog.

Now and then Pierre, ruder and louder as he warmed up to his work, poured brandy over the *châteaubriants* and set them alight. Dramatic flames shot into the air, making the customers look keener than ever in anticipation. Pop enjoyed watching this and made Angela Snow laugh ringingly by saying that he supposed this was the way you made hot dog.

"And coffee. What will you have with your coffee?"

Pop said he fancied a Rolls-Royce.

"One of your blinders?"

Pop said it was; though Red Bull was stronger.

"You think Pierre can mix it?"

"Easy," Pop said. "Half vermouth, quarter whiskey, quarter gin, dash of orange bitters."

"That'll suit me too," she said.

"Better make 'em doubles," Pop said. "Easier somehow."

Pierre seemed unexpectedly impressed by the privilege of mixing strange and special drinks and momentarily dropped all rudeness to become softly, almost obsequiously polite; probably, Pop thought, because it was another case of *très snob*.

Out in the bay the copper sails of departing fishing boats lit up the blue cornflower of sky with such intensity in the sunlight that they too were triangles of fire. All illumination too, Angela Snow's hair seemed to shine more beautifully when broken pine shadow crossed it and left it free again as the sun moved over the sand.

Soon the double Rolls-Royces had made Pop feel more like himself and he responded with an involuntary belch and a robust "Perfick!" when Angela Snow suggested a short siesta in the dunes.

"I'll get the bill," he said.

"No, no," she said. "My party."

"Not on your nelly," Pop said.

"Darling, that's not nice. I asked you."

"I'm paying," Pop said with all his charm. "You think I don't know my technique? Rhubarb."

When the bill came Pop looked at it and suddenly felt cold. There were so many items and figures that he could neither disentangle them nor add them up. His eye merely grasped at a few painful essentials and blinked the rest.

The portions of charred dog had each cost 1,200 francs; the *moules marinières* 700 francs; the cheese 500 francs; the double Rolls-Royces each 1,400 francs, making a final total, with tax on top of service and supplement on top of tax, of 11,650 francs.

As he fumbled to pay this, a last alarming item caught his eye.

"What's *couvert?*" he said. "What the blazes is *couvert?* We never had *couvert.*"

Angela Snow laughed in her most celestial fashion.

"That," she explained to him, "was just the breathing charge."

Pop, who was never one to be unduly miserable over the cost of pleasure, thought this was very funny and was still laughing loudly about it when they reached the dunes. He must tell Ma that one: the *très snob* lark and the breathing charge. Jolly good, both of them.

He was still more delighted when Angela Snow's first act on reaching the sand dunes was to cast off her shirt and drop her apricot slacks and stand before him in a yellow bikini so sparsely cut that nothing really separated her from pure golden nakedness.

"My God, this is good," she said, and lay flat on her back in a nest of sand. "This is good. Where are you?"

Pop didn't know quite where he was. He felt more than slightly lost and dazzled.

"Come and lie down with me, *chéri*. Come on."

This invitation was delivered with such bewitching languor that Pop was at her side, half in a dream, before he really knew it. Almost at once she closed her eyes. The deep olive lids, shutting out the large pellucid eyes that were always so warm and embracing, seemed now to offer him the further invitation to take in the whole pattern of her long slender body: the slim beautiful legs and arms, the sloping shoulders and the tiny perfectly scooped saltcellars below the neck, the small but upright breasts, and the navel reposing centrally below them like, Pop thought, a perfick little winkle shell.

As if knowing quite well that he was taking his fill of these things, and with some pleasure, she let her eyes remain closed for fully two minutes before opening them again.

Then she smiled, still a languid smile but also rather fixed.

"Suppose you know I'm madly in love with you?"

Pop confessed he didn't know. It was news.

"Outrageously. All-consuming," she said. "Night and day."

"Jolly good," Pop said. "Perfick."

"Not on your nelly," she said. "It's hell."

A recurrent lick or two of fire from the Rolls-Royce raced about Pop's veins and caused him to say that this was crazy.

"Right first time," she said. "Crazy. Mad. Mad as those hares."

For crying out gently, Pop thought. That was bad. By the way, had she ever seen those hares?

"No," she said. "Tell me."

Watching those pellucid olive eyes that now seemed to have added a look of mystery to their largeness, Pop told her about the hares: the strange wild gambolings that you would see in March, the leaping, dancing business of spring courtship.

"Fascinating," she said. "That would be a thrill."

"Bit mysterious," Pop said. "All that tearing about and dancing."

"Not more than us," she said. "What do we dance for? I mean all that stuff in Freud."

What, she asked, did he feel about Freud?

"Never touch it," Pop said.

"Scream," she said. "I love you."

She laughed so much at this that it was fully a minute before she was calm again and said, "Here's me madly in love with you ever since that virgin-firework lark and you've never even kissed me."

This was a state of affairs, Pop said, that could be remedied with no delay at all.

A second later he was lying at her side, kissing her for the first time. He had always been a great believer in first times, his theory being that there might never be another, especially where women were concerned, and now, with velvet artistry, one hand softly under her small left breast, he made the kiss last for ten minutes or more.

This experience left even Angela Snow slightly light-headed. She seemed to come around, already slightly tipsy after the wine, as if after a deep, passionate faint. Her large eyes blinked slowly, in a dream, and there might even have been a tear of emotion in them as she smiled.

He must save one of those for Iris sometime, she said in a languid attempt at light-heartedness, and what a lucky creature his wife was.

It was essential to keep all those things, Pop thought, on a light-hearted level. Else it wouldn't be fair to Ma. This now seemed the critical moment with Angela Snow and he laughed resoundingly.

"What's funny?" she said.

"Well," Pop said, "if everybody had their right I haven't got a wife."

"Joke."

It certainly was a bit of a lark, Pop said, when you thought of it. Him and Ma not married. And Ma on a separate passport an' all. Did Angela mean she'd never heard?

"Not a peep," she said. She'd concluded from the offspring alone that all was well.

"Must get it done some day," Pop said. "No good. You know we've had another since I saw you?"

Unsurprised, Angela Snow held him in a gaze fully recovered from its first emotional storm and said with languor, "Good show. Means you're still agile, virile, and fertile."

Pop said he hoped so and was so amused and even slightly flattered that he granted her the indulgence of a second kiss, holding her right breast this time, again with prolonged tenderness.

Passion and fervor left their mark on Angela Snow even more deeply than before and as she came around a second time she again felt it necessary to check emotion with yet another touch of flippancy.

"Don't know which I liked best. The one from the married man I had first, or the single one I had second."

"Mlle. Dupont knows I'm not married too. Rumbled it from the passports."

"Oh, she does, does she?"

And once again she gave him a smile of luscious, penetrative simplicity.

They lay on the dunes, watching the sun across the bay and occasional triangles of sail fire cut across the blue horizon, for the rest of the afternoon. As time went on her almost naked body grew warmer and warmer in the sun. The sand of the dunes became quite hot to the touch as the sun swung westward and most of the time Pop couldn't help thinking what a beautiful place it would be for Mariette and Charley to try out sometime. It might encourage them a bit.

At last, when it was time to go, Angela Snow said, "See you soon, poppet. Don't let it be long. The nerves won't stand it."

"Come and have lunch at the hotel one day," Pop said. "Ma'd love to see you."

"Even the hotel," she said. "Anywhere. But don't let it be long."

Finally, with a long quiet sigh, she drew on her slacks and Pop said good-bye to what he thought, with pleasure but detachment, was the nicest body he had ever seen since he first met Ma.

That night, as he sat in bed reading the *Times* and smoking his late cigar, he broke off several times from reading to tell Ma about Angela Snow, the terrible lunch, the bill, the *très snob* lark, and the breathing charge.

Ma said she was very pleased about Angela Snow; it had made his afternoon.

"Get around to kissing her?"

Pop confessed that he had, but Ma, huge and restful in transparent nightgown after a day that had been a strange mixture of religion and fair, French fish-and-chips and saints, remained quietly unperturbed.

"Says she's in love with me."

"That pleased you, I'll bet. Nice girl. I like her. Bit of a card."

For the third or fourth time that evening Pop remarked that he was thirsty. He expected it was the mussels. All shellfish made him thirsty.

"Well, go down and get a drink," Ma said. "Bring me one too."

Pop said this was a good idea and got out of bed to put on a silk dressing gown vividly embroidered in green and purple with vast

Asiatic dragons, a last-minute holiday present from Ma, remembering
something else as he did so.

"Ma, you remember that lot of pickled cucumbers, gherkins or
whatever they were, I had left over from that army surplus deal? The
one I made nearly six thousand out of?"

"The ones you got stored in the top barn?" Ma said. "I know."

Pop chuckled ripely.

"Hocked 'em all to one of the fishing boat skippers this afternoon
after Angela had gone," he said. "Seems they're just what they want to
pep up their diet with. Terrible monotonous diet they have, these
Froggy fishermen. Potatoes and fish all boiled up together. Saw 'em
doing it. And gallons of wine."

"Hope you'll get paid."

"Coming over to pick 'em up himself and pay me," Pop said. "Puts
in to Shoreham sometimes. What do you want—champagne?"

"Just what I could do with," Ma said.

Pop, going downstairs, found Mlle. Dupont going over her books in
the bureau. She got up to greet him in her customary nervous fashion,
fearing another complaint, but Pop at once put her at rest by explaining
about the champagne.

"And what mark of champagne do you prefer, Monsieur Larkin?"

The best champagne Pop could ever recall drinking was something
called Bollinger '29 at a big Hunt Ball at home, just before the war.

He mentioned this but Mlle. Dupont shook her head. "In all France
I do not think you could now find one bottle of Bollinger '29. All is
past of that year."

"Pity," Pop said.

"But I have Bollinger '34. That too is good."

That, Pop said, would do him all right.

Later he insisted on carrying it upstairs himself: ice bucket and bottle
and glasses on a tray. As he did so Mlle. Dupont stood in her habitual
position at the foot of the stairs and watched him in soft admiration,
dreamily thinking.

Day by day it was becoming increasingly clear to her that M. Larkin
was a milord. Only a milord could smoke such expensive cigars in bed
at night and ask for Bollinger '29. Only a milord could walk the
quayside with such an elegant lady as she had seen him pass the hotel
with that afternoon: so golden and aristocratic in her elegant apricot
slacks.

At the turn of the stairs Pop turned, cocked his head to one side, and
looked back.

"*Bonsoir, mademoiselle, dormez bien,*" he said nippily. "Sleep well."

"*Bonsoir,*" she said. "Sleep well, milord."

Pop thought that this milord lark just about took the biscuit and he told Ma all about it as he uncorked the champagne in the bedroom.

"Called me my lord, Ma," he said. "What price that?"

Ma, who sat up in bed popping Chanel No. 5 down her bosom, thought it was a scream.

"Lord Larkin," she said. "Sounds all right, though. Not half bad. I think it sounds perfick, don't you?"

Pop said he certainly did and, laughing softly, poured out the champagne. In fact it was more than perfick.

"I think it's jolly *très snob*, Ma," he said, "don't you? Very *très snob*."

6

Pop began to watch events on the *plage* with growing uneasiness, if not dismay. Things were not going well at all. It was clear as daylight that Mariette and Charley were right off hooks.

Periodically he talked to Ma about it, but Ma seemed quite indifferent, beautifully unperturbed. With great placidity she sat all day watching the sea, the French mamas, the leaping young gods, the tatty little French girls, and the fishing boats putting out to sea. She knitted, read magazines, sunbathed, and gave little Oscar the refreshment he needed, serenely unconcerned.

"What's Mariette sulking for?" Pop wanted to know. "Damnit, she hardly speaks to Charley nowadays."

Ma made the astonishing suggestion that it was probably lack of variety.

"Variety?" Pop said. This was beyond him. "Variety in what?"

"Before she was married she never had less than two or three running after her," Ma said. "Now she's only got Charley."

Pop, who had never looked at it in this way, had nothing to say, and Ma went on, "What do you think I let you run around with Angela Snow and old Edith Pilchester for?"

Pop said blandly he hadn't the foggiest.

"Variety," Ma said serenely. "Variety."

Pop still couldn't understand why Mariette should always seem to be sulking. At this rate he and Ma would be fifty before they had any grandchildren—a terrible thing. Why were them two always off hooks? Did Ma think that it was possibly some defect in Charley's technique? And if so should he have a quiet word with Charley on the matter?

"Don't you do no such thing," Ma said. "I've had a word already."

"With Charley?"

"No, with Mariette."

Setting aside the notion that perhaps the whole matter was bound up in some curious feminine secret, Pop said, "Give her any ideas?"

"Yes," Ma said. "I did. I told her to start flirting."

Pop whistled. Even he was stunned with surprise.

Ma said she didn't see that there was anything to be surprised about. Even the twins and Primrose flirted. Even Victoria had started. Didn't Pop use his optics nowadays? Hadn't he seen Zinnia and Petunia making eyes at those two little black-eyed French boys who wore such funny little pinafores? They were at it all day. They had them in a tizzy.

"Flirting's good for people," Ma said. "It's like a tonic. You ought to know."

Pop laughed and asked Ma if she'd thought of going in for a little herself.

"I might," she said. "Only it's a bit difficult with Oscar."

Pop was pleased at this and asked Ma if she thought a little drop of flirting now and then would do Charley any harm?

"Flirting with who?" Ma, who was sitting placidly on the sand, huge pale legs outstretched, indicated with a contemptuous wave of her heavily ringed fingers the pallid creatures who populated the *plage* on every side. "With this tatty lot? I pity him."

Pop said he was thinking more of somebody like Angela Snow. She could teach him a thing or two.

"You should know," she said. "He's not her type, though. Not like you are."

"She's got a sister," Pop said. "Very religious."

"Give the poor chap a chance," she said. "I'm trying to make it easy for him. Not—"

She broke off and looked at her wristwatch. It was ten o'clock: time to give Oscar a drop of refreshment. With a slight sigh she picked him up from where he had been lying with some of her own reposeful placidity on a large clean diaper and then dropped one side of her magenta bikini top and produced a handsome expanse of bosom like a full-blown milky balloon. Into this Oscar buried himself with eager rapidity while Ma went on.

"Oh, talking about flirting and all that, I think we're going to have trouble with our Primrose."

Primrose was eleven; even Pop, very faintly surprised, thought that was a bit dodgy.

"Trouble? How?"

"In love. Bad."

Pop said he'd go to Jericho. In love? How was that?

"How?" Ma said. "What do you mean, how? Naturally, that's how. Developing early, that's how. Like I did."

Ah well, Pop said, that was different. That was the right spirit. Nothing like starting young. Who was it? Not some French boy?

"Two," Ma said.

Pop, laughing good-naturedly, remarked that he supposed there was safety in numbers, to which Ma firmly shook her head.

"That's just it. Can't sleep at night. She's trying to give one of 'em up and can't decide which one it's got to be."

"Thought you said it was a good thing?" Pop said.

"Said what was a good thing?"

Pop, feeling himself to be rather sharp, laughed again.

"Variety."

Instead of laughing in reply Ma regarded him with something like severity over the top of little Oscar's bald dumpling of a head.

"Sometimes I'm surprised at you, Sid Larkin," she said. It was always a bit of a bad sign when she called him Sid Larkin. "It's a very tricky age. You'll have to be careful what you say to her."

"Me?" Pop said. "Haven't said a word."

Ma, deftly shifting little Oscar from one side of her bosom to the other, looked at him for some seconds before answering, this time with a glance more mysterious than severe, so that he was almost afraid she was going to call him Sid Larkin again. That would have been a bit much. She only did it once or twice a year—so's he'd know it really meant something when she did.

"No," she said darkly, "you haven't. But you will."

"Oh?" he said. "When?"

"When the time comes," Ma said blandly, "when the time comes."

Ma had him properly guessing now. He couldn't rumble her at all. There was something behind that Sid Larkin touch, he thought, and he was still trying to fathom what it was when Ma, in her habitually unruffled way, abruptly changed the subject by saying, "Going back to Charley. I think a walk would do him more good. He sits on this beach too long. He's moping. Take him down to the harbor and have a drink with one of your fishermen friends. Didn't you say you had another deal cooking?"

That was right, Pop said. He had. He'd got the Froggy skipper interested in a hundred cases of that tinned gherkins in vinegar that he hadn't been able to hock to anybody else up to now. It would show about 300 percent if it came off. Nothing very big, but it would help to keep the pot boiling.

"Good idea," he said.

He put one finger into his mouth and with a sudden piercing whistle, shrill as diamond on glass, startled the entire *plage* into thinking a train was coming. Mr. Charlton, who was idly picking up shells and trying not to notice the antics of the godlike young Frenchmen prancing all about him, recognized the sign at once and came strolling over.

"Put your top hat on, Charley old man," Pop said. "I'm taking you down to the harbor for a wet. Fit?"

Charley said he was fit and called a few words of explanation to Mariette, who had discarded her bikini for a remarkable strapless sunsuit in brilliant cinnamon with a boned front that uplifted and enlarged her bust to a sumptuous and thrilling degree.

The balls would be floating over any moment now, Charley thought, and he wondered suddenly if he had the courage to leave her there. She looked maddeningly beautiful, as she always did when sulky. Today she was all steamy voluptuousness, lying there languidly pouting in the warm morning sun, and he actually called, "You're really absolutely sure you don't mind if I go?"

Mariette made no sign. It was Ma who shook her head. Pop was, after all, right about Charley's technique. There really were some serious gaps in it. He really ought to use his loaf sometimes.

"Darling!" he called.

"Yes?" Mariette said.

"You honestly don't mind?"

"Have a good time. Don't get drunk," she said.

Probably not a bad idea, Pop mused as he and Charley walked along the harbor walls, watching the Breton fishing crews brewing buckets of fish and potatoes into one big steaming stew and loading red wine onto the decks by the dozen crates. It gave Pop great pleasure to watch all this and to gaze at the many furled copper umbrellas bright in the mid-morning sun above the crowded blue hulls.

"Don't see old Brisson about," he said. "Anyway, we'll have a snifter at the Chat Noir. He'll be along."

As he and Charley chose a pavement table at the café on the harbor's edge, Pop got the sudden idea that the occasion was one when they might try something a little special. It was too early for wine. It made him sleepy. And he was fed up with the eternal Dubonnet, Pernod, and Cinzano. What did Charley think about a real drink? Red Bull or something of that sort?

"First-class idea, Pop," Mr. Charlton said. "Absolutely first-class."

Pop, slightly astonished at the strenuous vehemence of Charley's tone, gave him a sharp glance of inquiry which he didn't bother to answer. Charley was feeling a private need for a strong pick-me-up. It depressed him increasingly each time he thought of the young French gods, their stupid great balls, and Mariette sunning herself in her sumptuous cinnamon.

"Rattling good idea," he said. "I've been waiting for somebody to ask me that one."

As Pop was about to call "Garçon!" and begin an explanation as to how to mix the Red Bulls, he saw Captain Brisson arrive. Pop always called him Captain. Huge, florid, and purple, he looked very much like a large bulldog with heart disease.

Charley, having been introduced, suddenly took off his spectacles and started polishing them madly. Pop, unaware of what made him do this, called to the waiter and at the same time started to explain to the captain about the Red Bulls and did he want one?

"Plizz, what name? Red Bull, you say?"

"Red Bull. It's a self-propeller!" Mr. Charlton said. "A blinder!"

"Plizz?"

The captain, like Pop, looked positively startled at the sudden vehemence of the small Englishman who, momentarily without his spectacles, looked so harmless, odd, and shortsighted.

"My son-in-law," Pop said, as if this explained everything.

Mr. Charlton rammed his spectacles back on his nose and in rapid French explained the composition of the cocktail that, only a year before, had knocked him flat. He was stronger now. He could take a dozen.

"Good," Captain Brisson said, presently tasting the Red Bull, which Charley had had the forethought to order double. "Good. I like. Good at sea."

Searching stabs of raw alcohol inspired Charley to fresh, almost rapturous enthusiasm for the virtues of the cocktail.

"Propel the whole ruddy boat," he said. "Nothing like it. Absolute blinder. Santé."

"Santé," Captain Brisson said.

"Cheers!" Pop said. "Santé."

"Cheers," the captain said.

"Santé," Charley said. "Down the hatch."

He already thought, as Pop and Captain Brisson sat discussing the question of sliced gherkins in vinegar, that he felt a great deal better.

Pop was feeling pleased with himself too. The captain had made a very reasonable offer for the hundred cases and the deal was now completed except for the formality of a little paper.

Since Pop was incapable of writing his name and the Captain incapable of writing English it devolved on Mr. Charlton to draw up a sort of invoice, agreeing price and quantity. For some reason he chose to do this in pencil. He couldn't think why, since he had a perfectly good pen in his pocket, except perhaps that the pencil needed sharpening and that the short rapid strokes of his penknife gave him the same nervous outlet for his emotions as the mad polishing of his spectacles.

"I am content," the captain said. His signature and Pop's cross, binding nobody and nothing at all, were added to Mr. Charlton's document, which the Frenchman kept. Pop never kept records. It was all in his head. "I sank you."

After this the captain and Pop shook hands. Then Pop knocked his Red Bull straight back, declaring that the proceedings called for another drink to which Charley added a kind of vehement amen.

"You bet!" he said.

"Plizz," the captain said. "I like to pay."

"Rhubarb!" Charley said. "This one's on me!"

After the second Red Bull he began to feel that the contemptuous memory of the young French gods and their stupid idiotic balls and still stupider prancings no longer disturbed him quite so much. He started to see the harbor through a viscous, rosy cloud.

Now and then he sharpened the pencil madly again and then, after a third Red Bull, actually started to sharpen it at the other end. About this time Captain Brisson said he ought to be going back to his boat and Pop said they ought to be going too.

"Rhubarb!" Charley said loudly. "Hell's bells. We only just got here."

"Please excuse," the captain said.

"Rhubarb!" Charley said again. "I thought the French were drinkers."

The captain again protested that he had to get back to his ship and Pop said very well, that was all right, and he hoped he'd see him soon. Perhaps in England?

"In England, yes," the captain said. "I come soon. When teeth are ready."

"What teeth?" Charley snapped.

Without embarrassment and with a certain touch of pride the captain slipped from his mouth what he explained to Pop and Charley were his temporary set of dentures. The new ones, he assured them, would be ready in a month or so, in England.

"National Elf lark," Pop reminded Charley.

"My mate," the captain said, "he have new wooden leg. Also it is true you can have cognac sometimes? *Oui?*"

"There's the National Elf lark for you. Charley old man," Pop said. "Free for all. Even the Froggies. Wooden legs an' all."

"Rhubarb to the National Health lark!" said Charley aggressively, "and double rhubarb to the Froggies!"

As if detecting in this a certain note of ill-concealed hostility Captain Brisson, whose face had now broken out in a rash of red and purple blotches, shook hands all over again with Pop and Charley, at the same time forgetting to put his teeth back. It was only when he had gone some yards along the quayside that he remembered the omission and slapped them back into his mouth with a blow so sharp that it knocked him off keel, making him stagger.

Soon after he had disappeared Pop was about to say for a second time that he and Charley ought to be going too when he saw across the street a figure waving to him with a white-and-chocolate scarf.

He did not need to hear the fluted call of "Darling!" that followed it to know that this was Angela Snow. She was dressed in trim pure white shorts and a coffee-colored linen blouse and white open sandals in which her bare painted toenails glistened like rows of cherries. With her was a girl in a pea-green cable-stitch sweater and a skirt of indeterminate color that might have once been mustard. Much washing had turned it to an unpleasant shade of mongrel ocher, rather like that of a mangel-wurzel.

"This," said Angela Snow, "is my sister, Iris."

Pop and Charley rose to shake hands, Charley unsteadily.

"Good. Splendid," Charley said. "Just in time for a snifter."

"Darlings!" Angela Snow said. "My tongue's hanging out."

Iris said nothing but "Howdedo." She was a solid, shortish blonde of rising thirty with a skin as hard as marble and more or less the color of an acid drop. Her eyes were almost lashless; the complete absence of eyebrows made her face actually seem broader than it was, as well as giving it a look of completely bloodless astonishment. Her hair was cut in a roughish homemade bob and she had small white ankle socks of exactly the kind that French girls wear.

Charley demanded of the two girls what would it be and presently Angela Snow was drinking Pernod and her sister a small bottle of Perrier with ice. Charley and Pop decided at the same time that this was as good a moment as any to have a fourth Red Bull and while this was being mixed Pop reminded Angela Snow of her luncheon promise and asked when she was coming.

"Whenever you say, dear boy. At the given moment I shall be there."

"Tomorrow?"

"Tomorrow, darling, as ever is. Bless you."

"And your sister," Pop said, giving Iris a rich perky look that would have melted Mlle. Dupont to tears but that had on Angela Snow's sister only the effect of heightening her appearance of bloodless surprise, "would she care to join us too?"

"I'm sure she'd adore to."

"Impossible," Iris said. "I go to Guimiliau to see the Calvary and then the ossuary at—"

The word "ossuary" startled Pop so much that he gave a sort of frog croak into his Red Bull, which had just arrived. He had as sharp an ear as ever for strange new words but this one had him floored.

"What," he said, "is an ossuary? Sounds *très snob*."

"Bone house," Angela Snow said.

"Same to you," Pop said.

"Scream!" she said, and everyone, with the solid exception of Iris, roared with laughter.

Even before the arrival of the fourth Red Bull Charley was feeling great. The bit about the ossuary served merely to put him into louder, cheerier, more pugnacious mood.

"Rhubarb!" he said to Iris Snow. "Of course you can come. It's *langoustine* day tomorrow. Have them every Thursday. Don't you adore *langoustines*?"

Iris, who thought eating had much in common with the other deadly sins and consequently existed mostly on dry toast, cheese biscuits, and anchovy paste, had no word of answer.

"You see she visits somewhere different every day," Angela Snow said in explanation. "Ah, the calvaries and the crosses, the dolmens and the menhirs, the *allées couvertes* and the tumuli—Iris has to see them all."

Pop sat openmouthed before what he thought was the oddest female he had ever seen in his life but was saved from pondering over her too long by a sudden, almost pugnacious question from Charley.

"And how," he demanded of Iris, "do you travel, Miss Snow? By car or what?"

Iris permitted herself the astonishing luxury of uttering fifty-six words all at once, speaking with measured solemnity.

"I think walking is the only true and right way of seeing these things. Walking leads to contemplation, contemplation to mood, and mood to meditation, so that when you get there you are one with the place you're visiting. So I walk to all the nearest ones and go to all the distant ones by train."

"By train?" Charley said. "What train? Not by any chance that *little* train?"

"Of course. What else? Whenever and as often as its—"

"My God!" Charley gave a positive shout of delighted triumph and gazed at Iris Snow with alcoholic rapture, as to a kindred spirit. "She knows my little train! Hear that, Pop? She knows my little train!"

Pop, who thought something must have got into Charley—he'd start spouting Shakespeare or that feller Keats any moment now, he thought—could only stare at Angela Snow, who gave him a split-second sporting wink, without the trace of a smile, in reply. He was too astonished even to wink back again.

"That train," Charley kept saying. "That little train. You remember, Pop, how that was the first thing that brought it all back again?"

Brought all what back again? Pop wanted to know.

"Me. This. Everything. All that time. All those years. The whole ruddy shooting match."

No doubt about it, Pop thought, Charley was as drunk as a newt. Pickled. Something had got into him. It reminded him of the time he had first met him and how Mariette had had to lend him pajamas and put him to bed. There was the same raving, rhapsodic light in his eyes.

"Chuffing away over the heather!" Charley said. He had started to wave his arms about in ecstatic recollection. "Chuffing away for miles. I remember once—where was it? St. Pol de Léon—no, not there. Somewhere else. No. Has St. Pol de Léon two cathedrals?"

Without knowing it, and for no sane reason at all, Charley had begun to sharpen his pencil again.

"You might almost say it has," Iris Snow said. "There's the cathedral itself, and then of course there's the *Chapelle du Creizker*. Much, much more magnificent."

"It was there!" Charley said with a rhapsodic jolt in his voice. "It was there!"

What was? Pop wanted to know.

"Charley's got a spider on the end of his nose," said Angela Snow, who loved practical jokes and who was dying to get the subject changed, since relics, saints, and *pardons* were her sister's food and drink, day and night. "I can see it dangling."

Charley did nothing about the supposed teasing spider except to snatch vaguely at the air immediately in front of him and then start stirring his Red Bull madly with his pencil, as if it were a cup of tea.

"First time I ever really saw the world," he said. "Consciously, I mean. Consciously. From that tower you can see—"

"Seventy other towers," Iris said. "Of course on a clear day."

"Never forget," Charley said. "God, you talk about 'a wild surmise—silent upon a peak in Darien'—"

"Charley's off," Pop said. "More Shakespeare."

"Keats!" Charley shouted. "Keats!"

"Same thing," Pop said.

"Whenever I go there again," Iris Snow said, "I shall think of you."

"Do," Charley said, "do," and started to sharpen his pencil madly again. "Think of me!"

Suddenly he was on top of the tower again, on top of the world. Everything was splendidly revelatory and wonderful. His insides felt rich with Red Bull. His veins were a jumble of wires that sang like harp strings. He heard himself order a fifth Red Bull in a voice that echoed inside his head as a cry might have done through one of the sepulchral *allées couvertes* that Iris found so fascinating.

Drinking it, he was aware that his intestines were on fire and he suddenly gave a belch of rude immoderation.

Magnifique, he kept telling Iris Snow. *Magnifique*. Rhubarb! And he didn't care a damn for any of the bastards. Did she?

Whether it had anything to do with this robustly repeated inquiry he never knew but suddenly he came to a vague realization that neither Angela Snow nor her sister were there any longer.

"Where have the Snows gone?" he said. "Melted?" Jolly good joke, he thought. *Magnifique*. "Snows all melted?"

Some time later he was dimly aware of walking back to the *plage* with Pop, still madly sharpening his pencil and still saying he didn't care a damn for the bastards, whoever they were.

"All Froggies are alike," he was saying as they reached the *plage*. "Eh, Pop? No guts. No Red Bull. No red blood. Eh? Can't take it, eh?"

Without waiting for an answer, he made a sudden spasmodic leap onto the sand, landing midway between Ma, who was giving further refreshment to Oscar, and Mariette, who, sumptuous in fiery cinnamon in the noon sun, was flirting madly with a muscular Frenchman bronzed as evenly all over as if every inch of color had been painted on.

Charley at once uttered a queer cry, half in warning, half in anger, and rushed across the sand, seaward, as if about to drown himself. The *plage*, it seemed to him, was full of balls. They were floating everywhere, maddening him as they had never done before.

Suddenly he started charging hither and thither with the violence of a demented buffalo. He was attacking balls everywhere as if they were monsters, stabbing at them with his open penknife, making them burst.

One of several loud reports startled a French woman into a scream and another startled Ma in the act of giving Oscar the other side. One ball as vivid a shade of mustard as Iris Snow's skirt had once been was floating in the water. Charley charged it with a dive, leaving it swimming on the surface of the waves like a deflated and forgotten tooth bag.

Pop, who didn't know what to make of it all, stared blankly at Charley giving the death blow to a big pink-and-purple ball that went up with a crack like a Roman candle, merely thinking that perhaps they'd better lay off Red Bulls for a bit, in case Charley got violent sometime. They didn't suit everybody, especially on an empty stomach.

Less than a minute later he was shaken out of this complacency by the sight of Charley rushing back with puffing frenzy across the sand, every ball now triumphantly punctured, to where Mariette, luxuriously lying on her back under the gaze of an admiring Frenchman who stood with hands on his knees, was testing the truth of Ma's shrewd observations on variety.

In full flight, Charley kicked the startled Frenchman twice up the backside. He was, however, less startled than Pop, who suddenly heard Charley, as he lugged an astonished Mariette to her feet, ripping out the challenging words, "And tomorrow you'll come on the little train! Hear that? You'll come with me on the little train!"

In bed that night, in the quiet of darkness, Pop was still trying to work out this violent episode for himself.

"So that," he said, "was what all the hoo-ha was about. That little train. Don't get it, Ma. Do you?"

Ma said of course she got it. It was as plain as a pikestaff.

"How? Don't get it," he said.

"Charley wanted to go on the little train and Mariette didn't. That's all."

Lot of fuss for nothing Pop thought. All over a little thing like that. All over a train.

"Not at all," Ma said. "It's always the little things. That train means a lot to Charley."

Pop said he thought it seemed like it too.

"It's connected with something in him," Ma said. "In his childhood."

"Never!" Pop said. "Really?" For crying out gently.

"It stands for something he's lost. Or else something he's never had. Not sure which."

Pop said he shouldn't think so either. Charley would have to take more water with it, that was all.

"It's psychology," Ma said. "You hear a lot about it on telly."

Wonderful thing, Pop remarked, telly. He missed it on holiday. It learned you something all the time. Every day. Ma said she agreed. She missed the *Mirror* too. Without it she never knew what her stars foretold and that made it awkward somehow.

At last, lying under the lee of Ma's huge mountain of a body, Pop found himself going back over the day and in the course of doing so remembered something else he thought remarkable.

"Heard a word today, though, Ma," he said, "I've never even heard on telly yet. And I'll bet you never have either."

Oh, and what word was that? Ma wanted to know.

"Ossuary."

And whatever in the world did that mean?

"Bone house to you," Pop told her.

"Do you mind?" Ma said, and kicked him hard under the bed-clothes. "Whatever next? You'll have the twins picking it up in no time."

"Sorry, Ma," Pop said. *"Dormez bien.* Sleep well."

"Sleep well, my foot," Ma said, and gave her handsome head a swift twist on the pillow, so that she was lying full face to him. "What makes you think I'm all that tired?"

Pop said he couldn't think and immediately set to work to demonstrate that he wasn't all that tired either.

7

But it was always Ma, in her unruffled way, who shrewdly remembered the best and most important things and it was she who, next morning after breakfast, called Pop's attention to an event a week ahead.

"You know," she said, "what it is next Thursday?"

Pop didn't, except that they were going home.

"That's Friday," Ma said. "Thursday the twenty-ninth, I mean."

Pop said he couldn't think what the twenty-ninth meant at all; he only knew that the month at St. Pierre le Port seemed to have gone like the wind. He could hardly believe that soon they were going home.

"Mariette and Charley," Ma said. "Their wedding anniversary."

"Completely forgot," Pop said.

"Forgot, my foot," Ma said slyly. "The trouble is you don't get much practice with wedding anniversaries, do you?"

Pop confessed that this was quite true but nevertheless suggested darkly that he and Ma made up for it in other ways.

"Good thing too," Ma said. "Anyway, I thought we ought to give them a party."

Perfick idea, Pop said. Jolly fine idea. Perfick. *Très snob.*

"I thought we could ask Angela Snow and her sister and perhaps Mlle. Dupont. How does that strike you?"

Pop said that nothing could have struck him better. It was just the job. Mariette would be thrilled too.

"By the way," Ma said, "what's Angela Snow's sister like? If she's anything like her we'll have a high old party."

She wasn't, Pop said.

"Oh?" Ma said. "What's she like then?"

Pop found it difficult to say. He could find no handy word to describe Iris Snow with any sort of accuracy. He thought hard for some moments and then said, "All I know is she wears false boosies and she's very pale."

What a shame, Ma said. She was very sorry about that. She always pitied girls who had to wear those things. Good boosies were a girl's crowning glory, as you could see from all the advertisements there were about them everywhere nowadays.

Pop heartily agreed and invited Ma to consider our Mariette for instance, which in turn made him remark that he was glad to see that she and Charley were well on hooks again.

"Like lovebirds," Ma said. "We must give them a good time on Thursday. The tops."

Best party they could think up, Pop said. What did Ma suggest?

"Well," Ma said, "I tell you what I thought. I thought that as we've got Angela Snow coming to lunch today we'd discuss it all then. We can get Mlle. Dupont in over coffee and all talk about what we're going to eat and drink and so on. Have a proper laid-out menu and the table decorated and all that. How's that strike you?"

Again Pop thought it struck him very well. They could get all the wines ordered too and he would try to think up some special sort of cocktail. The expense could be damned; the gherkins and the cucumber in vinegar lark would take care of that.

"Good," Ma said. "Now perhaps we'll get some real food."

At lunch, before Mlle. Dupont joined them for coffee, a small but quite unprecedented incident took place—in Pop's experience anyway. The day was coolish, with a touch of that bristling westerly wind that could blow fine sand into every corner and crevice like chaff from a thresher. Even Angela Snow had put on a thick red sweater and Pop noticed that in spite of it she shuddered as she first sat down.

"Let's give the vin rosy a rest, shall we, Ma?" Pop said. "Have something a bit more warming today."

Just what she felt like, Ma said. Pop must choose a good one.

"Sky's the limit," Pop said, and with infinite charm turned to Angela Snow and suggested that she should make the choice.

The customary Thursday *langoustines* not having arrived because the sea had been too rough, it presently turned out that for lunch there was *potage du jour* and *omelette au fromage* followed by *côtes de porc grillées* with *haricots verts*.

"In that case burgundy," Angela Snow said.

"A good one, mind, the real McCoy," Pop said. "No half larks. The best."

Angela Snow said she thought in that case that the Chambolle Musigny '47 couldn't be bettered.

"Fire away," Pop said. "Make it two bottles."

A waitress finally brought the wine in a basket cradle. A lot of dust covered the bottle and this, to Pop, was a sure sign of something good. The waitress then pulled the cork and poured out a little of the wine for Pop to taste but Pop was quick to say,

"No, no. Angela. Angela must taste it."

She did.

"Corked," she said firmly. "No doubt about it. Must go back."

A curious suspended hush settled on the table, broken only after some seconds by Primrose asking in a piping voice, "What's corked, Pop?"

Pop didn't know; he hadn't the remotest idea what corked was. Obviously this wine lark was a bit dodgy, he thought, and privately decided he must go into it a bit more closely. There were things he didn't know.

"Of course it can happen anytime, anywhere," Angela Snow said. "It's nobody's fault. It's one of those things."

Pop said he was relieved to hear it and was on the verge of saying that "corked" might not be a bad word to describe Iris Snow when he thought better of it and decided not to, in case Ma should somehow misunderstand.

The direct result of all this was that when coffee was brought Mlle. Dupont came to the table in more than usually nervous, apologetic mood. She apologized several times for the unfortunate incident of the Chambolle Musigny. Aware though she was of the ease with which it could happen at any time, anywhere, even to the best of wines, she would nevertheless have rather cut off her right hand than it should happen to milord Larkin and his family.

At the word "milord" Angela Snow was astounded into a silence from which she hadn't recovered by the time Ma was suggesting to an equally astonished Mlle. Dupont that the party wouldn't be complete if the children didn't have custard and jelly for afters.

Meanwhile the coffee filters had to be attacked. Pop always dealt with his, though never very successfully, by giving it a number of smart hostile slaps with the flat of his hand. Mostly these produced no visible result whatever. Charley's method was more simple. He merely pressed the top down hard and invariably spilled what coffee there was all over the place.

On the other hand, Mlle. Dupont seemed lucky enough to be blessed with a special sort of filter, for while everyone else was struggling messily to coax a few black drops of liquid into the cups she was sipping away with alacrity, trying to calm her nerves.

"First, to decide how many people."

Ma counted up the heads.

"Not counting Oscar and I think he's a bit young, don't you?" she said, "I think there'll be a round dozen. That includes you," she said to Angela Snow, "and your sister. And," she said to Mlle. Dupont, "you too."

Mlle. Dupont's pale olive face at once started flushing. She was most flattered, most honored, but really it couldn't be. Her French and English began to mix themselves hopelessly, as always at times when she was excessively nervous, and she could only blurt out that it was *très difficile, impossible,* quite *impossible.* There would be so much *travail* and Alphonse would need much watching.

"Who's Alphonse?" Pop said.

"He is the *chef.* He is not an easy man."

Drinks, Ma thought. She knew. Nearly all cooks drank. Like fishes, too, though perhaps you couldn't blame them.

"Alphonse will be looked after," said Pop, who had by now abandoned the struggle with the coffee filter and had lit up one of his best Havanas. "The main thing is the grub. Kids," he said to Charley and Mariette, "what do you fancy to start with?"

Mariette said she's been trying to think but it was Mr. Charlton, always so bang on the target in these things, who made the happy suggestion that he thought they ought to begin with *melon au porto.*

"With that," he pointed out, "you eat and get a drink at the same time."

It was cordially agreed by everyone, especially Pop, that *melon au porto* sounded marvelous. Mlle. Dupont thought so too, saying several times over that she thought she could get the lovely, small *charentais* melons, which were the best, if she tried hard.

"And then may I suggest *filets de sole aux truffes?*"

"Troof, troof!" the twins started saying. "Troof! Troof!"

"Quiet!" Pop thundered, and the twins stopped as if throttled.

"How do you feel about that, Mariette?" Ma said. "Wouldn't rather have lobster?"

"How is the *filet de sole* composed?" Charley said.

The rather grand word "composed" seemed to flatter Mlle. Dupont so greatly that she started to describe the contents of the dish with both verve and tenderness.

"*Vin blanc,* white wine, butter, *les truffes,* and *quelques autres choses très délicieuses*—"

"Sounds just the job," Pop said. "Chips with it?"

Mlle. Dupont recoiled from the suggestion of chips with silence, not really understanding exactly what it meant. The milord was a comic man sometimes.

Eventually everyone agreed that the *filet de sole aux truffes* didn't sound too bad at all, though Pop was privately disappointed that there was no further mention of chips. You always had chips with fish. What was wrong?

"And now as to meat? Or should it possibly be chicken? Or perhaps some other bird?"

Suddenly, while everyone was trying to concentrate on the problems of this, the main course, Victoria bit Zinnia sharply on the ear. Nobody took much notice of this except Petunia, who threw at Victoria a piece of *omelette au fromage* she hadn't been able to eat because it tasted of soapsuds. In a second all three girls were crying and Ma was saying seriously, as if there wasn't a ghost of sound to be heard, "I as good as told you so."

"Quiet!" Pop thundered for the second time in ten minutes, and there was instant silence at the table, so that Ma remarked with pride, as she so often did, that Pop had them at a word.

The effect of this was to impress Mlle. Dupont tremendously. The English milord was obviously a most masterful person. A man clearly born to command. You could tell these born, masterful, commanding aristocrats fifty kilometers away.

This was the season for *perdrix*, she was saying suddenly. There were now beautiful young *perdrix*. What was the English word?—partridge? Shouldn't they therefore select partridge—*perdrix*, perhaps, *à la mode d'ici?*

It suddenly occurred to Pop that he had heard these ominous words somewhere before. They struck a faint and unpleasant chord in his mind. And in a flash he remembered the pregnant sausage rolls with steam coming out of their ends.

Partridges—no—he said, he didn't think so. No *à la mode d'ici.*

"If it's all right with Charley and Mariette," he said, "I know what I want and what I should like to have."

"Go on. Say it," Ma said. "I know."

"Roast beef and Yorkshire."

"Biff! Biff!" the twins started saying, but this time a single look was enough to silence them.

"Can't wait," Charley said.

"Lovely!" Mariette said. "Couldn't be anything better. Oh, Pop, you always have the sweetest ideas."

Pop, feeling rather flattered by this, gave one of his perkiest, richest smiles at Mlle. Dupont, who responded confusedly by saying, "*Rosbif* of course. That we can arrange. But what else was this you said? This Jorkshire?"

Pop started to explain that this was, in his opinion, a pudding that had no equal. It was about the best in the world.

"I see," Mlle. Dupont said. "It is merely a question of whether Alphonse can make it. I doubt it very much."

"Then Ma can make it for him," Pop said.

Mlle. Dupont professed to be instantly and completely horrified. It was quite out of the question. It was unthinkable that a stranger should go into the kitchen, still less teach Alphonse how to make strange dishes. It would only offend him. He was at the best of times a temperamental man and sometimes, after drink, ran about with carving knives.

"Fetch Alphonse," Pop said. "I daresay he wouldn't say no to a brandy. I want one too."

Mlle. Dupont now fluffed over her coffee, which she had allowed to get quite cold. Alphonse also, she recalled, but not aloud, had a mistress in Morlaix and two in Brest. He visited the three of them in rotation and they too sometimes had strange effects on his stability.

Alphonse, duly called in from the kitchen, didn't say no to a brandy. He was a man of stocky proportions, inclined to be portly, with very black hair parted down the middle with millimetrical exactitude and polished with a great deal of violet brilliantine. His eyes were protuberant but handsome and in the space of three seconds from first entering the *salle à manger* he managed to give Ma, Angela Snow, and Mariette the quickest, most comprehensive once-over.

Since Alphonse spoke no English, it was left to Mr. Charlton, translating instructions from Ma, to explain the composition of what Mlle. Dupont called the *pouding à la Jorkshire*. These instructions, though simple in the extreme, were listened to by Alphonse with aloofness, not to say contempt, while he drank in the visionary beauty of Angela Snow, who had for a long time sat in a state of bemusement, not saying a word.

Suddenly Alphonse became unexpectedly voluble and first Mlle. Dupont and then Mr. Charlton translated his words for Ma.

"He says if you will write it down on paper it shall be made as you wish. And is it the same as for *crêpes?*"

"Pancakes," Mr. Charlton explained.

"Exactly the same," Ma said. "Couldn't be more right."

"*Ça va bien,*" Pop said. "*Merci beaucoup, Alphonse.*"

Alphonse said, "*Merci, monsieur,*" and immediately became suddenly voluble again. This time it was to offer the suggestion that the beef should be the *contre filet,* which Mlle. Dupont applauded as being absolutely right, quite excellent.

"And now what about afters?" Ma said.

"Ah!" Pop said smartly, picking it up in a flash. "*Les après.*"

Alphonse looked witheringly about him for a second or two and then held a short conversation with Mlle. Dupont, who said, "Alphonse is suggesting either *crêpes Suzette* for dessert or *bombe surprise.*"

It was at this moment that Angela Snow came out of her half dream to hear Ma insisting on jelly and custard for the children and to find herself being shamelessly and mentally undressed by Alphonse's over-large handsome eyes.

"I think myself the *crêpes Suzette,*" she said, staring straight through Alphonse. "They'll keep him busier at the time."

"That about settles it then," Ma said.

"No it don't though," Pop said. "What about the cake? Got to have a cake. Midnight, champagne, and all that lark."

"Oh, Pop, lovely!" Mariette said, and suddenly ran around the table in one of her moments of spontaneous delight to kiss Pop with luscious gratitude. "Cake *and* champagne—it's like being married all over again!"

"Second honeymoon, Charley, second honeymoon," Pop said, hoping the cheerful pointed words wouldn't be lost on him. "Second honeymoon."

Charley, using his loaf, looked as if he understood. Then Mlle. Dupont said Alphonse would be most honored to make the cake. And if there were any other things, any other thoughts—suddenly a great sense of excitement ran through her, as if the party were really her own, and she ended by half running out of the *salle à manger* into the bureau in another fluff, repeating half in French, half in English, a few uncertain sentences that nobody could understand.

For another half hour, while Charley, Mariette, and the children went to the *plage* and Pop for a gentle snooze on the bed, Ma and Angela Snow sat outside on the terrace, drinking coffee. By this time the sun had appeared but the air was quite autumnal. Already at the end of the terrace a few leaves of the plane trees pollarded to give shade in hot weather were turning yellow and even falling to the ground. The beadlike strings of colored lights, shattered by storm and still unrepaired, gave the trees an air of premature shabbiness that was like a small herald of winter. It was all too true, as Mlle. Dupont had remarked to Ma only that morning at breakfast, that the season was coming to its end. The guests were departing. Soon the hotel would be empty. The French had no taste for the sea when October began and in another week or two the little *plage* would be wrapped away for winter.

Presently Angela Snow was saying how much she was looking forward to the party and what a lot you missed by not being married—the anniversaries and that sort of thing.

"Suppose you do," Ma said. She'd never really thought of it.

"I'll have to settle down myself, I suppose, one of these days," Angela Snow said.

"Oh?" Ma said. "Why?"

She didn't mind a scrap everyone knowing that she and Pop weren't married—most took it for granted they were and anyway it looked the same, even if it wasn't—and she remained quite unperturbed and unsurprised when Angela Snow, who liked to be frank in everything, said in an offhand way, "Don't you ever think of marrying Pop?"

Ma threw back her dark handsome head and roared with laughter.

"What?" she said, "and give him a chance to leave me?"

"Scream," Angela Snow said. "Suppose he might at that."

"Off like a hare."

Angela laughed so much over her filtered half-cold coffee that she spilled most of it into the saucer. It was undrinkable anyway, as she had long since discovered filtered coffee always was. But she nevertheless supposed the French would always cling to it, just as the Scots did to herring and oatmeal.

"Well, must go," she said. "Must see what the adventurous Iris has been up to. Let me know if ever he does."

Ma laughed in her friendliest fashion.

"Who? Pop? I'll send you a wire. That'll give you a bit of a start on Mlle. Dupont."

"Oh, is she in the hunt too?"

Ma said she was afraid so. She'd be in a whale of a tizzy by the time that party was over.

"And not the only one."

Graceful and elegant, Angela Snow stooped to kiss Ma a sporting good-bye, telling her at the same time to give Pop her best love, which Ma warmly promised to do, with knobs of brass and tinkling cymbals, as Pop himself was so fond of saying sometimes.

"God bless," Angela said. "Have to fix a hairdo somehow before that party. For two pins I'd have my blasted face lifted as well."

"Where to?" Ma said, laughing again. "You keep it as it is. Pop'd never forgive you."

Angela Snow went back into the hotel on the pretext of telephoning a hairdresser but in reality on the off chance of running into Pop as he came downstairs. But the lounge, the reception desk, and the stairs were all deserted and she suddenly realized with unpleasantness that she might run into Alphonse instead. She didn't care for Alphonse. The process of being mentally undressed by strange men had never amused her. Nor, for some reason, did she like men who parted their hair down the middle. But now and then she couldn't help wondering what the virginal Iris would make of those too large, too handsome eyes.

"Did mademoiselle wish for something please?"

It was Mlle. Dupont who came at length to the door of the bureau and called the words. In reply Angela Snow said she was wondering about a hairdresser and was there one she could go to in the town?

"There is nothing exciting here. Nothing *soigné*. One must go to Morlaix or Brest."

"Oh? Then I might go to Brest."

"Philippe—that is the name."

"Philippe," Angela Snow said. "Do you go there?"

"I regret not often. I can't afford it."

"No? Not even for the party?"

Mlle. Dupont, who had been torn all day by the question of whether to have a hairdo or a new corset for the party and had almost decided on the corset, could only gaze in silence at Angela Snow's exquisitely smooth aristocratic yellow hair and wish that her own were like it, so that such difficult dilemmas and choices never arose.

"Got to make the party a success, you know," Angela Snow said.

"I think that Milord Larkin," Mlle. Dupont said rather loftily, "will see to that. He has the *flair*."

Drawn up sharply by the second mention of the word "milord" that day, Angela Snow had no time to make any sort of comment before Mlle. Dupont fluffed again and said, "I am right in thinking that? Yes? He is a milord?"

"Down to the ankles," Angela Snow said. "And like every Englishman he's sure his home is his castle."

At the mention of the word "castle" Mlle. Dupont was unable to speak. A castle—a *château*. There was something overpowering, *très formidable*, about the word "castle."

"You must ask him to tell you about it," Angela Snow said.

"I will ask that," Mlle. Dupont said quietly.

After Angela Snow had departed Mlle. Dupont went upstairs. In her room she took off her dress, as she did every afternoon, and lay down on the bed. Like Angela Snow she had hoped for the chance of running into Pop on the stairs but nothing had happened and she lay for an hour alone and in silence, thinking largely of Milord Larkin, the castle, and how altogether surprising the English were, but also of the entrancements of marriage and a lot of other things. She remembered the occasion when Pop had caressed her, brief and idle though it had been, with a warm swift hand, and how he would forever remember her bedroom when he caught the scent of *les muguets*.

At the end of it she decided there was nothing for it but to have her hair dressed at Philippe's and buy the new corset too. After all, she thought in typical French fashion, the bill for the party would be a big one and she would be able to afford it out of that.

She would have her hair done in that Empire style that was now so fashionable and that she knew would give her the illusion of height she needed so much. The corset must be a black one, trimmed with lace in parma violet at top and bottom, and every time she thought of it she started trembling.

8

The evening of the party was warm and sultry, only the softest westerly wind ruffling the sea into small white pleats on the sand along the *plage*.

Dinner, Mlle. Dupont had suggested, should be at eight-thirty. This would give the only two French families remaining in the hotel time to finish their food in comfort before retiring to the lounge. She had herself superintended the laying of the one long table, decorating it with bright orange dahlias, dark red rose petals strewn about the cloth, and sprays of asparagus fern.

Pop, who entranced everybody by appearing in a biscuit-colored light-weight suit and a yellow silk bow tie with large cranberry spots on it and a handkerchief to match, spent most of the time between six and seven mixing punch in the bar, tasting it frequently to see if it was any good at all. He finally decided it was a bit of a snorter.

He had seen the recipe for punch in some magazine Ma had bought. It was known as Colonel Bramley's Punch and you could have it either hot or cold, Pop deciding that since the evening was so sultry he would make it cold. Plenty of ice was the form.

The main ingredients were rum, white wine, Curaçao, lemon, and sugar, but after the first mixing Pop decided that the flavor of rum was, if anything, rather too prominent. Not everybody liked rum. He added brandy. This brought out a certain heaviness in the mixture. It needed sharpening up a bit. He tried a tumbler of kirsch for this and decided that it was exactly the right thing for giving the punch a subtler but at the same time more brittle tone. When the ice was added just before seven o'clock, when everybody was expected to arrive, he casually decided that another bottle of white wine and a second dash of brandy wouldn't do anybody any harm at all and these were added together with large slices of fresh orange and a scattering of cocktail cherries, which had the effect of making the whole thing look pretty, amusing, partyish, and at the same time quite innocuous.

Although Ma, Mariette, Charley, and the other children came down-stairs after seven o'clock and gathered in the bar, from which Mlle. Dupont had actually removed last year's heather and replaced it with bowls of dark purple asters, there was no sign of Angela Snow and her sister until a quarter to eight or of Mlle. Dupont until nearly forty minutes later.

Meanwhile the children drank Coca-Cola and orange juice and the four grown-ups sampled the punch. Sometimes Ma allowed the chil-dren to sample the punch too and also sneak a slice of orange or a cherry out of it with their fingers so that they could have an extra suck.

"Good pick-me-up on a wash day this, Pop," she said. Just what she wanted. "Wondered why you'd been so quiet since six o'clock."

Ma was wearing a low-cut dress in deep purple, much the color of the asters, with a narrow mink stole. She was drenched in a new perfume called Kick and was wearing a pearl-and-diamanté comb in one side of her hair and three handsome rows of pearls around her neck. Mariette was wearing a dress of stunning low-cut simplicity in burgundy velvet, effective in its sheer richness but also because there was so little of it, and a necklace of garnet and diamond that Pop had bought her in Brest for the anniversary.

Now and then Pop decided that the punch was going down rather too fast and added another harmless dash of rum, a little kirsch, or a glass of brandy.

By a quarter to eight, when Angela and Iris Snow arrived, the charac-ter of the mixture had changed completely, though Pop, by adding orange and cherries again, kept it looking much the same. Ma thought that, if anything, it was much nicer now.

"Very more-ish," she said, and settled down to a fifth glass of it. "And so cool."

As soon as Angela Snow and her sister arrived Pop remarked how warm the evening was and was quick to press them to a cooling glass.

"Ingredients?" Angela Snow said as she tasted it. "I think it's another of your blinders."

Cheers, she went on to say, if it was. If not there was plenty of time.

"Women's magazine recipe. Practically teetotal," Pop explained. "It's actually the coolth that makes it what it is."

Iris Snow, who liked Pop's word "coolth," sipped happily.

Their lateness in arrival was, she explained, entirely due to her. She had been to see a calvary at St. Thégonnec and had missed the train. She smiled with unusual readiness and apologized. Her hair looked less home-cut than usual, Pop thought, and the dark coffee-brown frock she was wearing, apart from the fact that in the haste of dressing she had evidently had some difficulty in balancing the two protuberances underneath it so that one was much lower than the other, suited her quite well and was modestly attractive.

But it was Angela Snow's dress that had everyone wide-eyed in admiration. Pop thought it a corker. If she had a stitch on underneath it he would be more than surprised. The embroidered purity of its line, somehow accentuated by her long drop earrings, was even more fetching than its color, a pale turquoise, and the fact that it fitted like a skin.

About eight o'clock M. Mollet crept in, molelike as ever, as if out of hiding. He had been sent to say that Mlle. Dupont wouldn't be long; she had been delayed by complications of the kitchen.

She had in fact been delayed by complications of the new corset. It was rather tight and the zip was awkward. Twice she had run down for one of the chambermaids to come to help zip her up but they were all giving a hand in the kitchen and it was M. Mollet who at last came up to her room, to face the unparalleled embarrassment of finding Mlle. Dupont less than half dressed, with a figure as white as marble under a shining sheath of pure black and purple frills.

The experience left him not knowing whether he was going this way or that. It was then crowned by the sudden vision of the tall English girl in long earrings and pure turquoise and the disturbing fact that though she was fully dressed she actually seemed to have far fewer clothes on than Mlle. Dupont had in her bedroom. A cosmic explosion could hardly have shaken him more. A kind of low seasickness rocked through him and Pop gave him a glass of punch, which he accepted in a nervous daze, confident only, as Mlle. Dupont already was, that things in the hotel had never been quite like this before and never would be again.

Nobody took much notice of the self-effacing little figure in a black coat and pinstripe trousers and presently he crept out again, head held timidly down, so that he accidentally knocked against Pop, who was ladling out a third glass of punch for Charley.

"*Quel twerp,*" Pop said, and there was laughter from everybody except Angela Snow, who suddenly realized that, for some unaccountable reason, she felt intensely sorry for the little reception clerk, who spent all his days burrowing between desk and bureau, forever like a mole.

It was twenty-five minutes past eight before Mlle. Dupont entered the bar. This was a strange experience in itself, since she could recall no one having had a drink there since Liberation Day. In traditional

French fashion she was wearing all black, with long pearl-drop earrings to give the illusion of that extra height she needed. Tonight she looked positively *chic* and was enveloped in a strong sensational cloud of lily of the valley.

Pop, whose progress in French had been quite marked—always so quick to pick everything up, as Ma said—went straight over to her, clasped her by both hands, and said, *"Mademoiselle! Enchantay!"* as if he had been doing it all his life.

"Delayed in the kitchen, my foot," Angela Snow thought and realized suddenly that she was madly, unreasonably jealous. It was quite unlike her.

"Fascinating tie," she said, and went over to finger Pop's large yellow-and-cranberry butterfly that made him look so dashing. "French?"

"English," Pop said.

"Has that air," she said. "The Froggies simply couldn't do it, dear boy."

The word "Froggies" made Mlle. Dupont bristle. She had begun the evening with nervous apprehension anyway, the complications of the kitchen being so great and those of the corset hardly less so. She felt all too conscious of the corset. She was sure it would make her itch before the night was gone.

"Drink up," Pop said. "Everybody have one more for the wagon train."

Mlle. Dupont, sipping punch, deliberately turned her back on Angela Snow and asked to be told what this cool, charming liquid was.

"In *Anglais*, punch," Pop said.

"Ah, le punch."

"Spécialité de la maison Larkin," Pop said. "Larkin Special. Goes down well, eh? *Très bon, n'est-ce pas?"*

"Extraordinaire. Excellent," Mlle. Dupont said, and then remembered how, in books about England, one always read of gentlemen drinking *le punch.* It was like tea and fog; it was part of the true English scene. Everyone knew, of course, that England was perpetually shrouded in fog, that the sun hardly ever shone there, and that no one ever, or hardly ever, drank anything but tea. But now she had recalled *le punch.* Undoubtedly it was an aristocratic thing.

She now suggested that they might, at any time, go in to dinner. Pop, ladling out the last glasses of punch and sending a final tumblerful to Alphonse in the kitchen, cordially agreed.

"Feeling quite peckish," he said, and hoped everyone else was.

The evening had begun well, he thought, and most people were laughing as they left the bar and went into the *salle à manger*. Everyone seemed properly warmed up, companionable, and happy.

Even Iris Snow, who had eaten nothing but two cream crackers since twelve o'clock midday, felt like a canary.

After the cooling punch the softer, warmer touch of *melon au porto* was like a velvety caress. Everyone agreed that that had been very well-chosen. Full marks. Absolutely. Even the twins mopped it up in no time, asking what it was called.

"There it is on the menu," Charley said. "You can read it. *Melon au porto*. Melon with port wine."

The menu cards had been specially printed in gold and Mademoiselle herself had also ordered little decorations of gold doves to be added at each corner. She had searched for a long time for some suitable symbol of marital love and had finally decided that doves were it.

"Porto! Porto! Old mother Shorto! Diddlum dorto!" the twins started shouting, and a smiling Pop, for once, had no word of reprimand.

A light white wine of the Loire, a little dry, accompanied the sole. It was colder, if anything, than the punch had been. Charley said he thought they married very well together and Pop said Charley should know. Ma remarked that she thought the sole was the best bit of fish she'd had in France and Mlle. Dupont beamed. Pop was sorry about the chips, though, and was on the verge of saying so when he changed his mind and said, "In front of snails anyway. Anybody want to change and have snails? Don't all speak at once. Twins? Snails?"

"You're a snail!" the twins said. "You're a silly old snail! Snail, snail, put out your horn—"

Pop, with happy restraint, merely smiled and Mlle. Dupont, who had always known how correct, undemonstrative, and reserved the English were, couldn't help thinking that their children, at table, sometimes enjoyed the strangest latitude.

Under these pleasantries and the cold white wine of the Loire, Iris Snow began to feel more and more like a singing bird. Now and then she became conscious of one of her protuberances slipping a little under her brown dress and she gave it a bit of a hitch.

Angela Snow began to wonder if she'd got a flea or something and gave her occasional looks of disapproval. She'd caught a flea once before at one of those wretched *pardons*. You never knew.

"And what's next? What's coming next?" Pop said, rubbing his hands. Things were going with a bang. "The *rosbif*. Yes? No? I sink so—yes!"

The roast beef was presently wheeled in on a sort of large, ancient perambulator. It reposed there under a kind of silver shed. This had not been used for thirty years or so and, like the coffee filters, had gone rather brassy at the edges.

The wheeler-in was Alphonse, complete with white hat, white choker, a gravy spoon of about quart measure, and a carving knife two inches wide. His too large, too handsome eyes darted rapidly about the room like jets, catching Iris Snow in the act of doing a twitch. This he interpreted as a sign of secret recognition and took good note of it as he turned up the spirit flame that sprang out of the bowels of the perambulator to keep the beef warm.

Presently Alphonse was carving the *rosbif* with pride among rising steam and sizzling gravy. Every red slice came off with a lofty, dandyish flourish. The *pouding à la Jorkshire* was helped to the plates with a touch of fire and almost reverent extravagance—typical Froggy, Pop thought.

Ma was given the first helping, Alphonse standing over her in a suspended bow to ask, in French, if Madame would taste and pronounce judgment on the *pouding* please?

Mlle. Dupont translated this request with bilingual flutterings and Ma took a good mouthful of Yorkshire. Everyone waited in silence while she slipped it down. It wasn't half as good as she knocked up herself on a Sunday morning, she decided, but wasn't bad really and she said, in a strong English accent, "*Très bon*. Very nice indeed. *Très bon*. Nice." Ma then speared a second piece of Yorkshire on the end of her fork and held it across the table to Pop. "Better pass your judgment too, Pop, hadn't you?"

Pop, who was feeling in the mood to praise anything, even *saucisson à la mode d'ici*, accepted the pudding nippily and tasted it with a loud elastic smack of his lips. A moment later, searching for a word to describe what Alphonse had created, he was fired by a moment of happy inspiration, remembering a word the brigadier had used.

"Delectable!" he said. "Absolutely delectable. Hot stuff. *Formidable!*"

As if at a signal, Alphonse started to leap up and down, spontaneously brandishing the carving knife, at the same time darting flaming glances at Iris Snow, who twitched her bosom again in reply.

A moment later she was astounded to see Alphonse start careering around the table, waving the knife with sweeps of expert extravagance, as if he contemplated chasing her. A sudden transcendent thrill went through her, moving her strangely. It was all a dream. In imagination she suddenly saw herself being pursued by Alphonse over miles of Breton heather, among wild rocks, toward the sea, finally hiding herself from the dark penetrative pursuing eyes in some far-distant *allée couverte*, among secret tumuli.

Mlle. Dupont was horrified. After a single second of relief that with the approval of the *pouding à la Jorkshire* the second of the night's ordeals was over, the first having been with the corset, she was now faced with the fact that Alphonse was about to have one of his temperamental fits. Something, as Pop remarked so often of Charley, must have got into him, and she could only think it was the large glass of *le punch* and two equally large *cognacs* that Pop had had sent into the kitchen for the purpose of encouraging him. It was too *terrible*, too *effrayant*, for words.

Ma, on the other hand, starting laughing like a drain. The children started shrieking too, especially Victoria, who was easily liable to accidents if she pitched her voice too high. Iris Snow was laughing loudly herself, uncertain what to do about the second transcendent thrill that went through her at an even faster, more ecstatically piercing pace than the first, making her quiver from throat to toe. All she could do was to giggle wildly whenever Alphonse brandished the knife, each time having a strange spasmodic recurrence of her dream.

Suddenly, after Alphonse had run around the table three or four times, the flame under the meat perambulator leapt up and then went out with an unseemly plop that sounded not at all unlike a belch. As if at a second signal Alphonse stopped running. Breathing hard, he abandoned the carving knife in order to relight the flame and in another second, as the glow sprang from beneath the brassy meat cover, Iris Snow experienced a third transcending rush of emotion that took her far beyond rocks and tumuli and even the roast beef and Yorkshire that everyone was now enjoying happily.

"I sank you, ladish and jentlemens," Alphonse said. He had learned these few words of English off by heart from the second cook, who had once worked in Whitechapel. "Blast and damn, *merci mesdames et messieurs*, blast and damn, sank you! *Vive les Anglais! Vive le Jorkshire!*"

At this he suddenly took off his tall chef's hat, raised it, bowed politely, and backed out of the *salle à manger*, giving a final dark undressing glance at Iris Snow, who was trying hard to conceal her emotion by hastily sliding Yorkshire pudding into her mouth. She was not very successful, though she had to admit to herself that she had tasted nothing like the rich red beef and its delicious melting pudding for years.

Rich food, even more than the unaccustomed punch, the port, the white wine, and the Chambolle Musigny that accompanied the beef, was now having a strange and unprecedented effect on her. Its stimulus was most marked where she might least have expected it. She was beginning to feel queer thumpings in the bosom, with sudden longings for air.

Her head on the other hand seemed quite light and clear. Her mind retained all its sane, rippling canarylike quality. She was sure she had been perfectly lucid as Alphonse constantly regarded her with those immense, buttery eyes. Alphonse, on the other hand, thought otherwise and had noted over and over again how often she twitched at him. It was very interesting, that twitch.

"I knew the French'd never do the custard and jelly properly," Ma said in a whisper to Angela Snow, who was sitting between her and Pop. "The custard's like billstickers' paste."

Angela Snow said she thought the French didn't really know custard, as custard, that was.

"Then it's about time they did," Ma said, with something like severity.

She was in fact merely tasting the jelly and custard for the children's sake while actually waiting for *crêpes Suzette* to come on.

It was past eleven o'clock when Alphonse arrived back from the kitchen to make the business of the *crêpes Suzette* a sacrifice of joy. That was the best part of the evening, Ma thought. So did the children, who sprang out of their chairs every time a pan of golden flame went up and shrieked that it was just like fireworks.

"Ought to have the lights out," Ma suggested. "Look very pretty."

When the lights were put out the flares of flaming liqueurs danced about the darkened *salle à manger*. The bright leaping light gave to the front of Angela Snow's skintight dress a remarkable effect of transformation. Her body looked no longer blue but silver and it would have been almost too much for Mlle. Dupont to bear if Pop, who was sitting next to her, hadn't thought it as good a moment as any to caress her thigh.

After that the dinner never seemed quite the same to her again. She gradually lost all hope of concentration. From that moment she never knew whether it was the fourth bottle of Chambolle Musigny they were drinking, or the fifth or what it was. In contrast to Iris Snow she had begun to feel quite light-headed and there was still champagne to come.

It came at twelve o'clock, together with the cake that Alphonse had made. Alphonse, more buttery-eyed than ever, bore the cake into the *salle à manger* himself and set it down, with pride and a flourish, before Mariette and Charley.

The cake was iced in bright soapy pink, with a single large red candle on it, and on top of it were the words imprinted circularwise, in red: HAPPY BIRDSDAY ANNIVERSAIRE AND GOOD LUCK

When she read these words Ma felt very touched and then everyone toasted Mariette and Charley with champagne. Even M. Mollet had crept out of hiding again, molelike and shy, to take part in the toasting, staring with filmy eyes at the blue vision of Angela Snow that had troubled him so much, and so increasingly, ever since he had first seen it at eight o'clock.

All through the toasting, Pop stood with swelling paternal pride, watching Mariette. No doubt about it, she was sumptuous—even more beautiful, he thought, than Ma had once been. Charley boy was lucky all right and Pop could only hope that he would, in the shortest possible time, show his appreciation of the fact in the right and proper way. Pop couldn't help thinking too of the day, perhaps, not all that far ahead, when Primrose, Victoria, and the twins would begin to develop too on those same impressive, luscious lines. Perhaps by that time Mariette and even Montgomery would be having children and—who knows?—him and Ma following suit again. He was all set for that. That would be the day.

As if in answer to his thoughts, as the hotel's old brassy gramophone started playing for dancing, he heard a soft voice say, "Wouldn't you dance with me, Pop? I'd love to have the first dance with you."

It was Primrose. There was an indefinable half-sad smile on her face, the sadness heightened by the fact that she had, Pop thought, put just the faintest touch of lipstick on and had crimped her dark hair down over her forehead in a curious little fringe, in the way the French girls did.

'Course he would dance, he told her, and she at once held up her slim sun-brown arms, again with a touch of sadness, the fingers rather drooping.

"Thought you wouldn't ask me," she said sadly as he swung her away to the tune of an old favorite, "La Vie en Rose." "I've been hoping you would."

Pop said he was sorry and also that it hadn't struck him that he'd been expected to ask his own daughter to dance. Laughing merrily, he said he reckoned she ought to have asked him.

"Oh, no," she said, and again the voice was full of her plaintive sadness. "I couldn't do that, Pop, it just shows how much you know."

"Oh, and what about?" Pop asked her.

"Women."

It was some seconds before Pop recovered from this withering blow. When he finally did so he suddenly thought it diplomatic to sidestep a second one—in case one should be coming—by neatly changing the subject with a ripple of a laugh.

"Well, home tomorrow. Old home sweet home."

Primrose, unsmiling, wasn't deceived a bit and showed it by looking him full in the face, her dark soft eyes so full of sad disapprobation.

"Why do you have to sound so glad about it?"

Glad? Pop said. Glad? Why not? It was nice to go on holiday but it was nicer still to go home. Everybody said so.

"Everybody?" she said. "Who's everybody? What do they know?"

Pop, unable to think of a sensible answer to this crushing question, found himself looking down at his daughter's bright yellow dress. He was surprised to find it cut rather wide and low at the neck, where she was wearing a double row of pearls. He was even more surprised to discover that the body underneath it was no longer quite that of a little girl, and that she had beautiful little saltcellars, very like Angela Snow's, just at the base of her olive neck, where the pearls were.

"Don't you want to go home?" he said.

He was up against it now all right, he thought. He remembered what Ma had said. He'd got a handful now.

"No, Pop," she said. "That's it. I didn't sleep a wink all last night for thinking about it. Nor the night before. Nor the night before that."

Pop, in his airy way, asked for crying out gently whatever was it that had done that to her. For the life of him he couldn't imagine.

"Pop," she said, and again she looked up at him, this time no longer with sadness but with a glance so swift that it had swung away again before he could catch it, leaving him looking down at nothing but the dark oval of her hair. She had very pretty hair and it curled fluffily in the nape of her neck, just like Ma's did. "I want to ask you something."

Ask away, Pop said. Fire away. Money, he supposed.

"Pop," she said, and her voice was sad again, with something like low passion in it, "do I *have* to go home? *Must* I go home?"

Didn't mean to tell him she wanted to stay here, in France, did she?

Pop said. All on her lonesome? All by herself?

"Not by myself," she said. "I won't be alone."

It wouldn't be much fun in the hotel, he reminded her. The season was practically over.

"I'll have someone to stay with," she said.

Before answering, Pop permitted himself the luxury of humming a few bars of "La Vie en Rose." Very good song, "La Vie en Rose." Good thing Mlle. Dupont had fished out some of these old favorites. They got you.

"Oh?" he said. "Who?"

"My boyfriend."

For once unsurprised, Pop was back as quick as a bird, laughing.

"Thought you had two?" he said.

Pained dark eyes held him for a sharp second or two, but whether in renewed sadness or sheer scorn for his brief burst of laughter and the little he understood about women he simply never knew.

"I've given one up," she said. "I had to. I had to make the decision."

Though he'd always held that there was safety in numbers, Pop hummed what he thought were a few consolatory, approving murmurs, mostly mere wordless echoes from "La Vie en Rose," but somehow they didn't seem to impress her. She was silent for once, unconsoled.

"What's this one's name?" he said.

"Marc-Antoine."

Typical Froggy, Pop thought. Very fancy.

"And how old's he?"

"A year older than me. Twelve."

"H'm," Pop said heavily, quite unlike himself. "H'm."

A second later he found himself looking down at her, but she at once looked away.

"He says I can go and live with him," she said.

"Eh?" Pop said. He spoke faintly. Good grief, bit early wasn't it? He knew from experience that Ma had been well forward and all that for her age, but damnit. After all, there were limits—

"I mean with his parents. His father keeps a confectioner's shop. A *pâtisserie*. I could—Oh please, Pop"—suddenly he couldn't help thinking that the voice was uncannily, disturbingly like that of the loveliest and most insinuating of all his daughters, Mariette—"please, Pop, couldn't I? Please?"

Pop, giving what he thought was a sagacious wag of the head, a gesture meant to be taken seriously, said simply, "You'd better ask your Ma."

Primrose, who like Mariette wasn't her father's daughter for nothing, was back as quick as a swallow.

"I asked her. She said I was to ask you."

Cornered, Pop took refuge in a few further light bars of "La Vie en Rose," but he knew that that lark couldn't go on much longer. There was a crisis about somewhere.

"Well, I don't know," he said, his voice heavy again. What the devil could he say? He simply didn't know. He could only wonder, in an unprofound moment, what Ma would say? Perhaps Ma didn't know either. "Well, I don't know——"

Profounder instincts than his own kept Primrose silent. She hadn't even another pleading, imploring please to offer and he knew he was in a spot.

"This wants thinking about," he told her in another heavy but not very deep excursion—damnit, what was all that psychology lark that Ma talked about? Didn't that come in somewhere? With something like a flurry of desperation, utterly unusual in him, he made an effort to sum up the kernel of the matter in a single phrase and came out with half a dozen words of brave simplicity that struck even him as being not quite what was wanted: "Long way from home, you know."

A second later she withered him with a glance both needlelike and wretched. Really downright wretched. He expected any moment to see big, sorrowful tears welling from her eyes. That would be the end. That would get him. Damnit, he was slap in the middle of it now all right.

"It's all very well for you," she said. Somebody had turned the record over or put on another one and now the gramophone was playing a tune he didn't know at all, but which Primrose did—a heart twister of yearning southern sorrow called "Anima Core." "You're grown-up. You've forgotten about things——"

Pop started to assure her that there were some things he hadn't forgotten about yet, but she said peremptorily, "You'd like to part us, I expect."

"Well, I—"

"Don't you ever hear that bit Charley's always quoting?" she said. "It's his favorite bit. 'Love is not love that alters when it alteration finds,'—we have it at school too sometimes."

Pop was silent. That feller Keats again. Charley boy all over. He had to hand it to Charley. Terrific influence on the family that chap had been. No doubt about it.

Gloom hung over him like a cloud and he was profoundly wishing he knew a bit more about psychology, if not Keats, when a cheerful languid voice hailed him and said, "Why the dark deep furrowed brow, dear boy? The *crêpes Suzette* not settling or what? Or shouldn't a girl ask? Cheer up, chum."

It was Angela Snow, dancing past him with Montgomery, and Pop, suddenly restored to his perky, normal self again, laughed back in typical rousing fashion.

"Only Juliet here," he said, stroking Primrose's soft dark hair— damnit, he wasn't sure he wasn't very nearly quoting Keats or Shakespeare or somebody himself now—"wants to stay in France with her Romeo."

"And rightly so," Angela Snow said. "Got the right idea. You're going to let her, of course, aren't you? I'll kick you if you don't."

"'Course," Pop said. 'Course. Got to start sometime."

"Sensible man," she said. "Anyway I'll be here for a while yet. I'll be a chaperone."

Unstartled by a word only vaguely familiar to him, Pop watched the turquoise, willowy vision float away and then found himself, a moment later, looking down at a pair of dark eyes brimming over, as he had feared they would be, with tears—except that they were now clear, bright tears of joy.

"Oh, Pop," was all Primrose could say. "Oh, Pop. Marc-Antoine will be thrilled."

French blood in the family now, Pop thought. Blimey, what next?

"It's just like the Sugar Plum Fairy," Primrose said softly, her olive lids quite closed. "I never imagined—"

"Like *who*?" Pop said.

"Tchaikovsky."

She was light-headed, Pop thought. Must be. It did that to you when you were young. You went off your grub and got to thinking you were floating about, empty.

He now hadn't the vaguest idea what his daughter, with eyes still lusciously closed, was talking about and he decided it could only be another of them larks they learned you nowadays at school.

And again, as if sensing his thoughts, she said, "It's about the little girl who goes to bed after a Christmas party and can't sleep and then comes downstairs and watches the Sugar Plum Fairy dance and all that. Just like this. Haven't you ever heard of it?"

Pop had to confess he hadn't. Bit out of his range, like that feller Keats and the rest of 'em. Nevertheless he was fascinated, as always, by the hint of an excursion into new upper worlds and asked her what else they learned them nowadays at school? You never knew.

"Oh, biology," she said. "Sex and all that."

For crying out gently, he thought. No wonder Ma had said she was developing early. It didn't surprise him, considering the help they got. Again, for the second or third time, he didn't know what to say and was saved the necessity of attempting any comment by another airy remark from Primrose, delivered this time with dark eyes fully open, roundly staring up at him, beautifully glistening.

"They don't teach them sex in French schools though," she said.

"Oh?" Pop said, "don't they? Well, well. Too bad." He laughed in his customary rousing fashion. He'd had an idea for a long time the Froggies were a backward lot. Even in sex. How did she know they didn't teach it?

"Because I asked Marc-Antoine," she said. "He was awfully surprised we had it."

Didn't wonder at it, Pop thought. Didn't wonder at all.

"Anyway, he was very interested and that's how we started to get to know each other better."

He must tell Ma all this. Ma would certainly have to hear all about this lark, Pop was thinking. At the same time he was wondering if another glass of champagne wouldn't do him all the good in the world, when suddenly the music stopped.

In the short ensuing silence he saw Ma talking to one of the French chambermaids. He guessed little Oscar was awake and was quite certain of it a moment later when he heard Ma say she'd be up in a minute to soothe him down and that if punch, white wine, red wine, champagne, and *crêpe Suzette* wouldn't do the trick nothing would.

With an involuntary rush of paternal affection he turned to pat Primrose on the head and was astonished to find that he stood with empty arms. A voice low with emotion thanked him with a few happy whispered syllables for the dance and everything. He stood without a coherent thought he could offer in answer, trying hazily to disentangle all that stuff about sugar plum fairies, Tchaikovsky, sex, biology, and what they learned you nowadays in school, so bemused that he probably wouldn't have heard the next record, which was that old favorite, "Night and Day" if it hadn't been that a curious thing occurred.

As Iris Snow heard the opening bars of the music something suspiciously like a sob sprang from her throat. A moment later she hastily pressed a tiny lace square of handkerchief to her mouth and started rushing from the room.

By one o'clock Pop had danced once each with Mariette, Ma and Angela Snow and was now having a waltz with Mlle. Dupont. Ma warned him several times of the virtues of equal shares.

"Got to treat all of us the same," she said. "It's Iris Snow after Mlle. Dupont. No favoritism. Don't forget."

Pop, who was ready to distribute favors everywhere, remarked that Iris Snow had disappeared somewhere and laughingly supposed she might have gone off to catch the flea.

"What flea?" Ma said.

Pop explained how Angela Snow, who was increasingly irritated by her sister, had jocularly told him about the twitch.

"Not a very nice thing to say," Ma said. "Still, don't you catch it though."

He left her to find Mlle. Dupont, who was in an excited mood. While she danced she kept breathing harder and harder and as the dance went on she threw back her head, laughing freely, and said she felt like singing.

Rather to Pop's surprise she actually burst into a few bars of song. Her voice came out as a rather pleasant not uncultured contralto and not a bit as if she had adenoids, as French singers often do. Pop then said jovially that he felt like having a bit of a warble himself and on the spur of the moment suggested she should join him in "It Had to Be You"—but she didn't know that masterpiece, a favorite of Pop's youth, and they sang "C'est si bon" instead, she singing the French and he, in a light falsetto, what he could remember of the English words. Soon everyone else was singing too and the bright noise was punctuated by the cracking volley of champagne corks.

Iris Snow could hear them as she stood on the terrace outside, talking to Alphonse, in French, under the plane trees. Every moment she felt more than ever like a wild canary. She had never had so much to drink in her life and in rapid sentences she was telling Alphonse how much she adored his country. France was her mecca. Everything about France was so cultured. There was nowhere in the world like France. She adored it, its people, its art, its manners, its wine, and its food.

From a woman who fed largely on soft-boiled eggs, dry toast, and anchovy paste on biscuits this was said with a remarkable degree of passion, and in the lights of the hotel windows Alphonse kept her held with remorseless charm in the overlarge handsome eyes that were now so like big, shining prunes.

Soon she was aware again of a transcendent rushing thrill, that strange, unsteady thumping in the bosom and the panting desire for air. She longed to rush down to the beach, she said. A few moments later Alphonse guided her unsteadily to the *plage*, where she found it much easier to sit down than stand up and where she suddenly found herself remarking recklessly, for no reason at all, in a voice that seemed not to belong to her, that the night was just like Grecian honey. It was all like new warm honey from the south, she said, and she longed to rush to the sea. A moment later she started to take off her shoes and stockings, going about it so ineptly that Alphonse, without asking, started to give help with the garters.

With a protesting shriek of joy she suddenly dashed across the beach to the sea. The little pleated phosphorescent waves were just like milk, she thought, and over in the western sky a great star—oh, no, a planet, she supposed—was hanging like burned gold above the sea—oh, so like a wonderful great big gingerbread, she called out crazily, with all the gilt still on!

Alphonse, who hadn't the vaguest idea what she was talking about, pursued her to the edge of the water. By the time he reached it she was already paddling, ecstatically westward, up to her knees. With the water rising up her legs she suddenly decided to tuck her frock in her knickers, which were the same shade of dark coffee-brown as the dress. Seeing this, Alphonse started to take off his shoes and stockings too and roll up the legs of his blue-and-white-striped chef's trousers, which Iris adored.

At this point the sea, as Charley had once explained, was shallow for half a mile from the shore, and Iris was still only up to her knees, thirty yards out, when Alphonse caught up with her. He at once embraced her passionately around the lower middle and started kissing her madly on one ear.

In the middle of this she felt her knees buckle underneath her. In a moment she was up to her armpits, kneeling on sand. Alphonse went under too and in this uncomfortable position, still crying out that the night was like honey and the stars like gilded gingerbread, Iris Snow surrendered gladly to whatever was coming, with low sobs of joy.

Back in the hotel, while Alphonse was also making the interesting discovery that the English could be surprisingly unrestrained, Mlle.

Dupont was taking advantage of Ma's absence upstairs to invite Pop into the bureau. There was something of importance she wished to say.

With shining eyes she asked him to accept a small green leather box from her. "A small thing. A little parting gift for you."

Opening the box, Pop found inside it a pair of silver cufflinks reposing on a bed of emerald velvet.

"Please to look. There is something—"

Pop took the cufflinks out and, looking more closely, found that Mlle. Dupont had had his initials engraved on the faces of the links in the form of a monogram.

"Very nice," he said. "Absolutely perfick—"

"It is just a small thing. Just—"

"Wonderful. Very *chic*," he went on, and said he didn't know how to thank her. "*Très snob.*"

Mlle. Dupont, without saying so, very much hoped he would thank her by kissing her and in fact he did. The kiss was of a kind she had never experienced before and presently knew that she probably never would do again. Under the long extremely well-directed pressure she several times thought the new corset would give way.

When it was all over she stood looking up at him with unsteady luminous eyes, holding his face in her hands.

"Tomorrow you will be back in England," she said. "Tell me about your house in England. Your *château.*"

Oh, it was perfick, Pop said. A paradise. You wouldn't find anything more perfick in the world nowhere, he told her, and then in that glowing hypersensory way of his, warmed up to the business of describing how the junkyard was in spring, with cuckoos calling, nightingales going glorious hell for leather night and day in the bluebell wood, water lilies gold and white in the stream, fields glowing with strawberries, meadows rich with buttercups and grasses, and all the rest of the marvelous, mad, mid-summer lark in England.

For some time she listened to all this as she might have listened to some sort of celestial revelation and then decided to ask a question. It was perhaps a rather indelicate question, but she knew that if she didn't ask it now she never would.

"And will you perhaps marry one day?"

Pop patted her playfully on the roundest part of the corset with an especially warm affectionate hand and laughed loudly. Mlle. Dupont had never known hands so warm.

"Shall if somebody asks me."

"Someone will," she told him with transfixed, shining eyes. "I'm sure that someone will."

Better give her the other half, Pop thought, and set the seal on the evening, the gift and her complete and luminous joy by repeating the kiss at even greater length, under even greater pressure.

"I have decided to reconstruct the hotel," she said. "To have an *ascenseur* and water hot and cold in all the bedrooms. It was you who gave me such ideas."

That was the spirit, Pop said. *Très snob.* Pull 'em down. Start afresh. He wouldn't mind putting a bit of money into it himself if it could be wangled.

"We could be partners?" she said.

"Could be," Pop said. "Could be."

"It is always you," she said, "who has such wonderful ideas. Before you came to stay here I had no courage for such changes—"

"Courage my foot," Pop said, and gave the corset a final semistroking amorous pat in the roundest part. "Natural. If you want an apple off the tree go and get the damn thing."

Still pondering on this remark as if it were some mysterious, mystical text for living, Mlle. Dupont went back with Pop to the *salle à manger*, where everyone except Angela Snow and M. Mollet was still dancing.

In an astonished spasm of jealousy Angela Snow watched her come into the room, holding Pop in a kind of aerial embrace of wonder. For a few electrified seconds she experienced an amazing impulse to rush over and smack Mlle. Dupont's face as hard as she could.

While she was still trying to resist it something surprising occurred. She suddenly found herself being asked to dance by M. Mollet.

M. Mollet had wanted to ask her to dance all evening but had lacked the courage. Now, shy and flushed, pince-nez sparkling, he began dancing with her in a way she hadn't experienced before. He held her consistently at arm's length, as if afraid of letting the front of his body touch the long sheathlike curves of hers. He was several inches shorter than she was, which meant that he was constantly forced to gaze up at her. In this way she found herself concentrating on his eyes. Behind the glasses the pupils were a peculiar midshade of brown, like partly roasted coffee beans. They were sad, mute, appealingly funny little eyes and suddenly she liked them.

After a speechless five minutes she suddenly felt a dreamy and extraordinary impulse to kiss M. Mollet bang in the center of the forehead. Fortunately the music stopped a moment later, waking her.

"And a damn good thing too," she thought. "If you'd have kissed him the poor dear would have dropped down dead. Don't be so lethal."

In a second all her flippancy was back. The jealous creature who had wanted to slap Mlle. Dupont's face had disappeared.

Meanwhile, on the far side of the room, in the electric light, the delicate little prisms of Ma's diamanté comb flashed with many colors as Pop paused to joke with her.

"It's time you had another dance with Angela," she told him. "Fair's fair."

It was nearly four o'clock, Pop reminded her. He wanted to sit down with a quiet glass of champagne somewhere. Even he was getting tired.

"Do as I say," Ma said. "Have one more dance with her and then get into bed."

Pop threw back his head and laughed uproariously.

"Ma," he said, "I think you'd better say that sentence in some other way, hadn't you?"

Ma shrieked, digging him joyfully in the ribs, realizing what she had said.

A moment later Pop found himself dancing with the same languid, casual, flippant vision who had long since endeared herself to him as a sporting, kindred spirit.

She, as if unable to recover from M. Mollet's technique of dancing at arm's length, let Pop hold her in that way too, looking straight into his happy, perky eyes and giving him a sporting wink or two.

"Well?"

"Well?" Pop said.

"Whale of a party."

Pop said he thought so too, and she said, "One thing missing, though."

"Oh?"

"That proposal."

"From me?"

"From you," she said. "Very nearly too late now. I've practically given myself to M. Mollet."

"Have a heart," Pop said. "For crying out gently."

"Love him. Adore him," she said. "He's sweet. Surprised?"

Pop admitted he was very surprised but remarked that there was no accounting for tastes.

"But I do, dear boy," she said. "He's so small. And moley. And brown and all that. One wants to hug the wretched man. Don't you fathom?"

Pop said he didn't fathom and told her, much to her surprise, that he thought it was a clear case of psychology. It was something she'd missed somewhere at some time or never had. See?

For answer she drew him nearer and laid her lovely head on his shoulder.

"This I wouldn't have missed for all the world," she said, "for all the world, my sweet. For all the world I wouldn't have missed it. It's been absolutely perfick. But then with you it always would be."

Impulsively she kissed him as she had wanted to kiss M. Mollet, in the center of the forehead, and an astonished Pop almost recoiled from a display of a technique with which he had been totally unacquainted before.

"That's for keeps," she said in a whisper. "Don't lose it, will you?"

Half an hour later the party was over. Nobody in the hotel was awake except M. Mollet, who had been so shattered by the evening's experiences that he was busy taking aspirin, and Mlle. Dupont, who lay full length on her bed in darkness, still in her corset, thinking over and over again of how she would reshape the hotel, put in an *ascenseur* and hot and cold water in all the bedrooms and how, perhaps, she might have a partner—and also of the fogless splendors of an England astonishingly revealed as abounding in strawberries, cuckoos, water lilies, nightingales, and *pouding à la Jorkshire*.

Outside the hotel nobody was awake either, except Iris Snow, who was walking slowly up and down the *plage*, watching the setting planet that was so like a gingerbread with all the gilt still on, trying to find a pair of lost stockings and all the time singing a happy barefoot song.

9

In the morning Angela Snow woke at eleven o'clock with a headache. She had been a miserable meany about Mlle. Dupont, she thought, and it wasn't like her. She felt very, very cross with herself. And without breakfasting or waking Iris, who hadn't come in till six o'clock, she went down into the town and ordered two dozen roses to be sent to Mlle. Dupont in the afternoon. There was nothing she could think of to say as a message and she sent them without a card.

Then she decided to go and say good-bye to the Larkins and then, a moment later, impulsively decided not to after all. Enough, after all, was as good as a feast. It was all over now and she could only send them a silent, sporting blessing, thinking as she did of the long, golden, light-headed afternoon on the dunes, when salt and sun had burned her lips and the blown breath of sea and pines had been strong enough to make her even happier and tipsier than Pop's cocktails and the wine had done.

The result was that when the Rolls finally drew away from the Beau Rivage at half past one only two people besides Mlle. Dupont and M. Mollet, furtive as ever, stood on the terrace, under the plane trees, to wave good-bye. Like two silent torchbearers, Primrose and Marc-Antoine stood solemnly holding large pink-and-chocolate ice creams in bright saffron-colored cones, giving the tops of them occasional licks with bright pink tongues. Neither of them uttered a single syllable in farewell and after Pop had been struck once again by the dubious distant prospect of having French blood in the family he couldn't help noticing that Marc-Antoine, who was the color of suet and wore large shining steel-rimmed spectacles, looked remarkably like a younger, smaller, Froggier Mr. Charlton. Funny how his daughters attracted the type.

When everything was finally packed and everyone was in the car—Ma quite imperial in the back, with little Oscar in her arms—Pop went up to the steps of the hotel and under the astonished eyes of M. Mollet gave Mlle. Dupont a prolonged parting sample of amorous affection that even had the children cheering from the car.

"Here, stand back and let the dog see the rabbit!" Ma called.

"*Au revoir!*" Pop said. "Good-bye, mademoiselle," and at last retreated from her dazed figure with several debonair waves of the hand. "*À bientôt! Au revoir, merci!* So long! Good-bye."

"Good-bye!" she called. "*Au revoir!* Good-bye! *Adieu!*"

"Good-bye! *Au revoir!*" everyone called. "*Adieu.* Good-bye!"

When Pop got back into the Rolls even Ma had to confess she was surprised at the length and generosity of Pop's prolonged farewell.

"You wouldn't be if you'd seen the bill," Pop said. "Damnit, might as well have my money's worth."

The bill was a blinder. He doubted very much if he'd ever get over the bill. Percentages for this, taxes for that, services for the other. Breathing charges. He doubted if even Charley, that master of figures, would ever be able to sort out all the dodgy squeezes in that bill. It had very nearly skinned him out, he told Ma, very nearly skinned him.

"Think we got enough to get home with?" Ma said.

"Might have to pawn the Rolls," Pop said serenely. "Well, so much for the French lark."

Still, he thought a moment later, it was all over, it was well wurf it, and he gave a final chorus of contrapuntal toots of the horn in debonair farewell as the Rolls moved away.

As soon as the Rolls was out of sight and Pop's cheerful tooting of first the melodious tune of the country horn and then the symphonic brass of the town one had died away, Mlle. Dupont rushed back into the hotel, determined that no one should detect the tears in her eyes. But when the red roses arrived at two o'clock there was no help for it and she lay for the rest of the afternoon on her bed, weepily watching the roses in their big glass vase and seeing over and over again the pictures Pop had painted for her of his home, his *château*, the lordly paradise, in England. Never again would she say that the English were frigid and reticent or restrained or that they took their pleasures sadly or that fog perpetually covered their land. She knew it to be otherwise.

Meanwhile, as the Rolls drove along the coast, Ma called Pop through the speaking tube.

"I don't know what you did to Mlle. Dupont last night but you got her in a proper tizzy."

"Nothing," Pop said airily. "Nothing. Not a thing."

"Did you ask her to marry you?"

Pop said he rather thought he had. Hadn't he ought to have? Ma wasn't offended? After all she'd given him the cufflinks. Had to encourage her a bit.

"Oh, it's not that," Ma said, and started laughing in her customary hearty fashion. "I was only thinking I hope she don't have to wait as long as I have."

Pop burst out laughing too. That was one of Ma's good ones. Well, bill or no bill, it had been a pretty good holiday. Done everybody a whale of good, he thought, getting to know how foreigners lived. Especially Mariette and Charley, who both looked in the pink. He'd expect results now.

"I expect you asked Angela too, didn't you?" Ma said down the tube.

"Shouldn't wonder," Pop said. "She said summat about it."

Ma said she wasn't worried about Angela. She was a sport. She could take care of herself. But she didn't want Pop going around putting people in a tizzy and breaking their hearts. You'd got to draw the line somewhere.

Pop agreed, but still when you were in Rome—

"Oh, talking about Rome, there's another thing," Ma said. "Have you thought any more about little Oscar's names?"

Pop was quick to confess he hadn't.

"Well, I know you've been busy, but we can't let the poor little mite go about all his life with only one name, can we?" Ma said. "That would be a nice thing, wouldn't it?"

"Terrible," Pop said.

"Well, I've been thinking a lot about it. Are you listening?"

Yes, Pop told her on the tube, he was listening.

"Well," Ma said, "I tell you what."

"Half a minute. We want something good. Something special. No half larks. Something a bit *très snob*."

"I know that," Ma said. "Anyway, I've thought what I'd like to call him."

"Oh?" Pop said. "What?"

"I thought we'd call him Oscar Livingstone David Larkin."

Pop was silent for some moments. All his strong paternal instincts came steeping warmly to the surface as he contemplated the proposed trio of names for his son. The names had got to be right, he thought again, no half larks.

Almost immediately he had a qualm about it and called back to Ma down the tube, "No, Ma. Won't do. Not them. Can't have them."

"Oh?" Ma said. "Why not?"

"Makes his initials O.L.D.," Pop said. "He'll be called Old Larkin all his life. Can't have that."

Ma cordially agreed, they couldn't possibly have that; and before she could think of anything else to say Pop called her again on the tube.

"Giving us a bit of trouble, this one," he said. "Good job it wasn't twins," and went on to shoot a sudden, uneasily pertinent question at Charley. "Twins run in your family, Charley old man?"

Not that he knew of, Charley said.

"Well they do in ours!" Pop said in direct, open challenge. "You want to watch what you're up to."

And what did that mean? Ma said. Watch what who was up to?

"Well, you know," Pop said darkly. "Somebody or other."

Mr. Charlton treated these exchanges with silence, not only because it was a silence he thought they deserved but also because he couldn't for the life of him think of anything remotely sensible to say.

"What was that you said about Rome, Ma?" Pop said. "Didn't you say once you wanted to call him after some Roman emperor?"

"I did an' all," Ma said. "But I'm blowed if I can remember which one it was now. Tiberius, I think."

Back in a flash of scolding breath came Charley, "Not on your life. Not that one. Not on your nelly."

"Why not?" Ma said.

"You'd hardly want to call him after a judicial murderer, would you?"

Charley at it again, Pop thought in silent admiration. Charley away again. Amazing feller. You never knew where Charley was off to next. He certainly used his loaf sometimes.

"I should think not," Ma said. "He's got a soft nature, this boy. Wasn't there one called Octavius, though? I remember him on telly once. In a play."

"You can't possibly call him Octavius," Charley said. "He's the seventh, not the eighth."

"Who is?" Pop said.

"Oscar. Besides Oscar Octavius sounds a bit much, don't you think? Call him Septimus if you want a Roman name."

"Septimus?" Ma said. "Why Septimus?"

"Septimus—the seventh. Sept—the same as in French. The same as September. The seventh month."

Mariette, who occasionally found it necessary to keep Charley in check, he was so clever sometimes, said quickly, "September isn't the seventh month, lovey. It's the ninth."

Back in a revelatory flash came Charley again, "Ah, but it used to be, darling, before the calendar was changed. Just as November used to be the ninth and December the tenth."

Pop was stunned again to silent admiration. Wonderfully clever feller, Charley. Terrific clever feller. No keeping up with Charley.

"I think Septimus sounds rather nice," Ma said, kissing Oscar on the ear, "it suits his nature. You like it, Pop?"

He did, Pop said. It had that rather *très snob* touch about it. What Charley sometimes called the *je ne sais quoi.*

"Not too difficult?" Ma said. "After all we want to give him names people can say."

Pop treated this remark with a short soft laugh of scorn. What was the name of that kid at the post office, he wanted to know. Horsa or something, wasn't it? Septimus was no worse than that. Who was Horsa anyway?

"Saxon King," Charley said blandly. "Had a brother named Hengist."

Altogether too taken aback to speak, Pop could only silently congratulate Ma on the swiftness with which she once again made one of her nippy changes of subject.

"What was the name of that other explorer?" Ma said, and then started laughing inconsequently, thinking of Charley. It would certainly be a bomb under Charley if Mariette had twins. That would make him use his loaf a bit. They could call them Hengist and Horsa too.

"Who?" Pop said. "Shackleton?"

"No, before him," Ma said. "A foreigner."

The word "foreigner" struck a certain discord in Pop, who found himself silent again, thinking hard but at a loss. Again Ma couldn't think of the name she wanted either and it was Charley who at last, as so often before, came to the rescue.

"Columbus. Is that the one you've got in mind?"

Columbus, Ma said. Of course. That was it.

"Oscar Columbus," Pop repeated several times over. "That's got class. Oscar Columbus. That's a bit of *très snob,* an' all, Ma. I like that."

Ma said she liked it too and should they settle on Oscar Septimus Columbus David then?

"Oh, not David," Mariette said. "I hate David."

Pop confessed he too wasn't all that gone on David either and urged Ma to put her thinking cap on. Ma was always the one who had the brain waves. She was a dabster for names.

Less than half a minute later Ma confirmed Pop's faith in her by laughing merrily down the tube and saying she wasn't sure but she thought she'd got it.

"How about Dupont?" she said. "Oscar Columbus Septimus Dupont Larkin?"

It tickled him to death, Pop said. Dupont—just the job. Perfick. It absolutely tickled him to death. *Très snob.*

"That's that then," Ma said calmly. "And if we can't have a wedding when we get home, at least we can have a christening, can't we? Fair enough?"

Fair enough, Pop said. Any excuse for a party.

"And I tell you something else I just thought of," Ma said.

Oh? Pop wanted to know. What was that?

"I thought we'd ask Mlle. Dupont to be godmother," she said. "Sort of bring her into the family."

That was a corker, Pop said. He wondered what Mademoiselle would think of that.

"Blessed if I know," Ma said. "You never can tell what these French-women are thinking, I always say," and then realized why. "After all, I don't suppose you can if you don't know their language, can you?"

A moment later the thought of little Oscar having a French god-mother set Pop slapping his knee and roaring with laughter. Joyful noises gurgled down the speaking tube and the sound of the Rolls's contrapuntal horns rang royally across the rocky slopes of heather, somewhere among which Charley's beloved little train, symbol of travel long ago, seemed to let out a terse and mocking toot in reply.

"Godmother Dupont," Pop said. "Well, I'll go to the bone house. I'll go to the ossuary."

"Which," Ma told him blandly but not uncordially, down the tube, "is just about where you'll end up one of these fine days," and then, with a sigh, settled serenely back on the Rolls's deep dove-gray cushions, a wide handsome spread of maternal bosom exposed, ready to give Oscar Columbus Septimus Dupont Larkin a little drop of the best.

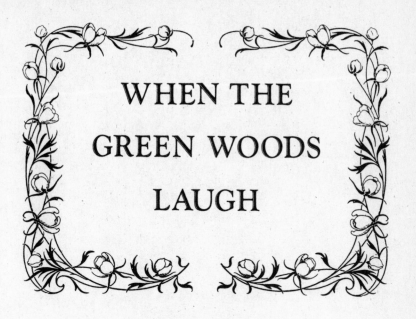

WHEN THE
GREEN WOODS
LAUGH

When the green woods laugh with the voice of joy,
And the dimpling stream runs laughing by;
When the air does laugh with our merry wit,
And the green hill laughs with the noise of it.

BLAKE, *Songs of Innocence*

1

After parking the Rolls-Royce between the pigsties and the muck heap where twenty young turkeys were lazily scratching in the hot mid-morning air, Pop Larkin, looking spruce and perky in a biscuit-colored summer suit, paused to look back across his beloved little valley.

The landscape, though so familiar to him, presented a strange sight. Halfway up the far slope, in fiercely brilliant sunlight, two strawberry fields were on fire. Little cockscombs of orange flame were running before a light breeze, consuming yellow alleys of straw. Behind them the fields spread black, smoking slowly with low blue clouds which drifted away to spread across parched meadows all as yellow as the straw itself after months without rain.

"Burning the strawberry fields off," Pop told Ma as he went into the kitchen. "That's a new one all right. Never seen that before. Wonder what the idea of that is?"

"Everything'll burn off soon if we don't get rain," Ma said. "Me included. As I said to the gentleman who was here this morning."

Ma was wearing the lightest of sleeveless dresses, sky-blue with a low loose neckline. Her pinafore, tied at the waist, was bright yellow. The dress was almost transparent too, so that Pop could see her pink shoulder straps showing through, a fact that excited him so much that he gave one of her bare olive-skinned arms a long smooth caress, quite forgetting at the same time to ask what gentleman she was referring to.

"Why I'm cooking on a morning like this, I can't think," Ma said. Her hands were white with flour. Trays of apricot flans, raspberry tarts, and maids of honor covered the kitchen table. A smell of roasting lamb rose from the stove. "I'd be watering my zinnias if I had any sense. Or sitting under a tree somewhere."

Pop picked up a still warm maid of honor and was about to slip it into his mouth when he changed his mind and decided to kiss Ma instead. Ma returned the kiss with instant generosity, her hands touching his face and her mouth partly open and soft, making Pop think hopefully that she might be in one of her primrose-and-bluebell moods. This made him begin to caress the nape of her neck, one of the places where she was most sensitive, but she stopped him by saying, "You'd better not get yourself worked up. That gentleman'll be back here any minute now. Said he'd be back by half past eleven."

"What gentleman?"

"This gentleman I told you about. He was here just after ten. Said he wanted to see you urgently."

Insurance feller, Pop thought. Or fire extinguishers. Something of that breed.

"What'd he look like?"

"Dark suit and a bowler hat and a gold watch chain," Ma said. "And in a big black Rolls. With a chauffeur."

"Sounds like a brewer," Pop said, laughing, and started to take off his biscuit-colored summer jacket. Thinking at the same time that a glass of beer would be a nice idea, he paused to ask Ma if she would like one too.

"Had two already this morning," Ma said. "Could face another one though."

Pop put the maid of honor in his mouth and started to move towards the fridge. Ma, who was rolling out broad fresh flannels of dough, looked up suddenly from the pastry board as he came back with two iced bottles of Dragon's Blood and laughed loudly, her enormous bust bouncing.

"You look a fine sketch," she said. "Better go and look at yourself in the glass before your visitor arrives."

Pop, looking into the kitchen mirror, laughed too, seeing his face covered with flour dust where Ma had kissed him.

"Good mind to keep it on," he said. "Might frighten this feller away."

He was, he thought, in no state for visitors; it was far too hot. He also had it in mind to ask Ma if she was in the mood to lie down for a bit after lunch. Mariette and Charley were at the market; the rest of the children wouldn't be home till four. There wouldn't be a soul to disturb the peace of the afternoon except little Oscar.

"Well, you'd better make up your mind one way or the other quick," Ma said, "because here comes the Rolls now."

Pop sank his Dragon's Blood quickly and Ma said, "Better let me get it off," and lifted the edge of her pinafore to his face, wiping flour dust away. This brought her body near to him again and he seized the chance

to whisper warmly, "Ma, what about a bit of a lie-down after lunch?"
He playfully nipped the soft flesh of her thigh. "Feel like it? Perfick
opportunity."

"Don't get me all excited," Ma said. "I won't know where to stop."

In a mood of turmoil, thinking of nothing but how pleasant it was
on hot summer afternoons to lie on the bed with Ma, Pop reluctantly
walked into the yard. It was so hot that even the turkeys had given up
scratching and were now gathered into a panting brood under an elderberry tree from which black limp inside-out umbrellas of berries were
hanging lifelessly. Over in the strawberry fields lines of flame were still
darting and running about the smoking straw and from the road the
sound of the Rolls-Royce door snapping shut was as sharp as a revolver
shot in the sun-charged air.

It was in Pop's mind to dismiss whoever was coming with a light-
hearted quip such as "Not today, thank you. Shut the gate," when he
stopped in abrupt surprise.

Ma's visiting gentleman in the dark suit, bowler hat, and gold watchchain had suddenly turned out to be a woman in a white silk suit
covered with the thinnest of perpendicular black pencil lines and with
a small black-and-white hat to match.

She came across the yard, plumpish, blond, chalky pink about the
face, and pretty in a half-simpering rosebud sort of way, with outstretched hands.

"Mrs. Jerebohm," she said. "How do you do?" She spoke with the
slightest of lisps, half laughing. "You must be Larkin?"

Pop, resenting the absence of what he called a handle to his name no
less than the intrusion on his plan for a little privacy with Ma, murmured something about *that* was what he always had been and what
could he do for her?

Lisping again, Mrs. Jerebohm said, with a hint of rapture, "Mr.
Jerebohm simply couldn't wait to see the house for himself. So that's
where he's gone and he wants us to meet him there. I hope that
dovetails all right? You know, fits in?" It was not long before Pop was
to discover that "dovetailing" was one of Mrs. Jerebohm's favorite and
most repeated expressions. She simply adored things to dovetail. She
simply loved to have things zip up, buttonhole, click, and otherwise be
clipped into neat and unimpeachable order.

"If we like it I hope we'll have it all zipped up this afternoon," she
said. "That's the way Mr. Jerebohm likes to do business."

Silent, Pop feigned a sort of ample innocence. What the ruddy hell,
he asked himself, was the woman talking about?

"They told us at the inn you wanted to sell and the minute we heard we had a sort of thing about it."

Inn? Pop could only presume she meant The Hare and Hounds and at the same time couldn't think what that simple pub had to do with her constant lisping raptures. She fixed him now with eyes as blue as forget-me-nots and a quick open smile that showed that two of her front teeth were crossed. That explained the lisping.

"Could we go right away? I mean does that dovetail and all that? We could go in the Rolls."

Pop, bemusedly thinking of roast lamb and mint sauce, cold beer, fresh apricot flan, and Ma lying on the bed in nothing but her slip or even less, suddenly felt a spasm of impatience and used the very same expression he had once used to Mr. Charlton, in the days when he had been as eager as a hunter to collect taxes.

"You must have come to the wrong house, madam," he said. "Or else I'm off my rocker."

"Oh no." When Mrs. Jerebohm flung up her hands with a rapturous lilt, which she did quite often, it had the effect of stretching the white suit across her bust, so that it momentarily seemed to puff up, tightly. It made her, Pop thought, with her smallish blue eyes and crossed teeth, not at all unlike a white eager budgerigar.

"Oh no," she said again. "That doesn't fit. There can't be two people who own Gore Court, can there?"

It had hardly occurred to Pop, quick as ever in reaction, what she was talking about before she fluttered lispingly on, "You can show us over, can't you? You do want to sell, don't you?"

"Going to pull the whole shoot down one of these days," Pop said, "when I get the time."

Mrs. Jerebohm expressed her sudden shock with prayerful lifts of her hands, bringing them together just under her chin.

"Oh, but that's awful sacrilege, isn't it? Isn't that awful sacrilege?"

Pop started to say that he didn't know about that but the first words were hardly framed before she went lisping on:

"But we could just see it, perhaps, couldn't we? At the inn they assured us you were keen to sell. You see we're mad to have a place in the country. Absolutely mad. So when we heard—"

"Big place," Pop said. "Fifteen bedrooms."

"That would suit us. That would fit all right. We'd want to have people down. My husband wants shooting parties and all that sort of thing."

"Ah, he shoots does he?"

"Not yet," she said, "but he's going to learn."

A sharp, searching fragrance of roast lamb drifted across the yard, causing Pop to sniff with uplifted nostrils. Ma, he thought, must be opening the oven door, and with relish he also remembered maids of honor, raspberry tarts, and apricot flans. He wondered too how many vegetables Ma was cooking and said, "Couldn't manage nothing just now, I'm afraid. My dinner's on the table."

"Oh? Not really?"

"Ma'll be dishing up in ten minutes and she won't have it spoiled."

"Oh, be an angel."

The appeal of the small forget-me-not eyes was too direct to resist and Pop answered it with a liquid look of his own, gazing at Mrs. Jerebohm with a smoothness that most women would have found irresistibly disturbing. It was like a slow indirect caress.

On Mrs. Jerebohm it had the effect of making her retreat a little. She seemed to become momentarily cool. She showed her crossed teeth in an unsmiling gap, much as if she had realized that her fluttering "Oh, be an angel" had gone too far into realms of familiarity.

"I can wait for you to finish your lunch," she said. "I'm perfectly content to wait."

"Oh, come in and have a bite," Pop said. "Ma'll be pleased to death."

Mrs. Jerebohm gave an answer of such incredible frigidity that Pop almost felt himself frozen in the hot July sunshine.

"No thank you. We never eat at midday."

Pop could find no possible answer to this astounding, unreal statement; it struck him as being nothing but a fabulous lunacy. It couldn't possibly be that there were people who didn't eat at midday. It couldn't possibly be.

"I will wait in the car."

"Have a wet then. Have a glass o' beer," Pop said, his voice almost desperate. He was feeling an urgent need for a glass, perhaps two, himself. "Come and sit down in the cool."

Mrs. Jerebohm, already cool enough as she surveyed the piles of junk lying everywhere across the sun-blistered yard, the now prostrate brood of turkeys, and the Rolls-Royce incongruously parked by the muck heap, merely showed her small crossed teeth again and said, "Have your dinner, Larkin. I'll be waiting for you."

Turning abruptly, she went away on short almost prancing steps toward the road. Instinctively Pop gazed for a moment at the retreating figure in its penciled white skirt. The hips, he thought, were overlarge for the rest of the body. As they swung fleshily from side to side they looked in some way haughty and seemed frigidly to admonish him.

Going back into the house, he felt something more than thirst to be the strongest of his reactions. The morning had suddenly become unreal. In a half dream he poured himself a glass of beer, drank part of it, and then decided he needed a real blinder of a pick-me-up to restore his sanity.

Ma was busy laying the lunch as he concocted a powerful mixture of gin, whiskey, and French vermouth, a liberal dash of bitters, and plenty of ice.

"Been gone a long time," Ma said. "What did he want after all?"

In a low ruminative voice Pop explained to Ma that his visitor was, after all, a she.

"Wants to buy Gore Court. Wants me to show her and her husband over after dinner."

"What's she like? No wonder you been gone a long time."

Pop swirled ice around and around in his glass, moodily gazing at it. He drank deeply of gin, whiskey, and vermouth, waited for it to reach his empty stomach, and then in tones of complete unreality revealed to Ma the shocking news that he had just met someone who, believe it or not, never ate at midday.

"Can't be right in her mind," Ma said.

"Fact," Pop said. "Invited her in to lunch but that's what she said. Never eats at midday."

"Why? Does she think it common or something?"

Pop said that could be it and drank solidly again. A moment later Ma opened the oven door and took out a sizzling brown leg of lamb surrounded by golden braised potatoes, so that the morning at once woke into new excruciating life, with pangs of hunger leaping through Pop like a pain.

"You hear something new every day," he said, "don't you, Ma? Something as shakes you."

Ma said you certainly did and then suddenly, with no warning at all, popped the leg of lamb back into the oven again.

"You mean she's still waiting out there? She'll faint off or something."

More than likely, Pop thought. Yes, she was waiting. Depressedly he poured another couple of inches of gin into his glass, hardly hearing Ma say, "I'd better take her a bite of something out. Glass of milk and a slice of flan or something. She can't sit out there on an empty stomach. She'll go over."

Less than a minute later Ma was away across the yard on an errand that was less of mercy than one of sheer correction. It simply wasn't right for people to do these things. It was as plain as the moon: If you didn't eat you didn't live. It was criminal. You faded away.

Pop had hardly mixed himself a third pick-me-up before Ma was back again, bearing the offering of apricot flan and milk, now rejected.

"On a very strict diet," Ma said. "Trying to get her weight down. Got a proper chart and pills and units and points and all that sort of thing."

Pop, remembering Mrs. Jerebohm's overrounded thighs, tight in the thin white suit, was suddenly jolted by piercing shrieks from Ma. Her great sixteen-stone body seemed to be laughing from every pore.

"I told her to look at me," Ma said. "I think it cheered her up a bit. She was no more than a sylph, I said."

Pop put the word away in his mind for further reference. Ma took the sizzling leg of lamb from the oven again and a few moments later Pop was deftly carving it into generous pink-brown slices, to which Ma added steaming hillocks of fresh-buttered French beans, two sorts of potatoes, new and braised, mint sauce, and vegetable marrow baked with cheese.

Bent over this feast in attentive reverence, Pop at last paused to drain a glass of beer and look up at Ma and say, "Ma, what did I pay for Gore Court in the end? I forget now."

"First it was going to be nine thousand. Then it was seven."

Pop helped himself to five or six more new potatoes, remarking at the same time how good they were in the long hot summer, and then sat in thought for a moment or so.

"What shall I ask? Ten?"

"Show a nice profit. Might be able to have that swimming pool Mariette keeps talking about if you brought the deal off."

There was a lot of land there, Pop reminded her. And all those greenhouses and stables and asparagus beds. To say nothing of the lake and the cherry orchard. He thought he'd ask twelve.

"Why not fourteen?" Ma said serenely. "You can always come down."

Pop said that was true, but was Ma quite sure it wasn't too much?

"Not on your nelly. Look at the paltry bits of land they ask five hundred for nowadays. Don't give it away."

No chance of that, Pop said. Not if he knew it. No fear.

"Go up a bit if anything," Ma said. "No harm in trying. Ask fifteen."

Pop, ruminating briefly, thought he detected sense in this and finally, with an airy flourish of a hand, said he thought it wouldn't choke him if he asked seventeen.

"Now you're talking," Ma said. "Now you're using your loaf." She laughed suddenly, in her rich, quivering-jelly fashion. "Might be able to have the swimming pool heated now. You know how I hate cold water."

Less than half an hour later, after eating three slices of flan, half a dozen maids of honor, and a raspberry tart or two, at the same time abandoning with reluctance the idea of a nice lie-down with Ma, Pop put on his light summer jacket again and went out to Mrs. Jerebohm, leaving Ma at the task of feeding little Oscar, now eighteen months old, with much the same lunch he and Ma had had themselves, except that it was all mashed up and in smaller proportion. Oscar, he proudly noted, was getting as fat as a butterball.

Out in the road a chauffeur in bottle-green cap and uniform held open the door of Mrs. Jerebohm's Rolls and Pop stepped into an interior of beige-gold, the upholstery softer than velvet.

"Well, here we are," Pop said. "Perfick afternoon."

"I see you too have a Rolls," Mrs. Jerebohm said.

"Oh, that old crate. That's a laugh."

Pop, who in reality adored and revered the Rolls with pride and tenderness as if it had been the eighth of his offspring, cheerfully proceeded to tear the car's paltry reputation to pieces.

"Took it for a small debt," he explained. "Wouldn't pull pussy. Knocks like a cracked teapot. You'd get more out of a mule and a milk float. Still, the best I can afford. Struggle to make ends meet as it is."

As the Rolls turned the last bend before the house faded from sight he invited Mrs. Jerebohm to look back on his pitiful junkyard, the paradise from which he scratched the barest of livings—if he had good luck.

"Like my poor old place," he said. "Just about had it. Falling apart and I'll never get the time to put it together again."

"Charming countryside, though," Mrs. Jerebohm said. "I adore the countryside."

Pop resisted a powerful impulse to praise the countryside. Nothing in his life, except Ma, brought him nearer to celestial ecstasies than the countryside. Instead he now started to concentrate, with a new warm glow, on fresh enthusiasms.

"Ah, but wait till you see Gore Court. Wait till you see that."

"I'm absolutely dying to. Absolutely dying. We've seen so many that haven't—you know—sort of dovetailed, but this one gives me a kind of thing—"

A moment later Mrs. Jerebohm took a handkerchief from her white suede handbag, releasing an unrecognizable breath of perfume on which Pop's hypersensitive nostrils at once seized with eager delight.

It was a wonderful perfume she was wearing, he said. Could she tell him what it was?

"Verbena. French. You like it?"

It was perfick, Pop said. It suited her perfickly. It was just her style.

"Thank you."

She smiled as she spoke, this time with her lips parted a little more, so that the edges of her mouth were crinkled. The effect of this was so surprisingly pleasant after the frigidities in the yard that Pop wondered for a moment whether or not to hold her hand and then decided against it. Even so, he thought, it might not be all that much of a hardship to dovetail with Mrs. Jerebohm one fine day.

He was still pondering on the pleasant implications contained in the word "dovetail" when the Rolls rounded a bend by a copse of sweet chestnut, beyond which were suddenly revealed a mass of baronial turrets taller than the dark torches of surrounding pines.

"There!" Pop said. He spoke with a studied air of triumph, waving a hand. "There's the house. There's Gore Court for you. What about that, eh? How's that strike you? Better than St. Paul's, ain't it, better than St. Paul's?"

2

Mr. Jerebohm, who had stayed the night with Mrs. Jerebohm at The Hare and Hounds, had been up that morning with the lark. He was not at all sure what sort of bird a lark was or what it looked like, but he knew very well it was the bird you had to be up with.

Numbers of small brown birds in the many thick trees surrounding the pub, which both he and Mrs. Jerebohm called the inn, had chirped him awake as early as half past four. He supposed these might have been larks. On the other hand they might well have been robins. He was a stranger in the country; it was a foreign land to him, distant as Bolivia, unfamiliar as Siam. He simply didn't know. Nor did he know anything distinctive about the trees that stood about the pub with tall lushness, almost black in high summer leaf. A tree was a shape. It had branches, a trunk, and leaves. In spring the leaves appeared; they were green; and in autumn they fell off again.

Grass was to be recognized because it too was green, or generally so. It grew on the floor, most conveniently, and cows grazed at it. Mr. Jerebohm recognized a cow. It had horns, teats, and gave milk. If it didn't it was a bull. He also recognized a horse because even in London, where stockbroking absorbed him day and night, you sometimes still saw one drawing a cart. You also saw them on films and television, running races. You also hunted foxes with them, which was what Mr. Jerebohm hoped to do as soon as he and Mrs. Jerebohm had finally settled on a suitable place in the country.

Finding a suitable place in the country had turned out to be an unexpectedly difficult and tedious business. The notion that you rang up or called on a house agent, described the kind of residence you wanted—Mr. Jerebohm invariably referred to houses as residences and their surroundings as domains—and bought it immediately was nothing but a myth. This was not in the least surprising, since myths were exactly what house agents dealt in. They were crooks and liars. Their sole idea was to sell you pups.

Mr. Jerebohm was determined not to be sold any pups. Nobody sold him any pups in the world of stockbroking and nobody was going to sell him any in the world of larks and cows. He was, since he was a Londoner, clever enough not to be caught by that sort of thing. People in London were naturally clever. They had to be; it was due to the competition.

On the other hand, everybody knew that people in the country were not clever, simply because there was no need to be. There were enough fields, trees, cows, horses, and all the rest of it to go around. You had ample milk, fresh from the cow. You kept hens and they laid multitudes of eggs. Farmers made butter. As to the people, you smelled innocence in the air. They were naturally simple. The sky, even when rainy, was full of purity. The fields had a sort of ample pastoral virginity about them, unbesmirched by anything, and even the manure heaps had a clean, simple tang that was good to breathe.

The exceptions to all this were house agents. Two weeks of trailing with Mrs. Jerebohm from one to another had made Mr. Jerebohm tired and angry. He was now constantly taking pills and powders for the suppression of bouts of dyspepsia brought on by viewing manor houses that turned out to be matchboxes, farms that were nothing but hen coops, and country residences of character that looked like disused workhouses or mental homes.

He wanted no more of house agents at any price and for this reason had been more than glad when the barman at The Hare and Hounds had told him that a fellow named Larkin had a very nice house that he was planning to pull down. It was a pity and a shame, the barman said, but there it was. Nobody seemed to want it.

"You're sure it's nice?" Mr. Jerebohm said. He had heard that word about houses before—it was the most misused, the most callous, in the language. "Has it class is what I mean?"

Class was what Mr. Jerebohm was looking for and class was precisely what couldn't be found.

"I ought to know," the barman said. "My missus goes in to air it twice a week and cleans and dusts it once a fortnight. You could walk in tomorrow. Class? It's a treat. All in apple-pie order."

Mr. Jerebohm thanked the barman and gave him a shilling. It paid to be generous to the yokels.

"Pinkie," he said that night as he folded his charcoal city trousers and hung them on the bedroom towel rail, "Pinkie, I've got a sort of hunch about this house. A funny kind of premonition. Have you?"

Pinkie was his pet name for Mrs. Jerebohm; it suited her much better than Phyllis.

Pinkie, who in nothing but panties and a brassiere was squatting on her haunches in the middle of the bedroom floor, hands on hips, balancing a Bible and a thick telephone directory on her head, going through her slimming exercises, said she thought so too, adding, "I think I've lost another ounce. I weighed myself today in the ladies' at that hotel where we had lunch. But I can't really tell until we get home and I can take everything off and get on the proper scales."

Mr. Jerebohm, saying good for her, got into bed, propped himself up on the pillows, and started to read the *Financial Times*. The night was exceptionally hot and stuffy and in any case he knew from long experience that there was no need yet awhile to think of shutting his eyes. It would take Pinkie the best part of another hour to do her balancing acts with books, stretch her legs, touch her toes, do push-ups, take off her makeup, and swallow her pills.

"Good night, Sunbeam," she said when she got into bed at last. She liked to call him Sunbeam last thing at night; it left a blessed sort of glow in the air. "Sleep well." She kissed him lightly on the forehead, barely brushing his skin, anxious about her facial cream. "I'm mad to see this house. It's so beautiful here. Don't you think it's beautiful?"

Mr. Jerebohm wasn't sure whether it was beautiful or not. Hot and restless, he found he couldn't sleep well. It was terribly noisy everywhere. The countryside not only seemed to be full of barking dogs. From the fields came a constant moaning of cattle and whenever he was on the verge of dropping off he was assailed from all sides by low asthmatic bleatings.

Later in the night he had a rough bad dream in which Pinkie lost so much weight that she became a skeleton and he woke in an unpleasant sweat to hear a whole eerie chain of birds hooting at each other from tree to tree. These, he supposed, might well have been owls, though he wouldn't have been at all surprised to hear that they were nightingales.

Whatever they were they kept him awake until dawn, when once again the larks started their maddening chorus in the ivy.

3

When Pop Larkin first saw Mr. Jerebohm, hatless and coatless in the heat, waiting outside the tall wrought-iron gates by Gore Court, it struck him immediately that his face seemed in some way curiously out of proportion with the rest of his body.

Mr. Jerebohm was shortish, squat, and slightly paunchy beneath watchchain and waistcoat. By contrast his face was rather long. It was grayish in an unhealthy sort of way, with thick loose lips and eyebrows that had in them bright sparks of ginger. He looked, Pop told himself, rather like a bloater on the stale side.

"Afternoon, afternoon," Pop said. "Perfick wevver. Hope I haven't kept you waiting? Hope you don't find it too hot?"

Mr. Jerebohm, who in sizzling heat had tramped about the domain of Gore Court for the better part of an hour, so that his dark city trousers were now dustily snowy with white darts of seed from thistle and willow herb, confessed to a slight feeling of weariness. But Pop was cheery.

"Cooler inside the house. Wonderfully cool house, this. Thick walls. I daresay," he said, "it's above twenty degrees cooler inside. Had a good wander around?"

Mr. Jerebohm confessed that he had wandered but wasn't sure how good it was. He had learned to be craftily cautious about houses. He was going to be very wary. He wasn't going to be sucked in.

"Had to fight my way through a damn forest of weeds," he said. "Look at me. How long has the place been in this state of disrepair?"

Pop laughed resoundingly.

"That seed?" he said. "Blow away in a night. One good west wind and a drop o' rain and it'll melt away. Put up any pheasants?"

When Mr. Jerebohm rather depressingly confessed that he hadn't put up a bird of any kind, Pop laughed and said, "Hiding up in the hot wevver. Place's crawling wiv 'em. Partridges too. And snipe. And woodcock, down by the river. Didn't see the river? I'll take you down there when you had a deck at the house. And the lake? Beautiful trout in the lake. Nice perch too. Didn't see the lake? Didn't get that far? I'll take you down."

Mrs. Jerebohm, following Pop and Mr. Jerebohm up the circular stone steps leading to the front of the house from a short avenue of box trees, found herself borne along on a mystical flow of lilting information that might have come from a canary. It was so bright and bewildering that she was inside the house before she knew it, standing at the foot of a great baronial sweep of oaken stairs.

"There's a flight of stairs for you," Pop said. He waved a demonstratively careless hand. "Handsome, eh? Like it?"

Mrs. Jerebohm, almost in a whisper, went so far as to say that she adored it. If anything clicked, that staircase did.

Cautious as ever by contrast, Mr. Jerebohm struck the banisters of the stairs a severe blow with the flat of his hand, as if hoping they would fall down. When nothing happened Pop startled him with a sentence so sharp that it sounded like a rebuke. "Built like a rock! Wouldn't fall down in a thousand years!"

With hardly a pause for breath Pop enthusiastically invited Mrs. Jerebohm to take a good deck at the paneling that went with the stairs. It was linenfold. Magnificent stuff. Class. There were walls of it. Acres. Talk about fumed oak. Fumed oak wasn't thought of when that was made. You could get ten pounds a square foot for it where it stood. And that was giving it away. And did she see the top of the stairs? The Tudor rose? The Tudor rose was everywhere.

Mrs. Jerebohm, speechless, stood partly mesmerized. At the very top of the stairs, lighting a broad paneled landing, a high window set with a design of fleur-de-lis, swans, and bulrushes in stained glass of half a dozen colors threw down such leaves of brilliant light, driven by the strong afternoon sun, that she was temporarily dazzled and had to pick her way from step to step, like a child, in her ascent of the stairs.

A man from Birmingham had offered him a thousand pounds for the window alone, she heard Pop say in a voice that reached her as an unreal echo, like some line from a far distant overromantic opera, but he had turned it down.

"Class," Mr. Jerebohm was half admitting to himself. "Class."

"How old is this house?" Mrs. Jerebohm brought herself to say. Her voice too was like an echo.

Pop said he thought it was Georgian or Tudor or something. Fifteenth century.

Mr. Jerebohm, with a bloaterlike smile, was quick to seize on these transparent contradictions and nudged Pinkie quietly at the elbow as they turned the bend of the stairs. It served to prove his point about how simple the yokels were.

"How many bedrooms did you say?" Mrs. Jerebohm unable to keep entrancement out of her voice, almost hiccupped as she framed the question. "Was it ten?"

Twelve, Pop thought. Might be fifteen. If it was too many they could always shut the top floor away.

"There's a beauty of a room for you!" he said with almost a bark of delight. A huge double door, crowned by a vast oaken pediment, was thrown open to reveal a bedroom half as large as a tennis court. "Ain't that a beauty? Didn't I tell you it was like St. Paul's?"

Mrs. Jerebohm, stupefied by the sheer size and acreage of paneling, heard three pairs of footsteps echo about her as if in a cave. Above them, at the same time, the chirpy solo voice of Pop was urging her to take a good eyeful of the view from a vast blue-and-pink window that might have come out of an abbey.

"Drink that in!" he said. "Take a swig at that!"

Mrs. Jerebohm, in half-ecstatic rumination, found herself positively gulping at two acres of thistles, willow herb and docks among which numbers of black conical cypresses and a half-derelict pergola of roses stuck up in the air like a sad fleet wrecked and abandoned. Beyond them a line of turkey oaks, black too in the blistering perpendicular light of full afternoon, cut off completely whatever view was lurking behind.

"In winter," Pop started to say with a new, more vibrant lyricism, "in winter, when the leaves are down, and the light's right, and it's a clear day, in winter, Mrs. Jerebohm, you can stand here and see the sea."

In a rush of disbelief, lyrical too, Mrs. Jerebohm several times repeated the words in heavy lisps.

"The sea—the sea? No? Really? The sea?" she said. "You mean we can really see the sea?"

"Smoke of ships in the channel," Pop said impassively, "coming from all over the world."

"Oh, Sunbeam," Mrs. Jerebohm said, lisping, "you hear that? You can actually see ships out there. Ships!"

Mr. Jerebohm, impressed though still wary, had no time to make any sort of comment before Pop struck him a resounding but friendly blow in the middle of the back. Mr. Jerebohm recoiled uneasily, but Pop, totally unaffected, merely told him, "This is the place where you got to use your loaf, old man. Get your imagination to work. Have a deck down there."

As Pop waved a careless hand in a quick flexible curve in the direction of the impossible thistles, Mr. Jerebohm half ducked, as if confident of another approaching blow, but Pop merely urged him, taking a great deep breath, "Imagine roses down there. Imagine acres of roses. Eh? A couple o' thousand roses."

Without another word he suddenly flung open a casement in the churchlike window, again drawing a long deep breath.

"What price that air, eh? Take a sniff at that. Like medicine. Old man, that's pure concentrated iodine."

"Iodine?" Mr. Jerebohm, incredulous, snapped sharp, bloaterlike lips. "Iodine? What on earth's iodine got to do with it?"

With stiff wariness Mr. Jerebohm waited for an answer, determined not to be caught by any cock-and-bull nonsense of that sort.

"Air here's stiff with it," Pop said. "Saturated. Due to being practically surrounded by sea."

To the speechless astonishment of both Mr. Jerebohm and Pinkie, he proceeded to toss off careless scraps of topography.

"Got to remember this country is almost an island. Didn't know that? Fact. Two thirds of its boundaries are water. It's an island on an island. Understand me?"

Before Mr. Jerebohm could begin to say whether he understood him or not Pop thundered out, "Nobody hardly ever dies here. People live forever, same as tortoises. Everything grows 'ell for leather. Cherries, strawberries, hops, apples, pears, corn, sheep. Everything! Not called the Garden of England for nothing, this place. Not called the Garden of England for nothing, old man."

Suddenly, after Pop had closed the casement with a gesture almost dramatically regretful, Mrs. Jerebohm felt quite overpowered, in a faint sort of way, by the projected grandeur of seascape, roses, iodine, and heights and asked diffidently if perhaps she could see the kitchens.

"Certainly!" Promptly Pop started to lead the way downstairs, freely admitting as he did so that the kitchens were perhaps a bit on the large side, though of course that wasn't necessarily a bad thing these days. It gave you a lot more room to put telly in for the maids.

That, Mrs. Jerebohm said, reminded her of something. Help. What about help? Could help be got? In London that, of course, was the great problem. Would she be able to get help in the country?

"Sacks of it," Pop said. "Bags." If his conscience pricked him slightly as he recalled the constant eager race of village women to get to the rich pastures of strawberry fields, cherry orchards, and hop gardens and all the rest, where families cleaned up sixty or seventy pounds a week, tax free, he momentarily appeased it by reminding himself that, after all, business was business. A fib or two was legitimate. You had to allow for a fib or two here and there. "All the help you want. Only a question of paying on the right scale and giving 'em plenty o' telly."

Lispingly Mrs. Jerebohm confessed that she was relieved to hear it. The question had been bothering her. It was the thing on which everything depended.

"Quite," Pop said blandly. "Quite."

A moment later he opened the door to the kitchens. A vast funereal dungeon opened up, half dark, its windows overgrown with rampant elderberry trees. The air was drugged with mold.

"Something would have to be done with this," Mr. Jerebohm said. "Not much iodine here."

Pop, severely ignoring the sarcasm about iodine, freely admitted once again that it was all a bit on the large side but anyway you could always put in a Ping-Pong table for the maids. Help 'em to keep their figures down. He laughed resoundingly. They got fat and lazy quick enough as it was.

Mr. Jerebohm, in turn ignoring the joke, started to retreat with relief from the dankness of the kitchen dungeons, saying, "You're quite sure about the help? What about chaps for the garden and that sort of thing?"

"Oceans of 'em," Pop said. "No trouble at all."

His conscience, pricking him slightly a second time, forced him to think of farm laborers who ran about in cars or mounted on splendid, glistening, highly expensive motorbikes and of how his friend the brigadier couldn't get a boy to clean his shoes, and he wondered, not for the first time, what Ma would say. Ma was strict about the truth. Still, you'd got to allow a fib or two here and there.

"Well, I hope you're right." Mr. Jerebohm told himself he wasn't sold yet. Much experience with house agents, the liars, cheats, and swindlers, had left him skeptical, cautious, and, as he liked to tell himself, sharp as a fox. "It's of paramount importance."

Pop, recoiling slightly from the word "paramount" as if it meant something shifty, said, "Well, now, what else?" He too was relieved to escape from the kitchens' dank elder-mold darknesses and he was bound to admit they ponged a bit. "What about a look at the outside?"

He searched the air for a breath of Mrs. Jerebohm's light and exquisite perfume and, as he caught it, made her smile with perceptible pleasure by saying, "That scent of Mrs. Jerebohm's reminds me of Ma's garden. She grows verbena there."

"You see, we'd plan to do a fair amount of entertaining," Mr. Jerebohm said. "That's why I spoke about the chaps. Shooting parties and that sort of thing. Lot of people for weekends."

"Beautiful shooting country," Pop said. "Marvelous. Bags of cover. What about a look at the lake now?"

Mr. Jerebohm said yes, he was ready to have a look at the lake if Pinkie was.

"You go," she said. "I'd like to wander around the house again."

As she started to go upstairs, Pop, in the moment before departing, called up after her, "If you change your mind it's straight down from the front of the house. You'll see the path. There's a white gate at the bottom."

As he skirted the seed-smoking thistle forest with Mr. Jerebohm Pop put to him what he thought to be an important question. "What business you in?"

"Stock exchange."

"Plenty o' work?"

"Mustn't grumble."

"Hot weather affected you at all?" Pop said. "It's caned a lot of people."

"Not really." Mr. Jerebohm couldn't help smiling behind his hand. Really the yokels were pretty simple. And when you thought of it, how could they be otherwise?

"There's the lake for you," Pop said. "Beautiful water lilies, eh? Always remind me of fried eggs floating about on plates." The lake, low after months of drought, stretched glassy in the sun. On banks of gray cracked mud, flies buzzed in thick black-blue swarms. An odd invisible moorhen or two croaked among fringes of cane-dry reed and out on the central depths great spreads of water lilies shone motionless in the sun.

Pop picked up a stone, aimed it at a distant clump of reeds, and threw it. It might have been a signal. A line of wild duck got up, circled, and headed for the center of the lake, crying brokenly as they flew.

"Thought so," Pop said. "Whole place is lousy with 'em."

Pheasants? Mr. Jerebohm supposed.

"Wild duck." Damnit, these Londoners were pretty simple when you came to think of it. "Like wild duck? Ma does 'em with orange sauce. Puts a glass o' red wine in too. I love 'em. Shot so many last winter though I got a bit sick of 'em by the end.''

For a painful moment or two Mr. Jerebohm's sharply watering mouth told him he would never, never get tired of wild duck. He longed suddenly and passionately for wild duck with red wine and orange sauce, tired as he was of living on yogurt, toast fingers, consommé, and undressed salads in order to help Pinkie keep her weight down.

"And all this goes with the house? The lake and everything?" he said. "What's beyond?"

"Parkland. See the big cedar?"

Mr. Jerebohm stared at a tall dark object on the skyline and might as well have been looking at a factory chimney. "Starts there. Quite a few deer in it still. Used to be a pretty big herd. Like venison?"

God! Mr. Jerebohm thought. Venison?

"Ma always does it in a big slow double pan in plenty of butter," Pop said. "Nothing else, just fresh butter. We always have red currant jelly with it. The meat fair falls apart. Perfick. I tell you, old man, perfick.''

Mr. Jerebohm, who had lunched exceptionally early, in unison with Pinkie, on thin slices of lean ham, butterless rye biscuits, and China tea, thought "God!" again in agony, feeling his stomach perform involuntary sickening acrobatics of hunger. There was something not fair about talk of food sometimes.

"Not sure how the trout are holding up," Pop said. He'd got to be fair about the trout. No use overpraising the trout. To be perfickly fair the herons fetched them almost as fast as you restocked and you never really knew how they were. "Caught sight of two or three fat ones though, last time I came down. Still, it's cheap to restock if you wanted to.''

Mr. Jerebohm, staring hard at the lake as if in hope of seeing a fish rise, resisted with great difficulty a powerful and insidious temptation to ask how Ma dealt with trout.

"Same with pheasants," Pop said. "You'd have to start thinking of restocking soon if you wanted to shoot this autumn."

"I thought you said the place was stiff with them?"

"Old birds," Pop said with swiftness, unperturbed. "Pretty wild too. You want a couple o' hundred young 'uns. It's not too late. They're well advanced this summer. Hot wevver."

Mr. Jerebohm, deeply tormented again by agonies of hunger, suddenly abandoned all thought of foxiness and dizzily saw himself as the proud master of all he surveyed. The whole scene was simply splendid. This, he thought, was it. Lake, trout, pheasants, park, deer, wild duck, venison—God, he thought, this must be it.

Rapture left him abruptly a moment later, leaving him rational again. "What, by the way, are you asking?"

"Going to farm?" Pop said.

The question, short and simple though it was, was an astute one. If Mr. Jerebohm was going to farm he naturally wanted to lose money. Pop knew most of the dodges and this was the popular one. You made it in the city and lost it on the land. The countryside had never been so full of ragged-trousered brokers—what he called the Piccadilly farmers—pouring their money down the furrows.

"Roughly the idea," Mr. Jerebohm said. "Pleasure too of course. Mrs. J. is mad keen to have a nice rural domain."

"I've been asking nineteen thousand."

That ought to dovetail it all right, Pop thought. Mr. Jerebohm, though speechless, didn't flinch. A few thistle seeds, borne on the lightest of winds, floated angel-wise down the bank of the lake, here and there settling on reeds and water. Mr. Jerebohm watched them with eyes that might have been idle but were sharp enough to see a fish rise in a startled circle, a moment later, far out among the water lilies.

"Big 'un there," Pop said. "Ever have 'em blue? The trout I mean. We had 'em in France once and Ma got the recipe. You want plenty o' brown butter. You get 'em fair swimming in brown butter and then they're perfick."

Mr. Jerebohm disgorged a low, hungry sigh. He felt he couldn't hear much more of the poetry of eating and wished to God Pinkie would come and help him out a bit. In vain he looked back in the direction of the house and then said, snapping, "I'll give you twelve." Sentimentality was out. Absolutely out. You had to be firm from the beginning. The class was there all right but you had to be firm.

Pop laughed in a certain dry, easy fashion.

"I think it's about time I went home," he said. "Ma'll be wondering where I've got to."

"Oh? It's a perfectly good offer in my view."

Pop laughed again, this time more loudly.

"Well, maybe in your view, old man," he said, "but that ain't mine, is it?"

Again Mr. Jerebohm wished to God Pinkie would come to help him out a bit. There were times when he needed Pinkie.

"To be perfectly honest, I really ought to consult my wife about it first and then let you know," he said. "I don't want to be precipitate."

"Should think not an' all," Pop said, at the same time wondering what the hell "precipitate" meant. It sounded like something catching.

"Shall we start to walk back?" Mr. Jerebohm said. The afternoon was really shatteringly hot. Sweat was pouring off him in uncomfortable streams. Where on earth was Pinkie? "I could give you word by Monday."

Monday, Pop said, might be too late. The chap from Birmingham was coming down again to look at the window and another chap was after the paneling. You didn't see linenfold like that every day. It was worth all of fifteen hundred if it was worth a bob and once these demolition rats got to work you wouldn't see the place for dust.

The expression "demolition rats" disturbed Mr. Jerebohm to the core. It was even worse than venison with red currant jelly and wild duck with orange sauce. God Almighty, where on earth was Pinkie? As he followed Pop up the path he again looked toward the house in vain.

With inexpressible relief he heard Pop say, less than a minute later, "Ain't that your missus standing up there under the trees?" Pop paused to point to a grassy knoll, a hundred yards away, crowned by a ring of big sweet chestnuts. "Waving her hand."

"Waving both hands!"

It was clear, Mr. Jerebohm thought, that Pinkie was in a state of some excitement, unless, as was possible, she was trying out some new slimming exercise. Both arms were waving madly above her head, the hands waggling like spiders.

"Sunbeam!" she started to call. "Sunbeam!"

The excited lisping call dragged Mr. Jerebohm up the slope of parched grass to the knoll as if he had been attached to Pinkie by a rope. He felt unutterably glad to see her and wondered, twice and aloud, what it could be that so excited her.

"Probably came across some buried treasure," Pop said. "They say Cromwell was here. One of his prisoners escaped from a window in the house—"

Mr. Jerebohm, utterly uninterested in Cromwell, half ran forward to meet Pinkie, who lisped liltingly in return, "Come and see what I've found. You wouldn't guess in a thousand years."

Pop started to follow Mr. Jerebohm and his wife through the chestnut trees. Masses of prematurely fallen blossoms, in dry pollened tassels, had fallen from the trees and clouds of pungent yellow dust were raised as Mr. and Mrs. Jerebohm ran.

"There! I discovered it. I just absolutely ran across it. I wasn't thinking of a thing and suddenly it sort of conjured itself out of nowhere. It just sort of dovetailed—"

A kind of pepperbox, in white stone, with a domed roof and a marble seat inside, sat with forlorn elegance among the chestnut trees. Black piles of decaying faggots were propped against one side.

"It's a summerhouse, isn't it? The sort they built in the eighteenth century?" Pinkie said. "Didn't they call them follies?"

Folly or not, Pop thought, the chap who built this thing was on my side.

"And the view. You must look at the view."

Turning, Pop had to admit that the view was pretty stunning. It was better than perfick. The lake, sown with water lilies and framed with long fingers of reed, could now be seen entire, with park and cedars spread out as mature, calm background. It needed only a herd of deer to run lightly across the cloudless blue horizon to set the last romantic seal on it and send Mrs. Jerebohm finally and sedately mad.

"Come and sit inside a minute," Pinkie said to Mr. Jerebohm. "You'll get the full flavor then."

Though the shady marble struck with ice-cold shock on Mr. Jerebohm's seat, Pinkie might have been cased in armor for all she noticed the chill on hers.

"Sunbeam, we've absolutely got to have it. What is he asking?"

"Nineteen thousand."

"Is it an awful, awful lot?"

"I offered him twelve."

"Would he split do you suppose?"

"I expect so. I could have a stab."

Mr. Jerebohm knew, in his heart, that whether he had a stab or not it really didn't matter. The folly had finally achieved what roses, paneling, iodine, and seascape had failed to do. Whatever doubt remained after trout, venison, duck, and pheasant had done their all-tormenting work had gone forever.

"Try him with fifteen," Pinkie said. "We've got to get it laced up somehow. I couldn't bear—"

A sudden dread of colic made Mr. Jerebohm rise quickly from the marble seat, his rump half frozen. It was a positive relief to get out into the hot, stifling air.

"Well, Larkin, my wife and I have talked it over. I'll give you fifteen."

"Couldn't do it," Pop said, speaking with great blandness. "The demolition rats would give me more than that."

Mrs. Jerebohm recoiled from the expression "demolition rats" as Mr. Jerebohm himself had done down by the lakeside. It was an expression so nauseating that she actually had a vision of real rats, live and repulsive, gnawing away the stone and marble of her beloved folly, and she pinched Mr. Jerebohm sharply on the arm.

"I'll split the difference," Mr. Jerebohm said.

"Fair enough," Pop said. "Seventeen thousand."

Mr. Jerebohm had no time to protest against the neatness of Pop's arithmetic before Mrs. Jerebohm lisped, "Oh! Splendid. Splendid. I'm so glad we've got it all sewn up."

Sewn up it was, an' all, Pop thought. Ma would be pleased. And Mariette. They could have the swimming pool easy now. And probably even heated.

"Well, that's it then, Larkin." Mr. Jerebohm shook Pop not uncordially by the hand. Mrs. Jerebohm, smiling with winning, crossed teeth, shook hands too. "Thank you. I'll tell my solicitors to contact you. Presume you'd like some sort of deposit?"

Wouldn't cause him no pain, Pop said. Couldn't manage cash, he supposed.

Mr. Jerebohm said he didn't see why not. There were times when it was better that way. The times being what they were, in fact, it actually suited him.

As the three of them walked back to the house, Pop turned to Mrs. Jerebohm's tight, white-suited figure and asked if there wasn't perhaps something else she wanted to see? The kitchen garden? The asparagus beds? The greenhouses?

"You could grow some beautiful orchids there."

Orchids were one touch of poetry too much for Mr. Jerebohm, who said rather peremptorily that thanks, there was nothing else they wanted. At the same moment Mrs. Jerebohm pointed across the valley, where smoke from the strawberry fields was still drifting across the blue brilliant sky.

"A fire!" she said. "Isn't that a fire?"

Yes, Pop said, it was a fire and went on to explain how, for the first time in living memory, they were burning off the strawberry fields. The strawberry lark was over for the year. In a couple of weeks harvest would be over too. Everything would be over. It would all be finished months ahead of time, thanks to the marvelous summer, and he offered Pinkie Jerebohm the final crumb of comfort needed to make her day supremely happy.

"The women'll all be coming in from the fields early this year. You'll get all the help you want in the house. Been a perfickly wonderful summer, don't you think, absolutely perfick?"

It certainly had, Mrs. Jerebohm said, it certainly had, and with one long ecstatic backward glance at the lake and its lilies she felt her eyes slowly fill with tears of joy.

This, she told herself, was paradise.

That night Pop felt the deal called for a bottle of champagne in bed with Ma and an extra good cigar. As he sat in bed, sipping and puffing and watching Ma brush her hair at the dressing table, he caught pleasant glimpses of her body, vast and soft, under the forget-me-not blue nightgown, thin as gossamer, he had bought her for Christmas.

"Think the kids were pleased about the swimming pool," he said, "don't you? I thought the twins would die."

At the supper table he had been surrounded by children choking with excitement. The twins were half hysterical. Montgomery, Victoria, and a fast-maturing Primrose—he wasn't sure she wasn't going to be the prettiest of the lot after all—were not much better.

"Didn't think Mariette and Charley sounded all that wild though," Ma said.

"No?"

"No. After all you promised you'd build 'em a bungalow with the stuff you pulled out of Gore Court. And here they are still living with us."

"Stuff's too good for a bungalow. You couldn't do it," Pop said. "I'll give Mariette a thousand for her birthday next month. They can start on that."

Well, that was nice and generous, Ma said, and got into bed to sip champagne, her nightgown giving off strong clouds of heliotrope, her new perfume.

"Thundering hot still," Pop said.

Still, he thought, they mustn't grumble. Been a pretty fair day on the whole. He hadn't expected to get more than ten or eleven for Gore Court at the best, but thanks largely to Ma he'd done much better. Ma was a sharp one really. By the way, he said to her, what about Mariette? Any sign of any increase and all that?

"Not yet," Ma said. "Charley's going to have a test."

"Test? Good God."

The subject of a test was so embarrassing that Pop felt both relieved and glad when Ma changed the conversation abruptly and said, "You didn't really tell me what Mrs. Jerebohm was like."

Ma, as always, was pleasantly curious, even eager, to hear more of Pop's female acquaintances.

"Fairish," Pop said. "Uses some funny expressions. Dithers a lot. Says things like 'dovetail' and 'zip up' and 'clock' and so on. Excitable."

Ma looked sharply up at him at the word "excitable" and said she hoped he hadn't been up to any hanky-panky of any sort.

"No, no," Pop said. "Nothing like that."

Ma said she was very relieved to hear it. Unabashed, Pop asked why.

"Because they're going to be our nearest neighbors," Ma said. "That's why. We'll be having them in for drinks and all that. You want to start off on the right foot, don't you?"

Pop, sipping champagne, said he didn't mean excitable in that way. He meant she got sort of emotional about little things. He recalled the tears he had seen in her eyes at the lakeside. She was all excitable about the joys of country life and all that lark.

"Except she thinks eggs grow on trees," Ma said, "and cream comes out of a tap."

Well, it wasn't quite so bad as that, Pop said, but it was a damn cert Mr. Jerebohm didn't know a duck from a jackdaw. Typical Piccadilly farmer—every pea pod was going to cost him a bob and every pheasant a tenner.

"Well, if he don't mind," Ma said.

Oh, he didn't mind, Pop assured her, it was all part of the game. But what a world, wasn't it? What a world when you had to lose a lot of money so as to make more? What a world, eh?

"Certainly is," Ma said, and went on to say that there were times when she thought we were all half crazy. "Not sure we haven't forgotten what it's all about sometimes."

Forgotten what all what was about, Pop wanted to know.

"Oh, you know," Ma said, "just being here."

The sudden conscious reminder that he was alive on a hot summer evening full of stars was enough to recall to Pop something he had meant to ask Ma earlier on.

"Had a good mind to ask you to have a lay-down when I got back this afternoon," he said, "but you were watering your zinnias."

"Well, I'm not watering my zinnias now," she said, "am I? You never want to spoil a good mind."

Pop thought that this, like so much that Ma said, made real sense and presently, after getting out of bed and drawing back the curtains and gazing with his own special sort of rapture at the blazing summer stars, got back into a world of chiffon and heliotrope in order to demonstrate to a silently waiting Ma what a good mind he still had.

4

Several weeks later, about five o'clock on a warm October evening, Pop, in his shirt sleeves, was sitting comfortably in a deck chair on the south side of the house, a quart glass of beer at his side, occasionally potting with a shotgun at odd pheasants flying over from the Jerebohm domain to roost in the bluebell wood beyond the yard.

It was just the sort of shooting the doctor ordered. You sat in comfort, with a nice supply of beer at hand, and picked off the birds like one o'clock. Perfick sport. Like fishing for trout with worms, he didn't suppose it was the real and proper sporting thing to do, but at the same time he reckoned it was streets in front of tramping over sodden stubbles on rainy winter afternoons, waiting for birds to be beaten out of copses at ten quid a time. The pheasant tasted no different anyway and he was very glad he'd managed to persuade Mr. Jerebohm to buy a couple of hundred young ones at precisely the right time. Well fed on corn, the birds had fattened beautifully in the extraordinary warm autumn weather and were now as tender and tasty, he thought, as young love. Now and then you missed a bird because at the critical moment you had the beer up to your lips, but on the whole he couldn't grumble. He'd bagged a brace already.

It was not often that he was alone about the house, but Ma and the children, together with Charley and little Oscar, were still hard at the strawberry lark. It was the first time in living memory that the strawberry lark had extended into September and October. There were years when a few odd pounds ripened in autumn but now, thanks to the long hot summer that seemed as if it would never end, there were whole fields of them. Splendid fruit was being gathered in tons. The burned fields of July had been fed by August thunder rains and had woken into sudden blossoming, as deserts do. It was the most remarkable lark he'd ever known. Ma and Charley and the kids had been at it for six weeks, making pots of dough.

In the fading evening light he missed a bird that planed over too low and too fast for him and then, a minute later, found himself without beer. For a few minutes he sat debating with himself whether to fetch another bottle or to give up shooting altogether and was finally saved the necessity of making a decision by the sight of two figures crossing the yard.

The sudden arrival of the brigadier, who dropped in quite often, left him unsurprised. It was the sight of Angela Snow, silky-haired and lovely as ever, wearing the dreamiest of thin summer dresses, a shade deeper than pale sherry, that made him leap up from his chair. He hadn't seen her since that tenderest of holiday farewells in France, a year before.

"Lambkin," she said. "Darling. Given me up for dead or lost or as a bad lot or what?"

Pop, kissed first on both cheeks and then with a light flowering brush on the lips, was actually at a loss for words.

"I was waffling into town to buy an evening paper," said the brigadier, who did a great deal of walking, not from choice but necessity, since he couldn't afford a motor, "and Angela picked me up in the car. Must say I wasn't sorry either. Been damned hot again."

The word "hot" set Pop hurrying to the house for drinks, ice, and glasses, which he brought out on a tray vividly scrolled in magenta, orange, and scarlet scenes violently depicting Spanish dancers.

"The brigadier, poor lamb," Angela said, "has been crying on my shoulder."

The brigadier, angular, thin, and shabby as ever, the elbows of his alpaca actually looking as if gnawed by mice, coughed several times in embarrassment, quite shy.

"Come, come," he said. "Now really."

"Honest to God," Angela said. "And I was the great stupid. I hadn't heard about his sister."

On a morning in April the brigadier's sister, going upstairs with a small pile of ironing and suddenly lacking strength to reach the top, had simply sat down on the middle steps and quietly died.

"Nice brace of birds," the brigadier said, eager to change the subject. "Got them in the meadow, I suppose?"

Pop, pouring large whiskeys onto hillocks of ice, laughed resoundingly and explained how the birds, flying over from the Jerebohm domain, were on the contrary picked off in comfort, from the deck chair.

"Good God," the brigadier said. Shocked, he relapsed after the two words into immediate silence. It was really a bit beyond the pale. By Jove it really was. Even for Larkin.

"And what," Angela said, "is the great big hole doing in the garden?" She laughed flutingly, pointing across the garden to where, beyond the flaming yellows and scarlets of Ma's zinnias, a vast earthwork had been thrown up, dry as stone from the heat of summer. "The grave for the poor wretched birds as they fall?"

"Swimming pool," Pop explained.

"Good God," the brigadier said again. Whiskey in hand, he stared incredulously across the garden, prawnlike brows twitching. The apparent vastness of the pool, seemingly half as big as a public bath, shocked him even more than Pop's unsporting habits with pheasants. Coughing, he tried a dry joke of his own. "Quite sure it's large enough?"

"Got to be big to take Ma," Pop said.

"Scream," Angela Snow said. "And when do you hope to use it?"

"If the wevver's nice, early next spring," Pop said. "Going to have it heated."

The brigadier did his well-mannered best not to choke over his whiskey. Angela Snow laughed in her incomparably musical fashion, on bell-like notes, her pellucid eyes dancing.

"And shall we be invited for a dip?" she said. "If we're not, I shall write you off as a stinker."

"'Course," Pop said, "probably have a party to christen it," and went on to say, yes, Ma would have it heated. If it wasn't heated, she said, she'd have to have a mink bathing suit and what about that? The trouble with Ma was that she wasn't all that much of a swimmer and got cold very quickly. She floated mostly and if it was warm she had more fun.

"I heard of a bathing party once," Angela said, "where all the bathing suits melted as soon as the chaps jumped in. How about that?"

Perfick idea, Pop said. He'd have to think about that. Eh, General?

A certain shyness, not shock this time, left the brigadier speechless again and it seemed to Pop that Angela Snow, laughing no longer, looked at him with a touch of pity. He suddenly felt overwhelmingly sorry for the general himself. He had heard stories of a daily help serving him bread and cold bacon for lunch or leaving him to dine alone on cold pies of sausage meat as hard as rocks. He felt a chill of loneliness in the air and made up his mind to give the general the brace of pheasants when he left. He could knock off some more tomorrow.

"Another snifter?"

The invitation cheered the brigadier considerably, though not nearly so much as Pop's sudden recollection of a dish Ma had made that morning and of which there was some left in the fridge. It was a sort of open cheese tart decorated with thin strips of anchovy. It was equally delicious hot or cold. He'd go and get it.

"Ma got the recipe from Mlle. Dupont, in France, on that holiday last year," he said on coming back from the house with the tart, which Ma had cooked in a baking tin a foot wide. "By the way, Angela, did you go again this year?"

Pop cut handsome wedges of tart and proceeded to hand them to the brigadier and Angela, who said, "Couldn't, dear boy. Had to stay at home and look after Iris."

Pop said Oh? He was sorry about that. Ill or something?

"Nothing so simple, darling. Married."

For crying out gently, Pop said. That was a surprise. He hadn't thought she was the type.

"Nor did she. Not until that party of yours at the Beau Rivage. That altered the outlook. She lost a precious possession there."

Pop laughed. He must remember to tell Ma that. The brigadier, by contrast, showed no sign of amusement at all, not because he was shocked again but merely because he wasn't listening. Chewing with almost excruciating relish on the wedge of cheese tart, he stood bemused, a man lost. Two sandwiches of crab paste at lunch time hadn't shown much staying power.

"What about staying for supper?" Pop said suddenly. "I daresay Ma'll find a couple o' braces o' pheasant. I shot ten or a dozen last week. Expect there'll be strawberries and cream too. Ma generally brings back a few pounds from the field."

The brigadier, silent still, felt he could have wept. A prick or two of moisture actually pained his eyes, in fact, as he gave a low cough or two and finally said, in tones intended as cryptic but polite in refusal, "Oh, no, no, Larkin. Really mustn't. Thanks all the same. No, no, no."

"Oh, you're a sweetie," Angela Snow said, and the brigadier looked perceptibly startled, as if thinking or even hoping for a moment that the remark was meant for him, "of course we'll stay. I'm absolutely starving anyway. Aren't you, Arthur?"

The brigadier himself had never looked more startled than Pop did at the sudden mention of the general's Christian name, which he had never heard before.

"Good," he said. "Good. Ma'll be tickled to death. Especially when she hears you're starving."

The brigadier, who was always starving, had nothing to say. The light was fading rapidly now. The scarlet and yellow of Ma's zinnias were like burning embers dropped from the heart of the sunset, the quiet air still like summer, the sky unfeathered by cloud, the sweet chestnut leaves hardly touched by a single brushstroke of brown or yellow. Perfick evening, he heard Pop say as he poured yet another whiskey and offered another wedge of tart—that touch of anchovy was masterly, the brigadier thought, it started all your juices up—and then, a moment later, he heard the first laughing voices of the Larkin family coming home from the strawberry field.

Half a minute later he was aware of a young vision crossing the yard in the twilight. The dark head and olive skin of Primrose were exactly like those of her mother. For a few seconds it actually hurt him to look at her, taller by several inches than when he had seen her last, growing rapidly, her bust ripening. She seemed to him like a younger, less vivacious Mariette. The dark eyes were shy, big, and serious, even a little melancholy, and suddenly his heart started aching.

It was uplifted a moment or two later by Ma, carrying in her arms a little Oscar looking as fat as a young seal. Boisterous as ever, brown from weeks of sun, she breezily invited the brigadier to have a strawberry. In the twilight the baskets of lush ripe berries looked almost black.

"Not surprised to see you here, General," Ma said. "But Angela too! Going to stay for supper, aren't you?"

"Already fixed," Pop said. "Already fixed."

"Lovely to see you," Angela said. "Can't think what's come over this man of yours, though. Been behaving like a curate. Never a caress."

"Wait till he gets you in the swimming pool," Ma said, and, laughing like a jelly, went away to put the pheasants into the oven and little Oscar into bed.

The appearance of Mr. Charlton, looking astonishingly healthy and brown as a chestnut, startled the brigadier even more than that of Primrose had done. Charley had filled out a lot too. He was big, even muscular.

"Look remarkably fit, young man," the brigadier said, and Pop could only think, gloomily, that appearances could be pretty deceptive. He'd begun to think there must be very grave defects in Charley. It was all of two months since Charley had had his tests and neither he nor Ma had the foggiest notion what the results were. The worst of it was Mariette looked astonishingly healthy too. It was a bad sign.

A few moments later he was shepherding everyone into the house, himself carrying the drinks tray, when the telephone rang. Soon afterwards Ma appeared at the door and called, "Mariette says it's Mrs. Jerebohm, wanting me. Will you talk to her? If I'm to get Oscar down and the meal cooked I can't stand there nattering half the night."

"Charley," Pop said, "tot out. Give Angela and the brigadier another snifter," and went into the house to answer the lisping voice of Mrs. Jerebohm, who said:

"We'd like it so awfully much if you and Mrs. L. could come to dinner one evening soon. Thought perhaps the twenty-sixth might be nice. It's a Monday—awfully awkward day, I know, but we're down for a long weekend. Hope it dovetails with your plans. Know you're always terrifically busy."

Pop, thanking her, said he was pretty sure it would be all right and if it wasn't he'd ring her back very soon. After he had said this there was a long pause from the other end of the line and he said, "Hullo. Still there?"

Yes, she said, she was still there.

"Thought you'd gone. Nothing the matter?"

No, she said, nothing was the matter. She giggled briefly. It was just his voice.

"Oh? Well, can't help it," Pop said, laughing too. "It's just beginning to break, that's all."

Mrs. Jerebohm giggled again, seemingly as nervous as a puppy.

"No, seriously, it sounds so different. Awfully different, actually. One doesn't connect it with you."

"Ah, well, sorry about that," Pop said. "I'll try to do better next time."

It was the sort of conversation he forgot as quickly as it was made and after going back into the living room, where the brigadier already had a third stiff whiskey in his hand, he let it go completely from his mind. He would talk to Ma about the dinner later on, probably in bed, over a final snifter.

Wearing a yellow pinafore, Angela Snow floated gaily from kitchen to living room, helping Mariette to lay the supper table, talking as she did so in high musical overtones. This, she declared, was her idea of fun. The brigadier, already feeling the third whiskey lifting depression from him like a cloud of dark smoke, watched her going to and fro with eyes looking every moment less and less jaded. The juices of his senses had started waking as sharply as those of his mouth had done over anchovy and cheese, so that he began telling himself over and over again that she was a beautiful, beautiful creature.

Soon the delicious unbearable fragrance of roasting pheasant was
filling the house. Every few minutes the brigadier sniffed openly at it
like a dog. It seemed as if a long night, a gray mixture of solitude,
sandwich lunches, bone-hard apple pies, and cold bacon, was at last
breaking and passing him by. He hardly noticed the arrival of a fourth
and then a fifth whiskey and it was from the remotest ends of a waking
dream that he heard Pop calling with ebullient cheerfulness to Mr.
Charlton, "Shall we have pink tonight, Charley boy? Why not? Get
three or four bottles on the ice quick. Ought to go well with the
pheasants, I think, don't you?"

"Darling, if that was champagne you were referring to I shall remain
faithful to you forever," Angela Snow said. "I adore the pink. It's
absolutely me. Quite my favorite tipple."

The brigadier might well have wept again except that now, by some
miracle, there was nothing to weep for. Had there ever been? He simply
couldn't believe there ever had. He was beginning to feel alive again,
terrifically alive. Pink champagne? By God, that took him back a thousand aching years. He was again a crazy subaltern on Indian hill sta-
tions, lean and active as a panther: dances and parties everywhere, polo
and pig sticking, affairs with two married women running at the same
time, servants everywhere as plentiful as beetles. He was the gay dog
having champagne for breakfast, with a certain madness in the air, and
nobody giving a damn.

"Glad to see you're perking up, General," Ma said as she passed him
with two deep glass dishes of strawberries, each containing half a dozen
pounds. "Got your glass topped up?"

"Splendid," the brigadier said. "Splendid. Absolutely splendid."

"Don't spoil your appetite, though, will you?" she said. "Supper'll
only be ten minutes or so."

The brigadier found it suddenly impossible to believe how swiftly
the evening had gone. The time had whipped along like prairie fire. He
took his watch out of his breast pocket and discovered it to be already
eight o'clock. Spoil his appetite? He could have eaten horses.

Ma had cooked two braces of pheasant, together with chipolata
sausages, thin game chips, potatoes creamed with fresh cream, and the
first Brussels sprouts with chestnuts. Brimming boats of gravy and
bread sauce came to table as Pop started to carve the birds, the breasts
of which crumbled under the knife as softly as fresh-baked bread.

"Tot the champagne out, Charley boy," Pop said. "And what about
you, General? Which part of the bird for you? Leg or bosom?"

The brigadier immediately confessed to a preference for bosom and a moment later found his eye roving warmly across the table, in the direction of Angela Snow, who met the gaze full-faced and unflushed, though with not quite the elegant composure she always wore. This started his juices flowing again and with a brief peremptory bark he found himself suddenly on his feet, champagne glass waving.

"To our hostess. I give you a blessing, madam. And honor. And glory. And long, long health—"

The unaccustomed extravagance of the brigadier's words trailed off, unfinished. Everybody rose and drank to Ma. The brigadier then declared that the pink champagne was terrific and immediately crouched with eager reverence over his plate, the edges of which were only barely visible, a thin embroidered line of white enclosing a whole rich field of game, vegetables, sauce, and gravy.

Somewhere in the middle of a second helping of pheasant he heard Pop recalling his telephone conversation with Mrs. Jerebohm.

"Wants us to go to dinner on the twenty-sixth," Pop said. "I said I thought it was all right."

"Having staff trouble, I hear," the brigadier said.

"Oh?" Ma said. "The women'll all come back in the winter."

"Has to do the cooking herself, I understand."

"Well, that won't hurt her, will it?" Ma said. "If she likes good food she'll like cooking it. Same as I do."

"I can only say," the brigadier said, gazing solemnly into the winking depths of his glass, "that if the dinner she gives you is one tenth as delectable as this—no, one thousandth part as delectable—then you will be feeding on manna and the milk of paradise—"

Once again the extravagant words floated away. With them went the piled plates of the first course, carried out by Mariette and Angela Snow, who brought back bowls of strawberries and cream to replace them.

Soon the strawberries lay on the brigadier's plate like fat fresh red rosebuds, dewed white with sugar. The visionary sherry-colored figure of Angela Snow came to pour the thickest yellow cream on them, her voluptuous bare forearm brushing his hand. Then as she went away to take her place at the table a sudden spasm of double vision made him see two of her—a pair of tall golden twins of disturbing elegance who actually waved hands at him and said, "You're doing fine, Brigadier, my sweet. Does my heart good to see you. This afternoon I thought you were for the coalhole."

What on earth she meant by the coalhole he didn't know and cared even less. He only knew he was doing fine. The strawberries were simply magnificent; they came straight from the lap of the gods. Only the gods could send strawberries like that, in October, to be washed down by champagne, and soon he was eating a second dishful, then a third.

"The general's away," Ma kept saying with cheerful peals of laughter, "the general's away."

Then a renewed and stronger bout of double vision made him miscount all the heads at the table. The twins and Victoria were already in bed, leaving eight people eating. But now sometimes he was counting sixteen heads, then eighteen, then twenty, all of them dancing around the table like figures in a chorus. Behind them the television set glimmered a ghastly green and Pop's extravagant glass and chromium cocktail cabinet shimmered up and down like some impossible garish organ at a fair.

It was to these figures that he found himself saying hearty and newly extravagant farewells just after eleven o'clock, the brace of newly shot pheasants in his hand.

The evening had been great, he kept saying, swinging the pheasants about with grand gestures. Absolutely great. Straight from the gods. He kissed Ma several times on both cheeks and clasped Pop and Charley with tremendous fervor by the hand. After this he kissed both Primrose and Mariette, saying with unaccustomed gravity, followed by a sudden belch, that Ma and Pop were a million times blessed.

"A million times. A million times. Ten million times."

Still swinging the pheasants, he started to climb into Angela Snow's car and then paused to give several pleasurable barks in final farewell.

"By God, Larkin, I must say you know how to live!" he said. "I'll say that for you. I'll say you damn well know how to live."

Once again he started to swing the pheasants madly about his head and Pop treated him to a sudden clout of affectionate farewell plumb in the middle of the back. The gesture pitched him violently forward and through the open door of the car, unlocking fresh barks of laughter, in which Ma and Angela Snow joined ringingly.

"Sleep well, General!" Ma called. "Sleep well!"

"Sleep be damned!" the brigadier said. He waved a majestic hand from the car window, splendidly reckless, eyebrows martially bristling. "Shan't sleep a damn wink all night! Shan't go home till morning!"

Pop said that was the spirit and urged him not to do anything he wouldn't do. The brigadier yelled, "Bingo!" exclaiming loudly that he wanted to kiss Ma again.

"Must kiss Ma!" he said. "Got to kiss Ma. Never sleep if I don't kiss Ma."

Pop again said that this was the stuff and urged Ma to come forward and give the brigadier a real snorter, one of her specials.

Ma immediately did so, fastening her lips full on the brigadier's mouth with powerful suction. The brigadier, half suffocated, made a rapid imaginative ascent skyward, unable to breathe.

Then Angela Snow called, "Here, what about me? What have I done? What about this little girl?" so that Pop, not quite knowing at once whether it was his services that were being called for or those of the brigadier, simply decided that it must be his own and proceeded to give Angela Snow three minutes of silent and undivided attention on the other side of the car.

Pop, who didn't believe in doing things at any time by halves, felt quite prepared to prolong things even further, but even Angela Snow thought there were limits and finally struggled out of the embrace gasping for air, as if half drowned.

"One for the road?" Pop said. "Come on, one more for the road."

"One more like that and I shall be away. There'll be absolutely no holding me."

"I'm away already!" the brigadier said. By God, he was too. He had never known sensations like it. Not, at any rate, for a long time. He was sailing heavenward on imaginary clouds of bliss. There was no stopping him.

"Got your pecker up all right now, haven't you?" Ma said. "Not down in the dumps now, are you?"

Not only was his pecker up, the brigadier thought. Everything else was.

"Good-bye, darlings," Angela Snow called at last to the Larkins. "Farewell, my lambs. Bless you both ten thousand times. And the same number of the sweetest thanks."

The brigadier, not quite fully conscious, felt himself being driven away into a night voluptuous with stars, the good-byes still sounding behind him like a peal of bells. Soon afterward, with a reckless hand, he was grasping Angela Snow somewhere in the region of a smooth upper thigh and to his very great surprise found there was no whisper of protest in answer.

"Must come into the cottage and have a nip of brandy before you go," he said, "eh? Let's broach a keg. Bingo?"

"Bingo," Angela Snow said. "You have absolutely the sweetest ideas. I'm dying for a nip."

Angela, still recoiling slightly from the velvet impact of Pop's long-drawn kiss, felt half light-headed herself as she stopped the car at the cottage, got out, and stood for some minutes waiting for the brigadier to find his latchkey. All the time he was still swinging the pheasants about with careless gestures.

"Got it." Key in one hand, pheasants in the other, the brigadier groped gaily to the cottage door. It was a bit tricky here she heard him explaining as she followed, and heard him trip on a step. "Got to find the lights. Should be a torch somewhere."

The door of the little cottage opened straight into the living room and the brigadier, unlocking the door, went inside, unsteadily groping.

"Stand still," he urged her. "I'll have a light in a couple of jiffs."

Suddenly he turned and, in the darkness, ran full against her. A powerful recollection of Ma's divinely transcendent kiss bolted through him in such a disturbing wave that a second later he was urgently embracing her.

The sudden force of it made him drop the brace of pheasants and trip. Angela Snow, caught off guard, tripped too and they both fell over, the brigadier backward, across the hearthrug.

Dazed for a moment, he found it impossible to get up. Then he realized, flat on the floor, that he didn't want to get up. He told himself that only a fool would want to get up. The silk of Angela Snow's dress spread across him in a delicious canopy and finally he put up a hand and started touching, then stroking, her bare left shoulder.

It might have been a signal for Angela Snow to get up too but to his delighted surprise she, apparently, didn't want to get up either. This prompted him to start stroking the other shoulder and a second later, in response, he heard her give a series of quiet, thrilling moans.

"Heavenly," she told him. "Keep on. Just between the shoulders. That's it. Just there."

Great God, the brigadier thought. He stroked rapidly.

"Slower, slower," she said. "Slower, please. Around and around. Slowly. That's it. Heavenly."

A moment later, with sudden abandon, the brigadier grasped the zip of her dress and pulled it with a single stroke down her back. In response she kissed him full on the mouth, more softly and tenderly than Ma had done but still with the instantaneous effect as of veins of fire lighting up all over his body.

Something about this electrifying sensation made him say, when the kiss was over, "By Jove, the Larkins know how to do it, don't they? By Jove, they know how."

"And they're not the only ones."

The brigadier, urged on, began to think that nothing could stop him now and presently he was caressing her shoulders again and unhooking the clip of her brassiere.

"Around and around," he heard her murmur. "That's it. Around and around. Oh, that's heavenly. How did you find my weak spot? And so soon?"

The brigadier hadn't the faintest notion. He was only aware of the entire evening flowering into madness.

"By Jove, I could lie here all night," he said. "I could see the stars out. I don't want to go to bed, do you?"

"Oh, no?" she said. "Don't you?"

Halfway up the stairs the brigadier, at the end of an evening of revolutionary sensations, none of which he had experienced for a generation, felt yet another one rise up, out of the darkness to greet him.

Without warning five of Pop's whiskeys, ten glasses of pink champagne, and several large brandies joined their powerful forces. One moment he was grasping at the bare voluptuous shoulders of Angela Snow; the next he was sitting on the stairs, at more or less the same place where his sister had sat herself down and left him in final solitude, and passed out swiftly and quietly, without a sigh.

When he came to himself again he was alone, fully dressed, on the bed. The autumn dawn was just breaking and in the middle of it a huge and spectacular planet was shining, winking white as it rose.

5

A week later Ma was sure the long, hot summer was at an end. The nights and mornings, she said, had begun to strike very parky. The last of the strawberries were finished; there was frost in the air. She had begun to feel very cold across her back in bed at night, so that she was glad to tuck up closer to Pop, and already by day she was sometimes glad to wear two sweaters, one salmon, one violet, instead of none at all.

"Think I'll slip my mink stole on when we go to the Jerebohms tonight," she said.

And by eight o'clock, when she got out of the Rolls outside the big oak front door of Gore Court, she was very glad she had. A cold, gusty, leaf-ridden wind was beating in from the west. Twigs of turkey oak and branches of conifer were flying everywhere.

"I'm duck skin all across my back already," Ma said. "You feel it worse after a hot summer. I hope it'll be warm inside."

Pop, who had taken the precaution of having three Red Bulls laced with double tots of gin before coming out, said he hoped so too and pulled the big brass bell knob at the side of the front door.

A clanging like that of a muffin bell echoed through the house very far away, as if at the end of cavernous corridors. For the space of two or three minutes nobody answered it and presently Pop pulled the bell knob again. By this time rain was spitting in the wind and Ma said she was freezing to death already. Pop said he wasn't all that hot himself but that was how it was with these enormous houses. The servants always lived half a mile away.

A second or two later the big front door was opened by a girl of nineteen or twenty, blue-eyed and very fair, with her hair done up in the shape of a plaited bread roll. She gave Pop and Ma the slightest suspicion of a curtsey and said, "Good evening. To come in please," in an accent so strong that Pop, fixing her with a gaze like a limpet, told himself she must be Froggy.

Inside the huge baronial entrance hall, lit only by a big brass lamp hanging over the head of the stairs, the air struck cold as a vault. It smelled moldy too, Ma thought, and a bit mousy into the bargain, rather like that hotel they'd stayed at in Brittany.

"No, I'll keep my stole on," she said to the girl when she offered to take it, "thank you."

"*Bitte,*" the girl said, and then corrected herself. "Please."

Bitter it would be an' all, Ma thought, if you had to live in this place all winter and couldn't get it no warmer than it was now. She'd get pleurisy in no time.

She thought the drawing room, huge though it was and with all its treacle-brown paneling about as cheerful as a church vestry, seemed a little better. A fire of birch logs a yard long was sulkily smoking— burning was too definite a word for the thick pink mist gushing out of the silvery pile of wood—in a brick fireplace as large as a cow stall. The heat that came out of it might possibly have warmed a fly, Ma thought, but not a very big one.

"Ah, Larkin." Mr. Jerebohm, with outstretched hand, advanced from the smoky regions of the fireplace. "Mrs. Larkin."

Mr. Jerebohm, who was wearing a black velvet jacket and a claret-red bow tie, said of course they both knew Pinkie, who now simpered rather than walked across the drawing room to lisp, "Good evening," and shake hands. Pinkie was wearing a silk evening dress of an indefinite brown color, rather like stale milk chocolate. It was sleeveless, off the shoulder and rather low at the bust, so that some inches of a dough-colored pouchy bosom were revealed.

"It'll be pride that keeps her warm," Ma thought. "Nothing else will."

Pinkie lisped that it was awfully nice to see them and did they know Captain and Mrs. Perigo.

Still clinging to him, is she? Ma thought. Thought she'd run off with that feller Fanshawe long ago.

"Evening," Pop said. "Think we've met a couple o' times."

Captain Perigo said, "Really?" in a voice remarkably like the groan of an unoiled gate, and said he didn't believe they had. In expressing his words his bony jaw, which was much the color of pumice stone and about as fleshless, unhinged itself with rusty difficulty and then remained emptily open, unable to hinge itself back again.

"Often seen you ride at the point-to-points," Ma said. "My daughter Mariette rides a lot there."

"Really?" Captain Perigo said.

This monosyllabic eagerness of welcome was in direct contrast to Mrs. Perigo, who spoke heartily and had eyes like ripe black olives. If Captain Perigo, from continuous association with horses, looked remarkably like an undernourished hunter himself, Mrs. Perigo had all the plushy creaminess of a cow. In tones like those of a deep-blown horn she drawled good evenings, at the same time giving Pop a look of openly inviting greeting, eyes in a deep slow roll.

High society now, Ma thought. There was a certain mannered stiffness in the air quite foreign to her nature and she was glad she'd brought her mink.

"Our summer seems to have left us, don't you think?" Mrs. Perigo said. "Absolutely heavenly. We'll never have another one like it, ever, will we? I mean ever? You been away?"

"Not this year," Ma said. "Been too busy strawberry picking."

"Really?" Captain Perigo stared at Ma in openmouthed pain, as if she had been doing time.

The unmistakable chill in the air prompted Pop to think that a large snifter would go down well. A moment later he found himself confronted with a tray held by Mr. Jerebohm. On it were three or four pink glasses, each about the size of a thimble.

"Care for sherry?"

Pop thanked Mr. Jerebohm, raised a thimble of pale amber liquid, and stared at it dubiously, not certain whether to knock it back in one go or husband it for a while. He decided on husbandry. Something told him there might not be another.

"Admiring your mink," Mrs. Jerebohm said to Ma, who was also holding a thimble. "Hope you don't mind? Quite gorgeous. That lovely new color."

"Bought it with the money I made in the strawberry field," Ma said. "Put in a lot of extra time this year."

Pop, overhearing this, was ready to laugh aloud and was only saved from doing so by the sudden languorous appraoch of Mrs. Perigo, who bore down on him with dark still eyes and swinging hips. Pop knew all about Mrs. Perigo, who was wearing a tight evening dress of geranium-leaf-green that fit her like a pod, and he was already on his guard.

"You sort of live next door, don't you?" she said.

Sort of, Pop said. Half a mile along the road.

"Never see you around anywhere. How can that be?"

That, Pop said, could only be because she didn't keep her eyes open, a remark that caused her to give him another slow inviting glance, openly ripe and full.

"I will in future though," she said.

Pop laughed and then was silent. He wasn't going to be drawn by Mrs. Perigo. There were men in every village for a radius of ten miles around who wished with all their hearts they'd never met Corinne Perigo.

"Silly to be so near and never have a peep of anybody," she said. "That's the worst of the country though, there's so damn little fun."

Pop, drinking sherry in sips so minute that he could hardly taste it at all, thought that if any woman had had any fun it was Corinne Perigo, who had in her time run off with a naval commander, a veterinary surgeon, and an agricultural inspector. The naval commander had shot himself and the inspector was in a home. Pop didn't know about the vet, but in the process of her adventures the forbearing Perigo had turned into a monosyllabic horse.

"Heard you say there was no fun in the country." It was Pinkie Jerebohm, offering a plate of the snippiest of cocktail snippets to Pop and Mrs. Perigo. "Have one of these. And what about your glass?"

What about it? Pop thought and was dismayed to hear Pinkie say as she peered into his glass, "Oh! You're still all right, I see."

Pop simply hadn't the heart to say anything and he could only suppose there was so little recognizable difference between a full and an empty thimble that you really couldn't blame her.

"Well," Mrs. Perigo said, "do *you* think there's any fun?"

"My husband does," Pinkie lisped. "He adores it. He thinks the days are so long. Much longer than they are in town, miles longer. Perhaps it's because he's always up with the lark. The only thing is that you can't get help for love nor money. I had to get this Austrian girl in. She can't cook though and even she's been spending her days off in the strawberry fields."

All would be well, Pop assured her, now that the strawberries, potatoes, and sugar beet were finished. She'd get plenty of help now.

"I profoundly hope so."

A moment later, over in the fireplace, a heavy gust of wind came down the chimney and erupted in a pungent cloud of birch smoke, so that Captain Perigo, in the act of trying to get a little warmth into his haunches, seemed visibly to rise up, exposed as on a funeral pyre.

This seemed like a signal for Mrs. Jerebohm to muster her chilly guests together, which she did with the simpering of a hen gathering stray chicks.

"Shall we go in? I think we might, don't you? I think all's ready. Shall we? Shall we go in?"

Pop gave his thimble sherry a final despondent glance and then switched his gaze to Ma, who was shivering. Better knock it back, he thought, profoundly glad at the same time that he'd insured himself with three Red Bulls. He didn't care for sherry much at the best of times and he was quite right: It was perfickly obvious there wasn't going to be another.

The dining room was vast too, with polished oak floors that echoed hollow with every step and a big stone fireplace that sheltered yet another pile of smoking birch. If the air didn't quite take your breath away, Ma thought, it wasn't very much better. It was like a stable in wintertime.

The dining table looked nice though, she thought. Tall red candles rose from green china bowls filled with scarlet hips and haws. There were rose-pink dinner mats, cut wineglasses, pretty silver saltcellars, and butter knives with painted handles, all looking discreet and pleasant under golden candlelight.

Everything looked very *très snob*, Pop thought and only hoped the food would be up to the same standard. He was pretty well starving.

Half a minute later, sitting next to Mrs. Perigo, he found himself staring down at a small green glass dish in which reposed a concoction consisting of five prawns, a spoonful of soapy pink sauce, and a sixth prawn hanging over the edge of the glass as if searching for any of its mates that might have fallen overboard. You could have eaten the lot, Pop thought, with two digs of an egg spoon.

"I hope everybody likes prawn cocktail?" Mrs. Jerebohm said. A wind whined and whooped like an owl in the chimney as if giving answer. "I hope you'll forgive me if I don't join you. I'm not allowed. I have my yogurt."

"Don't agree?" Ma said. "Onions get me that way too."

Mrs. Jerebohm looked frigid. "Not exactly. It's my diet. I have to watch it all the time."

"Ma went on a diet once," Pop said. "By the time she'd got the diet down her every morning she was ready for a good square breakfast."

"Really?" Captain Perigo said. "I mean to say—"

What Captain Perigo meant to say nobody discovered. Mrs. Jerebohm toyed with yogurt. Pop toyed with a prawn, thinking it tasted more like a bit of last week's cod than anything else he could name. Ma sniffed the chilly air, hoping she might catch a smell of steak or something cooking. She rather fancied steak tonight but she merely felt a sense of denial when she remembered how far away the kitchens were.

Presently Mrs. Jerebohm swallowed a pill, washing it down with a glass of cold water, and Mr. Jerebohm walked around the table, filling glasses with chilled white wine.

Pop, who had made the prawn cocktail last as long as possible, decided he couldn't put off the end any longer and sucked at the last meager spoonful just as Mrs. Perigo dropped her napkin on the floor.

"Do you mind, Mr. Larkin? I've dropped my napkin."

Pop poked about under the table. The napkin had dropped between Mrs. Perigo's not unshapely legs, which were held generously apart. The temptation to caress one of them or even both was a strong one which Pop successfully resisted just in time.

When he finally retrieved the napkin and put it back in her lap he was not surprised to notice that she was eyeing him with a keen but voluptuous sort of disappointment. He wasn't at all sure there didn't seem to be a hint of annoyance there too and with a nippy gesture toward Mr. Jerebohm he changed the subject.

"Had many pheasants yet, Mr. Jerebohm?"

Mr. Jerebohm confessed, with a certain air of annoyance too, that he had, in fact, not had many pheasants. Hardly a damned one.

"Oh?" Pop expressed a most fervent and sympathetic surprise. "How's that? Thought you had plenty."

So, confessed Mr. Jerebohm, did he. But where did the bounders get to? You could walk all the way to the lake and never see a brace.

"Knocking the stoats off?" Pop said, airily.

What on earth had stoats got to do with it? Mr. Jerebohm said.

"And what about jackdaws?" Pop said. "Eh?" Bigger menace than stoats. "And magpies?" Bigger menace than jackdaws. "And hawks?" Bigger menace than the lot. Deadly.

Mr. Jerebohm, who didn't know a lark from a sparrow, let alone a magpie from a hawk, sat almost as openmouthed as Captain Perigo while listening to Pop's fluent recital of the pheasant's countless deadly enemies.

"You mean—?"

"Perfickly obvious," Pop said. "Your birds are being taken by summink or other."

Pop stared hard at Ma as he spoke, but Ma didn't move an eyelash in reply.

"Really?" Captain Perigo said. "I mean to say——"

"No doubt about it," Pop said. "You'll have to get among the stoats and things. Won't he, Ma?"

Ma cordially agreed. And the foxes.

"Damnit," Mr. Jerebohm said, "I thought the hunt took care of the foxes."

"Half and half," Pop said. "The hunt takes care of the foxes and the foxes take care of the hunt."

"Had a fox fetch a goose the other night," Ma said. "Right under our noses."

"I think we fed 'em too well in the first place," Mr. Jerebohm said. "They simply didn't want to fly."

"Never. Got to feed 'em. Got to fatten 'em up a bit," Pop said. "After all, what's a pheasant if it's all skin and bone?"

Mr. Jerebohm said he simply didn't know; he hadn't even seen one. He hadn't seen a snipe, a deer, a hare, or a damn rabbit either. Had Larkin?

"Caught sight of a few in the distance once or twice," Pop said. "Too far off, mostly."

"Really?" Captain Perigo said.

While all this was going on the blond Austrian maid had been clearing away the cocktail dishes. She was rather a fresh, pretty little thing, Pop thought, and recalled that he hadn't seen her about the village at all. He must look out a bit more and as she picked up his dish he turned and gave her a short warm smile.

She gave him the hint of a smile in reply and a second later he felt the air between himself and Mrs. Perigo positively dry up, parched by a withering glare.

While the girl was out of the room Mrs. Jerebohm daintily swallowed another pill and drank another glass of water. Pop tried the white wine, all flavor of which appeared to have been chilled out in some deep and distant tomb.

"What about wild duck then?" Pop said.

As if unprepared to discuss the subject of wild duck, Mr. Jerebohm went over to the sideboard and started sharpening the carving knife. No, he said rather tersely, he hadn't seen any wild duck either. He doubted in fact if there were any wild duck about the place. If there were they were damn widely scattered.

"They come and go," Pop said. "We had a brace last week, didn't we, Ma? Not much on a wild duck, but they're beautiful with orange sauce. Perfick."

Tortured by the renewed description of Ma's wild duck with orange sauce, Mr. Jerebohm found himself faced with the task of dismembering three small larded partridges brought in on a dish by the Austrian maid. They not only looked on the small side but they seemed, he thought, rather crisp. He gave the girl a look of slightly curt reproval and then with sinking heart proceeded to thrust the carving knife hard into the breast of the first partridge.

Under this first prod the bird gave a sharp leap about the dish. A second made it dance sideways, skating in gravy. The knife grated against bone as hard as ebony, setting Ma's teeth on edge, and with depressing insistence Mr. Jerebohm attacked it again. This time it skated into the two other birds, one of which leapt completely from the dish and slithered full circle around the sideboard.

After the Austrian maid retrieved it deftly Mrs. Jerebohm called, lisping, "Not for me, dear, you know I mustn't. I have my peanut pâté."

On Mrs. Jerebohm's plate there reposed the smallest portion of brown-gray pâté, looking not at all unlike a mouse nibbling at a solitary lettuce leaf. A still smaller portion of grated celery, together with one sliced tomato, covered some part of the rest of the plate and for a few moments Mrs. Jerebohm stared at it all either as if in disbelief or as if wondering whether something, possibly, could be missing.

Watching her, Ma thought she had the clue.

"Salt?" she said. "Looking for the salt?"

"Oh, never salt," Mrs. Jerebohm lisped. "Salt is absolutely fatal."

Never? Ma said. She hadn't heard.

"And pepper. They both put on more weight than bread. Oh, I never, never eat salt. Never, never pepper."

"Really?" Captain Perigo said. "I mean to say—"

By this time the first of the partridges, tortuously dismembered by Mr. Jerebohm, was coming to table, garnished with frozen peas and game potatoes. The birds looked, if possible, more charred than ever and as each meager portion was set down in the pool of glass and silver and candlelight Ma's customary epitaph "Shan't get very fat on this" flashed sadly through her mind. No doubt about it—they wouldn't either.

"Absolutely delicious," Captain Perigo said, uttering his first real original sentence of the evening.

In return Mrs. Perigo gave him a look of flat-iron contempt, as if he were not supposed to utter sentences of originality. His jaw, falling open suddenly, expressed a pained acquiescence that showed no sign of receding until he presently found time to pick up slowly, one by one, three or four peas on the end of a fork. Even these remained for some time poised before the empty gap, in air.

"Anyone going hunting on Thursday?" Mr. Jerebohm said.

He hadn't hunted much yet. The midweek meets were awkward and not, it seemed, very well patronized. These days, it appeared, you couldn't get the chaps.

"I'll be there," Captain Perigo said. The peas had only just gone in when his mouth opened again.

This time there was no answering look of contempt from Corinne Perigo, who merely half glanced at Pop and said, "I know I can't. I've got a perm."

"You going, Larkin?" Mr. Jerebohm said.

Pop, rather uncheerfully, said, yes, he thought he might. He was struggling with elastic bits of partridge, longing for a cheese pudding or something, a steak and kidney pie or something, to fill him up. Had to take a day off now and then, he said, and he hadn't hunted once this year.

At this point some instinct made him turn and look at Corinne Perigo, who to his considerable surprise was attacking a piece of rubbery breast of partridge with silent fury. The normally soft, sensuous lips were being bitten hard and white and for the life of him he couldn't imagine why.

One thing he hadn't any doubts about, however, was the partridge. He hadn't the heart to ask if the birds had been shot on the estate. Once, as he struggled to get a mouthful of flesh here and there, he saw Mrs. Jerebohm smile at him across the table. Half in sympathy rather than anything else he gave her a warm and winning smile in reply.

"Like being in the country?" he said.

"Oh, yes."

Secretly, in fact, she had begun to hate it. The grounds were still full of thistles and willow herb. The kitchen garden looked sordid and try as you could you couldn't get help. The locals were independent, rude, and treacherous and it would be late spring before she could have asparagus. Even the Austrian girl, simple and nice as she had been on arrival, had started on the path of rural corruption, thanks largely to the strawberry fields.

"Perfick here," Pop said. "Wouldn't change it for nowhere else in the world."

"Never, never want to live anywhere else?" Corinne Perigo said.

"Never," Pop said, and with such resolute finality that Mrs. Perigo's lips finally untightened and broke into a smile.

All through the sweet course, which consisted of ice cream crowned with a solitary half of walnut, the westerly gale rose in the chimney. Smoke gathered into the fireplace in thicker and thicker clouds, until at last a light gray fog hung about the room. Ma found herself shivering more and more often and began to wonder how soon she could get home and cook herself some good hot eggs and bacon. She wasn't sure she wouldn't jump into a bath too.

"Shall we find more comfortable chairs?" Mrs. Jerebohm said, "and some coffee?"

Through increasing fog, with hollow footsteps, Mrs. Jerebohm and her guests filed back to the drawing room, where Mr. Jerebohm began to dispense minute thimbles of crème de menthe and brandy.

The Austrian maid was also there, serving coffee and actually smiling with unexpected pertness at Pop as she said, with her strong accent, "Sugar? One lump or two?"

"Four," Pop said, and while she was still laughing, went on, "Are you Froggy? From France I mean?"

"I am from Austria."

"Very nice," Pop said, and was not unastonished, in view of the luscious smile he gave her, to see that she served the four sugar lumps to him herself, smiling with a separate movement of her lips at each one.

These gestures were not lost on Corinne Perigo, who presently cornered him at a safe distance from the smoking fireplace and said, "Sorry I won't see you at the hunt Thursday."

Pop said he wasn't all that sure he could go. Might not find the time.

"No? I'd go if I could change my perm."

Pop didn't answer. The hunt really didn't interest him this season. He was very busy and the present crowd were pretty ragtag and bobtail. The country, too thickly wooded, with too many orchards, wasn't really good for hunting either.

Nor did Mrs. Perigo interest him very much. Nobody could say he wasn't interested in women; he was ready and willing for them any time you cared to name. But Mrs. Perigo wasn't quite his kind. Something about her, more especially the voluptuous glances, irked him. He didn't want to go hunting with her either, one way or the other.

"Well, anyway, even if I can't go," she said, "you could drop in for a stirrup cup in the morning, before you went, couldn't you?"

"Never drink in the mornings."

"No? Simply can't believe it."

Captain Perigo drank like nobody's business, starting an hour after breakfast.

"Honest fact," Pop said, straight-faced as an owl. "Blood pressure."

Mrs. Perigo gave him another deep, slow smile, this time both disturbing and enigmatic too.

"I suffer from it myself," she said. "Sometimes. Depending on circumstances."

Whatever the circumstances were Pop didn't bother to ask and he was glad to hear Ma's warm, friendly voice inquiring of Mrs. Jerebohm, "Get to know many people since you've been here? Made many friends?"

Mrs. Jerebohm was too reticent to point out that her poverty in country friendships was only too well reflected in the number of guests at her dinner table. She had conceived, once, the idea of having eight or ten guests that evening for dinner, or perhaps even a cocktail party, but somehow country people seemed to close themselves up, oyster-like, slow to accept you.

"Not too many," she confessed. "I did invite a Miss Pilchester to tea last week, but she didn't even answer my note—"

"Batty," Mrs. Perigo said. "She probably didn't even open it. Or she wove it into a scarf on her loom."

Ma, who wouldn't have such remarks at any price, rose to Edith Pilchester's defense swiftly and sharply.

"She's not been well, poor thing. Appendix or something. One of those grumbling ones. The sort you have to put up with because they're not bad enough to have out. I keep telling Pop he'll have to go and massage it for her."

Ma found her rich loud laugh enveloped in a chilly cloud, out of which Corinne Perigo's voice inquired with slow sarcasm, "Oh? Does he make a habit of massaging appendixes?"

"Oh, he'll massage anything for a lark," Ma said, laughing in bountiful fashion again. "He's got a waiting list a mile long."

The frigidity with which the Jerebohms received this announcement sprang less from shock than confusion, which was not improved by Pop saying, with a fresh laugh, that he'd never massaged an appendix in his life.

"Oh, really?" Captain Perigo said. "Well, I'm damned."

"You'll have to come over and have a bite and wet with us one day," Ma said, "and meet a few people. We'll get the brigadier and a few more in one Sunday—"

"That's it," Pop said. "We'll knock off three or four geese and Ma'll stuff 'em with sage and onions."

Painfully in a low voice, Mr. Jerebohm said, "Thank you. We'd be glad to."

This uncordial acceptance threw another chilling mist over the conversation, which stopped completely for half a minute, until Mrs. Jerebohm said, "I hear you have several children, Mrs. Larkin. Your house must be full already."

"Seven so far," Ma said. "Quite a little brood."

"Little? You mean you'd like to have more?"

"Oh, Pop would," Ma said. "There's no holding him back."

In the cool, smoky drawing room there was no sound but that of coffee spoons stirring at sugary dregs in cups and a few sharp sniffs from Captain Perigo struggling with some obstruction in his nose.

Almost at once Pop's own nose started to sniff out the increasing chill in the air and he was suddenly half afraid that somebody would soon be asking him and Ma if they were married or not and he turned the conversation smartly.

"Seen any hares at all, Mr. Jerebohm?"

Mr. Jerebohm confessed stiffly that he hadn't seen any hares. He was about to remark that he thought hares in fact were extinct, like wild duck, deer, pheasant, woodcock, and a lot of other things, but Pop broke cheerfully in with,

"Tell 'em how you do hares, Ma. That French recipe, I mean. The one with burgundy and prunes." In his sudden enthusiasm for the French way with hares he lifted a hand in air, as if about to strike Mr. Jerebohm in warm comradeship in the middle of the back. "That's a beauty. That'll make your gills laugh."

The prospect of Mr. Jerebohm's gills ever laughing again seemed an utterly remote one. The coffee spoons tinkled emptily again in their cups. Captain Perigo sniffed again and then actually brought out his handkerchief and blew at his nasal obstruction, loudly, with a single trumpet snarl that earned him a fresh look of contempt from Mrs. Perigo.

"Play crib?" Pop said with great cheerfulness. "What about a couple of hands at crib?"

Crib? What was crib? Mr. Jerebohm was unfamiliar with crib.

"Card game," Pop explained. "Very old card game."

"Perhaps it's getting a little late for cards," Mrs. Jerebohm started to say, and was suddenly saved the necessity of continuing by a violent crash of timber or masonry, or both, somewhere in the region of the back door.

"Getting damn windy," Captain Perigo said, and added that he wasn't sure he liked it.

A moment later the agitated Austrian maid burst into the room to say excitedly that half a tree had fallen on the stable roof and that she was getting very frightened. She wasn't used to such winds. They sounded like the sea.

"Better be going," Ma said. The sudden opening of the door, bringing a driving draft, had set her shivering again. "Don't want to get myself steamrollered under a beech tree. That'd be a jammy mess."

"Well, be seeing you!" Pop said, as they shook hands all around. "Thank you, Mrs. Jerebohm. Thank you, Mr. Jerebohm. Don't get doing anything I wouldn't do."

Mr. Jerebohm received this cheerful advice in further silence. The sound of yet another crashing tree branch startled Pinkie Jerebohm into almost running across the wide baronial hallway with Ma's mink stole and Corinne Perigo's big white sheepskin jacket, which she clutched closely about her shoulders as she turned to Pop to say, "Well, don't forget that stirrup cup. If you can find the time."

"That's right," Captain Perigo said. "Roll up for a noggin at any time."

After Ma and Pop had driven home under a sky of lashing rain and a falling barrage of autumn boughs. Pop was dismayed to find that television had already closed down and that only Charley and Mariette were still up, studying plans for a bungalow on the kitchen table.

While Ma sipped at a good gin-and-mixed and started to fry eggs and bacon, "because if I don't eat soon my stomach'll drop out," Mariette said, "Ma, we can't quite decide. What do you say? Shall we have one bathroom or two?"

"Oh, two, dear," Ma said with not the slightest hesitation. "After all, you might not always want to bathe together." She and Pop quite often did.

For crying out gently, Pop thought. What next? He gave Ma a severe and disapproving look which she, over the frying pan, completely ignored. He didn't go much on that lark. It was almost as bad as having separate bedrooms. He stood a fat chance of becoming a grandfather if Ma was going to start putting obstacles like that in Charley's way.

Over the eggs and bacon, together with a few glasses of port, Ma warmed up, saying several times, "Thought I'd never get the circulation back in my feet. I think I'm going to have a hot bath even now."

Pop said good idea. He thought he might hop in with her.

"Well, do," Ma said cordially. "Why not?"

Ma always got into the bath first, for the simple reason that she displaced such an enormous amount of water that Pop could gauge the depth better when he followed her. Tonight the waterline came almost up to the top of the bath, so that not much more than Ma's handsome dark head, wide olive shoulders, and upper bosom was revealed.

"Well, that was an evening," Ma said. "I thought I'd never get warm again."

"Me too."

Pop was feeling human now. A bath with Ma was about the cosiest, pleasantest thing in the world.

"I shouldn't have thought you were cold," Ma said, "with the steamy way that Mrs. Perigo kept looking at you. I hope you didn't get any ideas about her?"

"Not my type," Pop said. "She's sour."

Ma, washing her neck and shoulders with a flannel impregnated with special French soap, said she was very glad to hear it and at the same time asked Pop if he could reach the Schiaparelli bath oil from where it stood on the stool. She'd like a drop more in.

"I'll have to get a bigger size next time," she said as she peppered the water with a generous spray of oil, "I use so much of it."

"Soap at your end?" Pop said.

"Somewhere. Had it a moment ago."

With adroit hands Pop started a swift search for the soap, but Ma's body occupied such a large space of water that there was very little area left to search in. His hands kept finding Ma instead, so that presently she was half shrieking, "Sid! If you do that again you'll have me under. You know what happened last time."

Once Ma had laughed so much that she slid suddenly under, unable to sit up again until Pop climbed out of the bath and pulled her up.

"Sid! I told you. You'll have me under."

"Got to find the soap, Ma," Pop said. Ma, all pink and olive, seemed to him to blossom through hot clouds of perfumed steam. "Can't very well get clean without the soap."

"Well, it's not down *there*!"

"No?" Pop said, and confessed he was surprised. "Thought you might be hiding it."

"What's that against my left foot?" Ma said. "Is that it? Or is it you?"

Slightly disappointed, Pop found the soap beside Ma's left foot, the sole of which he tickled lightly, making her shriek again, so that she slapped him playfully in protest. In return he started splashing her with water, saying at the same time, "Wonder if Mr. and Mrs. Jerebohm ever bathe together? What do you think, Ma? Doubtful?"

"Never," Ma said. "She locks herself in and does exercises. She told me."

Laughing, Pop said some people never had any fun and started tickling Ma again about the soles of her feet, so that she suddenly wallowed backward like a huge handsome olive seal, laughing too.

Almost prostrate, she lay for some moments helpless and shrieking, half the global map of her body revealed, until finally with an ecstatic rush of joy, telling himself that this was perfick, Pop stretched out his arms toward the familiar continent of pink hills and olive valleys and fished her up again.

6

By ten o'clock on Thursday morning Pop decided that he wouldn't go to the hunt meeting after all. Something big was brewing up in the way of another Army surplus deal and it would take him most of the day to sift the prospects out. Probably show something like 500 percent if it came off—anyway, wurf while.

Nevertheless as he drove away from the house in the Rolls he told himself there could be no harm in stopping off at The Hare and Hounds and saying hello to one or two people, just to see what sort of rabble had turned up. The weather had turned very mild again. The first elm leaves were coloring a clear bright yellow and above them the sky was a sharp northern blue, washed clean of any trace of cloud. If anything it was too blue, Pop thought, and as he got out of the Rolls his hypersensitive nostrils instinctively sniffed the morning air for the smell of rain.

Outside the pub hounds were prancing and snuffling about the paddock, tails raised like a collection of pump handles. A few pink coats loped to and fro. Captain Perigo, blue of chin and already slightly watery-eyed, was having a whiskey outside the bar door, his hard hat sitting well down on his ruby ears. Mr. Jerebohm had turned up too and was clearly not used to riding very much. His pose of squatting on his horse, posterior pushed out like a rudder, looked part of a game of leapfrog.

Corinne Perigo had, after all, also turned out and was talking to a man named Bertie Fanshawe, the man whom Ma had mistakenly suspected she had run away with. Perhaps Ma had mixed her up with Freda O'Connor, who also often had a fling. She was a girl of spanking bosom and voice of low husky passion, who was now talking to Colonel Arbor, a shortish man who rarely talked much but, like a bronchial horse, merely guffawed in a rusty sort of way. Bertie Fanshawe was beefy. You could have cut his face up into prime red steaks. He guffawed too, but brassily, on coarse trumpet voluntaries all his own.

They were a pretty ripe old lot, Pop thought. The cream of county society, eh? It was a good job, he thought, that Mariette had turned out, neat and beautiful as usual, with Montgomery as escort. He was proud of them both. He was glad too to see the brigadier, though on foot, the poor devil not being able to afford a secondhand motorcar, let alone a nag. It would have been pleasant to see Angela Snow appear too but it was, he feared, too much to expect. She lived too far away.

Then to his great surprise, he saw, less than a minute later, a Jeep-drawn horse-box draw up, and out of the Jeep, bright as a quince among a collection of sacked potatoes, Angela Snow.

She was a bandbox of a girl if you liked, he thought. She even had the knack of being able to choose a horse that perfickly matched herself. Today she was riding a brilliant burning chestnut, lean and silky of body as she was.

It showed Mr. Jerebohm's lean black mare up, Pop thought, as rather a poor old bag of bones, an animal with a decidedly uncharitable look in its eye.

"My sweet." In a moment or two Angela, unabashed by public gaze, was kissing Pop full on the mouth, to the extreme consternation of the brigadier, who had not been quite the same man since the passionate upheavals on the hearthrug, and the unpleasant surprise of Corinne Perigo, who started flashing glances of jagged glass on all sides, blackly. "Not going to come with us today? Abysmally disappointed."

Pop, who hadn't seen Angela since the gay evening with the brigadier, blandly explained that he was only a working man.

"Can't afford the time to go gallivanting. Got to scratch a living somehow. Been up since five as it is."

"Suppose so. And how's the swimming pool? Coming on?"

Slow, Pop said, slow. They didn't work all that hard these days. The heating apparatus had been held up too.

"You stand there, you croaker, and tell me it's going to be *heated*?"

"'Course," Pop said, and laughed in his most friendly, rousing fashion. "Can't have Ma catching cold."

"Naturally not. Didn't you murmur something too about having a party to celebrate the opening?"

"In the spring," Pop said airily. "In the spring."

Presently a horn flashed copper in the morning sun, a signal to remind Pop that the hunt would soon be away and that therefore there was precious little time left in which to get outside a snifter.

"Come and have one," he said. "We'll get the brigadier in too."

He took Angela softly by the arm, steering her through a thickening crowd of people, cars, bicycles, horses, and horse-boxes to the door of The Hare and Hounds, at the same time tapping the brigadier on the shoulder as he passed him.

"Going to buy you a drink, General old boy. Come on. Angela's here." he said, and was surprised for the briefest moment not to hear the brigadier's customary grunt of polite refusal in reply.

Nor had the brigadier the slightest intention of giving it. A storm of volcanic emotions had swept over him at the mere sight of Angela Snow's lips pressing themselves on Pop's. He knew only too well what that felt like. He could once again feel his hand gyrating on Angela's pulsating naked back. He was overwhelmed by a returning rush of every detail of that stormy session on the hearthrug. If ever he needed a drink, he thought, it was now.

"First you're coming. Then you're not coming. Fickle man."

A languorous hand held Pop in check three or four yards from the lounge bar door. It was Corinne Perigo, looking at him in a pretense of friendly calm not confirmed by the fact her nostrils were dilating with unusual quickness.

"Couldn't manage it," Pop said. "Business to do."

"And here am I changing my hair appointment."

For the life of him Pop couldn't think what that had to do with him, and was almost ready to say so when she went on, "And who's the tall blond piece? Haven't seen her before."

"Old flame."

Pop didn't laugh as he said this, but Mrs. Perigo did.

"Old I suppose is right. Still, I see she appeals to the brigadier too. The poor old thing was having palpitations."

Pop, suddenly tired of a conversation in which his nearest and dearest friends were being put through a mincer, turned abruptly and went into the bar, leaving a stunned Corinne Perigo standing in lethal silence, alone.

Inside the pub he decided he had a call to pay before joining Angela and the general at the bar. It took him only a couple of minutes to pay it, but meanwhile the brigadier was glad of even that short respite. It gave him a chance to recall the shattering experience on the hearthrug.

"Rather an evening we had."

"Momentous."

Ever since that time an important gap in his memory had bothered the brigadier very greatly and with a sudden rush of courage he decided that this was as good a moment as any to fill it in.

"I found myself on the bed," he said, "and you not there."

"A girl has to go home sometime."

The brigadier said he knew. But it was the time before she went home he was now referring to.

"You were asleep, darling. Very asleep."

"And you?"

"I was having that brandy you promised me. I needed it too."

My God, the brigadier said, half on fire, had the whole affair had that sort of effect on her?

"Devastating, dear boy."

The brigadier, completely on fire now, pitched his voice in a low whispered key, expressing everything in a single cryptic but palpitating sentence.

"Folly to repeat it?"

"What do you think?" Angela said, and gave him a long, languid smile.

The brigadier was saved the necessity of answering this enigmatical question by the breezy entrance of Pop, who floated up to the bar, called the barmaid his little Jenny Wren, ordered himself a double Johnnie Walker, and urged Angela and the brigadier to knock theirs back and quick. The hunt would soon be moving away.

"Wish you were coming," Angela said. "Both of you."

"I'm afraid," the brigadier said, "my hunting days are over."

"Oh?" she said, and laughed on high, belling notes. "Must have been rather something when you were in full cry."

The brigadier felt suddenly halfway to heaven again. A late peacock butterfly, roused by the warmth of autumn sun, fluttered at the bar window, danced among the bottles, and flew across the room. The brigadier watched it settle and cling delicately, its wings brilliant, to the edges of a curtain. Nobody could have felt more like a peacock than himself at that moment and it was in a dream that he heard the barmaid say, "Sounds as if they're moving off, sir. Yes, they are."

"One for the road," Pop said, and pulled a roll of fivers from his pocket about the size of a pint mug. "Double for the general. Large Madeira for Miss Snow. Another double for me."

Already horses were moving off outside. Cars were starting up. A couple of pink coats flashed by. The peacock flew again and Pop said, "Madeira. Don't think I ever tasted it. Any good?"

"Sweet. And warm without being sordid."

The brigadier laughed, alternately watching the butterfly and the edges of Angela Snow's extremely fine smooth hair. The two of them were so beautiful that it positively hurt him to look at them and as he sipped his whiskey he wished to God his hunting days weren't over. But damnit, it was no use, they were; he was past pretending; and he knew the best he would get for the rest of the day would be the far cry of hounds and that queer tugging bleat of a horn being blown across bright autumn fields.

"Well, cheers," Pop said. "Down the hatch. Have a wonderful day. Even if you don't kill nothing, I mean."

It was soon after three o'clock in the afternoon that Mr. Jerebohm, with growing discomfort, decided that he was far from having a wonderful day. He thought it was developing, on the contrary, into a hellishly unpleasant day. Unlike the brigadier, he was beginning to wish his hunting days were over. As rain began to fall, at first in mere biting spits, then in a steady chilling downpour, he even started to wish they had never begun.

It wasn't merely that the countryside, under teeming rain, looked and felt more uncharitable with every step he took. The hunt wasn't running very true to form either.

He knew perfectly well what a hunt ought to look like. He had seen it so often in old prints, on Christmas cards and in advertisements for whiskey. It was gay; it positively bounced with cheerful life. Against charming rural backgrounds of woodland and pasture, in winter weather always crisp and beautiful, riders and hounds galloped at full invigorated stretch, all together, well-drilled as an army, in pursuit of a small red animal framed against the far blue sky. The pink coats were as bright as holly berries at Christmastime and the laughing tails of the hounds as happy as children at play.

But today there was nothing cheerful or well-drilled or invigorating about it. Not only was the rain becoming colder, drearier, and heavier every moment, there was something very wrong with his horse. He had bought it under the impression that it was a hunter; he had paid what he thought was a stiffish price for it—he liked its color.

Pinkie liked its color too; she even thought it handsome. There had even been a time, a day or two since, when Mr. Jerebohm had thought it handsome too, but now he could have cheerfully hit it with a shovel.

All day the animal had behaved like an engine without steam; it continually lacked the power to pull itself off dead center. After desultory canters of thirty or forty yards or so it would suddenly draw up, give a congested cough in its throat, and then release breath in hollow bursts of pain. Afterward it stood for some time staring with cautious eyes at the dripping hedgerows, autumn woods, and bare, sloppy stubbles before with amazing instinct, turning for home.

It had been, in fact, turning for home all day. Three times during the morning Mr. Jerebohm had been blisteringly cursed with words such as "If you can't keep up, bloody well keep out of the way!" From time to time he found himself several hundred yards, even half a mile, behind the pack. He was continually losing hounds behind distant woods, where they wailed like lost souls, mocking him. Several times he got off and walked. It seemed quicker that way.

By half past three in the afternoon he knew, with miserable certainty, that he was lost. Pack and riders were nowhere to be seen. It was raining more and more fiercely on a driving wind and his horse held its blowing frame like a sieve to the rain. Mr. Jerebohm in fact, felt like a sieve himself. The rain was driving large holes through his face, chest, legs, shoulders, and buttocks, and the wind, colder every moment, followed the rain.

A growing conviction that the countryside was one big, evilly devised swindle started to come over him as he turned his horse to the west, the direction where he thought home lay. The supposed pastoral nature of it was a ghastly myth. The deer, pheasant, wild duck, hares, and snipe were all a myth too. The fox itself was a myth. There was no such animal. It was extinct, like the dodo. People rode to hounds merely in the hope of seeing the resurrected ghost of one.

Soaked to his chest, he crossed an unfamiliar piece of country that seemed like a barren land, a heath with neither hedgerows nor fences, roads nor telegraph wires. Occasionally Pop Larkin cantered over it with Mariette; it was open and quiet and Pop thought it perfick. Groups of pine covered the farthest slopes. Young birches, yellow with late autumn now, had sown themselves among brown acres of bracken. In summer, cotton grass blew like snow among pink and purple heather.

Traveling across it on his breathless horse, Mr. Jerebohm merely thought it harsh and uncivilized. It was another part of the great country swindle. It was wild, miserable, and shelterless. Oh, for a hot bath, he kept thinking; God, for a hot bath.

On a road at last, under the civilized protection of telegraph wires, he heard a car coming up behind him in the rain. A second later his horse reared, gave a skyward flip, and threw him. He landed heavily on a grass verge that, though soft and sodden with rain, felt as hard as a cliff of rock.

It was Pop Larkin who ran forward, hailed him, got him to his feet, and tried to comfort him with the words, "Lucky you fell on grass, Mr. Jerebohm. Might have been a bit hard if you'd gone the other way. Had a good day?"

Dispirited and shaken, Mr. Jerebohm merely groaned.

"Better come in to my place and have a drink," Pop said. "It's only just down the road. I'll mix you an Old King Cole."

What the hell, Mr. Jerebohm asked himself and then Pop, was an Old King Cole.

"New drink I found the other day," Pop said. "Mostly rum. It'll put fire into you."

Mr. Jerebohm groaned again. He didn't want fire put into him. In terrible pain, he was sure his back was split in two. He was convinced his kidneys were ruptured and that his spleen was not where it ought to be. Trying to limp back to his horse he felt one leg give a crack underneath him and could have sworn that it was broken.

In sympathy Pop said, "Tell you what. You drive the Rolls back. It's perfickly easy—gears are as smooth as butter. I'll ride the horse."

Mr. Jerebohm, too far gone in agony to argue with this or any other solution, merely dragged his creaking body into the Rolls and let Pop recapture the horse, which reared again in ugly fashion as he did so.

"See you in five minutes," Pop said. "Ma's there."

He seized the bridle and looked the horse firmly in the face. Not only was it an uncharitable animal to look at, he thought, it was downright ugly. It wanted teaching a sharp lesson. It needed a damn good clout and he promptly gave it one, so that the horse, enormously surprised, at once calmed down.

"Nothing but a bag o' horsemeat," Pop said. "D'ye hear me?"

At the house he found Mr. Jerebohm standing in front of the kitchen fire, a glass of rum in his hand, steaming gently. Ma had also given him a good big wedge of cheese and bacon tart on which he was now chewing slowly but with silent gratitude. Ma had been deeply sympathetic about the fall. She thought she didn't like the look of him all that much and she was just saying, as Pop came in, "You look a bit peaky, Mr. Jerebohm. It's shaken you up. Why don't you sit down?"

Mr. Jerebohm knew he couldn't sit down. He felt that if he did sit down he would never get up again. His bones would lock.

"Shall I telephone the doctor?" Ma said. "I think I ought to."

In low murmurs Mr. Jerebohm said no, he didn't think so; he merely wanted to go home.

"Get outside that one," Pop said, looking into Mr. Jerebohm's glass, "and I'll mix you another."

Gratefully Mr. Jerebohm got outside the remainder of his Old King Cole. He was steaming more noticeably every moment. His riding boots were half full of water. His ribs ached every time he drew breath and only Pop's large rum cocktail, mixed double as usual to save time, gave him any sort of comfort.

It was the warm rum too that started his brain slowly working again and presently caused him to remember something. It was probably just one more example of the big country swindle, he thought, but he would soon find out.

"Most grateful to you, Larkin," he said. "By the way, I've got a bone to pick with you."

"Pick away," Pop said. "Perfickly all right."

"Didn't you tell me when I bought Gore Court," Mr. Jerebohm said, "that there was a boat on the lake?"

"Perfickly true," Pop said, laughing. "But it ain't there now."

"Oh? So you know? Then where is it?"

"In my boathouse," Pop said. "Just before you took over the house Montgomery found a gang of kids throwing bricks at it, so we rowed it up the lake, carried it over the sluice gates, and brought it up the river. It's safer under cover. I meant to have told you."

Mr. Jerebohm listened in silence, but nevertheless didn't want to seem ungrateful. The rum was marvelously comforting.

"I'll row it back in the spring." Pop said. "I daresay Montgomery'll give it a coat of varnish in the meantime."

Overwhelmed with kindness, Mr. Jerebohm could still find nothing to say. Nor, for another moment or two, had he any words to answer another remark from Pop, who presently disappeared into the pantry and came out holding a brace of pheasants.

"Little present for you," he said. "Knocked 'em off in the medder last Monday afternoon. They'll want hanging a couple o' days."

Searching for words, Mr. Jerebohm felt he could have wept. "Wonderfully kind" was all he managed to mutter. "Very, very kind."

"Make a nice change from pills and diets," Ma said, "won't they? I don't hold with all those pills. The world takes too many pills by half."

It damn well did too, Mr. Jerebohm thought, it damn well did too.

Blessed with pheasants and rum and Pop's final injunction "to clout the bounder if he plays up again," he managed to ride slowly home in the dying light of an afternoon across which, at last, the rain was slackening.

There was even a break of light in the west and as he rode past The Hare and Hounds, with the pheasants slung across the saddle, he could distinctly see the faces of Corinne Perigo and Bertie Fanshawe as they cantered slowly past him.

"Good night!" they called, and he said, "Good night" in reply, having just enough strength to raise a hand in courtesy to his hat.

"By God," Bertie Fanshawe said to Mrs. Perigo, "they shoot 'em from horseback now, do they?" The unexpected vision of a man riding home from a fox hunt with a brace of pheasants slung across his horse was altogether too much to bear. Damnit, it wasn't the thing. "Next thing you know we'll be having electric hounds and mechanical horses or some damn lark."

Mr. Jerebohm, if he could have heard, might well have thought it a good idea, especially about the horses. As it was, he merely limped on toward home, silently aching from boots to collar, wind-stung eyes on the sky.

Unfamiliar though he was with the passage and change of country seasons, he knew perfectly well that it was winter that now stared at him out of a cold watery sunset, and that it looked, if possible, even more uncharitable than the rain, his horse, and the darkening countryside.

7

Walking slowly along the lakeside on a shimmering afternoon in late April, the warmest so far of the year, Pinkie Jerebohm saw in the middle distance across the water a floating object, pale primrose in color, to which for some moments she was unable to give a name.

After staring at it steadfastly for some time, just as incapable as Mr. Jerebohm of detecting the difference between one bird and another, she finally decided that it must be, of all things, a yellow swan. She had always supposed that swans were white, but perhaps they turned yellow in the mating season or something of that sort. You never knew with nature.

A few moments later, to her intense surprise, the yellow swan started waving a hand. A sudden impulse made her wave in reply and it took her only a few seconds longer to realize that whatever changes of color nature might effect in swans at springtime it worked no such miracles on Pop Larkin.

Pop, gay in a yellow sports shirt, hatless, and fully ready to greet the first fresh burst of spring, was rowing Mr. Jerebohm's promised boat, gay itself with new golden varnish, across the middle of the lake. The day was absolutely perfick for the job, as he had told himself over and over again that morning. It couldn't possibly have been more perfick: cuckoos calling everywhere, the sky quivering with larks, the woods rich with blackbird song, his favorite of all except the nightingale's. Even the wood doves were talking softly away on those wooing notes that were the first true voice of summer.

"Afternoon, Mrs. Jerebohm!" Pop's voice was quick as a leaping fish as it crossed the water. "Perfick day. Decided I'd bring the Queen Mary back. Sorry to have been so long."

It was most kind of him, Pinkie lisped as she watched him ship oars and let the boat drift into the bank. But there really hadn't been that much of a hurry. You couldn't say it had been much like boating weather, could you?

"Perfickly true," Pop said. "It is today, though. You'll have to get Mr. Jerebohm to give you a trip around the lake before dark."

Mr. Jerebohm wasn't at home, Pinkie said. Moreover she wasn't at all sure that he rowed.

"Pity," Pop said. "Very nice little boat." With a neat half wink he invited Mrs. Jerebohm to give the fresh-varnished boat the once-over. Montgomery, he thought, had done a very good job on her. "Even had the carpet sweeper on the cushions." The cushions, a bright plum-purple with lemon piping, looked very gay and springlike too.

"Like me to give you a trip?" Pop said. Perky as a terrier, he skipped from boat to bank, where he tied the painter to a tree root, laughing freely. "Beautiful afternoon for it—might never get another one like it for weeks."

Pinkie Jerebohm, who was dressed in a close-fitting lavender jersey suit that only succeeded in showing how fruitless all her fond hard work at slimming had been, said that she had, as a matter of fact, actually started out to look for primroses.

"Come to the right place," Pop said, and with an extensive sweep of a hand enthusiastically indicated the woods that came down to the very edge of the shimmering lake at its farthest end. "Woods are full of 'em. Crowded. Fick as fick. You can even smell 'em as you go by. Hop in. I'll take you over."

Mrs. Jerebohm hesitated. She wasn't at all sure about hopping in. She had Corinne Perigo coming in to tea at four o'clock and wondered what time it was now.

Impressively Pop's wristwatch flashed gold in the sun. "Only three o'clock," he said. "Bags o' time."

For another apprehensive second or two Mrs. Jerebohm hesitated. Among other things was the boat safe? It didn't leak or anything of that kind? She couldn't swim. She was, in fact, terrified of water.

"Pity," Pop said. "I mean about the swimming. Oh, the boat's perfickly safe." After a succession of unobtrusively quick glances at Pinkie's figure, he decided that, slimming or no slimming, she wasn't at all bad in the right places and would probably look quite passable in a bathing costume. "Thought you might like to come over and use our swimming pool when we get it open next month. Lovely pool. All blue tiles."

Mrs. Jerebohm thanked him for thinking of her, but said that it wasn't all that much fun, was it, if you couldn't swim.

"Ma can't swim," Pop said, "but she has fun all right. Trust Ma. Come over one afternoon and I'll learn you. In a couple o' days I'll have you going."

Well, Pinkie said, she didn't know about that. Though she didn't say so there were, after all, limits. There were certain proprieties. Mr. Jerebohm wasn't often home in the afternoons and he mightn't think it quite nice if his wife took swimming lessons with Larkin when he wasn't there.

"Good for your figure," Pop said with some enthusiasm and several more rapid glances at it. "Not that it's not good now."

An unusual flutter sprang through Pinkie Jerebohm. Some seconds later, almost without knowing it, she was accepting Pop's offer of a hand and in a fraction of a minute afterward she was in the boat, facing Pop, who began rowing her away.

"But you *will* keep an eye on the time, won't you?" she said. "What I mean is—I mean I must absolutely dovetail in with Corinne. I simply mustn't keep her waiting."

Damn Corinne, Pop thought, determined not to spoil a perfick afternoon worrying about Corinne, who several times during the winter had put his back up in no uncertain way. At the Hunt Ball, at two o'clock in the morning, she had cornered him in a half-lit drafty corridor on the pretext of getting him to take out a subscription to a new country club about to be started up by Bertie Fanshawe. In reality it was merely an excuse to start pawing his neck. On an evening in January she had somehow winkled him out of the bar of The Hare and Hounds on the pretext that her car wouldn't start. On that occasion, without ceremony, she began pawing him all over and then turned like a snake, actually hissing, when he told her to stop it and quick. "You need a good belting," he told her on a third occasion when she telephoned twice in one evening to invite him over for a drink because the captain was away. That, she told Pop with savage sweetness, was exactly what she hoped he was going to give her. She wouldn't rest, in fact, until he did.

She'll rest a devil of a long time, Pop thought and a second later put Corinne Perigo completely from his mind by asking Pinkie Jerebohm if she could smell the primroses yet? In his own hypersensitive way he had already caught the lightest breath of them across the water.

"No," she said, and in fact the boat was already drifting in to the far bank where young hazel and sweet chestnut and a few high, gold-flowered oaks came down to the water's edge, before she actually detected the first scent of them floating on the lightest of airs.

"Wonderful scent," Pop said. "Fancy there's a few bluebells there too." He drew deep breaths, with selective sharpness. Yes, you could smell the bluebells too. "Get 'em?"

Pinkie Jerebohm, helped out of the boat by Pop's two outstretched hands, had to confess that she couldn't get them. It was all too elusive for her. It was wholly impossible to separate one scent from another, especially when she scarcely knew which was which, and suddenly at the woodland's edge she was deeply aware again of an uncommonly nervous flutter darting through her, leaving her slightly uncertain at the knees.

For the rest of the afternoon, at irregular intervals, she kept experiencing that same sensation without ever being able to decide what caused it. Crowds of white anemones and primroses covered the whole floor of the wood with endless drifts of the softest unwinking white and yellow stars. The tops of the trees were gold-green belfries of buds pouring down birdsong in tireless peals. From across the lake cuckoos called continually, bell-like too. The notes taken up, transformed, and repeated in the wooing moan of doves that Pop adored so much.

Pinkie, bending among primroses, sometimes even kneeling among them on patches of big dry papery chestnut leaves, gradually felt intoxicated and absorbed to a point where time no longer mattered. Nor did Pop remind her. It was pretty nearly perfick by the lakeside on such a day. It was his idea of heaven. The only thing that could perhaps have made it more perfick still, he thought, was the chance of having a short, gentle squeeze with Pinkie.

He wondered how she'd take it? Just the same as Edith Pilchester did? He wondered, and then suddenly found he couldn't be sure. They were rather *très snob*, the Jerebohms. She might go sour.

Still, a casual brush among the primroses, accidental or otherwise, would soon tell him. Couldn't do no harm. It wasn't every girl, after all, who got the chance of being stroked in the middle of a primrose wood on a hot April afternoon.

Several times afterward he found himself watching the bending, rounded figure of Pinkie, plumpish and smoothly tight in its lavender jersey suit in spite of all her slimming, and told himself that the time had surely come when a little bit of dovetailing might be fun.

Each time she suddenly straightened up and walked away. Each time, too, he told himself he couldn't be absolutely sure about her. Something about the big bunches of primroses that she had gathered and now held in front of her as she walked gave her an odd look of innocence that he couldn't quite get over.

All this time he himself had been gathering violets, mostly fat white ones, but also a score or two of the dark purple kind. Every now and then he buried his nostrils in them, draining them of scent. All the nerves of the spring afternoon seemed to vibrate tautly as he smelled the flowers and once he felt impelled to call out, "Beautiful, ain't it? Nowhere like the country."

Pinkie, who was now gathering separate bunches of white anemones, said she agreed, though in fact the winter hadn't taught her so. The winter had been a trial, hard to bear. That was largely because Mr. Jerebohm still insisted on living in Gore Court not because it was pleasant, convenient, or in any way desirable but merely as a means of losing money. Mr. Jerebohm in fact was now raising pigs. Palatial sties had sprung up everywhere and Mr. Jerebohm found a certain satisfaction in feeding the animals on pig swill made of gold. Pinkie, who didn't understand the reasoning behind making money on the stock exchange and giving it to pigs to eat in the country, couldn't help feeling she would have preferred a maisonette on the front at Brighton, where she could occasionally parade in her best hat, gossip over morning coffee, and gaze at the sea.

Here there was hardly anyone to gossip with except Corinne Perigo. The natives, she thought, were uncommonly hostile. They kept themselves steadfastly to themselves. Friendliness seemed no part of their nature. The Austrian maid had left two weeks ago in a huff and now, with the arrival of spring, all the women of the village were planting potatoes, hoeing strawberries, or doing strange jobs in hop fields. She knew now that she couldn't get any help for months and suddenly as she thought of it for the fiftieth time that week she gave a long, uncertain sigh.

Pop, hearing it from some distance off, came over to her bending figure, carrying his bunch of white and purple violets like an offering.

"Surely not sighing on an afternoon like this?" he said. "Too perfick by half for that. Smell the violets."

Laughing, he thrust the violets up to Pinkie Jerebohm's face and for a delicious second or two she dreamed over them, drinking the scent. Broken sunlight fell like a light veil on her face, which was not unpretty in its simpering way, and on her two hands, clasping almost more primroses and anemones than they could safely hold.

This, Pop told himself, might be just the moment for a trial run. Perhaps he should try her under the chin first and see what happened? But suddenly Pinkie, from being almost completely unbalanced one moment in scent and sun and flowers, darted out of herself with a lisping exclamation, "Oh, you know it's really awfully awfully sweet of you to bring me over here. I do appreciate it. Spending so much of your valuable time—"

Pop, still locked in indecision, uncertain whether to brush her lightly under the chin or go in for a proper squeeze where there'd be no mistaking what it meant, hadn't a second longer in which to make up his mind before she almost threw up her flower-crowded hands in the air.

"Time! But whatever time is it, pray? We must have been here half an hour or more."

Pop, laughing, flashed a look at his watch and said, "More like hour and a half. It's nearly half past four."

"Oh my goodness. Corinne will be frantic!"

To Pop's intense surprise Pinkie broke into running, actually dropping flowers as she scurried under the trees to the waterside. He followed her on light springy steps, hoping she might possibly slip and fall in a harmless sort of way so that he could have the pleasure of picking her up but to his disappointment she made the boat without a trip or stumble.

A moment later he was there too, catching her lightly by the soft upper flesh of her arm as he helped her into the boat. To his further surprise a couple of extra velvety squeezes had no effect at all on Pinkie, who seemed utterly oblivious not only of Pop but of everything else as she half stumbled into the boat and flopped rather heavily down on the plum-and-yellow cushions.

"Don't rock the boat," Pop said.

"Whatever can I have been thinking about? An hour and a half! Whatever *was* I thinking?"

Pop, taking up the oars and quietly starting to row the boat out into the lake, where silver shoals of small fry were leaping up like little fountains in the sun, noticed that Pinkie in her haste and distraction hadn't had a moment in which to put her dress straight. Her lavender skirt had ridden up well above her knees.

Charmed and slightly excited by the unexpected vision of Pinkie's rather plump silky legs, Pop found himself paying less and less attention to her lisping self-chastisement as he rowed her across the lake in the sun. Except that he damned once or twice the irritating and oppressive entry of Corinne Perigo into the conversation, he was enjoying himself very much, both actually and in anticipation. Pinkie, he decided, wasn't half a bad shape after all. Her legs were quite pretty and he could see an awful lot of them.

"I'll never, never forgive myself. It really is a granny knot, isn't it? Inviting people to tea and then just not being there. Oh! I *am* a careless fool."

"You'll be at the house in ten minutes," Pop said, full of airy comfort. "Women are always late anyway."

"That remark doesn't help," Pinkie said. The social strain, keeping her at full stretch, almost made her voice break. "You don't see any sign of Corinne, I suppose?"

No, Pop said and told himself that he was damned if he wanted to. There was something crude about that woman. After all, as Ma often said, you had to have a bit of finesse about you.

The boat was still thirty yards from the opposite bank when Pinkie, hands full of flowers, sat forward on her cushions with all the appearance of a frog ready to leap.

"You wouldn't mind awfully if I absolutely made a dash for it, would you?"

Not much time now, Pop thought. The golden afternoon was slipping away. His chances were disappearing as rapidly and surely as the boat was drifting through shoals of unfurling water lily pads into the bank.

"Sit still," Pop said, "Don't stand up." Pinkie had actually, in her anxiety, tried to stand up in the boat. "Wait till I tie her up. You don't want a wet tail, do you?"

Utterly oblivious of her risen skirt, Pinkie sat on the very edge of the cushion, an inch or so of bare thigh revealed above her stockings.

Now or never, Pop told himself. "Don't move until I say," he warned her. "It's a bit deep just here."

Momentarily calmed by sensible advice, Pinkie sat precariously still on her cushion while Pop, yellow shirt fluttering, nipped on to the bank and pulled the boat in.

"Hold hard till I tell you!"

A second offering of sensible advice was completely lost on Pinkie, who suddenly leapt up and staggered forward to the bank and into the unready arms of Pop, who still had the boat's rope in his hands. Staggered too, Pop dropped the rope, felt Pinkie begin to slip down the grassy slope toward the lake, and managed to catch her firmly with both arms, just in time.

"Neat bit o' rescue work," Pop thought, and in a moment had Pinkie in a swift and uncompromising embrace, at the same time caressing her with one hand some inches below the back waistline.

For some moments a light but intoxicating perfume of half-crushed violets, primroses, and anemones filled the air and Pinkie, almost breathless, gasped as she caught at it. At the same time her lisping mouth had opened in what Pop thought was a gesture of encouragement. Stimulated, he gave the roundest part of one thigh an extra nip of affection and was on the point of kissing her full on the lips when, to his pained surprise, she started screaming madly.

He hadn't ever heard anyone, he thought, scream quite so loud. You could surely hear it a mile away. On high, full-throated notes Pinkie lifted her face to the sky and for nearly half a minute wailed wordlessly, at the same time dropping every flower she held.

"Better try to comfort her a bit I suppose," Pop thought, and was just wondering how to start this delicate operation when he saw a new figure running toward him along the lakeside.

It was Corinne Perigo, advancing in a hatless charge.

"Wherever have you been? Whatever has happened?"

Pinkie Jerebohm, white-faced, standing in a pool of stricken flowers, allowed herself a moment of deathly silence before answering in a whisper, "This man has just tried to violate me."

Pop had hardly grasped the words before Corinne Perigo gave him a venomous, curdling look.

"You absolute swine," she said. "You absolute swine."

Pop, for once, was at a loss for an effective reply. No one had ever called him that before. It was rather much, he thought. A moment later he was startled to hear Corinne Perigo's voice again, now speaking in tones of even colder venom.

"Have him charged, Pinkie. Put him in court. Let the police deal with him. The swine. It's high time. I'll be a witness for you."

As a weeping, flowerless Pinkie was led away along the lakeside Pop found himself staring with mild disconsolation at the lake, dismayed to find that the boat, which he hadn't had time to tie up, was drifting away.

One way or another, it was a bad end to a perfick afternoon.

"Not sure you haven't gone and torn it this time, Sid," he told himself. "Not sure you haven't gone and torn it now."

8

On that same shimmering April afternoon Edith Pilchester, succumbing at last to the grumbling appendix that had been troubling her for weeks, went into the hospital to have it out. When Ma heard of this nearly a week later she was not only full of sympathy for the wool-gathering Edith, always so lonely, but at once urged that Pop must pay her a visit as soon as possible, at the same time taking something nice with him to cheer the poor thing up.

"You'd be worth a dozen boxes o' pills to her. She'd be up and about in no time."

Pop agreed and presently, on a showery April evening full of thrush song, took Edith Pilchester two bottles of port; a basket of fresh peaches, pears, grapes, and apricots; a box of milk chocolates; a large bunch of deep yellow freesias; and several slices of cold breast of turkey. All spring came flowing richly into Edith's room on the strong fragrance of freesias and Edith, pale and meager, wept.

This, Pop said, they couldn't have; it wouldn't do at all, and immediately sat down on the bed and held her hand. This warm and unexpected gesture merely had the effect of making Edith weep afresh, not quietly now but in a loud, spinsterish blubber, so that soon, when a nurse came in to fuss with a chart, there was cold severity in the air.

"And what," she said, "have you been doing to my patient?"

"Making love to her," Pop said, quick as a jackdaw. "Like a sample?"

"That will do. I must ask you not—"

"See what he's brought me!" Edith Pilchester sobbed. "Freesias. Wine. Gold, frankincense, and myrrh—"

The effect of this outburst was so touching that the nurse suddenly felt like weeping too and hastily remembered she had something to do in another ward.

When Pop now suggested that Edith should dry her eyes and have a grape or something she said no, no, no thank you, she couldn't touch a thing.

"Have a drink then," Pop said, and immediately poured out half a tumbler of red port, advising Edith to get it down her at once, so as to warm the vital parts.

Edith, taking the port in one quivering hand and dabbing her eyes on the corner of her flannelette nightgown with the other, apologized several times, begging that Pop wouldn't think her too silly, and said it wasn't merely that the gifts had overwhelmed her. It was a combination of things.

"Oh?" Pop said. "For instance what?"

"I heard the most awful news about you. It was absolutely ghastly."

Awful news? Pop, cheerful as ever, couldn't think what that could be.

"This awful woman. This Mrs. Jerebohm. They tell me you're actually being prosecuted."

Pop laughed with a bucolic sort of bark that actually reached the young nurse in another ward.

"Oh, that," Pop said. "That's a real lark, that is."

"But *did* you—I mean *is* there any truth in it?"

" 'Course," Pop said. "Case comes up in two weeks' time."

"Ghastly," Edith said. "Absolutely ghastly."

Pop, treating the matter with renewed levity, wondered if Edith would mind all that much if he joined her in a glass of port? With birdlike joy, tears drying now, Edith begged him to do so, adding, "But what *is* it all about? What *are* you supposed to have done?"

Pop, still sitting on the bed, adroitly poured himself a glass of port.

"Pinched her bottom. She was getting out of a rowing boat."

Edith, halfway between tears and laughter, could only give a froglike croak in answer, silently wishing it might have been her. No such opportunities had come her way for some time, not even at Christmas.

"But aren't you at all *concerned*? You don't seem to be worried about it one little *bit*."

Pop, she thought, seemed to be taking life in a spirit of jollier, livelier levity than ever. Incorrigible, remarkable man.

"I'll worry when the time comes," Pop said. It was a major part of his rather loosely made philosophy to cross bridges when he came to them. "After all, anything might happen before then."

It might indeed, Edith thought. It might indeed.

"I only hope," she said, "you've got a good solicitor."

Pop, purporting to be utterly unconcerned, gave her one of his sudden smoothly mischievous glances that had the immediate effect of making her toes tingle sharply at the bottom of the bed.

"Going to conduct the case myself," he said. He laughed rousingly, winking. "Counsel for the defense—that's me."

Edith, sipping port, didn't know whether to be alarmed or delighted. "But do you know *how*? I *mean*—"

"Seen it all on telly!" Pop assured her blandly. "Court cases nearly every night of the week on telly."

"But how you *dare*! I should *die*."

"Well, I shan't. Going to enjoy myself that day. Drink up."

Edith drank up, raising her glass to Pop at the same time.

"I can only wish you all possible success," she said, looking Pop straight in the face with a refreshed swallowlike glance, eyes glowing. "Oh, I *know* it will be. I *feel* it. I've got that sort of *thing* about it."

Whole thing would go like a bomb, Pop said. Would she be well enough to be there? He hoped so.

"I shall be there if it *kills* me. And so will all your friends. We'll absolutely *band* together."

Such fervent promises of support had Pop chuckling again. With charm he started lightly urging Edith to peel herself a grape or a peach or something. In reply, Edith had to confess, as she gulped down deep rich breaths of freesia perfume, that she was really altogether too nervous to eat anything for the moment.

Something, she said, biting her lips, had just come to her.

"Oh?" Pop said, and looked at her bitten lips with concern, wondering if perhaps she had had a sudden postoperative twinge.

"I've just thought that if it could be of any help at all I'd cheerfully appear as a witness," she said. "I mean as to character or something—"

Or something? Pop thought. Good old Edith. Very nice of Edith. But he wasn't sure about that something.

"Haven't quite got the case worked out yet," he said. "Haven't got the order of battle ready."

Edith, who was sure it was going to be an absolute battle royal when it came, suddenly felt herself go unreasonably coy. She shrank perceptibly into her nightgown, feeling her toes tingle sharply again at the bottom of the bed.

"By the way, what *are* you charged with? I've asked myself over and over again."

"Indecent assault or summat," Pop said. "It's all in the summons."

The word "indecent" immediately seemed to whir and flash about the room like a dragonfly on a hot afternoon, making Edith flush in her throat. She knew perfectly well now that all night long she would lie awake and wonder about what could possibly have happened in that rowing boat.

"I never have liked that Mrs. Jerebohm," she said. "Such people don't belong in the country."

Oh, old Pinkie wasn't bad, Pop said. You could hardly blame Pinkie. It was Corinne Perigo that was the snake in the grass.

"That woman!" Edith said. "I could kill her!"

The magisterial vehemence of this remark made her suddenly flop back on the pillows, surprised, flushed, and weakened. Pop had to confess to himself that he was surprised too. It was very strong stuff for Edith. Probably the drink had got into her, like it sometimes did into Charley.

"It's women like her who bring disgrace on our sex," she said. "They make you—oh, I don't know *what* they make you—"

Edith, completely crimson in the face now, broke off helplessly, impotent to express another thought. Pop, slightly alarmed that she might start up a temperature or have a relapse of some sort, urged her to take it easy, at the same time holding her hand.

"Easy," he urged her softly. "Easy. Easy."

Easiness came to Edith Pilchester in the form of a long quiet thrill. The last deep sigh before sleep could never have quietened her more effectively than that single repeated word or the clasping of Pop's hands.

"Got to trot along now." Pop told her some time later. "Come and see you again soon."

Light cold April showers were falling on the window. The cloud that dropped them was slate-dark, bringing on an early twilight in which the freesias, the peaches, and the apricots all glowed a curious, almost phosphorescent orange.

In a low voice, though not tired, Edith several times thanked Pop for coming. He would be very much in her thoughts, she said. Very much. Never, in fact, out of them.

Pop, who had made up his mind to treat her to a good-night kiss, then remembered something himself.

"Forgot to tell you about our swimming pool. Going to have a party when we open it next month. What about a donkey race in the water? Eh? Men and girls?" He laughed with his customary carelessness. "That's if they don't put me inside."

"Inside?" Her mind vibrated madly with alarm. "You don't mean prison?"

He meant prison, Pop said. Well, why not? It was warm. It was free. He believed they even had telly there too nowadays.

"Awful man," she said. "I believe you're really trying to frighten me."

"Not on your nelly," Pop said, and a second later, pressing her back on the pillows, gave her a faultless dream of a kiss that couldn't have acted more like a sedative, so much so that when the nurse came back, twenty minutes later, she found Edith peacefully sleeping, the half-drunk glass of port still in her hands.

"Visitor for you," Ma said, when Pop reached home half an hour later. "And I'll bet you'll never guess who."

Pop could guess all right; he knew.

"Sergeant Buzz-whiskers."

Sergeant Wilson, that was. He was the policeman who had originally served the summons. Hated doing it to Sid, he confessed, but there it was. Duty.

"Well, it's not the sergeant," Ma said. "That's caught you."

It had caught him too, Pop said, and after two or three guesses decided he might as well go into the sitting room and see for himself while mixing a decent pick-me-up at the same time.

He had hardly decided on this before a small figure, not unlike Pop but twenty years older, nipped into the kitchen. He looked very much like an artful gray terrier who had spent a lifetime gnawing an infinite number of bones, a practice that had knocked several of his front teeth out. His bony yellow forehead had a perceptible hollow in the center of it. If by some chance this had been filled with a third eye it could hardly have increased the strong magnifying qualities of the rest of his face. The lively little gray eyes were telescopic lenses, picking up every detail. The ears were bulbous earphones, tuned to every breath.

"Uncle Perce!" Pop said. "Haven't seen you since Mariette's wedding day."

Uncle Perce, in a voice no less diamond-sharp than his eyes and ears, said Perce it was and shook Pop's hand with a restless rattrap of wiry fingers.

"Calls for a drink, this," Pop said, and had just started to mix a couple of Red Bulls when his son-in-law, Mr. Charlton, came in. After an evening hanging curtains with Mariette at the new bungalow in the meadow Charley was thirsty too. So, Ma said, was she. Pop consequently found himself mixing about a gallon of Red Bull, well iced, to which Ma added an offering of fresh cheese straws and a bottle of Worcestershire sauce.

"Well, what's it all about, Perce?"

"Hear you're in trouble, Sid boy."

A combination of owl and fox gave Uncle Perce's half-toothless mouth a remarkably impressive twist.

"Oh, that," Pop said.

"They were chewing it over at The Hare and Hounds when I dropped in on my way over," Uncle Perce said. "First I'd heard on it. Why didn't you tell me?"

"Nothing to tell," Pop said, bland as ever. "Nothing to it."

One lid of Uncle Perce's searching eyes dropped like a trap.

"Allus come to Perce when the flag's down," he said. "You know that."

"Who was nattering at the pub?" Ma said, carefully sprinkling Worcestershire sauce on a length of cheese straw. "Anybody you know?"

Uncle Perce cast a pair of artful eyes on Ma and said, "Some I did and some I didn't."

"Oh?" Ma said. "Who didn't you?"

"There was a piece there," Uncle Perce said, "calling herself Mrs. Perigo."

Ma's bosom, in outrage, was suddenly swollen like a pouter pigeon.

"Don't talk about her! That woman's got no finesse," she said, pronouncing the word "finesse" to rhyme with highness. "She's the one who started it all."

Uncle Perce went through the startling act of closing both eyes, as if actually thinking, thus looking more artful than ever.

"I've seen that piece somewhere before," he said. "And it won't be long afore I remember where."

"Sooner I forget her the better," Pop said. "Drink up, Perce. You're slow."

"I'm thinking," Uncle Perce said, drinking up. "I'm always a bit slow when I'm thinking."

"What about you, Charley boy?" Pop said. "Room for another?"

Charley was readily agreeing that he had room for another when Pop suddenly remembered something. He hadn't set eyes on Charley all day, not since breakfast. Had Charley been egg hunting or something?

"No, as a matter of fact," Mr. Charlton said, "I've spent a good deal of the day at the public library."

"God Almighty," Pop said, almost exploding over the glass-and-chrome expanse of the cocktail cabinet. "Anythink wrong?"

It alarmed him to think that Charley and Mariette might be off hooks again. He could think of no other reasonable excuse for a man spending all day at the public library.

"Better get outside that one quick," he said, handing Charley a large second Red Bull. "That'll put you right. You look a bit dicky."

Mr. Charlton, looking both calm and healthy, said that there was in fact nothing wrong with him at all. He had merely been doing a little legal research.

In fresh amazement Pop asked Ma if she'd finished with the Worcestershire sauce for a moment. Ma said she had and passed the bottle, into which Pop dipped a fresh cheese straw. There was no fathoming Charley boy sometimes. Legal research?

"I thought I might get a few tips for you," Mr. Charlton said. "For the case, I mean."

Pop, supremely confident that he didn't need any tips, merely laughed in an easy fashion and went on to say that it was very nice of Charley, but—

"You see," Mr. Charlton said, "it isn't as if you'd done this sort of thing before."

Pop cheerfully admitted as much, but after all he'd seen it often enough on telly.

"Yes," Mr. Charlton said, "but you've never been in court—"

"Should think not," Ma said. "The idea."

"Might have been a couple o' times if it hadn't been for me," Uncle Perce said. "Remember that time—"

"We don't want to hear it!" Ma said. "Do you mind?"

Uncle Perce, artfulness momentarily crushed out of him by the second peremptory rising of Ma's pouter bosom, hadn't a syllable to say in answer and merely stared into his glass, thinking.

"The essence of this case," Mr. Charlton said, in a sudden flush of words so professionally assured that Pop wondered if he oughtn't to let Charley boy do the defending after all, "seems to me this. The case of the prosecution must rest almost entirely on corroborative evidence. Corroborative evidence there must be, otherwise Mrs. Jerebohm, as I see it, can stand there until the cows come home."

What the pipe was corroborative evidence? Pop wanted to know. A bruise or something? Where he'd pinched her?

"That'll have worn off a bit by now," Ma said, huge body bouncing with laughter.

"Corroborative evidence," Mr. Charlton said, "is evidence from some person or persons able to substantiate the accusation Mrs. Jere-bohm is making against you. In other words, did anyone else see what happened? For instance Mrs. Perigo?"

"She was there all right," Pop said, "shrieking at the top of her voice. Calling me an absolute swine."

"No finesse, that woman," Ma said. "No finesse whatever."

"I shall remember where I've seen that piece in a minute," Uncle Perce said. "I shall remember all right."

"As I see it," Mr. Charlton said in another rush of supremely calm assurance, "you need call only two witnesses. Mrs. Jerebohm and Mrs. Perigo, of whom Mrs. Perigo is the most important. Alternatively you can elect to go into the box yourself and speak on your own behalf. That, however, I wouldn't advise."

Temporarily startled, Pop recovered enough to remind himself, as so often before, what a marvelous feller Charley was. You had to hand it to Charley sometimes.

At this point Uncle Perce, dropping an artful eyelid, suggested he might come as a witness too. How about that?

"Why?" Ma said, and to this rather cryptic challenge Uncle Perce had no answer except to look immensely thoughtful again.

A moment later a cry from upstairs reminded Ma that little Oscar was awake and with her own calm assurance she left the kitchen to see what she could do for the baby, licking her fingers clean of Worcester-shire sauce as she went, half wondering if a bit of sauce on a cheese straw wouldn't help to soothe him down. She hoped Pop wouldn't be put inside. She really did. It would make it rather awkward in many ways.

"Well, I must go too," Mr. Charlton said, "or Mariette'll be won-dering where I am."

"That's it," Pop said, terrifically cheerful, "off to bed."

"Do you mind?" Mr. Charlton said. The April evening, its showers finished, still glowed faintly golden outside. "I haven't had supper. It's hardly bedtime yet."

"Then it ought to be," Pop said smartly, and wished Mr. Charlton a very good night, with pleasant dreams and all that lark, hoping the urgent hint wouldn't be lost on him.

Alone in the kitchen with an increasingly thoughtful Uncle Perce, Pop suggested another snifter and didn't Perce think the Worcester-shire sauce went well with the straws? Idea of Ma's. Uncle Perce agreed and got outside another snifter in very fast time. This encouraged Pop to mix a fourth and for the next half hour or so they sat drinking in steady contentment, one or other of them occasionally dipping a straw into the bottle of sauce.

Finally Uncle Perce said he ought to be getting back and Pop said he would run him home in the Rolls. Perce, who was boots and odd-job man at a hotel called The Three Swans five or six miles away, had walked over for the exercise but confessed he didn't feel like walking back. The snifters made him sleepy.

In the Rolls he fell into a sudden doze and it was only when the car stopped at the end of the journey that he abruptly sat up, sharply awake, and said with all the old compelling artfulness, "Sid. I just remembered who that piece is. She's no more Mrs. Perigo than I'm the Duke o' Wellington. You're going to want me as a witness after all."

Driving the Rolls back into the yard, in darkness, Pop couldn't help feeling, on the whole, rather pleased with himself. What with Charley's legal research and all that lark, and now Uncle Perce, things were looking rather more rosy.

These pleasant reflections were shattered, almost as soon as he was out of the car, by a voice.

"Hullo there," Corinne Perigo said.

"The gate's over there," Pop said, hardly bothering to look at the hatless, mackintoshed figure leaning against the front wing of the Rolls. "Or there's a shortcut over the fields. It's quicker."

"Suppose we take the shortcut? What I've got to say won't take long."

"Tell it to the marines."

"Look, let's not be silly," she said, "shall we? Why be silly?" .

"Speak for yourself," Pop said. "I'm off to have my supper."

"Listen," she said. "Supposing I said I thought the whole thing was a ghastly mistake?"

"Suppose you said the stars were potato crisps?"

"All I wanted to say was this." Her voice was low and languid in the darkness. "If you and I could come to terms I might—"

"Terms?"

"Well, an arrangement. Just you and me. Strictly *entre nous* and all that." Pop heard the dry rustle of the mackintosh as she suddenly swung away from the car and came closer in the darkness. "After all, what quarrel have we?"

Pop, thinking that so stupid a question didn't require an answer, started to walk away.

"No quarrel at all. All you've got to do is to give me the signal and I think I can persuade Pinkie to call the dogs off."

"Signal?" Pop paused halfway across the yard. "Dogs off? What signal?"

"Come back and I'll show you."

"Good night," Pop said.

Again he heard the dry rustle of the mackintosh in the darkness.

"After all, it's only a question of pride with her. I don't believe she really wants to go on with it. After all, who does? Nobody really does, do they?"

"You'd be surprised," Pop said, and a moment later left her standing there, a ruffled bundle alone under the April stars.

9

Although the regular Friday Petty Sessions at the Police Court in Fordington opened at half past ten it was nearly half past twelve before Pop heard a police constable calling his name.

By that time he was feeling decidedly peckish and couldn't help wishing he'd nipped across the road to The Market Arms for a glass of beer and a piece of pork pie or a couple of sandwiches. The court had taken what he thought was a damn long two hours to deal with three straightforward drunks, a speeding motorist, a dustman accused of stealing twenty-three boxes of cigars, and a barrel of a woman, arrayed in a man's cheese-cutter cap, who had hit her next-door neighbor over the head with a coal bucket.

"Call Sidney Charles Larkin."

Pop, who was wearing a natty black-and-white-check suit with a hacking-style jacket and a yellow tie, at once stepped briskly forward and said, "That's me!" and stood in the well of the court facing the magistrates' plain mahogany dais at the far end.

That morning five magistrates were sitting and a pretty ripe old lot they looked too, Pop thought. Sir George Bluff-Gore, the chairman, in a dead-black suit and plain gray tie, looked more like a dyspeptic pallbearer than ever and regarded Pop with a cheerless oyster eye. On his left sat a Miss Cathcart, a tall, mannish, peglike woman wearing pince-nez, a thorn-proof suit of nettle green, and a matching hat with a pheasant's feather stuck in the side. Miss Cathcart shared a house with a tiny nervous brown sparrow of a companion named Emily, whom she unmercifully bullied night and day, at the same time devoting much of her time to moral welfare.

On Sir George's right sat Major Sprague, a maroon-faced comatose bull of a man with staring eyes, who appeared to be continually searching for something to ram his head against. A Mrs. Puffington, a miniature overneat lady with a shining mother-of-pearl face, sat tucked under the broad flanks of the bull rather like a newborn calf sheltering from the morning's stinging wind. The fifth magistrate was a round soapy bubble of pink flesh named Portman Jones, a retired local preacher, bald as an egg, who quavered at the very end of the bench with an air of impending doom, rather like a pirate's victim quaking at the plank's end.

Pop, already damn certain he wasn't going to get much change out of that crew, presently heard the clerk of the court, a tallish man in a charcoal-gray suit, reading out the charge against him.

"Sidney Charles Larkin, you are hereby charged that on the twenty-third day of April of 1959, at Gore Court, you unlawfully and indecently did assault a certain female, namely Phyllis Monica Jerebohm."

The clerk then proceeded to point out to Pop that he had the choice either of being tried by a jury or of having the case summarily dealt with, to which Pop replied promptly that he would have it dealt with there and then.

"Very well. Do you plead guilty or not guilty?"

"Not guilty o' course. What do *you* think?"

"Never mind the of course. Nor what I think. Are you represented in court?"

"Course I am," Pop said, and waved an airy hand to the little public gallery at the back of the court, where Ma was sitting with Mr. Charlton, Mariette, Edith Pilchester, the brigadier, Angela Snow, and the landlord of The Hare and Hounds. If they weren't representing him nobody was.

"What I mean is this—are you represented by a solicitor?"

"Yes," Pop said. "Me."

"Do you mean by that that you are conducting your own defense?"

"I am."

"You are quite sure?"

"Sure?" Pop said. "'Course I'm sure." Moses, for crying out gently.

"Very well." As the clerk, with a withering look, turned his back on Pop, a solicitor named Barlow bobbed stiffly up and down again in front of Pop like a small tarred cork and said, "I appear for the prosecution."

"Defendant conducting his own case?" mumbled Sir George Bluff-Gore.

"Yes, sir."

"Very well. Proceed."

A moment later Mr. Barlow rose and, in a matter-of-fact tone of voice, proceeded.

"The facts in this case are very simple, sir, and are as follows. On the afternoon of April the twenty-third last Mrs. Phyllis Monica Jerebohm, who resides with her husband at Gore Court, was walking alone by the lake in the grounds of the mansion. It was a fine warm afternoon and it was her intention to gather primroses. As she walked along the lake she observed the defendant rowing toward her in a boat—"

Pop, bored already, found himself going off into a dream. He felt ravenous already and wondered what Ma had for lunch today. At any moment his belly would rattle emptily.

It actually did rattle, and quite audibly, a minute or two later, so that Mr. Barlow, in the act of finishing his recital of the facts, glared sharply at Pop as if accusing him of manufacturing a deliberately insulting noise.

"I will now call Phyllis Monica Jerebohm," he said.

"Phyllis Monica Jerebohm!" called a police constable in the passage outside, and in the space of a few seconds Pinkie, clearly unable to see very straight, was up in the witness box, grasping the book in her gloved right hand and already starting to read the words of the oath in rapid, nervously simpering scales.

"Remove your glove, please."

More nervous than ever, Pinkie removed her right glove, keeping the other one on.

Pop, who knew as well as anybody what had happened by the lake, wasn't worried very much by the questions put by the prosecution to Pinkie, who all the time stood clasping the front of the box with both hands, on one of which she still wore a white glove while holding its mate in the other.

The only time he had occasion to feel in the slightest degree apprehensive was when she was asked if, at any time that afternoon, she had been afraid, and she said yes, she had been afraid. He hadn't thought of that. She did in fact drop her glove on the floor of the witness box as she answered the question and when she rose again after stooping to pick it up her face was gray.

"Were you in fact more than afraid?"

"I was."

"Were your reactions in fact those of any decent, respectable woman face-to-face, alone, with unexpected and undesirable interference from a molesting interloper—or, for all you knew, an attacker?"

Before Mrs. Jerebohm could answer, Ma's voice rang out sternly from the back of the court.

"I beg your pardon!" she said. "I beg your pardon."

"Silence!" called a policeman, and at the same time another policeman heaved himself toward the public gallery.

"Silence my foot," Ma said.

"Silence in court!"

"Whoever is interrupting from the public gallery will have to be
removed," Sir George Bluff-Gore said, "if this continues."

"Come and do it," Ma said, well under her breath this time, "it'll
need three of you and a crane."

Sir George, who knew quite well who was interrupting from the
gallery but was reluctant to do anything serious about it, simply
coughed several times in an important sort of way and said, "Proceed,"
which Pop presently did by rising to put his first question to Pinkie.

"Mrs. Jerebohm—"

He paused abruptly and rather lengthily. You had to stand back and
let the dog see the rabbit—that was how they did it on telly. He knew.
He'd seen it scores of times. It kept the witness on the hop.

"Mrs. Jerebohm," he said, "I want to ask you a very simple question. Can you swim?"

The question startled not only the court but Mrs. Jerebohm, who
almost dropped her glove a second time, and in the public gallery Ma
started choking.

"No. I can't."

"Are you afraid of water, Mrs. Jerebohm? I mean," Pop explained,
"the sort you fall into?"

Several people at the back of the court started laughing, with the
result that a police constable shouted, "Silence!" and still another
policeman moved on cautious feet toward the gallery.

"I suppose I am."

"Either you are or you aren't," Pop said blandly. "No supposing. In
fact I put it to you, Mrs. Jerebohm, that you are terrified of water."

"I wouldn't say exactly terrified."

Pop, smiling in his cool, perky fashion, wondered if Mrs. Jerebohm
would mind casting her mind back to the afternoon in question.
Weren't almost her first words to him on that day "I can't swim. I am
simply terrified of water"?

"They may have been."

"Mrs. Jerebohm, do you feel you are lucky to be alive today?"

"I suppose we all do," Pinkie said, her gloved hand clutching hard
at the edge of the box. "It's only natural."

"Never mind about all of us," Pop said. "Do you?"

Pinkie, who had already been more than surprised by several of

Pop's questions and couldn't for the life of her see the point of this one, almost inaudibly murmured yes and then was still more startled to hear Pop say, "Have you any idea, Mrs. Jerebohm, how deep the lake is?"

Mrs. Jerebohm, growing more nervous every moment, confessed that she had no idea at all.

"If I told you it was fifteen feet in places, even twenty," Pop said, "would it upset you?"

"It possibly would."

"Give you bit of a turn like?"

Pinkie simply stared straight in front of her, in silence. No answer was forthcoming and none was necessary. She was clearly having a bit of a turn already.

"Now, Mrs. Jerebohm, do you recall that when I rowed you into the bank that afternoon—that's where the lake's fifteen feet deep, by the way—I warned you on no account to move until I got the boat moored?"

"You may have. I was in a great hurry."

"To go where?" Pop said. "To the bottom of the drink? Because, strike me, that's where you would have gone if I hadn't grabbed hold of you when I did."

Pinkie, more pallid than ever, looked suddenly sick.

"I disagree," she said, after a moment or so, in a remote voice that she hoped sounded dignified, if not calm. "I could well have looked after myself."

"Not on your nelly!" Pop said.

"What was that strange expression?" Sir George Bluff-Gore mumbled. "I didn't catch that."

"It's an expression," the clerk said, "in the current vernacular."

"I beg your pardon?" Pop said. He had no intention of being insulted and put so much severity into his voice that the clerk, biting his lip, seemed to recoil visibly.

"Just two more questions," Pop said. "What did you do after the alleged attack?"

"I screamed."

"Why," Pop said, "didn't you attack me?"

"Because you were holding both my hands."

Pop gave the swiftest, perkiest of smiles at the same time only wishing he could telegraph it to Ma and his friends in the gallery.

"So now," he said, "I've got three hands, have I?" He held up his hands for all the court to see. "One to pinch you with and two to hold you with." Pinkie's face had suddenly gone from extreme gray pallor to boiling crimson. "Adam and Eve and Pinch Me, eh? Thank you very much, Mrs. Jerebohm."

After the pale and shaking Pinkie the next witness, Mrs. Perigo, looked icy, almost arrogant, by contrast. She was wearing a tailor-made tweed suit in a sort of dull rhubarb shade and a close-fitting hat to match.

The questions he wished to put to her, Mr. Barlow said, were very simple in themselves but, nevertheless, very important. First, did she see the attack? Second, was the nature of it as described by Mrs. Jerebohm herself? And third was the reaction of Mrs. Jerebohm that of a lady in a state of most alarming and acute distress?

To all three questions Mrs. Perigo answered yes, merely adding to the last of her answers that Pinkie was hysterical. This, Pop knew, was the corroborative evidence stuff that Charley had briefed him about and he listened eagerly as the solicitor for the prosecution went on.

"One more question. Did the defendant at any time offer, in your presence, any sort of expression of regret or apology for his action?"

"No."

"None whatever?"

"None whatever. He merely laughed."

"He merely laughed, you say. Thank you."

This, Pop knew, was the tricky part of the business and when he finally rose to question Mrs. Perigo he stared her straight in the face and opened with a question like a bullet, not bothering to pause for emphasis, as he had done with Pinkie.

"You are Corinne Lancaster Perigo?"

"I am."

"You're quite sure?"

"Naturally."

Nothing could have been more haughty than the word "naturally" and at the back of the court Ma felt her blood starting to boil.

"Absolutely certain?"

"Of course I'm absolutely certain!"

When the fury of the words had died down a bit, Pop went on.

"You say you saw the alleged attack?"

"Certainly."

"Can you tell the court from what distance?"

"Several yards."

"Can you tell the court how many yards is several?"

"Oh, three or four. Half a dozen."

Pop, pulling himself erect, wagged his finger at Mrs. Perigo with accusing severity.

"I suggest to you, madame," he said, "that if you had a neck as long as a giraffe's and a fifty-foot extension ladder and a three-inch telescope you couldn't have seen pussy from where you were."

"Indeed I could. And did."

Ma, in a fury of her own now, could bear it no longer.

"Wheel her out!" she called.

"Remove that person from the court at once."

"All right," Ma said. "Don't touch me. I'm going. I'll be over at The Market Hotel, Sid. I'll see if they've got some decent steaks for lunch. I forgot to ring the butcher."

"Good egg!" Pop said. "See if they've got some smoked salmon too."

"Right!"

While Ma was being removed from the court, as large as ever but more dignified, the clerk rose stiffly to ask with great acidity if Pop had quite finished with his personal catering arrangements. If so, could the court proceed.

"No more questions," Pop said.

Mrs. Perigo, haughtier and colder than ever, withdrew from the witness box, sweeping across the well of the court on a positive breeze of perfume, leaving the solicitor for the prosecution to rise and say, "That is the case for the prosecution."

"Do you wish to call any more witnesses, Larkin?" the clerk said.

"I do," Pop said. "Uncle Perce."

"What was that?" Sir George Bluff-Gore said. "Uncle who?"

"Call Percival Jethro Larkin!"

Quick as a fox, Uncle Perce nipped into court and was already halfway through a toothless recitation of the oath before the book had actually been handed up to him.

"Morning, Sid. Cold for the time o' the year."

"The witness will refrain from making observations," the clerk said. "Either about the inclemency of the weather or any other matter."

"Yessir. Sharp 'un this morning, though."

"Quiet!"

Uncle Perce was instantly and obediently quiet, though not for long.

"Well, I wouldn't be anybody else, would I?" He said in answer to Pop's question as to whether he was in fact Percival Jethro Larkin.

"And do you at the present time live at The Three Swans hotel at Wealdhurst?"

"That's me."

"Where you are employed as handyman and boots?"

"That's me."

"The witness will answer the questions either in the negative or the affirmative," the clerk said. "And not by observation."

"Yessir."

Pop, before addressing Uncle Perce, again made one of those timely and dramatic pauses he had so often seen enacted, and with such effect, on television.

"I want you to glance around the court. Take your time. Have a good long look."

"Yessir. Sid, I mean."

Uncle Perce took an all-embracing, owllike stare around the court, at the same time picking one of his few good teeth with a fingernail.

"Do you see in court," Pop said, "anyone known to you as Mrs. Perigo?"

"No, that I don't."

"Quite sure?"

"Sure as I like a nip o' rum on a cold morning."

"Take a good look at the lady in the dark red costume who sits over there."

"Her with the red bag on her head?"

That was the one, Pop said. Did he know her as Mrs. Perigo? No, Uncle Perce said, he'd be blowed if he did.

"Quite sure?"

"Sure as I like a—"

"Answer yes or no!" the clerk said.

"Yessir."

"Very well. You don't know her as Mrs. Perigo," Pop said. "But you do know her?"

"Oh yes, I know her."

"Mr. Larkin," the clerk interrupted. "Can you tell us what all this is designed to show? Where is it meant to lead us?"

"To the truth!" Pop thundered.

"Very well. Proceed."

"Now," Pop said, "can you tell the court when you last saw the lady?"

"About three weeks ago."

"And can you say," Pop said, "where you saw her?"

"In bed." Uncle Perce spoke with smart emphasis, almost with a snap of his jaws.

"Alone?"

"With a gent."

Several people in the gallery broke into spontaneous laughter but the various policemen, the clerk, and Sir George Bluff-Gore seemed momentarily mesmerized and offered no word of reprimand. Nor was there any word from Corinne Perigo, who was now as gray and tense as Pinkie still was.

"You say you saw the lady in bed. Can you tell us where this was?"

"At The Three Swans o' course. I took their early-morning tea up. One of the maids'd got bronchitis and we were shorthanded at the time."

Pop permitted himself a smile. He was really starting to enjoy himself. The court lark was a drop o' good after all.

"But the lady, you say, is not Mrs. Perigo?"

"No. Her name's Lancaster. Mrs. George Lancaster."

A sensational tremor seemed to go through the court and Sir George Bluff-Gore sat forward on the bench by more than a foot, eager for every word.

"Are you quite sure the name is Lancaster?"

" 'Course I am. I had another dekko at the visitors' register yesterday."

Pop waved an airy, modestly expansive hand.

"So the lady describing herself in this court, on oath, as Mrs. Perigo, did in fact register herself at the hotel as Mrs. Lancaster?"

"That's a fact," Uncle Perce said. "Yessir."

"Which amounts to this, does it not"—Pop, television-taught, paused for emphasis again, convinced that this was the right time, if ever, to let the dog see the rabbit—"that either at the hotel or in this court the lady has been telling a lie?"

"You're right, Sid!" Uncle Perce said. "And a thundering big 'un too, if you ask me."

"Bingo!" the brigadier said softly, and gave a smile of winning triumph to Angela Snow, who returned it affectionately.

Ten seconds later Pinkie Jerebohm suddenly fell forward in a bumping faint. Corinne Perigo, chalk-faced, rushed from the court as if scalded. Two policemen lifted Pinkie bodily and carried her out through a door, closely followed by a buxom policewoman carrying her handbag and flapping a big white handkerchief. The clerk scratched among his papers rather like a black-and-white hen searching for a mislaid egg and Sir George Bluff-Gore conferred for some moments with his magisterial colleagues, all of whom looked suddenly like hens too, their heads slightly to one side, clucking under their breaths.

From somewhere at the back of the public gallery Mr. Jerebohm, breathing like a train on a difficult gradient, pushed with flapping arms past ushers, policemen, solicitors, and clerks and finally disappeared in the direction Pinkie had gone. In the confusion everybody seemed to have forgotten Pop, who stood not unconfused himself in the well of the court, and it was not until Sir George rapped sharply on the bench in front of him that order was restored. Then a policeman shouted, "Silence!"

"Mr. Barlow," Sir George said, "do you feel in the circumstances that you can carry this case any further?"

"No, sir," Barlow said. "In the circumstances I do not."

"Very well. The defendant is discharged."

"You may go," a police sergeant said to Pop, who went without delay, finding himself two minutes later in the bar of The Market Hotel, where Ma, Mariette, Charley, Montgomery, Miss Pilchester, Angela Snow, the brigadier, and the landlord of The Hare and Hounds were all waiting, glasses in hands, ready to give him a chorus of acclamation.

"Everybody's staying to lunch here," Ma said, giving him her own personal greeting in the form of a kiss laid on his lips like a cushion. "I've got it all fixed. Smoked salmon and steaks for the lot."

"Well done, Larkin," The brigadier said. "Damn good staff work."

"Sweet man," Angela Snow said, kissing him lightly on both cheeks. "Blistering success. Had 'em cold from the word go."

"Don't they call it purgatory?" Ma said, laughing splendidly over a Guinness, "or is it perjury? I never know. By the way, where's Uncle Perce?"

To her almost stupefied surprise, Uncle Perce came in a moment later with the old enemy, Mr. Barlow, who immediately came up and shook Pop by the hand, told him he had done well, in fact, very well, and asked what he and his good lady were going to have.

Ma, remembering the word "attacker," thought for a moment she'd a good mind to sue him for defamation of character and then abruptly changed her mind and said, "A large Johnnie Walker," instead. That would learn him.

"Yes, you did well, Larkin," Mr. Barlow said. "Congratulations."

"Oh?" Ma said. "You didn't help much, did you?"

"All in the day's work," Mr. Barlow said. "All got to live."

"I couldn't bear it," Edith Pilchester said. "It was absolutely terrible. Every minute was ghastly."

"Uncle Perce is the one we got to thank," Pop said, gratefully accepting a quart of light ale from Mr. Barlow, at the same time catching him a fraternal blow in the ribs with his free elbow. "Thirsty work, our job, eh?"

Mr. Barlow laughed, proving to be as human as anyone else after all, and Uncle Perce, finding a brief moment when he could lift his face from his own quart glass of ale, laughed too and said, "I told you I'd remember that piece, didn't I, Sid? I knew I'd remember. I can see her now in that bed. She'd got a black lace nightgown on—that's what brought it back to me."

"Don't talk about that woman," Ma said. "Don't spoil the party. I always said she'd got no finesse."

"Well, cheers," Angela Snow said, her voice more than ever cool and languid. "It only goes to show."

Show what? Ma wanted to know.

"The truth," Angela Snow said, "of the old Chinese proverb."

What proverb was that? Pop wanted to know, and a second later heard Angela Snow, to the accompaniment of golden peals of laughter, telling him the answer.

"If you're going to be raped," she said, "you might as well relax and enjoy it while you can."

10

It was not until a warm Saturday evening in early June that Angela Snow, in a pure white swimsuit gleaming as a snail shell, dived with cool grace from the springboard of the Larkin swimming pool and swam the whole length of the bath under water before finally surfacing and turning on her back to float motionlessly in the sun.

"Pool's christened!" Pop shouted. "Everybody in!"

Soon everybody was in the water, which shone clear and blue as turquoise. The brigadier, spidery of leg, his middle covered by what looked like a discarded length of faded pink face flannel, duck-paddled to and fro in the shallow end, where Ma, in a bright magenta bikini that seemed to sit on her body like an arrangement of well-inflated balloons, was playfully teaching little Oscar a gentle stroke or two. Little Oscar, fat as a balloon himself and wearing a startling costume of blue-and-yellow stripes, wasn't very interested in strokes and spent most of his time bobbing out of the water to lick at an ice cream, a melting super-bumper in thick layers of chocolate and raspberry.

At the deep end of the pool the twins, together with Victoria, Primrose, Mr. Charlton, and Montgomery, were either diving off the board or the edge of the pool. Primrose, grave and bewitching in a bikini of emerald green, sometimes sat on the edge for long periods in a dream, staring mostly at Mr. Charlton. She wasn't at all sure she wasn't in love with Mr. Charlton, who in turn thought she was growing more and more like Mariette every time he looked at her. Mariette was in the house, occupied with the final touches of preparation to ham and fresh salmon sandwiches, prawn vol-au-vents, sausage rolls, asparagus tips, cheese tarts, salads, and things of that sort. She was being helped in the kitchen by a more than usually shy, fussy, and indeterminate Edith Pilchester, who was trying without success to summon enough courage to change into a swimsuit, a royal blue one, which she'd bought specially for the day. She hadn't worn a swimsuit for years.

"You see I'm not all that frightfully good a swimmer," she was explaining, "and somehow—"

"Ma isn't either," Mariette said. "What's it matter? Go up and change in the bathroom. Pop won't like it if you don't try the pool."

"You don't think he'll take offense?"

"Not offense exactly," Mariette said. "But you know how Pop is. He adores people to enjoy themselves. He's been waiting a long time for today."

"I know. I absolutely long to. It's just that I—"

It was just that she was so dreadfully shy about that sort of thing, she persisted in explaining several times. She wasn't used to it. She supposed she was getting too old for it or something, she said, and it was not until Mariette finally made the suggestion that what she needed was a little Dutch courage to stimulate her that she allowed herself the luxury of a whiskey and said she'd have a stab at it after all.

In the pool, in an evening growing more and more embalmed every moment, the air a pure light gold, Pop was enjoying himself by giving imitations of a porpoise or riding little Oscar on his shoulder. Sometimes he dived under Ma, brushing her body playfully on the way up or down.

The brigadier, watching this sportive play and listening to the steam valve of Ma's laughter shrieking into air every time Pop touched her, couldn't help wishing he had the courage to try something of the kind on Angela Snow, but a queer sort of diffidence had come over him too. Every time he watched her white cool figure cutting the water or diving from the board in the evening sunshine he knew he could have done with a little Dutch courage himself.

All this put him into a daydream of his own and when he finally came out of it some time later it was to see with relief that Pop, in his customary fashion, was handing around drinks on a tray.

"Drink, General? Everybody enjoying themselves? Help yourself. Eats are coming in a moment. Everybody here? Where's Edith? I don't see Edith nowhere."

"She was in the house helping Mariette a few minutes ago," Ma said.

"Time she was here," Pop said. He liked his guests on the spot; he liked a party to go with a bang. You couldn't have people missing when the party was just warming up. "The grub'll all be gone if she don't soon get here."

"You'd better go and find her, hadn't you?" Ma said. "If you don't want her to starve."

Pop, agreeing that this was something like the right idea, went into the house, deciding to renew the trayful of drinks at the same time.

"Help yourself to another before I go, General," he said. The brigadier didn't hesitate and then, with a drink in either hand, padded on thin white legs to the far side of the pool, where Angela Snow sat gazing at a half-empty glass, softly splashing her long legs in the water.

A palpitating rememberance of all that had happened on the hearthrug swept through the brigadier as he sat down beside her and she said, "Hullo, my lamb. Thought you were never coming to talk to me. Afraid you'd jilted me."

She was hardly his to jilt, the brigadier thought. He only wished to God she were. A twinge of loneliness nipped him and then was gone for a moment, banished by the sudden pleasant realization that he was sitting only a bare inch or two from her smooth long limbs.

"How are you, my sweet?" she said. "You look sort of pensive to me."

The brigadier, with a rumbled bark of heartiness that didn't deceive her at all, said that he was actually in fact splendid. Absolutely splendid.

"Sweetie, you're in a dream."

"Oh?" The brigadier was greatly startled. "Really?"

"I've been watching you."

The sentence was of such direct simplicity that the brigadier, momentarily unnerved, said, "Your glass is half empty. Have some of mine—allow me? May I?"

With a hand on the verge of trembling he poured a generous part of his second glass into hers and then added the remainder to what was left of his first. As he did so she felt an inexplicable twinge of her own, a sudden bristling at the nape of her neck, which caught her unprepared. She remembered then how the brigadier had surprisingly found her weak spot in the darkness and she started wondering what she would do about it if he found it a second time.

"Well, cheers, honey," she said. She lifted her glass to him, turning on him her pellucid, almost overlarge olive eyes. "Nice, sharing your drink with me. That's made my day."

The brigadier, for the first time, found himself looking straight into her eyes. He hadn't realized before how remarkably sympathetic they were. It struck him that they were like wide, warm pools. They held him closely, with a great stillness, and he couldn't get away.

"It's rather made my day too," he said, and to his infinite astonishment she started running one of her fingers along the back of his hand.

Meanwhile, in the house, Pop had searched both kitchen and living room for Edith Pilchester without success. Mariette had vanished into the garden too and he was about to follow her with a second tray of drinks when an alarming sound, like that of a battering ram, brought him to the base of the stairs.

Edith, in shy haste, bathing cap in hand, had slithered down the full flight of stairs and now lay, a vision of royal blue and purest white, prostrate on her back.

"Oh! I do feel a ghastly fool."

"All right?" Pop said. "Not hurt?"

Edith in her bathing suit, relieved of the encumbrances of tweed, corset, and heavy woolens, was suddenly revealed as having a figure of modestly good proportions. Her legs were smooth and hairless. She had very white, sloping shoulders.

"No, absolutely all right. Absolutely."

Eager not to miss anything, Pop hastily set down the tray of drinks and helped her to her feet. Edith, clumsy as ever, half jumped, half rolled from the stairs, to find herself a moment later in Pop's arms, held in a palpitating squeeze.

"How's your operation today?"

Pop whispered and held her so uncompromisingly close that Edith, who had never been so unashamedly near to anything male in her life, had hardly breath enough left to say, "I won't put you in court. You know that don't you?"

"Wouldn't stand a chance if you did," Pop said, laughing. "No corroborative evidence. Once more?"

"One more. Please."

Pop kissed her for the last time and a moment or two later, with a final spirited slap from him, she was in the garden, flushed and feeling almost naked as she half walked, half ran to the pool.

Pop, following with the drinks, met Primrose coming into the house, graver than usual and with only half a sentence to offer him in answer to his "Not going to bed? Party's only just begun."

"Just going to the wood for a walk," she said dreamily, "and—"

From her visit to the wood she came back, half an hour later, carrying a bunch of butterfly orchids, like palest green wax insects, which for some reason she gave to Angela Snow, who said, "Sweet. Thanks, my pet," and then tucked them into the bust of her bathing costume.

The intoxicating, almost too sweet breath of them rose at Angela's throat. The little swarm of greenish flower wings seemed at the same time to give fresh lightness to her splendid bare skin, so that the brigadier, who had never seen anything remotely like it in his life, suddenly realized that even the most arid moments had magical impulses, the power to bloom sensationally.

He wanted suddenly, in a wild moment, to ask her to marry him, but he either daren't or couldn't frame the words. Instead he started to murmur something about whether she could cook or not, then suddenly felt it was all too obvious and said instead, "Perhaps you'd come and have dinner with me one night, I mean?"

"Adore it."

"Which night would suit you?"

"Oh, any night, honey," she said, saying the words as if she were making a personal sacrifice for him alone.

He could hardly suppress his joy and in a lyrical moment thought of how he would give her scampi, asparagus, and veal cutlets or something of that kind. You could get them all, even the scampi, at the village shop nowadays. It was part of the rural revolution. He would try to cook all the meal himself. He would do his damnedest to make it nice for her.

All of a sudden the tranquillity of the evening was heightened by the sound of church bells. Across the meadows the pealing changes, in practices ready for Sunday, came in waves of crystal clearness, pursued by their own echoes.

"Do you go to church?" she said.

"Very occasionally."

"Would you come to church with me tomorrow morning?" she said, "if I came and fetched you? And then come to lunch with us? I've always wanted my father to meet you."

Almost before his stuttered "Yes, most kind of you, delighted" was out of his mouth an ebullient Pop had arrived, loudly uttering reproaches about empty glasses.

"This won't do, General. This won't do. Refills all around, come on!" he said, and then to his utter surprise saw that Angela Snow had actually laid two fingertips on the back of one of the general's hands.

Back with Ma, who was sitting on the edge of the pool holding little Oscar on one enormous knee and a Guinness on the other, Pop confessed that you could knock him down with a feather. It was perfickly stunning. Angela and the general were sitting holding hands.

"Why shouldn't they?" Ma said. "Perhaps he's going to ask her to marry him. Lucky girl."

Pop, ignoring whatever slight reproach about matrimony there might have been in Ma's voice, said, "Good egg!" and shouldn't he go over and give 'em a bit of encouragement or something like that?

"Something like what?" Ma said.

"I dunno," Pop said. "Like champagne."

"Give us a chance," Ma said. "I'm still on Guinness," and turned to give a sip to little Oscar, who in fact took several sips and then solemnly wiped his mouth with the back of his hand.

"Let's leave the champagne till it gets dark," Ma said. "Why don't you get some fun and games organized? I thought you said we were going to have races."

Pop, leaving Ma to carry on with the business of filling up glasses, suddenly became more acutely aware of the sound of bells. For some reason they always reminded him of Christmas. They made him think of snow on holly, musical chairs, Paul Jones, and Postman's Knock. They inspired him to fun. And suddenly in a brilliant burst of enthusiasm he was laughing in his most rousing fashion and shouting, "Everybody in the pool! Going to have Blind Man's Buff in the pool!"

Ma laughed rousingly too. That was a good one. Trust Pop to think of that.

"Who's going to start it?"

Pop was tempted to say Edith, but suddenly realized that he'd better do it himself, so as to hot it up from the start.

"I will," he said. "Come on, everybody in. Kids an' all. Angela, Edith. All in. General, where are you?"

Presently everybody was in the pool except, it seemed, Mariette. Somehow this evening Mariette was always missing. Where was Mariette?

"She's gone to fetch Oscar a woolly," Ma said. "She'll be back."

Presently Pop was in the pool, eyes bandaged, playing Blind Man. With one corner of the handkerchief ever so slightly raised he could easily tell the difference between Edith, Ma, and Angela and so knew which of them to chase at the right time. Not that he could miss Ma very well; she took up such an expanse of the pool. Several times Edith shrieked, stumbled in escape, and wildly went under but there was a time when he grabbed lusciously at what he thought was Angela Snow, only to find that it was Mr. Charlton.

When it was finally Mr. Charlton's turn to be Blind Man it was Primrose who allowed herself to get caught. Mr. Charlton was exactly the right type for her, she had decided. He was her dream. In the wood she had actually shed a tear or two and now to be caught by Mr. Charlton made her confusedly happy. In her joyful confusion, when it was her turn, she immediately caught the brigadier, who then wandered about the central parts of the pool like a searching spider, desperately hoping it would be Angela he touched. His singular misfortune at running several times into the large bulk of Ma finally made her so sorry for him that suddenly she pushed him flat into Angela's arms and for a suspended second or two he remained there until Pop shouted in lyrical encouragement, "Kiss her, man! Kiss her!"

To everybody's astonishment the brigadier actually did, still with the handkerchief over his eyes, standing in water up to his armpits, half as if at a baptism, half as if embalmed.

The whole thing, so unexpected, made Ma laugh so much that she had to go and rest at the side of the pool. While she was there, choking afresh at the sight of Mr. Charlton passing and finally torpedoing Edith Pilchester at the deep end, Pop joined her and said, "Charley boy's getting fresh tonight. Mariette'll have to watch out. By the way, where is she all this time?"

"I expect she's gone to have a lie-down."

"Good God. A lie-down? What's she want to lie down for?"

"She's just resting."

"Resting? What's she want to rest for? It's only eight o'clock."

"The doctor says she's got to," Ma said blandly. "Anyway for the first month or two."

In a positive whirlwind of joy Pop raced twice around the pool before finally jumping in, feet first, at the deep end. As he landed almost on top of Edith Pilchester, blindfolded now, he told himself in a shout that he hoped it would be a girl. Another Mariette. No, he didn't. He hoped it would be twins. He hoped in fact that all his family would one day have twins. He hoped that if Angela and the general ever got married they too would have twins. He hoped even Edith Pilchester would have twins. Why not? He wanted them all, every one of them, to have a life of double richness.

In a second whirl of excitement he grabbed Ma from the side of the pool and ducked her four times in rapid succession, at the same time shouting to Charley, "Get the champagne, Charley boy. Pink and red! Plenty of ice. It's your night, Charley boy."

With a thump on the back that almost broke Mr. Charlton in two he urged Charley boy on his fruitful way to the house and then found himself standing, some moments later, in a sort of delirium of suspense, on the diving board.

For some seconds longer he stood there gazing down at the blue water and all the faces of the people he loved. Across the golden evening the peal of church bells, together with the song of a late blackbird or two and in the near woods a bubbling call of pigeons, drifted in on a high chorus of midsummer sounds that exhilarated him like laughter. This was life, he told himself. This was how it ought to be.

A moment later, laughing too, he dived. The evening air flowed past him like silk and from across the meadows came the scent of drying hay.

H. E. Bates was born in 1905 at Rushden in Northamptonshire and was educated at Kettering Grammar School. He worked as a journalist and clerk on a local newspaper before publishing his first book, *The Two Sisters*, when he was twenty. In the next fifteen years he acquired a distinguished reputation for his stories about English country life. During World War II, he was a squadron leader in the R.A.F. and some of his stories of service life, *The Greatest People in the World* (1942), *How Sleep the Brave* (1943), and *The Face of England* (1953), were written under the pseudonym of "Flying Officer X." His subsequent novels of Burma, *The Purple Plain* and *The Jacaranda Tree*, and of India, *The Scarlet Sword*, stemmed directly or indirectly from his experience in the Eastern theater of war.

In 1958 his writing took a new direction with the appearance of *The Darling Buds of May*, the first of the popular Larkin family novels, which was followed by *A Breath of French Air* (1959), *When the Green Woods Laugh* (1960), *Oh! To Be in England* (1963), and *A Little of What You Fancy* (1970). His autobiography appeared in three volumes, *The Vanished World* (1969), *The Blossoming World* (1971), and *The World in Ripeness* (1972). His last works included the novel *The Triple Echo* (1971) and a collection of short stories, *The Song of the Wren* (1972). Perhaps one of his most famous works of fiction is the best-selling novel *Fair Stood the Wind for France* (1944). H. E. Bates also wrote miscellaneous works on gardening, essays on country life, several plays including *The Day of Glory* (1945), *The Modern Short Story* (1941), and a story for children, *The White Admiral* (1968). His works have been translated into sixteen languages and a posthumous collection of his stories, *The Yellow Meads of Asphodel*, appeared in 1976.

H. E. Bates was awarded the C.B.E. in 1973 and died in January 1974. He was married in 1931 and had four children.

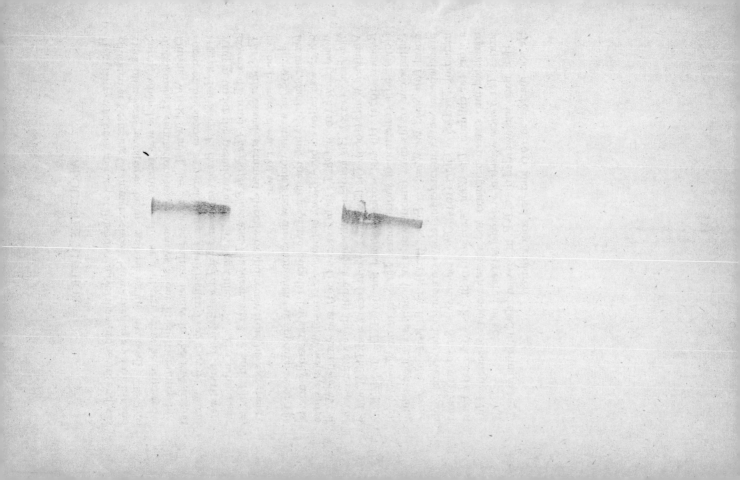